A
PLACE TO
HIDE

ALSO BY RONALD H. BALSON

An Affair of Spies
Defending Britta Stein
Eli's Promise
Karolina's Twins
The Girl from Berlin
The Trust
Saving Sophie
Once We Were Brothers

A
PLACE TO
HIDE

Ronald H. Balson

ST. MARTIN'S PRESS
NEW YORK

First published in the United States by St. Martin's Press, an imprint of St. Martin's Publishing Group

A PLACE TO HIDE. Copyright © 2024 by Ronald H. Balson. All rights reserved. Printed in the United States of America. For information, address St. Martin's Publishing Group, 120 Broadway, New York, NY 10271.

www.stmartins.com

The Library of Congress Cataloging-in-Publication Data is available upon request.

ISBN 978-1-250-28248-4 (hardcover)

ISBN 978-1-250-28249-1 (ebook)

Our books may be purchased in bulk for promotional, educational, or business use. Please contact your local bookseller or the Macmillan Corporate and Premium Sales Department at 1-800-221-7945, extension 5442, or by email at MacmillanSpecialMarkets@macmillan.com.

First Edition: 2024

10 9 8 7 6 5 4 3 2 1

To Monica
Ik heb je lief

A
PLACE TO
HIDE

CHAPTER ONE

Tel Aviv, Israel
2002

AT A SMALL table in the corner of a Tel Aviv bakery, a man sat studying financial papers and enjoying his morning cup of coffee. Suddenly his attention was drawn to two little giggling girls. The minute they entered the store, they excitedly rushed over to the bakery display, and pointed out their selections. The man watched them and smiled. They reminded him of his grandchildren. The woman with the girls tried her best to calm them down, but she had limited success. She leaned forward, had a short conversation with the salesclerk, and then pulled her girls aside to discuss their behavior. A moment later, the girls were handed their sweets in paper packets. The older of the two walked by the man's table, held out her doughnut, and said, "I got chocolate!" Not to be outdone, the younger child rushed over to show him her selection, but she stumbled, tripped, lost control over her sweet roll, and flipped it right onto his stack of papers. The little girl froze, turned around, and burst into tears.

The woman hurried to the table, took her child's hand, and smiled apologetically at the man. "I'm so sorry, sir," she said in Hebrew. "Becky's excitement sometimes gets the best of her. Allow me to clean it up."

"No, no, it's not necessary," he said, returning her smile. "No harm done." He gestured to the salesclerk to prepare another sweet roll for the little girl.

"You are so kind," the woman said. "They get so riled up. They love doughnuts."

"So do I," he replied, patting his stomach. "Maybe a little too much. And you have delightful children."

"Very kind of you," she said. "But they're my *grandchildren*."

His smile widened. "My goodness, you could have fooled me. By the way, I notice that you speak Hebrew with a Dutch accent."

She nodded. "That's true. Are you Dutch?"

"No, but I spend quite a bit of time there on business. In Utrecht. Are you familiar with Utrecht?"

"I should say so, that was my childhood home."

"Really," he said with raised eyebrows, "what a small world. Maybe I've come across your family in business. What is your father's name?"

"My father?" she said, then paused. Tears formed in the corners of her eyes. "It's a long story. I don't know my *real* father. I have only scant memories of my real mother, my real father, or my sister. They tell me I was born in Amsterdam, but I don't remember much about that either. I was raised in Utrecht by my second family. But I didn't call them *vader* and *moeder*. I called them *tante* and *oom*."

He nodded. "Aunt and uncle."

"Yes, they preferred it that way, in case my real mother and father should ever come for me. When I came to live with them, they changed my last name and called me by their family name. I'm not sure why. Their name was Leisner. I don't know what my name was before that." She shrugged.

"Well, it's very nice to meet you, Ms. Leisner. But regretfully, I have never met the Leisner family in Utrecht."

"Well, it's nice to meet you, as well. Actually, I'm Karyn Sachnoff now, not Leisner. My married name is Sachnoff."

"And my name is Burt Franklin," he said, holding out his hand. "It's very nice to meet you, too, Karyn Sachnoff. And I apologize for being so nosy."

Karyn smiled. "Oh, you're not nosy. It's kind of refreshing to talk to someone about the early years. I try to remember them from time to time, but I was very young. My aunt and uncle refused to talk to me about the years when I came to live with them. Whenever I brought up the subject, they shook their heads. Even when I was older, they still refrained from discussing the Netherlands in the '40s. Just that they were difficult times. I know I had a sister, but she didn't move with me. Even though I longed to find out what happened to my sister, the subject was closed. Those years were too depressing, they said, and they didn't know my sister, we weren't adopted together. So, I never knew what happened to her."

Karyn was lost in a thought or two, and then she looked at Burt and she smiled. "My sister's name was Annie, and I loved her very much. I can't tell you my real mother's or father's names, but I sure remember Annie."

"Did she move anywhere near you?"

"Not that I'm aware, I'm afraid. We were split up. I have no idea where Annie went. She could be anywhere now, and I have no idea where, or what her name would be. But I'm sure she's alive."

Burt showed a bit of surprise. "Really?"

Karyn nodded affirmatively. "Oh yes. We were alive together when they came to take me, and Annie was taken by someone too. Somewhere. I don't know where, but I know she's alive. I can feel it. There is a connection between sisters; it's mystical. I hear her talk to me sometimes at night." Karyn smiled. "I know she's alive."

Burt raised his eyebrows. "Well, she certainly could be. There were a lot of children adopted during the war years."

Karyn paused for a moment, and her lower lip quivered. "I'd give anything to find her. I've tried and tried, I've almost given up hope. It's impossible."

"Maybe not," Burt said. "There are records . . ."

"No, no, no, I've searched all the official records," Karyn said with a dismissive wave of her hand. "It's all a waste of time."

"Well. I'm not really talking about *official* records," Burt said. "There are some people who privately retained records, or who have remarkable memories. In fact, I know such a man. He's an American. He worked in Amsterdam for the State Department before the war, and then he stayed on during the war. The details of his life are something of a mystery."

Karyn brushed away a tear. "Would he talk to me if I called him?"

Burt squinted his eyes. "To you? I doubt it. He's an old man and rather grouchy. He doesn't like to talk to people. In fact, he has an unlisted number and very few know it."

"But *you* could talk to him?"

"And I do, he's a cousin of mine, and in some ways, he's like your aunt and uncle. He doesn't like to talk about the war years, even with me. They say he was a hero, but I don't know what he did. The war was very painful to him. In the few times when he does talk about the war, his memory is very keen. He has a photographic memory, and those pictures are stored away. His sense of recall is remarkable. He can see the things he is talking about."

"I understand. Just like my *tante* and *oom*. Good memories, but locked away. Well, thanks for talking to me and—"

"Wait," Burt said, holding up his hand. "Let's do this: I'll try to get in touch with my cousin and see if he'll agree to talk to you. If he agrees, I'll call you. But there is one problem: he refuses to speak Dutch anymore. It's too painful."

"That's all right," Karyn said. "I speak English. And French and Hebrew, and of course, Dutch. I used to be a features writer for the *Jerusalem Times*."

Burt stood up. "Then let me reach out to him, Karyn. No promises, but you never know. Let me have your phone number, and I'll call you."

She bent down and wrote the number in his notebook. "Burt, I am very appreciative, but I have to tell you, I've researched and researched." She shook her head. "It's not possible."

"Well, don't give up. Teddy is quite the man. Let me talk to him."

Karyn smiled. "Very well. If you are successful, I promise I won't take up much of his time, just a moment or so to find out if he knows anything at all that would lead me to my sister."

CHAPTER TWO

SEVERAL WEEKS PASSED without a word from Burt Franklin. Karyn didn't really expect to hear. For a while, she harbored thoughts of reuniting with Annie. They filled her mind day and night. She recalled the few memories she still held of the two of them. Only fragments of memories: a birthday party; a boat ride on an Amsterdam canal; the two of them singing songs on the floor of their home; being taken in a truck to some big, smelly room; and those days where Karyn sat silently at some crowded day care facility wrapped up in Annie's arms. She had loved Annie and her family so much. Being ripped away from them had hurt deeply. It still did. But she carried her memories; at least she had those. That's why the phone call was such a total shock.

"Karyn, it's Burt. Burt Franklin. Remember me?"

"Do I remember you, of course I do. From the bakery."

"Right. Well, Karyn, I have good news."

Karyn listened and her heart jumped. "Oh, Mr. Franklin, I'm not sure what to say. What is the news? Will the gentleman agree to talk to me, even just for a few minutes?"

"Oh, he'll talk to you, all right, but not on the telephone. He doesn't like telephones, remember? And please, call me Burt."

"Okay, Burt. But if he won't use a telephone, how am I supposed to converse with him? Am I to give you messages to take to him?"

Burt chuckled loudly. "Burt, the carrier pigeon? No, I'm afraid not. If you want to talk to him, you'll have to come to Washington. He'll only talk to you in person. He said he would give you as much time as you needed."

Karyn was floored. "I can't believe it. That is incredible. I really didn't expect this at all."

"Neither did I," Burt said. "As I was returning to Washington, I was thinking about you and about our conversation, and I thought if anyone could help you, it would be Teddy. His name is Teddy Hartigan. I hadn't seen him in a while, and I owed him a visit anyway. So, I drove out there. He now resides in an assisted-living facility in Silver Spring, just outside of DC. And there he was, just as cranky as ever, but I have to tell you, he still looks pretty damn good. I do love the old guy. I told him all about you and your darling granddaughters, and about your futile search for your sister. He didn't seem all that interested. I told him how I detected a Dutch accent in your Hebrew, and it still didn't spark an interest. I told him that you write for the *Times*, that you were very personable and a delight to talk to, and he just stared into space. Then I asked him if he'd agree to talk to you, and lo and behold, he shocks me by saying yes. But . . . here's the catch: he'll only meet with you on two conditions. One, the meetings must take place in Silver Spring, at the home—"

"Yes, of course," Karyn said. "And what was the other condition?"

"Well, you see, I told him you were a writer for the *Jerusalem Times*, and—"

"I used to, Burt, I don't work for them anymore. I'm freelance now."

"That doesn't matter, Karyn, that's even better. He wants you to write up his life story. He says he's getting old and he wants to leave something behind for his grandkids. You know, like a lot of people who survived World War Two, he hasn't been able to tell his story to them face-to-face. Throughout their whole life, he has not been able to talk to them about what happened to their grandfather. So, now he wants them to know who Grandpa Teddy was during the war. And in exchange for that, he will do his best to find out as much as he can about your sister."

"Wow! That's amazing," Karyn said gleefully, "but how is he going to do that? I can't even tell him the names of any of my real family members. Except Annie. I don't even know what my family name was."

"I told him that, and shrugged. He said he still has his connections back in the Netherlands. There are strings that he can pull. He's pretty good at what he does, Karyn, and I have faith in him, even though he admitted it's going to be a long shot."

"So, he wants me to write his biography, and for that he'll reach out to his contacts? This is crazy, Burt."

"For sure. But, if I know Teddy, he would do more than just reach out. Hell, Karyn, I'd do it if it was me, I mean, if I was you. If there was a chance of trying to find my sister, even the slightest chance, I'd turn it over to Teddy. What do you have to lose? You'll sit with him for a few days, give or take. You'll jot down some notes, learn about his life, and draft a story for his grandchildren to read. And in exchange . . . well, he's your best hope, maybe your last hope. Not many of them are alive anymore. Listen, he's brilliant, honest, and cranky as all hell. But I'll bet you'll love him just like I do."

"Okay, it's a deal. When do we get started?"

"Well, I'll be in Washington for the next two weeks. It would be best if I took you out there myself and introduced you in person."

"I can't thank you enough, Burt. Let me take care of a few things here and I'll call you with an arrival date, maybe next week."

"Great. See you then."

CHAPTER THREE

Silver Spring, Maryland

BURT DROVE KARYN out to the Greenview Retirement Home in the afternoon. He had picked her up at Dulles International that morning and taken her to a hotel in Silver Spring where she would be staying. On the way, he told her again that Teddy could be grouchy and testy, and she shouldn't take it personally. "That's just the way he is. He's not dangerous in any way, just caustic from time to time, and sometimes that hurts. If he gets like that, you tell him, and he'll stop."

"I've been a reporter for twenty-five years," Karyn said, "I can take care of myself." They parked the car in front of Greenview, entered the stately home, and walked down the corridor to Teddy's apartment. Their knock was followed by a sharp "Who's there?"

Burt and Karyn entered Teddy's small one-bedroom unit, and Burt made the introduction. "Karyn, this is Teddy Hartigan, and Teddy, this is Karyn Sachnoff, the woman I've been telling you about."

Teddy nodded his understanding, but did not comment.

"That's her married name, Teddy. Her maiden name, or should I say her adopted name, was Leisner. I don't know what her birth name was. I don't think she knows either."

Teddy waved an impatient hand back and forth, and in a raspy voice said, "She is perfectly capable of telling me her own name, or should I say, her set of names. So, let's not waste any more time. I'm not getting any younger."

Teddy sat down in his usual seat, a blue upholstered captain's chair placed directly opposite a yellow upholstered chair. They were six feet apart. He pointed for Karyn to sit down, turned to Burt, and said, "Thanks for bringing her by. So long."

Burt flashed a tentative smile at Karyn, as if to say, *Are you sure you want to stay here?* She nodded her approval. "See you later," she said with a smile. "He's not so tough. I'll be fine." Burt had agreed to meet for dinner later that evening.

Alone together, Karyn took her seat and looked at Teddy. He was thin, visibly bony, dressed in a plaid wool shirt and dark-wash pants. As Karyn had been told, he was at least ninety years old, and the type of man who would say, *Let's get started. I don't have much time to waste.*

Teddy pointed to her writing pad and said to Karyn, "I want you to write down every single thing you can remember about your early life in Holland. Especially, all you can recall about the time before you came to live with the Leisner family in Utrecht."

Karyn nodded. "It's not much."

"I figure," he said. "And write down how you came to live with the Leisner family, if you can remember that. Write down whatever the Leisners may have told you about your adoption."

"You want me to do that right now?"

Teddy wrinkled his forehead. "Hell no. Do it on your own time. Maybe instead of going out to dinner with Burt."

Karyn giggled. "Don't worry, it won't intrude upon my personal life, there isn't much to write anyway. So, let's get started with Teddy's life story. For posterity."

"Hmph. Posterity indeed. My grandkids rarely visit me and probably won't read the damn book anyway."

Karyn smiled. "Hm, hm, hm." She put her pen in her hand, and her writing pad on the table to her right. "Then let's not waste time, right? Where were you born, what were your parents' names, and where did you live?"

Teddy gave her a grouchy shake of his head. "Who cares? Why is that interesting? Why do biographers always start with baby pictures?

What's so interesting about a baby? My grandkids, who are in their thir-
ties, couldn't give a damn about my early life. They may or may not be
interested in what happened later."

"Okay," Karyn said, "where did you go to college? Anything interesting you want to tell me about that? You start where you want."

He nodded. "I grew up in Washington, so the logical place to attend
college, and graduate school, was at Georgetown. That's where my father
insisted I attend, and he made all the decisions. He was the boss. He was
a Georgetown alum and he made sure that I enrolled in ROTC, 'Hoya
Battalion,' just like he did. Like father, like son, but that was okay."

"What did your father do in Washington, DC? What was his business?"

"Politics, that was his business. He was an adjutant to Major General
Leonard Wood. Does that name mean anything to you?"

"I think there is a Fort Leonard Wood somewhere, an army post?
Am I right?"

Teddy scrunched his lips, showing his limited amount of patience.
"General Wood could have been president of the United States, and you
know what, my father would have been the vice president of the United
States." He stopped and scowled. "General Wood should've been the
Republican nominee for president in 1920. And he would've won; Republicans were favored. But Warren Harding beat out General Wood
in the primaries. It took ten ballots, but he beat him. That's the Republicans for you; always pick the wrong man. Anyway, my father never held
national office, but he remained influential in the Republican Party."

"And did you follow in his footsteps?"

"Some of them, but we didn't always believe in the same political
theories."

"So, tell me, what did you do when you left Georgetown?"

"Went into the army, of course. I was Hoya Battalion, remember?"
Teddy looked at Karyn with a frustrated glare, as though she should remember all the details and he shouldn't have to repeat himself. "When
you graduate ROTC, you owe the army two years. When I was com-
missioned as a second lieutenant, the army sent me to The Hague in the
Netherlands as an adjutant to Colonel Williams, who was involved in
a large legal matter. The Hague, as you know, is home to the Interna-

tional Court of Justice. I spent eighteen months in The Hague. When I returned back home, I was stationed as a military security guard at the Supreme Court for six months."

Karyn studied Teddy's weathered face for a moment, sat up, and said, "I think that's fascinating, Mr. Hartigan. If I were one of your family, I'd love to know all that. And I'd be so proud." Then for the first time since she met him, he smiled. Not a big smile, but one of those small, appreciative smiles. He tipped his head to the side, and said, "You might as well call me Teddy, my few acquaintances do."

"And please call me Karyn. You haven't mentioned any of those acquaintances. Would you like to tell me about them?"

Teddy hesitated a bit and finally said, "It would be painful, but I suppose I should, if it's going to be my life's history." Karyn nodded. He continued, "Well, there was Billy Foster, he was a friend and a pitcher on our baseball team. There was George Armstead, and there was Mitchell Willkie, Wendell Willkie's son."

"Wendell Willkie, the man who ran for president?"

"Yep, lost to Roosevelt fifty-five percent to forty-five percent. I met him through my father, of course. And then there was Betsy McCutcheon." His eyes drifted up to the ceiling and blinked a bit. "Boy, that's a long time ago. Another lifetime. The McCutcheons and the Hartigans were very close friends. Mr. McCutcheon and my father both belonged to the same country club, not to mention belonging to the same political ideology. Very conservative, if you know what I mean. When the two families would get together for a dinner, or a holiday, or a social event, and when they brought their kids, Betsy and I would play, and we became the best of friends. The relationship took a step up when we were fourteen or fifteen, if you know what I'm saying." Karyn smiled and nodded. "It was always one of those givens that Betsy and I would marry someday. I dated her all through college, although she went to Virginia. We chose to wait until I finished my master's and my army obligation before setting a date."

Karyn was interested in the romantic angle of the story. "So, when did you set a date? Did you get down on one knee?"

Teddy shook off the question. "Not exactly. That will all come later in the story. It was expected that when I returned to Washington from The Hague and finished serving out my term at the Supreme Court, I would pursue a career in government. That's what the Hartigans did."

"What do you mean, expected?"

"My father and his compatriots, like Mr. McCutcheon, would arrange what needed to be done to foster my political career. As a first step, my father arranged for an interview with Cordell Hull, the US secretary of state, with the anticipation that I should begin by working for the Department of State. After all, I did have a master's degree in political science. Since I had spent eighteen months in the Netherlands, Sumner Welles, the undersecretary of state, thought that I would be most helpful if I were a staff member assigned to the section supporting the Western European delegations. So, I found myself sitting in the basement of the State Department building doing research, collecting data, and preparing memoranda for our consulates in Belgium, Denmark, and the Netherlands."

"Oh, that must have been exciting."

"Let me tell you, the job was tedious and boring as all hell; that is, until I was reassigned." He stood. "Do you care for a cup of tea?"

KARYN ACCEPTED HER tea in a Wedgewood cup, inhaled the fragrance, and smiled. "Mmm. That's delightful."

"I have it shipped to me from England. It's my one vice."

"Are you curious about how I became a reporter?" Karyn asked.

Teddy took a sip of tea, looked up at her, and said, "Not really."

CHAPTER FOUR

"IT WAS LATE summer of 1938, and I had been working for the Department of State, Western European section, for a little over two years. Every day, there I was, sitting in the basement, studying embassy dispatches, foreign government position papers, and collecting foreign newspaper articles, when they were informative. I'd categorize them and file them away with internal State Department memos on matters concerning Belgium, Denmark, and the Netherlands.

"Throughout my two years, the dispatches, memos, and articles became more and more concerned with Adolf Hitler, and Germany's increased militarization. The Treaty of Versailles, which ended the First World War, prohibited Germany's military buildup, but what did Hitler care? He did whatever the hell he wanted to, and the other European countries let him get away with it.

"Hitler's saber-rattling and militarization didn't seem to terrorize Belgium, Denmark, or the Netherlands. His threats weren't directed against any of them. At that time, he was focused on the Slavic countries: Czechoslovakia, Austria, and Poland. Those were the countries with the largest concentration of Jewish residents. Hitler didn't seem to care about the Netherlands or the Scandinavian countries because they were traditionally neutral. Besides, they supplied Germany with oil, minerals, and raw materials. If there was a European war, those countries would no doubt declare their neutrality and continue to do business with anyone who wanted to buy, just like they did in World War One. So he was focused on the Slavic countries and on the people of the Jewish religion. He had a sick obsession with the Jews. It was in his writings. In any event, that was the opinion of the State Department.

"I admit, I had a boring job, sitting in the basement, but given the sluggish economy, I was glad to have a solid job at all, one that I could be proud of. Moreover, my father and his cohorts were proud of me, and Betsy was proud of me, though in her mind, the State Department was just a stepping stone to a much bigger and better job, so she said. Betsy dreamed of her own mansion in the upscale Washington neighborhoods where all her friends lived."

Karyn looked at her notes and then at Teddy. "You said, 'Until I was reassigned,' didn't you, Teddy? What was that about?"

"Yeah, right. It was late in the summer of 1938, at the end of August, I believe, that I received an interoffice message that Undersecretary of State Sumner Welles would like to see me in his office. Immediately. *Oh hell*, I thought, *what did I do wrong now?* I had no idea why I was being called and it made me nervous. I dashed up there as quickly as I could, and announced myself to his secretary, Ruth Henning.

"I knew Ruth very well. She would hand diplomatic packets to me from time to time and ask me to distribute them to other cabinet members. It made me feel important, and it got me out of the basement. And from time to time, I would bring her coffee and a pastry. We would sit and talk. She was a cutie, though older than me. She always had a steno pad in one hand, a pencil poking out of her tightly curled hair, and she was always chewing on a piece of gum.

"When I came over that afternoon in response to that message, she smiled at me coyly and bit her lower lip. She told me to take a seat while she walked into Undersecretary Welles's office to announce me. A few minutes later she returned with a little shrug. 'It will be a while,' she said. 'He's talking to somebody.'

"'I really don't know why I'm here,' I said to her in a tremulous tone. 'Why does he want to see me?' She raised her eyebrows, carefully looked around the room, and returned a conspiratorial glance. She reached into her drawer and pulled out a group of papers. She motioned for me to come have a seat next to her. 'These are my notes from this morning's meeting between Undersecretary Welles and Secretary of State Cordell Hull.'

"She leaned over and spoke very softly. 'I'm going to tell you why you've been sent for.' She picked up her notes. 'First, Sumner had me place a call to Cordell and request that he come over when he had a chance. A little while later, Secretary Hull came, said hello to me, and walked into Sumner's office. As usual in these meetings, I was asked to join them, bring my steno pad, and take notes.

"'Sumner began by saying in an angry tone, "The bastard gave his notice, effective immediately, and took the evening flight back to New York."

"'Cordell asked, "Who?"

"'"I don't remember his name," Sumner answered. "An official at our Amsterdam consulate. He was important because he was one of two or three men in charge of processing and approving visa applications." Cordell asked, "Do we know why?" and Sumner answered, "No, not specifically, but I suspect he couldn't handle the pressure. Of course, you know things are getting hotter by the day in all of our Western European consulates. There are huge increases in applications for visas, passports, family visits, emergency medical visas, blah, blah, blah. Which all exceed the quotas."

"'Cordell shrugged his shoulders and said, "Not much we can do about that. Immigration quotas are set by Congress." Sumner answered, "Well, that doesn't make it any easier for our consular officials. They take in the information, and if the application is approved, then their names are placed on a waiting list a mile long, knowing there's damn little chance of them getting a visa. Right now, there are a hundred and thirty thousand names on the German waiting list alone. And it's getting worse every day. Most of the applicants, especially those from Germany, Austria, Czechoslovakia, are refugees, and they list 'persecution' as the reason." And Cordell asked, "Jews?" and Sumner shrugged and said, "What do you think? Hitler passes some new restriction on Jews every day. But it's not only the Jews."

"'"Well, there's not much we can do about it," Cordell said. "Blame Congress, they're the ones that set the quotas. So why did you call me over here?"

"'"Because we need to fill the Amsterdam consulate post immediately. There are no applicants for the position and it's only getting worse.

I was hoping you could help. Hitler has the whole continent on edge. He boasts all he wants is peace, and then last March he swallows up Austria. Tens of thousands of Austrians start flooding our consulates, begging for visas. Then Hitler calls up a million reserves. Bear in mind, no enemy armies are sitting on Hitler's doorstep, no country has threatened Germany. There is no reason for him to call up a million troops. It leaves one to wonder, where is he going to send them? So, everyone is scared to death, and you can imagine what that does to our consulates."

""Yeah, yeah, what else is new? Hitler's front page every day," Cordell said. "Why did you call me over here?" And Sumner said, "Because I was hoping you knew someone who would fill that spot." Cordell twisted his lips and shook his head. "I don't get it. Foreign Service is a dedicated profession, not to be taken lightly. A consular office is a great honor. As it stands, there are no threats against the Netherlands. Don't you have anyone in the State Department you can transfer over there?" Sumner shook his head. Cordell said, "George Gordon is our ambassador to the Netherlands. Who does he recommend? In fact, why don't we just let George fill it? He must know of someone."

"'Sumner kept shaking his head. "I sent him a wire, Cordell, but he has yet to respond. He may be traveling. So, I wired Frank Lee. He's the consul general in Amsterdam. I met with him when I was there last spring. He tells me that he frequently corresponds with a young man in Washington, here at State, a researcher and analyst who sends him information."' At that point, Ruth stopped reading her notes, looked at me, and smiled. 'Guess who?'"

Karyn molded her lips like a whistle. "So, they intended to ask you to fill the position?" Teddy nodded and spread his hands wide open. "Me, and nobody else. It was pretty obvious that's why they sent for me. I said 'Me?' out loud to Ruth, and she quickly put her finger to her lips. 'Shhh.'

"I leaned over and whispered to her, 'I don't want the appointment, Ruth. I'm going to turn it down.'"

CHAPTER FIVE

"RUTH WALKED AHEAD of me and knocked on the door of Sumner Welles's private office. There stood Welles, a neatly dressed man with a receding hairline, gray along the edges, the same color as his brush mustache. I walked timidly into the room.

"'This is Mr. Theodore Hartigan, sir,' Ruth said, 'and he is here for this afternoon's impromptu appointment.'

"Undersecretary Welles stepped over to me and stuck out his hand. 'Come on in and have a seat, son.' I took a nervous step and Welles directed me to take the seat right beside his desk. 'Thank you for coming over on such short notice.'

"'Yes, sir, of course, sir,' I answered, though I really wasn't positive why I was there, no matter what Ruth's narrative told me. Maybe this was an interview.

"'Are you acquainted with Frank Lee at our consulate in Amsterdam?' Welles said.

"'Oh, yes, sir. I generally have a fair amount of contact with Consul General Lee, but not in person,' I answered. 'From time to time I correspond with him. I supply him with data and other information that he thinks is relevant. It's kind of my job and—'

"Welles smiled and nodded. 'Relax, son. Take it easy. You seem nervous.'

"And he was right on that account. I was nervous as hell, and I answered, 'A little. I don't know why you've called me here on an emergency basis, and—'

"'So, Theodore, or should I say Ted?'

"'Uh, actually my nickname is Teddy, not Ted, but Theodore would be just fine, sir.'

"'So, Teddy, or Ted, whatever, how is life in the Foreign Service, specifically the European section? How long have you been here now; three years?'

"'No, sir, two years. And it's more accurate to say *Western* European section, sir. Denmark, Belgium, and the Netherlands. That's where I sit every day, in a basement office, along with fourteen other men and women.' Then I quickly corrected the impression. 'But I'm honored to have the position, sir.'

"'I believe you are an analyst, is that right, Ted?'

"'Yes, sir. We follow European political currents, analyze data, read the daily publications, analyze comments, try to identify trends.'

"'Predict policies?'

"'Well, it's hard not to, but mostly we research and organize the data, identify trends, in order to pass the information up the line. Like to Consul General Lee. In that way, we *assist* in predicting policies.'

"'Pretty deep think-tank stuff, right, Ted?'

"I shook my head. 'I wouldn't go that far, sir. I'm just collecting data, reading newspapers, listening to speeches, trying to stay up to date on what the foreign governments are publishing, that sort of thing.'

"Welles sat back and nodded nonchalantly. To me, this meeting was bizarre. It appeared that Welles wasn't really interested in any of my answers or qualifications, no matter what I said. Perhaps he already knew the answers. Or didn't care. Maybe Ruth was wrong about the appointment. He continued, 'Do I understand that you speak Dutch?'

"'Yes, sir. I picked it up when I was assigned to The Hague four years ago, and frankly, it would be essential in my position. Much of what I'm reading is in Dutch.' I was nervous, and my knees were knocking. If I was the one who was interviewing to hire an official, I would never choose a nervous Nellie like me. I gazed around the room uncomfortably, totally confused why he would ask all these simple questions. And he didn't care about the answers.

"Finally, Welles leaned forward. 'We have a staffing shortage in our Amsterdam consular office,' he said. And I thought, *Oh Jesus, here it comes.*

"Welles shook his finger for emphasis. 'Right at a time when they are exceedingly busy,' he continued. 'They can't handle the overload. The only American staffer who processed visa and travel applications has resigned. Can you believe it? Other staffers are Dutch, and don't have the requisite clearance. We need a US boy in charge of processing our applicants. Making decisions. Following our quotas. Did you know about the man's resignation?'

"I cleared my throat. 'Yes, sir. But I don't know why he would resign or . . .'

"Welles waved me off. 'You're not getting my point, son. I want to send *you* to Amsterdam, Ted. I want *you* to fill that vacancy.'

"'Me?' I said. 'You want to put me in a leadership position in the Netherlands? Sir?'

"'Sure. A bright young man like you, familiar with the language, a man who has been—what is it you say—analyzing their data and predicting policies. And I can tell you have leadership potential. I can see that in you, Ted. You'd be perfect. It's a hell of an appointment for you, Ted. You'd be jumping ahead of a lot of people.'

"Well, no need to tell you, Karyn, I was a deer in the headlights. I mumbled, 'I don't know what to say, sir.'

"Welles smiled broadly. 'Then say, "Thank you, sir. It would be my honor, sir."'

"I bit my lip. How was I going to turn this down? That was the hard part. 'Well. I am certainly honored by your confidence, sir, it's just that right now, it's probably not a good time for me to be leaving Washington. When would you need me to go?'

"Welles looked at me like I hadn't heard a word he said. 'When? When? This is an emergency, son, haven't you been listening? We need you there right now.'

"'Sir, this is a bad time for me.'

"Welles creased his brow. 'Are you ill?'

"I shook my head. 'No, no. I'm fine, I mean I'm healthy, but this would be a bad time for me to leave Washington.'

"Welles leaned forward. 'You're in the Foreign Service, son, and after only two years, the undersecretary of state is putting a helluva promotion in your lap. And you are fumbling the ball, son. What is your problem?'

"'I'm appreciative, really I am, sir, but this is quite a shock. I hadn't put in for a transfer. My personal life is kind of unsettled at the moment, and I'm thinking what a disruption it would be. Not just for me, but for my girlfriend. She's planning on a big engagement party early this fall. And we're also very involved in a local theater production.'

"Welles scrunched his brow. 'A theater production? An engagement party? Are you engaged, Teddy?'

"'Not yet, but we both know we will be soon, and probably a wedding next June. She is a kindergarten teacher, and she loves the theater. She was a theater minor at college, and—'

"Welles had now had enough. 'Look here, this is a once-in-a-lifetime opportunity for you, young man. A giant step up the Foreign Service ladder. It'll get you out of sitting in the basement every day with those fourteen other men and women. It's a career advancement. I need you. Your government needs you. And we don't want to be derailed by kindergarten or amateur theater. Tell your girlfriend she can move to Amsterdam with you. A lot of guys do that, son.' Welles stood up. 'You'll leave in two weeks. Settle up your affairs here, it'll be a great move for you.'

"Welles reached over to shake my hand. 'This is a pivotal time in Europe and a pivotal time for you. Our last consular officer couldn't handle the pressure. Times are dicey, Ted. People need us. Go over there, son, and make a difference. You hear me?'

"I nodded, but I was hesitant.

"'Two weeks, son,' he said, giving me a pat on the shoulder. "My secretary, Ruth, will put in for your credentials. Congratulations.' He smiled broadly. 'Bon voyage, Theodore.'"

Karyn looked up from her notes. "Bon voyage? That's it? Leave in two weeks or forget about a government career?"

Teddy pursed his lips and nodded softly. "Yup."

"Well, what an asshole, excuse my French. What happened to Betsy?"

CHAPTER SIX

"I LEFT MY meeting with Undersecretary Welles in a state of shock. I walked around the block for an hour trying to figure out what to do. I wanted a career in the State Department. My father and all of his important friends had put me there. That was my future. But, sitting on Germany's border in 1938? I just wasn't prepared for that. What was I going to do? And I certainly couldn't quit the State Department. My father would never stand for that. And he couldn't go over Welles's head; there was no one over Welles and Hull but the president himself. And talk about the wrong time, I had to tell Betsy in the gentlest way possible, 'Honey, we're going to Amsterdam.' Of course, I expected her to protest, but I expected her to say that she would join me as soon as she could."

"You were that confident about Betsy McCutcheon?"

"Well, let's say I was hopeful. We had been going together for fifteen years, in a manner of speaking. We knew each other all our lives. Yes, I was confident, but nervous. I told you, I walked around the block for an hour. Maybe more."

Karyn set down her pen. "I want to respect your privacy here, Teddy. You don't have to tell this part if you don't want to. It's personal. It's private. This is a story that will be read by your grandkids, and who knows who else? Maybe you don't want them all to know your personal life with Betsy."

Teddy nodded. "Thank you, but it's a part of my life. This was a critical juncture of my life, and they should know about it. Is it going to embarrass me? I'm ninety-two years old. Who cares? So, include it."

Karyn was surprised, but she picked up her pen.

"It was time to talk to Betsy, no putting it off. My taxi pulled up to a stop in front of the McCutcheons' house, and I just sat there. The driver finally said, 'Hey buddy, are you getting out or what? I ain't got all day.' I had been rehearsing my talk with Betsy all the way from the State Department. I knew that no matter how I delivered the news, it wouldn't go over well. *Betsy, you won't believe the amazing meeting I had this afternoon. Undersecretary Sumner Welles called me into his office, me, and after praising my work* . . . I stopped and shook my head. Who was I kidding? She'd know that was baloney. She knew me too well.

"I looked out the window at Betsy's house and my nerves were tied in knots. I needed a few more minutes. Betsy was a hard woman. I had to build up my courage. I smiled pleadingly at the driver and threw a few extra bucks onto the front seat. He nodded and shrugged his shoulders. So, I conjured up another approach. *Undersecretary of State Sumner Welles, aware of my value to the Western European section, summoned me to his office today and* ordered *me to report to the Amsterdam consular office next week. They are in desperate need of me. I know that* Anything Goes *opens in a month, but this is a great opportunity for us, Betsy. I'm sure they have theater in Amsterdam.* I clenched my teeth. I thought that could work. It was quick, to the point, sounded good. And it was the truth. I just prayed that she'd be in an understanding mood.

"The driver turned his head. 'Sooner or later, fellow. We're at the address you gave me; 329 Greenwood. And I gotta go to work.'

"I sighed, got out of the cab, and walked toward the door. Maybe I'd be better off easing into the subject, a little at a time. I'd just have to find the right moment to let her know. Oh, who was I kidding, she was going to blow a gasket. But it had to be done, like ripping off a Band-Aid. I had to leave in two weeks. Probably alone.

"The McCutcheon house was a white-and-blue colonial in an exclusive section of Washington, DC. Bushes were neatly trimmed, and pots of geraniums lined the walkway. Everything was so well cared for. Betsy's father was an important businessman, but I didn't know exactly what he did. Mr. McCutcheon wasn't overly friendly where I was concerned. He wasn't exactly mean to me, just indifferent. I assumed that I didn't meet Mr. McCutcheon's high expectations where his daughter was concerned, but who would?

"I reached the door, still rehearsing a few alternative storylines, and

rang the bell. The McCutcheons' housemaid answered and showed me to the vestibule where I was to wait while she announced me to Betsy. In a few minutes, Betsy descended the spiral staircase and waltzed into the room. As always, my face blushed. She was adorable in her plaid A-line skirt and white Peter Pan collar, perhaps the most adorable girl in DC. Her smile was infectious. She was a little shorter than me, so she raised up on her tiptoes to give me a kiss." Telling the story, Teddy's eyes got a bit glossy. "That's how she always greeted me."

Karyn smiled on being introduced to the softer side of Teddy Hartigan.

"'Bets,' I said excitedly, 'you'll never believe what happened to me today. I couldn't wait to come over here and tell you.'

"Before I could say another word, she held up her palm to cut me off. 'Wait,' she said. 'I want you to meet someone.' She took me by the wrist and walked me quickly into the study, where her father was talking with another man. Both of them were dressed in conservative dark gray suits, narrow striped ties, and highly polished shoes. They were each holding a snifter of brandy. I was pretty sure I had seen the other man before. Maybe in a newsreel. He had an odd bowl haircut.

"'Theodore,' Mr. McCutcheon said, 'come on over here, I'd like to introduce you to a dear friend of mine.'

"I turned to Betsy, who fluttered her eyebrows and nodded her approval, as if to say, *This could be your big break.* 'Go on,' she said quietly, and gave me a nudge.

"I stepped nervously forward. *What now?* I thought. *What's my next surprise? It's been that kind of day.* 'Good afternoon, Mr. McCutcheon,' I said, extending my hand to Betsy's father.

"'Theodore, I'd like you to meet Senator Gerald Nye.' I remember he pronounced Gerald with a hard *G*. Then the light went on, and I made the connection. Senator Gerald Nye, powerful conservative isolationist, and author of the Neutrality Acts of 1935 and 1937, which were clearly designed to keep America out of European affairs. 'America First.' I had read the transcripts of Nye's addresses to Congress blaming the arms manufacturers and the international bankers for America's involvement in World War One. Along with Senator Robert LaFollette, Nye had recently formed a group that advocated the theory that a Jewish conspiracy was pushing America into the next foreign war. And there was Mr. McCutcheon sitting with his *very, very dear friend*.

"Mr. McCutcheon poked me hard on the chest with his forefinger. 'Senator Nye tells me there might be an opening in his congressional office next year.' He tipped his head in Nye's direction. 'Isn't that right, Gerald?'

"'Yes, indeed. Two of my young staffers are going into industry after the first of the year, thanks to you, Henry. I understand that Betsy's young man is a political science student. Is that right?"

"'Well, not exactly a student,' I said, 'but yes, sir. I have my master's in political science and right now I'm working at the State Department. Western European section: Belgium, Denmark, and the Netherlands.'

"Senator Nye's lips curled downward. 'Hmph. You'd be smart to steer clear of that area. Nothing but trouble for us. Mark my words, young man, there's going to be a war over there before you can say Jack Robinson. And if my committee has anything to say about it, the United States of America isn't going to be drawn anywhere near it. Not with dollars, not with arms, and certainly not with troops. Let those European warmongers fight over their territories as they've been doing for the last five hundred years. Before you know it, it will be 1914 all over again, and if Roosevelt has his way, we'll be sending shiploads of troops. That's exactly the kind of recklessness my Neutrality Acts will prevent.'

"'Y-yes, sir,' I stumbled.

"'Keep in mind, Theodore, there just might be a position on my staff come next February. I will need a secretary. I want you to apply,' he said.

"I looked over at Betsy, who was struggling to suppress her delight. 'Oh, that's very exciting, Senator,' she said. 'Thank you so much.'

"Nye nodded patronizingly at her. Then to me he added, 'Submit your résumé, young man, and we'll talk about it in the winter.'

"I was standing before one of the most powerful US senators, and my future father-in-law, and all I wanted to do was get the hell out of there. I wouldn't work for Nye if he paid me a thousand dollars a day! But I was shaking in my boots. I said, 'Thank you, sir.' Nye nodded, took a sip of his brandy, leaned back, and crossed his legs. Conversation over. Betsy took my arm and led me from the room.

"'What do you think about that?' she said quietly, once we were alone. 'Senator Nye is very important, you know, and he's practically offering you a job. You could have been a little more gracious.'

"I answered carefully, or so I thought. 'I understand, sweetheart, but my father wouldn't stand for that. He would never let me quit my job at the State Department, even if it's overseas. Besides, I'm not sure I would want to work for Senator Nye. He and I don't think alike, you know, on world affairs. He's way to the right and—'"

"'Who cares if you think alike?' she said, putting her foot down. 'Working with Senator Nye would do a lot more for your career than researching data files in the basement.' My responsive expression was somewhere between crestfallen and exasperated. Betsy picked up on it and backtracked. 'I'm sorry, sweetie, I didn't mean to hurt your feelings, or say that your work isn't important. It's just that you would be working directly for a senator in Washington.'

"'I work for the State Department in Washington, Bets, in the European section, and Nye is an isolationist. He'd just as soon we didn't have a European section at all. He doesn't want anything to do with Europe.'

"She tipped her head to the side and shrugged as if it was no big deal, a gesture I referred to as a tilted shrug. 'I'm talking about you, Theodore Hartigan,' she said, 'and our future together. Sometimes you have to bend a little, Teddy, and make some sacrifices. You know, sometimes you have to stand on your own two feet. You know, we've said this before, don't be a spineless teddy bear.' And she gave me a kiss. 'You don't have to work for the State Department anymore. You could get out of that basement, and get a *higher-paying job*.' She smiled at her joke and kissed me on the cheek. 'So,' she said, 'what's your big news today, honey? What did you rush over here to tell me? I'm all ears.'"

Karyn looked at Teddy. "Uh-oh," she said.

"Oh, you're right, Karyn. I turned to Betsy and answered, 'Maybe this isn't such a good time to have this discussion.'

"'C'mon, Teddy,' she said, 'you can always talk to me. You can tell me anything. We're as close as two people can be. What's the big news? Did you get a promotion? Oh boy, I hope you got a promotion.'

"I clenched my teeth. 'Well, there's no easy way to say this,' I said softly. 'I'm going to Amsterdam.'

"Betsy's response was totally unexpected. She clapped! 'That is so amazing! Gathering data in Amsterdam, when do you get to go? How long do you get to stay? Oh, I wish I was going to Amsterdam. Maybe you could take me with you?'"

Karyn gave Teddy a thumbs-up. "Boy, did you get lucky."

Teddy's lips twisted. "Not really. When I heard what she said, I smiled at her and gave her a hug. 'That's what I wanted to hear,' I said with a sigh of relief. 'The State Department is transferring me to our consular office in Amsterdam.'

"Then in a split second, Betsy's smile disappeared. 'Transferring? What does that mean? For how long?'

"'Well, it's a permanent transfer, Bets. It's a reassignment.'

"Betsy took a step back. 'Reassignment? I don't understand. I thought the plan was for you to move up the State Department ladder. Your career, remember?'

"I took her hand. 'Well, I am, honey. It's a promotion, a huge promotion. I'm going to be a consular official in Amsterdam. The appointment came to me personally from Undersecretary Welles.'

"'Amsterdam, Holland?'

"I nodded sharply. 'I'll be moving there. *We'll* be moving there.'

"Betsy looked dazed. 'Hold on a minute, Teddy,' she said with a tremor in her voice. 'This is life-changing. You . . . you can't make that kind of decision for me. I mean, we won't be in America.' She shook her head from side to side. 'Oh sweetheart, tell them you don't want this reassignment. You don't want a damn transfer. To hell with the promotion. They can't force you to take it, can they? I mean, it's not like you're in the army. You could . . .'

"'It's done, Bets. I accepted it. They want me to leave in two weeks. Look, it'll be a great career move for us.'

"Betsy was on the verge of hysteria. 'Us?' She continued to shake her head. 'You keep saying "us." For *you*, maybe, but *not for me*. I don't want to move to Amsterdam. I have a nice home here. And friends. And I have a nice teaching job here, with some great kids. Did you forget all that before you accepted? And what about *Anything Goes*? The curtain goes up in six weeks. You're playing Billy Crocker, for goodness' sake. He's the *lead*. What about that?'

"'I know, but Jimmy can step in, he's the understudy. And Andrea can play Hope.'

"Betsy stomped her foot. 'That's *my* role. I'm Hope Harcourt! Oh, Teddy, how can you do this to us? How can you be so thoughtless? You didn't even consult me; it was so damn selfish of you. We have plans, a life *together*.'

"'We still have a life together, Bets. Only we'll be in Amsterdam for a while. You'll come with me. Undersecretary Welles even suggested it. He said, "Bring your girlfriend with you."'

"'What?!'

"'The State Department approves of my bringing you with me. I'm sure they'll take care of all the arrangements. I'm sure they'll give us a bigger stateroom. You can come with me and live in Amsterdam.'

"'I don't want to live in Amsterdam! I don't even know where it is. If you showed me a map, I couldn't find it. We have a future *together*, Teddy, and it's right here in Washington, DC, and in the St. Andrews Church Theater Group. And what about *my* engagement party? Did you forget about that, too?'

"'Betsy, it's my engagement party too,' I said, though meekly.

"'It sure is! We're supposed to have a lavish engagement party in December. I've been planning it with Susie and my mother for weeks. What am I supposed to do about that?'

"I took a deep breath. I was becoming irritated at her. Talk about selfish. 'We can still have an engagement party,' I said. 'Or a wedding party! We can just have them when we come back.'

"I thought saying 'wedding party' would close the deal. Boy was I wrong. Betsy set her hands on her hips. Her shoulders were back, her lips were taut, and her jaw was clenched. 'Move back? Oh, is that right? And when will that be? Two years? Maybe even after we're married by some Holland priest? Or maybe I should wait two years to have my engagement party. You're not making any sense.'

"My frustration was growing. 'No, Betsy, you're not supposed to wait. You're supposed to come with me.'

"'Oh, now I'm *supposed to*? Who says I'm *supposed to*?' Betsy began to cry. 'Leave my family, leave my job, leave my friends, leave *Anything Goes*, all because you say I'm *supposed to*? Why? Because it's good for your career? Well, your career doesn't care if it ruins my life, does it?'"

Teddy suddenly stopped his narration. It was apparent to Karyn that he was becoming emotionally rattled. His lips were quivering. "Why don't we stop there for today," Karyn said. "I'm kind of tired, and I can tell you are too."

Teddy nodded in agreement. "Just a little bit more and we'll finish this for the day," he said, and Karyn nodded.

"I could tell I wasn't going to win my argument with Betsy," Teddy said with strain in his voice. "I kept thinking, what's going to become of our relationship? I didn't want to lose Betsy. I couldn't give up. 'Bets,' I pleaded, 'I'm ordered to report to Amsterdam in two weeks. Arrangements have been made, tickets are being issued. That's when my new job starts. As an important embassy official. A promotion. If I don't go, I'll lose my job. Welles even told me that my career in the State Department would be over. Please understand, honey. I have to go.'

"Betsy stomped her foot. 'Then go! But don't look for me to go with you. Get that through your thick skull.'

"'Aw, c'mon, Betsy, just think about it. I can't lose you, honey. Just think about it.'

"'I'm not going to think about it. Not for five minutes. This whole thing is crazy. You have a lot of nerve busting in here and saying all that stuff. Why can't you stand up on your two feet and tell them you don't want to go? Why are you so damn timid?' Betsy, now hysterical, turned and ran up the stairs and slammed her bedroom door. That was it."

Karyn put down her pen and closed her writing pad. "Then we should call it a day, Teddy. That's enough, don't you think? And Teddy, tonight, think about whether you want to include all that in your written biography. It'll be seen by . . . who knows how many."

Teddy took a breath before he responded. "My life's story would be incomplete without it. You will understand."

CHAPTER SEVEN

KARYN ARRIVED AT her hotel, kicked off her shoes, and flopped down on the bed. This had been an exhausting day. What must it feel like for Teddy? It was a lot for him to reveal in a single day. And it must have been depressing for him, at least some of it. It brought back some tough memories, that was obvious. Why would Teddy want his relatives to know all the details of his broken relationship? Why not just tell the story of his life as an embassy official at the onset of World War II? There must be several accounts of danger and heroics and war stories enough to make an interesting book for his grandchildren or great-grandchildren. Not a broken love affair. And this was certainly not what she had expected. Yet, she'd made a bargain. She would write his story, and in exchange, he would reach into his contacts and learn what he could about Annie. That was the deal, and she was determined to keep her end of it.

Karyn's cell phone chimed. There was a text message from Burt Franklin. *Hi Karyn: After a day with my cousin, you must need some refreshment. Feel like going to dinner? If so, give me a buzz.* Followed by his cell phone number. Maybe an evening with Burt would brighten her mood. He might be able to shed some light on why Teddy felt a need to memorialize his dating history.

"I'm glad you called me back, Karyn," Burt said. "I was worried that after a day with my grouchy old cousin, you might have thrown in the towel."

"He hasn't been grouchy at all," she said calmly. "But it must have been a very emotional day for him. I'm sure he is drained. I know I am. But I'm not going to throw in the towel."

"Are you still in the mood for dinner?"

"You bet I am, and maybe a cocktail to boot."

"Italian?"

"Perfect."

"I'll pick you up at seven."

"I DIDN'T FIND him to be grouchy at all," Karyn repeated over a glass of sauvignon blanc. "In my career, I've interviewed hundreds of people, many of them as disagreeable as you can imagine, but Teddy is not one of them. And I've interviewed plenty of people who want to discuss their personal relationships, for notoriety or some other publicity reason, but Teddy didn't come across as one of those either. Truthfully, I don't know his motive for baring his soul. Maybe he needs some internal reconciliation. Maybe this is a catharsis of some kind, I don't know."

"You're a very sensitive woman, do you know that? You must have a background in psychology."

Karyn smiled and shrugged her shoulders. "No, not really. I just sit and listen, but it was obvious that the session was emotional for him. It certainly was for me. He's near the end of the road. Why go through this? Why does he want his relatives to have those memories of him? Weren't there more heroic episodes in his life?"

"Well, he doesn't talk much about the early years of his life," said Burt. "Not even to me. I told you that. I do know that he received the presidential medal of something from President Truman at the end of the war. And some honorary royal commendation from Queen Wilhelmina of the Netherlands as well. So he must have done something."

Karyn pressed her lips and shook her head in frustration. "Goodness' sake, then why doesn't he tell me about that?"

"Give him time. Maybe he will. You know, it's his business. His story for posterity, or whatever."

DINNER WAS SERVED and the conversation turned to small talk. "What kind of work do you do in the banking business?" Karyn asked.

Burt smiled. "Always the reporter."

Karyn shrugged. "You don't have to answer if you don't want to." She smiled coyly and leaned forward. "Maybe it's international espionage."

That elicited a hearty laugh, and Burt blotted his napkin on his mouth. "Oh, I'm sure, if you think trading currencies is all that covert. Really, it's boring as hell. But it does allow me to travel. And meet pretty reporters in Tel Aviv."

Karyn smiled. "Well, look at me. I get to travel too. Who knows how long this interview will take? I could be here for weeks."

"What does your husband have to say about that?"

Karyn gave a little shrug. "I'm not married," she said matter-of-factly.

"Oh, I'm sorry. But you have children and grandchildren. I met two of them. I mean, I assumed you were married. I'm sorry."

Karyn didn't immediately respond. She just shrugged a little. Burt quickly said, "Please forgive me. That was intrusive of me and boorish and I apologize."

"That's all right," she said quietly as she looked down toward her dinner plate.

Burt tried to make things right. "You could ask me the same thing. Does my wife object to all my traveling? And I would have to answer, 'Um, not really. We're still married, sort of, but my travels don't matter to her.' He spread his hands. 'And then we would have exchanged two inappropriate, painful questions and answers. So again, I'm sorry, Karyn, I didn't mean anything other than small talk."

Karyn lifted her gaze and said, "So, can I ask you a personal question in return?" Burt took a breath. Karyn said, "Do you have a favorite baseball team? Or, have you seen any good movies lately?" Which caused them both to laugh, and lightened the mood.

CHAPTER EIGHT

"IN MY MIND," Teddy said, "I replayed the final conversations with Betsy over and over during the few days prior to departing Washington." Teddy was wearing the same plaid button-down shirt he'd worn the day before. He just picked up where he left off, as though there were no time lapse at all. The only thing different was the weather.

"Up until that time, Betsy was my first and only relationship. In the days following our blowup, I tried and tried to reason with her. I begged her to consider it further and give me a chance. My father told me not to worry, she'd get over it. 'She'll understand that you are in the State Department serving your country,' he said. 'I'll put in a good word with her father.'

"I reached out to a couple of her friends. 'Tell her it won't be the end of the world, just a couple years. She will soon realize what a wonderful adventure it could be for the two of us. She loves social engagements, and there are bound to be a number of them at the Amsterdam consulate.' I urged her to change her mind, and she urged me to turn down the appointment. I told her I couldn't do it, that I had accepted the appointment. And that was it. We were at an impasse, and there was no hope. I prepared for my flight to Amsterdam.

"Three days later, she came over to my apartment. I was packing my suitcases and a trunk. I was totally surprised when she showed up, and I thought maybe she was having second thoughts. She came to me, and we hugged and kissed just like two people in love. I held her tightly and we both cried. But it was soon evident that she was still hoping to change my mind.

"'Teddy,' she cried, 'I can't bear the thought of you leaving me. Day and night I've been an emotional mess. My mother's been consoling me, and so has my father. I told them I was considering going with you. My father asked me if I could just wait for a few days while he checked it out. Then, last night my father and Senator Nye came over to talk to me. They asked if I was aware of the dangers if I moved to Europe? Don't I remember that the United States fought a war with Germany not even twenty years ago? Did I know that we lost three hundred and twenty thousand young American boys in that war and it wasn't even about our country?'

"Betsy sniffed and continued. 'I told them that we were not going to Germany or anywhere near it. I said that there were no wars going on in Amsterdam or even anywhere else in Europe that I knew of.'

"'Don't be naïve,' Senator Nye said to me, 'the Netherlands is right next door to Nazi Germany.' He said, 'Have you been paying attention to what that bastard Hitler has been saying? Do you know about the people he's already killed, or put into prison camps?' Then Senator Nye pounded his fist and said in very strong tones, 'I'm telling you that Hitler will soon start a war with Czechoslovakia over the Sudeten Mountains and then with Poland and then who else? He'll go through all Europe. And when he does, it will draw in every country in Europe, and that includes the Netherlands. Holland may make all the noise it wants about how it's a neutral country, but Hitler'll take it when he wants it.'

"Betsy continued, 'Nye handed me a copy of a speech that Hitler gave at the Berlin Sports Palace just the previous Monday night. September 26. He circled the part he wanted me to read to you, Teddy. Senator Nye said these are the words of a warmonger.'

"Of course, I knew what she was talking about. Even though I had heard the speech at the State Department, I let her read the circled portion to me. It was the part where Hitler had warned President Beneš of Czechoslovakia that if he didn't give the Sudeten region to Germany, they would take it anyway. The circled part of Hitler's speech said, 'The decision now lies in his hands: peace or war. He will either accept this offer and now at last give to the Germans their freedom or we will go and fetch this freedom for ourselves.'

"I nodded. 'I know all about this,' I said, 'I listened to that speech.

Hitler's always making blustery remarks. And they shouldn't be taken lightly. Irrespective, we have an embassy and consular offices in the Netherlands, which is still at peace. And the United States will protect our embassy.'

"'Not according to Senator Nye,' Betsy said. 'We may be allies, but we will not go to war to defend Holland from Hitler. Senator Nye said you can depend on that. And then he looked at me and said, "I would never let a daughter of mine go to Europe. Not these days."' At that point, Betsy broke into tears and ran out the door.

"I went to my best friend. That was my mother. I asked her if I was being unfair to Betsy. My dad had set me up in a fabulous Foreign Service career. It was my career, my life, but Betsy wouldn't even consider it if it meant going overseas. I said, 'What if I took her out to dinner, to that fancy French restaurant she loves? I could present it in a more suave way. An assignment in Europe, in Holland, the land of windmills. You know, the two of us, hand in hand, through fields of tulips. Blah, blah, blah?'

"My mother shook her head and answered softly. 'No, Teddy, I don't think you're being unfair to her, you're just not the same people. You like your career and you have a right to keep it. And working for Senator Nye is not a career move you can handle. Betsy has her friends, her social circle. They mean a lot to her.' And I realized that her social group wasn't my social group. Things that were important to her weren't important to me. My mother finally suggested that maybe my assignment in Amsterdam, spending this time apart, would put things into perspective for each of us. Two days later, I boarded the ship and left for Amsterdam."

"I REMEMBER THE rainstorm when we landed at the Amsterdam airport. I gazed out of the window and watched the ground crew wheel the passenger stairs for the plane. I disembarked and followed the group. Standing at the ramp was a man in a khaki raincoat holding a sign that read, HARTIGAN.

"I waved. *'Welkom in Nederland,'* the man said. 'I'm Mitchell Jessup.'

"'Thanks for coming to meet me,' I said. 'I would have no idea where to go. Frankly, this whole thing was put together so suddenly, I don't know even where I am supposed to stay. I was told to report directly to the consulate. To Consul General Lee.'

"Jessup smiled. 'Well, you got this far. Don't worry about the details. The consul general has taken a personal interest in you. He sent me to meet you and bring you in. He has also tasked me with the responsibility of familiarizing you with our operations. Pretty much a red-carpet treatment, I would say. You were lucky they chose you over the other candidates for the job.'

"*There were other candidates?* I thought. *He could have chosen someone else?* 'To tell you a secret, Mitchell, I didn't really put in for this assignment. I didn't ask to come here. Isn't that crazy? One day I'm collecting data in the State Department basement, and the next I'm on a plane to Amsterdam.'

"'Well, lucky you,' Jessup said. 'In the US Foreign Service, Amsterdam has always been considered a prime posting. A real feather in your cap. Great staff, great city. Are you single?'

"I shrugged. 'I don't know. Probably. Don't get me wrong, I'm thankful for the assignment, but coming so abruptly like it has, it's kind of jumbled up my life. My fiancée feels abandoned, in fact she's probably history, and the entire cast of *Anything Goes* is furious with me for walking out a month before we open.'

"'You're engaged?'

"'I don't know. It wasn't official, I hadn't given her a ring. I was waiting until I paid it off. It was on layaway.' I shook my head. 'I hope I can get my money back.'

"Jessup seemed unsympathetic. 'Sorry, mate, but things are bound to turn around. Believe me, you could be stuck in a worse place. You'll soon see what I mean. It's always been one of the top destinations for Foreign Service workers. The icing on the cake, so to speak. There's always a waiting list for transfers. Well, at least there was until recently.'

"'When I interviewed for this position, or when I was forced to interview, Undersecretary Welles told me that you have a staffing shortage right at the time when the consulate is extremely busy. He attributed it to pressure from the increased demand for visas.'

"'Sumner said that?' Jessup curled his lips. 'He knows better. Oh, it's true that we're understaffed. We've lost three consular officers in the last few months—two Dutch and one American—and it's true there are lines at the door at all hours, but Mr. Hershman did not walk out last week because of workload pressure. That's bullshit.'

"'Then what was it?'

"Jessup raised his eyebrows. 'Workload pressure? Oh, Hershman wouldn't say that. He had some other excuse; I think he said it was family problems back home. But if you ask me, it was nerves, plain and simple. Everyone here is a bit on edge. I'll grant you, some of it has to do with the workload—trying to process thousands of visa applications— but look around, mate, we border Germany, a country with the largest, most well-equipped military in the world. And they're not afraid to deploy it. It is understandable if a worker opts for more peaceful surroundings, isn't it?'

"We grabbed my luggage and headed out to Jessup's car. He continued, 'Truthfully, I don't get it. I realize I'm not an American, I've lived in Holland all my life, but I work for an American outfit. I feel pretty calm because America doesn't take any shit. America is not afraid of anybody. Twenty years ago, America jumped into a European war that didn't even concern it, and won the war.'

"It was pretty clear to me that Jessup was naïve when it came to America's 1938 political state of affairs. I guess he never heard of 'America First.' 'Things have changed, Mitchell. America's not so quick to jump to anyone else's aid anymore.'

"'Well, maybe we don't need it. In the last war, the one they call "The Great War," the Netherlands stayed neutral the whole time. In fact, we prospered. So, there's no reason for Dutch citizens to be nervous. I know that Hitler could start another war tomorrow if he wanted to, but why would he start one with the Netherlands? He makes money with us. We make money with Germany. That's the way we are. There are constant assurances coming out of The Hague and the Royal Palace of our continued neutrality. We have nothing to fear from Hitler's military.'

"I shook my head. 'Maybe you're right,' I said. Inside I thought that Jessup was living in some fantasy world. Hitler was a madman. Totally unpredictable. For two years, every day, I had been reading *De Telegraaf* for Dutch news, *De Standaard* for Flemish news, and *Der Völkischer Beo-bachter* for German news. I had listened to taped radio reports sent twice weekly. I had listened to tapes of Hitler's speeches and public addresses. Hate speeches. Warmonger speeches. It was my job to study them, analyze them, and form opinions of trends and policies.

"Jessup said, 'Yeah, I ain't worried about it. Like, if he wants a coastline, he could just invade France. They're a traditional enemy of his and they have a much better coastline than we do. Right? I ain't worried, Teddy.'

"I smiled and slowly shook my head. 'You're probably right, Mitchell. He just might invade France. Just like his predecessor Kaiser Wilhelm did in 1914. He invaded your neighbor Belgium so that he would have a straight line right into France and their coast. And guess what? Belgium had declared their neutrality too.'"

"'Yeah, but he didn't invade the Netherlands, did he?' Mitchell said with a sharp nod.

"The car rolled along toward Amsterdam City Center, and I gazed at the lush fields and storied windmills. Beautiful country. Jessup waved his arm and proudly said, 'Look, we're not a warring country; we don't take sides. Ask around, talk to the people, and you'll see that everyone feels pretty comfortable and secure here in the Netherlands. Ask around.'

"'Hmm,' I said. 'I bet they believed the same thing in Vienna before he rolled in. And you better believe they don't think that anymore in Prague. No one knows what the mad paperhanger is going to do next. Ask around? Well, it might depend on who you ask. I'm here to fill an empty position, a shortage in our staff that exists because of Hitler's aggression. Nancy Kalish, one of your brightest and hardest-working staffers, recently returned to the States because her nerves were shot. She was scared as hell. I know that because I was corresponding with her.'

"Jessup shrugged his shoulders. 'It's true, but Nancy was different. She was Jewish.'

"'There are a hundred and thirty thousand Jews in this country right now, Mitchell. Amsterdam is referred to as the Jerusalem of the West. Do you think that Hitler and Himmler and Goebbels are content living next door to the Jerusalem of the West? And what about those hundred and thirty thousand Jews that live in the Netherlands? Do you think they're content living right next door to countries burdened by the Nuremburg Race Laws?'

"Mitchell answered, 'Wait till you're here a while. You'll find that the Dutch are a happy, calm people. It's the immigrants who stand in line, the ones trying to get visas, that are nervous. Not the Dutch. They're neutral, and Hitler said he respects their neutrality. It's Poland that should be worried, not Holland.'

"'They would be if they had any sense. Especially the Jews. They know what the Nazis have done to Jews in Germany and in the countries that they occupy. And it's like they can see the one million Nazi soldiers standing on the Netherlands' eastern doorstep just waiting for the word. Do you think those Jews feel happy and calm because The Hague and the Royal Palace have announced that the Netherlands will remain neutral?' I shook my head. 'That's why there are long lines at the US consulate door. That's why there's a waiting list a mile long for a visa. And isn't that why I have been sent to fill the vacancy?'

"Jessup shrugged. It was hard to argue with someone like me, someone who had the facts. But he said, 'The long lines are refugees from Germany, Austria, Czechoslovakia, and other countries. They're not Dutch.' Jessup waved his hand to change the subject. He'd had enough of this talk. He might be wondering why the hell I took this job, if I was so damn scared. And I would have to think hard to come up with an answer to that one.

"Mitchell ended the talk on a high note. 'Look at it this way, Teddy, you've been assigned to a great consular office. You're here, so enjoy it! We have terrific people here and great support from the US Department of State. I understand if you're a little nervous right now—new job, new city—that makes sense to me. But you'll get along great in Amsterdam. Everybody does.'

"We traversed the bridge at Leidsestraat and parked in front of a building on Keizersgracht. I stood outside on the narrow sidewalk and gawked at the scene. There were blocks and blocks of buildings and houses, tightly packed, wall-to-wall, along skinny sidewalks. A kaleidoscope of pastel colors. Narrow streets fanning out in an arc, separated from each other by rings of bike paths and concentric canals. I smiled as a statistic came to mind. 'One hundred and sixty canals and seventeen hundred bridges.' And I said to Mitchell, 'You just said Poland should be worried, not Holland. So what is the difference between "Holland" and "the Netherlands"?' He laughed and said, 'There's no difference. I mean there is, but most people use the terms interchangeably.'

"We had stopped in front of a redbrick building, four stories, with a sculptured roof. A dignified building with a large American flag waving on a pole, and a brass plate to the right of the doorway that read 'Consulate of the United States of America.' True to my anticipations, a large number of men, women, and children stood quietly in a line at the front door.

"'Home sweet home,' said Jessup. 'Let's go meet the family.'"

CHAPTER NINE

"THE LOBBY OF the consulate was relatively small. A young woman, her blond hair pulled back, walked down the hall, carrying a stack of papers clipped together. 'Good morning, Julia,' Jessup said cheerfully. 'May I introduce you to our newest consular official, Theodore Hartigan?'

"Julia stood and held out her hand. 'Julia Powers,' she said in perfect English. 'So nice to meet you, Mr. Hartigan. We've been waiting for you. It's wonderful that Washington was able to fill our vacancy so quickly. It was much quicker than we expected. As you can see, we are very, very busy these days.' She swept her arm in the direction of the doorway. She had a cute manner about her. I stepped up and shook her hand. It was soft and pretty. 'It was quick for me as well, Julia,' I answered. Then I leaned forward and whispered, 'Totally unexpected, I should say. It's still a blur.'

"Julia noticed the two suitcases that lay at my feet. 'I can see that,' she said with a glint. 'Are you moving into the consulate?'

"Jessup laughed. 'Consul Lee told me to bring him straight here from Schiphol. He doesn't even know where he's staying, and neither do I.'

"'My, my, Mr. Hartigan, you're in quite a fix,' Julia said playfully. 'I guess it's too late to go back home, and I hear that all the rooms in Amsterdam are full.'

"I rolled my eyes. 'I guess I'm just going to have to bunk with my buddy Sumner Welles, or have him come here to solve my dilemma.'

"'Oh, the undersecretary would love to come back here,' Julia said.

'He was here a few months ago and he, Mr. Jessup, and Consul General Lee made a serious withdrawal from Amsterdam's beer reserve.'

"Jessup laughed. 'Ha. What is it you Yanks say; I refuse to answer on the grounds I could criminalize myself?'

"'Something like that,' I answered.

"Julia tipped her head toward the elevator, 'Right now, Mr. Hartigan, I think Consul General Lee is waiting to meet you. He's on the second floor. You can leave your bags here. When you're finished, Mr. Jessup will take you to your apartment.'"

"CONSUL GENERAL LEE sat in his well-appointed office with wood paneling. His windows overlooked the Keizersgracht canal with a corner view of the Museumplein, one of Amsterdam's classic public squares; a beautiful grass field bordered by several cultural and administrative buildings, museums, theaters, a day care center, and a teachers' training college. He stood as I entered, and offered a warm handshake. 'Glad to have you on board, Hartigan. Your presence at this time is most welcome.'

"'It is my honor, sir. It appears the consulate is quite busy.'

"'So, you saw the line at the door? How many are there?'

"'You mean standing in the line? I didn't count, sir. Quite a few.'

"'It's the same at our consular offices in Rotterdam and The Hague. We are besieged with applications for immigration visas and nonimmigrant visas. They line up before dawn and we process them all day long until we close. The ones that aren't seen today are given a number and told to come back tomorrow. Almost all of them are German or Austrian, maybe some Czechs and Poles. And the majority are Jewish, which is understandable, given the present state of affairs in the German-occupied countries. Sadly, the US quota for applicants of German nationality, which now includes German-occupied Austria, is less than twenty-eight thousand per year. As you can imagine, that quota was filled a long time ago.'

"I was puzzled. 'But we continue to schedule appointments for them?' I asked.

"'Of course; we are a United States consulate. What does Lady Liberty say? 'Give me your tired, your poor, your huddled masses yearning to breathe free'?' He pointed to a plaque on the corner of his desk on which Emma Lazarus's poem was framed. 'Unfortunately, for the last fourteen years, since 1924, she lifts her lamp until the congressional quota for the applicant's home country is full. Nineteen thirty-eight's quota is filled for Germany and Austria. Unless Congress decides to increase the quota, which is very unlikely, it's filled for 1939 and 1940. So, most of those people you saw today will be assigned a place on the waiting list.'

"'How many are on the waiting list?'

"'As of last month, one hundred and thirty thousand people were on the German waiting list alone. Since the Anschluss, that includes the Austrians. The Netherlands borders Germany, so the vast majority of applicants are German.'

"I was beginning to feel overwhelmed. 'And my job is to schedule appointments for them?'

"'No, they'll do that downstairs. Your job is to meet with them at their scheduled appointment time. You'll meet with them, interview them, provide the information for their formal application, and forward the package to Washington.'

"'And if everything is in order,' I responded, 'and providing the quota hasn't been reached, will I be notified they'll be issued a visa and they can move to the United States?'

"Consul General Lee nodded. 'For immigration visas, that is true. As you know, immigration visas are issued to foreign nationals who intend to live permanently in the United States. Nonimmigration visas are for foreign nationals wishing to enter the United States on a temporary basis—for tourism, medical treatment, business, temporary work, study, or other similar reasons. But we must be very careful. Entry into our country is very serious. Your job is to interview each and every applicant. In addition to your initial screening and review of the application, we must carefully examine each of the documents required for each applicant.' Lee reached into his desk drawer and pulled out a printed sheet of paper. He slid it across his desk. 'This paper is given to each applicant who is a German national. There's another one for Poland, for France, and so on. It's a list of the documents we require for a person to apply for a visa. And each of those documents must be carefully examined and verified. Not an easy job, is it, Theodore?'

"I stared at the list and my eyes bulged as big as half dollars."

DOCUMENTS REQUIRED BY THE UNITED STATES TO OBTAIN A VISA: GERMAN NATIONAL

- Five copies of the visa application
- Two copies of the applicant's birth certificate
- Quota number (establishing the applicant's place on the waiting list)
- Two sponsors, each of whom is US citizen or a permanent resident
- Six copies of an Affidavit of Support and Sponsorship, fully completed and notarized from each applicant's sponsor
- A certified copy of each sponsor's most recent federal tax return
- Sworn affidavit from applicant's bank regarding the balances in applicant's accounts
- Affidavit(s) from any other responsible person regarding other assets (affidavit from sponsor's employer or statement of commercial rating) which may be used for the support of applicant
- Certificate of Good Conduct from German Police authorities, including two copies of each of:
  - Police dossier, if applicable
  - Prison record, if applicable
  - Military record
  - Other government records that may exists concerning the applicant

"I held up the printed list and cleared my throat. 'All those people downstairs . . . the ones on the street, the ones in the line . . . are they all bringing the supporting documents with them?'

"Lee shook his head. 'Probably not. Most of them don't know about this list or the documents required to apply. It's our job to explain the requirements when we meet with them. I mean, when *you* meet with them. It's *your* job now.'

"'I assume that many of these people are refugees, aren't they? I mean, why else would they be fleeing Germany? They're not seeking tourist visas, are they?'

"Lee shrugged. 'Well, that's their business, but some might be. A few. We have requirements for those visas as well. But generally speaking, almost all of the applicants are fleeing Germany, Austria, or parts of Czechoslovakia, the areas occupied by the Nazis.'

"This procedure made no sense to me. 'I'm sorry, sir, but I'm a little confused. The ones who are refugees, they have already fled Germany. How can we possibly expect them to have gathered all of the documents on the list before they fled? Are they supposed to sneak back into Germany, go to the nearest Polizei station, and tell them that they escaped but they forgot to get their certificate of good conduct? Excuse me, sir, but that's insane.'

"Lee shrugged. 'We don't write the immigration laws, nor do we specify the requirements for issuing a visa. That's up to Congress and the Department of State. It's our job to implement them. I could give you the reasons. I could tell you that America has security concerns. I could tell you that right now there's a depression going on, and our elected representatives don't want immigrants competing with Americans for jobs. American sentiment is solidly anti-immigration. In a poll conducted last May, only twenty-three percent of Americans were in favor of giving German refugees immigration status. And like I just told you, a large proportion of those applicants are Jewish. Do I have to tell you what percentage polled were anti-Jewish?'

"'That's not fair. Jewish people are the most persecuted in Germany. They should be given a preference.'

"'I suppose that's true,' said Lee. 'But we don't make the rules. We are but an arm of the Department of State, and we are bound to follow the rules.'

"'So, it's our job to meet with these people every day, and exhibit a positive attitude even though we can't help them? How are we supposed to sleep at night?'

"'Well, that's not quite true; we are helping people every day. Some people get visas. At least almost thirty thousand Germans will get one

this year. And there are other types of visas. Keep in mind, you are a Foreign Service officer and there are many other functions to fill other than
adjudicating foreign visa applications. Representing the United States
of America is one. The consulate serves and assists American citizens
abroad. We protect American commercial interests here in the Netherlands. We analyze our host country's economic and political conditions
and pass our analyses on to State. I'm not telling you anything you don't
know, am I, Theodore?'

"'No, sir.'

"Lee stood and reached out for another hearty handshake. 'It's not
all that overwhelming, Theodore. You'll get used to it. Just say, 'I have
to follow United States government policy.' That's your fallback position, your daily response. You're only following regulations; your hands
are tied. Remember that. Right now, my suggestion is to let Mr. Jessup
show you to your residence. You've had a long day. If you need anything
at all, just ask Jessup or Ms. Fairchild to help you. Julia can work miracles in this town. We'll see you back here first thing in the morning.'"

CHAPTER TEN

"I WALKED BACK into the lobby, and I must have had a dazed look on my face," Teddy said to Karyn. "But I did manage a weak smile for Julia."

"'You look like you ran into a windmill,' she said.

"'Right, that's a good description.'

"Julia's eyes were bright. They twinkled. 'I take it that Consul General Lee gave you a clear overview of our operations. And by that, I mean all of the work that you will be expected to do. Was he able to answer all of your questions?'

"'At this particular time, I don't think that anyone but the Almighty could answer all of my questions, if I even knew what questions to ask. I'm beginning to understand why Mr. Hershman left so precipitously.'

"Julia opened her eyes wide and nodded in agreement. 'Mark Hershman, the man you are replacing, is Jewish,' she said. 'And a sensitive man. Meeting with visa applicants on a daily basis, most of whom were Jewish with children, was very stressful for him. The rumor was that he left because he feared the Nazis and the possibility that Germany would overrun the Netherlands.' She shook her head. 'But I know differently. I knew Mark pretty well. He was a good man. Being unable to issue visas to all those families was breaking his heart. He couldn't sleep at night. Did he fear the Nazis? Of course, any sane person would, but that's not why he left.'

"'That makes sense to me, and I'm not Jewish,' I said. 'It's no secret that Jews are persecuted in Germany and they flee, if they can. Back in Washington, we've been following that for five years, since Hitler took office. Many of those refugees end up here in the Netherlands as permanent residents, or they seek immigration to the US. Consul Lee told me that it was Mr. Hershman's job to listen to their desperate stories every day. And I agree that putting them on a never-ending waiting list would be very difficult for him. Still, Jessup thinks that Hershman feared for his family's welfare in the event the Germans occupied the Netherlands. And if they did, they would undoubtedly impose their harsh racial laws here, just as they have done in all the other countries they've occupied. Don't you think that's a possibility?'

"'A German takeover? Well, I suppose it's a *possibility,*' Julia said, "but I hope to hell it never happens. If they wanted Holland, they'd take it. They are much bigger than we are, though I don't know the exact population numbers.'

"'I do,' I said. 'Germany is ten times bigger than the Netherlands. You are a country of eight million people. Germany is seventy million, and to that, you may add ten million more in German-occupied Austria. More importantly, the German army is four million strong, strongest in the world by far. I believe the Netherlands' army is less than twenty thousand. Do you want me to give you the comparative numbers between the German Luftwaffe and the Royal Netherlands Air Force?'

"'You're missing the point,' Julia said. 'Germany would take us if they wanted to, but they don't want to. We are a neutral country. We have always been a trading partner and at peace with Germany. That's why they didn't occupy us in the last war. There is no reason for Germany to invade or occupy our country. We do not pose any threat to them, and we do business with them. Why in the world would Germany want to invade a friendly country? Mark Hershman left because his job was breaking his heart. I know that for a fact.'

"'I guess it really doesn't matter,' I said. 'Mark is gone, and now I'm here. After a long flight, I'm glad to be on solid ground. Do you know where Mitchell Jessup is? He's supposed to take me to my apartment.'

"Julia shook her head. 'I think he went home.'

"My head flopped down. 'It's been that kind of day. I should say *month.*'

"'Aww,' Julia said sympathetically, her lower lip protruding. 'It has indeed been that kind of day for you. But don't worry, I'll walk you over there as soon as I can. Let me get my coat.'"

* * *

"JULIA AND I exited the consulate and walked over to the Museum-plein. It was a sunny afternoon, and the lovely quarter, one of Amsterdam's most popular gathering places, was bustling. Julia offered to take one of my two suitcases, but I waved off her request with a quick 'Thanks, but no thanks.' After all, I am a man. 'Your apartment isn't very far,' Julia said. 'It's just a couple of bridges away.'

"She pointed to the right. 'That is the Rijksmuseum, one of the world's finest art museums. Maybe *the* finest, at least I think so. On the left is the Concertgebouw, if classical music is your taste. Of course, if you're looking for something a little more lively, Amsterdam is known for its nightlife. You won't have much trouble finding it in almost any direction.'

"We crossed over a canal and through a commercial area. Julia was so easy to talk to. She possessed a wealth of information about Amsterdam. After a few bridges, she noticed that I was growing a little tired, carrying a suitcase in each hand. 'One more block,' she said with a smile. Finally, we came to a redbrick building. 'I believe your apartment is on the second floor,' Julia said. 'Let me help you with the bag. I insist.' She took one of the suitcases and proceeded up the stairs.

"My apartment was a tiny three-room unit, with an alcove kitchen, a small bedroom, and a living room. One might call it 'cozy.' Two of the windows overlooked a small plaza that included a tavern with several outdoor tables. Given the fact that it was now five o'clock, the tables were busy and conversation was bright. An illuminated Heineken sign displaying the tavern's name, De Lege Mok, hung above the tavern door. The Heineken sign was so bright, it cast a green glow through my windows and all throughout my apartment. Julia looked over at me and bit her lower lip to stop from giggling. ' You can always draw the shades,' she said.

"I rolled my eyes. 'It's true, I can, but I have to tell you that right now that sign is making me thirsty. Can I buy you a beer at the Empty Mug?'

"Julia's smile was the answer."

CHAPTER ELEVEN

KARYN SET DOWN her tablet and took a sip of tea. "It seems to me that you were quite lucky to have such pleasant company on your first day in the Amsterdam consulate."

"Julia was charming, the city was charming, but I didn't want to be there. My first day consisted of abruptly leaving Washington and the people that I cared about, traveling halfway around the world to Amsterdam, being dropped in the middle of an extremely pressured job, one that caused my predecessor to resign, and then I was given a depressing matchbox to live in. I suppose having a tavern next door was lucky."

"I meant Julia Powers, Teddy. Lucky to meet Julia. I assume your descriptions of her are accurate."

Teddy's half shrug confirmed. He answered, "It wasn't like I was out shopping for a charming girl. I had a girlfriend back in Washington, remember? Or so I thought, even though we didn't exactly part on the best of terms. But yes, Julia was a delight, and she spoke perfect English."

Karyn held back her grin. "I didn't mean anything, Teddy. I'm just doing my job, listening to your narrative, that's all. I assumed Julia spoke perfect English, she worked at a US embassy, maybe she was American, just like you. So tell me, what happened between the two of you at the Empty Mug?"

"Hmph. Between the *two of us?* It was just a get-acquainted kind of thing, that's all. Julia was interested in what was happening back home. You're right, she was an American. She was born in Detroit, went to the University of Michigan, and after graduation, she studied abroad. After traveling around, she took a job at the consulate."

"Was she married?"

Teddy showed a bit of annoyance. "That wasn't a topic of discussion right then. We were just getting acquainted over a beer. During our small talk, I asked her how she came to work at the consulate. She told me that she met a Swedish guy while at Michigan and they became very good friends, but his family had duties for him to fulfill back in Sweden. Julia's degree was in international studies and she decided to find a position in Europe. She traveled around, and settled in Holland. She applied at the embassy at The Hague, was well qualified, and was assigned to a position at the consulate in Amsterdam. And I found out later that she wasn't married, but she was dating a guy at the Majestic Hotel.

"I was interested in what there was to do in Amsterdam," Teddy said. "I wanted to know more about the people, how the unsettled state of affairs in Europe impacted Holland, and what the Dutch thought about it all. I asked her if Germany was on their minds all the time—after all, they shared a common border, and Germany was in the news every day. I asked her if it made her nervous, and she confessed it did.

"Eventually our discussion got around to the people I would be working with at the consulate. She told me, other than processing dozens of applicants applying for visas, and checking their documents, and answering a million questions every day, the consulate was a terrific place to work. The people were great. 'We interact with the American embassy in The Hague,' she said. 'It's the best place to learn about what's happening back home. There are a number of diplomatic events and foreign social affairs there. You'll love it.' Of course, Hershman obviously didn't."

"What did she ask *you* about," Karyn asked.

"Well, at first I was a little shy. I was hesitant to talk about my personal life back home. You can understand why. She said that I had a formal name, very distinguished. I responded that my father was a tried-and-true Republican, and he named me after President Theodore Roosevelt, whom he knew quite well. Then she asked me if I was a tried-and-true Republican as well. I hesitated, then said, not exactly.

"After a couple of beers, and the fact that she was so easy to talk to, she freely told me about her life. So, I started to loosen up a little. I told her about my family, and my job, and well, I told her about Betsy. Given how we left it, I wasn't sure where our relationship stood, but I hoped we would somehow patch it up. Then I talked about the experience I was having at the church theater group. I was playing the lead role in *Anything Goes*.

"With that Julia slapped the table and said, '*Anything Goes*? I love that musical! I saw it in 1935 at the Alvin Theatre on Broadway. Ethel Merman was in it. And now you're in it!'

"'Well, I *was* in it. Not anymore, which accounts for my stormy relationship with Betsy. I played Billy Crocker, a starring role, opposite the same role Ethel Merman played; Hope Harcourt. Betsy was playing that role. I also saw it at the Alvin Theatre. Of course, our production was just a small little church thing. An amateur thing. But we were quite good, I thought.'

"Julia's face was all aglow. 'You're into theater, that is so wonderful! I have a connection for you here in Amsterdam. I met a man last spring, a recent immigration applicant. He and his wife and daughter escaped from Germany. He's presently working as a writer and a producer at the Hollandsche Schouwburg. That's Amsterdam's theater. His name is Walter Süskind. I don't know what production they're working on right now, but they just finished a musical, *The Pirates of Penzance*. Of course, they did it in Dutch, but you'd never know the difference. Besides, you understand Dutch. If you're interested, I can put you in touch with him. He's a very nice fellow. He'll probably be at the Schouwburg tomorrow. It's right on the other side of the Museumplein.'

"Now, for the first time since arriving in Amsterdam, *my* face was aglow. If I could get involved in the theater, at the Schouwburg, then maybe Betsy would get excited about it. She might visualize herself as a star in an *international production*, and come to Amsterdam. Well, she might. Who knows? Then she wouldn't say to me, 'I don't even know where it is on a map.' Betsy loved to act and she loved theater. My spirits were lifting. 'I would like very much to meet Mr. Süskind,' I said, 'if you could arrange it.'

"I ordered another round for the two of us. Things were definitely looking up for me in Amsterdam. She told me that Walter Süskind, his wife, and child were Jewish. 'They couldn't wait to get out of Germany,' she said.

"As we sat there that evening on October 5, 1938, and as a smile was covering my face from ear to ear, a buzz suddenly circulated among the patrons at the Empty Mug. They were jumping out of their chairs, throwing money down on the table, and heading directly for the doors. The waitress came over. 'We just heard that Germany invaded the Sudeten Mountains in Czechoslovakia,' she said, giving us our check. 'We're closing.' The tavern customers, fearing the worst, cleared out in a matter of minutes.

"I offered to walk Julia home and she shook her head. 'No, thank you, I don't live far,' she said. 'Amsterdam is like a small town.' But I insisted, and we walked along the narrow streets toward her apartment building. People were buzzing, like in the tavern, hurriedly walking in all directions. You could tell that anxiety had gripped the Netherlands. No telling where Hitler would go next. If he captured one territory, he could capture more. Even though Czechoslovakia was on the other side of Germany, some five hundred miles away, the fear was palpable. How far would Hitler's invasion go? Would Czechoslovakia resist and attack Germany? Czechoslovakia had allies. Would they join in their defense? Would it quickly spread into a full-scale war? Would this become World War II?

"As far as I knew, and I was current with his speeches, Hitler hadn't ever mentioned the Netherlands. There was no reason to believe that the Netherlands would be next. But, Germany hadn't mentioned Belgium in the last war before attacking it and taking it over. The attack that occurred on my first day in Amsterdam was a demonstration that Hitler could and would act on a moment's notice if he felt like it. And he was making noise about Danzig, the territory that sat on top of Poland, a port in the Baltic Sea. Hitler had his eyes on that port. The 1919 Treaty of Versailles, bringing an end to the Great War, made Danzig a 'Free State.' The majority of people in Danzig were ethnically German, but it was to be administered by Poland. Hitler was clamoring that it should be annexed into Germany. But it remained Polish territory.

"Julia lived two or three bridges away. It was true that the area around the consulate was like a small town. When we arrived at her apartment building, I offered to walk her upstairs and stay with her until things calmed down, and I apologized if she thought that was too forward of me. She thanked me very much, but said it wouldn't be necessary, she would be just fine. She gave me a peck on the cheek, and I went home.

"All the way home, I kept remembering Senator Nye telling me that Hitler had threatened to invade Czechoslovakia and take over the Sudetens. And I remembered the newspaper article that Betsy read to me, where Hitler stated, 'With regard to the problem of the Sudeten Germans my patience is now at an end! Peace or war.' Either Czechoslovakia would give the Sudeten Mountains to Hitler, or he would take them. And now he had gone ahead and invaded them. Nye predicted that all of Czechoslovakia would be next. He repeated what everyone else was saying, that Hitler was a madman and if he wanted more, he'd take it. There was no holding him back. Good thing the US was on the other side of the globe. At least that's what Nye and his Republican counterparts said.

"Remember, Nye was an isolationist. Like many in Congress, isolationists insisted that the US stay as far away from European affairs as it could. When I was sitting with Nye, right before I was about to leave for Amsterdam, he said, 'Why don't you tell me, Theodore, why do we need immigration offices in our European consulates at all? We don't want the immigrants, and they're bound to get us into trouble.' He held his finger up, and chanted his favorite slogan: 'America First.'

"Now, as Nye predicted, the Sudeten Mountains had been invaded. A couple of days later a cable was delivered to me at the consulate. You'll never guess who it was from."

Karyn shook her head. "I give up. Senator Nye?"

"No. It was from Betsy. I couldn't believe it. She said that her father had told her all about the Nazis' invasion of the Sudeten Mountains. He told her that the Nazis could, and probably would, invade the rest of Czechoslovakia, and from there, who knows? Betsy said she was afraid for me and if I had any sense at all, I'd come back home. She said, and I quote, 'You don't need that job, you can get a better job. We can talk to Senator Nye, and if not for him, then one of my father's friends will help you. Have some courage, Teddy. I miss you. We used to have such fun. Our being apart is not working. It's not working for me at all. There is a dance at the country club in three weeks and what am I supposed to do about that? Am I supposed to have no social life because you want to work in Holland? Really? I miss you so badly, and I worry that something dreadful will happen to you. As it is, I think about you all the time. Do you think about me? Teddy, please come home. I love you. Your Bets.'"

Karyn lifted her hand to cover her mouth. "Oh my goodness. And you thought you two had broken up."

"I was totally shocked, Karyn. Truth was, I missed her too, I just didn't think she missed me as much. I sent a cable back to her right away. 'Bets. Don't worry, I'm fine. Everything is safe here in the Netherlands. The Nazis aren't anywhere near us. You know I can't leave the consulate right now. But I think about you and I can understand why you don't want to come to Europe at this time. Please wait for me. I love you, Teddy.'"

Karyn closed the cover of her notebook. "That's enough for me today," she said.

Teddy nodded and they broke for the day.

CHAPTER TWELVE

IT WAS LATE in the afternoon when Karyn arrived back at her hotel, ready for a nap. She found a message from Burt. *Give me a call.* She thought about it for a moment and wondered where this was going. Was he looking for a date? *He's a pleasant enough fellow, but maybe he's too pushy? He lives on one side of the world, I live on the other. His questions seem very personal, but are they really? It's been a long time since I dated.* She stared at the phone, tipped her head a bit to the side, and then shook it. "No." Then she dialed Tel Aviv.

Her daughter Beth answered the phone. "Mom? How are you doing? How is your project going in Washington? Are you discovering anything about your family?"

"Not yet, honey. Mr. Hartigan has made a few phone calls and is reaching out to a few people he knows, but he just doesn't have anything for me yet. The story of his life, on the other hand, is very interesting. At first, I was a little hesitant. A man of his age, I mean, how much would he remember? Then I calculated: he spent four years in college, two years in grad school, two years in the army, and two years in the basement of the State Department in Washington, before coming to Amsterdam. So, I figure he was about twenty-eight or twenty-nine, maybe thirty, when he was transferred to the American consulate in Amsterdam. And now it's 2002, so he must be ninety-two or ninety-three years old. Still, I have to say, for a man of his age, he has a remarkable memory."

"When will you be finished?"

"God, at the rate he's going, I'll be ninety-two. How are my darlings?"

"Sound asleep. I'll tell them Grandma called, but they'll just want to know when you can take them to the bakery."

"Ha. Tell them as soon as I can. I love you, Beth. Say hi to Ben."

Karyn set the phone down, stared at it, took a breath, and then said, "Oh, what the hell?" She dialed Burt.

KARYN AND BURT were sitting in an Italian restaurant in Silver Spring when he said, "I wondered if you'd return my call. After getting you involved with my cousin, I thought maybe you'd never want to speak to me again. Is he driving you nuts?"

"Hmm, sort of, but not really. He's pouring his heart out, there's no doubt about that. He's telling me his story chronologically, and he's a fountain of factual details, of which there are many. But his recollections are also about the way he felt, about his emotions at the time, and they're very personal. I'm wondering if he wants all that to be part of his memoir. Do you want to know something funny? I get the feeling that his story, his memoir, is not so much for his grandchildren as it is for himself."

"Writing a story for himself? What do you mean by that?"

"His memory, his recall, they're so vivid, so keen right now. He remembers the smallest details, even conversations. Much better than I can do. I can't remember that much about what happened last week. He is a library of everything that makes up his life. Not just his feelings, but what was happening in the world. I get the feeling that he fears age-related forgetfulness will creep in and chip away at his memories. Maybe he'll suffer from a kind of dementia. And he doesn't want to lose his memories. They are so dear to him. And there's no one left who knows all of those things, no one who can remember for him. What if he can't remember someone who was very dear to him? Then that person would no longer exist. I think he wants this story written for himself, and stored away on his personal bookshelf, and I'm going to help him do it."

Burt was moved and his lips were tight. "You are a wonderful person, Karyn."

Karyn shrugged. "So are you. To answer the question you asked me yesterday, I am a widow. My husband died eight years ago, and now I am wishing that we wrote a story too." A tear came to her eye. "Because there are things I wish I could remember."

CHAPTER THIRTEEN

"IT WAS ABOUT three weeks later, and no further threats had come out of Germany," Teddy said. Julia asked me to stop by her desk at lunchtime. It had been a very busy morning, and I had trouble communicating with some of the applicants. In most cases, they spoke only German, but this morning's applicants spoke only Yiddish, and neither the interpreter nor I could understand them. My interpreter spoke fluent German, and Yiddish as well, but the applicants' dialect was so strong, we ended up making hand signals of what we wanted to say.

"Finally, I broke for lunch, and I was hungry. I wondered where Julia wanted to go. 'Do you remember the man I told you about,' she said, 'Walter Süskind, the theatrical producer?'

"'Yes, of course.'

"'Walter, his wife Hannah, and their child came here as refugees last March, remember? It took every cent they had, but they had to get out of Nazi Germany. They're Jewish and they've applied for a visa. Of course, we put them on the waiting list, but unless something changes, they'll never get a visa. Back in Germany, Walter was the manager of a food company. Because of his experience, he recently got a job here at Unilever. He's a great guy. But I think I told you that he was a stage manager of a local theatrical company in Germany, and now he is currently at the Schouwburg.'

"'I remember,' I said.

"'A few of us were out last night with Walter and Hannah, and Walter mentioned that they were contemplating a new production at the Schouwburg. Either an Ibsen play or a musical, but they didn't know which one. I told them that you were starring in a musical in Washington before you were transferred over here.'

"I winced. '*Starring* is a little out of proportion. I mean, we were only practicing to put on an amateur church production. We were still weeks away.'

"'That doesn't matter. I also mentioned that you would love to become involved at the Schouwburg, no matter what play they were going to do. I hope I wasn't out of line, but that's what I said. I told him about you and your girlfriend and how you were scheduled to play leading roles in *Anything Goes*. He said he loves that musical and the Schouwburg should consider doing it.'

"'No way!'

"'Yeah. So, he asked me to drop by at lunch today and bring you along.' When I heard that, I was thrilled.

"The Hollandsche Schouwburg was just across the square from the consulate. On the way over, I mentioned sending a cable to Betsy that I was meeting with Walter Süskind. I would ask him if he would consider doing *Anything Goes* in Amsterdam. 'That sounds very exciting,' Julia said. 'Maybe that would be enough to convince your girlfriend to come over here and join the company.'

"'She makes a great Hope Harcourt,' I said.

"The Hollandsche Schouwburg was an immense stone building with a gabled roof. The front façade was lined with columns. The classic architecture reminded me of Washington. I had never been to the Schouwburg and I was awed. I don't have to tell you that it was far more impressive than St. Martin's, the church where our theater group was going to perform. Wouldn't Betsy love to be Hope Harcourt at the Schouwburg?

"Walter was there to greet us. He was a young man, with short black hair. I think he was just a few years older than I was. He was thirty-two at the time. He said there was nothing in production yet, but they were considering any number of plays. I asked him which ones. He said they had talked about Henrik Ibsen's *A Doll's House*. It was quite popular in the Scandinavian cities. I didn't know much about *A Doll's House*.

"I told him that Betsy and I loved theater. We had been practicing in the lead roles of *Anything Goes* at our local community theater. We had memorized our parts. What's more, we had the costumes and all of the scripts and maybe Betsy could bring them out with her. He said that was certainly something to think about. The difficult part would be assembling the music. He didn't know if sufficient members of the symphony or the jazz band were available. Would they have the time, or would they even consider a production at the Schouwburg? Then I took a chance. I mentioned that Betsy's father was very wealthy, and he helped underwrite *Anything Goes* in Washington, and maybe he would help out here. That got Walter's attention."

"And did Betsy's father agree to fund *Anything Goes*?"

"No, not exactly, but he agreed to seriously consider it and present it to the board."

"My goodness," said Karyn. "Quite a sales job."

"I thought so, though I thought it was a little nervy. I didn't have the go-ahead from either Betsy or her father. The possibility, even remote, that Betsy would come over was slight. But maybe if she loved me enough and if she could star in *Anything Goes*? Who knew? In fact, Walter asked me how certain I could be that Betsy would come. I told him I couldn't be certain, but I would push hard to get her here. She loved to perform, especially in *Anything Goes*. Privately, I had to concede that her family wasn't very fond of Europe, especially these days. There was bound to be some resistance. I told Walter that I'd push hard, and that might be enough. He nodded like he understood, but I don't think he was convinced. So, we ended by Walter saying that if Betsy would confirm that she would come to Amsterdam to play in *Anything Goes*, he would push hard to have the board approve it. I thanked him. I told him, even if we couldn't put this all together, I would like to be a part of the company, even if it was just as a stagehand. And he told me to come by the next week, he was sure there would be a spot for me.

"Later that night, I remember lying awake wondering if Betsy's love for me was strong enough to overcome all the resistance she would encounter. I know that her father and Senator Nye would be solidly against it. But she was an adult, and maybe she'd get a chance to star in the international production of *Anything Goes*! Wouldn't all that be enough to

bring Betsy to Amsterdam? If not, then what did that say about our relationship? Would Senator Nye's warnings be a more powerful deterrent
than her love for me? But then I thought, that's not fair. I wouldn't be
here either if I didn't have to be. But we'd see. Unfortunately, the very
next day, the deal was sealed.

"The next day was November 7, 1938. A seventeen-year-old Polish
Jew, Herschel Grynszpan, purchased a gun in a Paris gun shop. His
parents had sent him a note that they were expelled from the Eastern
German town where they lived, along with twenty thousand other Polish citizens, just because they were all Jewish, and they were now pen-
niless. They asked Herschel if he could send them any money. They had
no food or place to go. Herschel was furious. Germany would pay for
this. He walked straight into the German embassy and demanded that
something be done. When they turned him down flat, he fired a fatal
shot at Ernst vom Rath, a German secretary in the embassy. Two days
later, on November 9, 1938, Hitler learned of the shooting. His retaliation became notorious. In what came to be known as Kristallnacht,
Night of the Broken Glass, two hundred and sixty-seven synagogues
and seventy-five hundred Jewish shops throughout Germany were destroyed, and fourteen hundred more were damaged. Even more serious,
ninety-one Jews were killed, and twenty-five thousand more were arrested and put into a concentration camp. News of Kristallnacht spread
throughout the world.

"I received a cable from Betsy two days later. Naturally, she was in-
censed at what Hitler had done. She insisted that I come home immediately. She said that she hadn't slept a wink since she heard the news.
She was a nervous wreck, for which she blamed me. How could I put
her through this? How could I continue to work in Amsterdam? It was
thoughtless of me to do this to her. Her father told her that Kristallnacht was only the beginning of Hitler's madness. There would be more.

"A few days later I received another cable. Betsy wrote, 'Do you expect me to cry myself to sleep every night? If you truly love me, like you
say you do, then you wouldn't put me through such misery. You would
come home to me immediately. Tomorrow! How dare you even suggest

that I come to Amsterdam, even if I was given the role of Hope Harcourt in Amsterdam's *Anything Goes*? You are an inconsiderate man. Cold and insensitive.'"

Karyn tipped her head to the side. "Teddy, I sympathize with you. That must have been very painful, but she was a young girl, very immature. From what you tell me, she was a little spoiled. She'd had her own way for a long time. She didn't know how to deal with denial. Her fiancé was in Europe in 1938. It sounds to me like she wasn't strong enough to handle it. I feel bad for you, but it's understandable. Did you respond to her cable?"

"No, how could I? What could I say? I was hurt. She didn't express one word about the death and destruction inflicted on these innocent people during Kristallnacht. To be frank, she didn't express any concern about me, or anyone but herself. I know it was hard on her, but it just didn't sound like the Betsy I knew. Or thought I knew. Maybe her father and Senator Nye put her up to it, I don't know. So I wrote to my dad. Remember, he and Betsy's father were very close friends. The Hartigans and the McCutcheons. I asked him if he and Mr. McCutcheon could talk to Betsy and calm her down. I knew my dad would be on my side. After all, I was following in his footsteps serving in the Foreign Service. He was proud of me.

"He wrote, 'Theodore, I feel for you, but talking to Mr. McCutcheon is not the answer to your problem. He was never in the army, and he doesn't support the State Department issuing visas in Europe. He's an isolationist. He won't be much help.' Then a couple of weeks later I received another letter from my father. Once again, he said he was proud that I stepped into such a prominent position. 'Men like you will make a difference.' Then toward the end of the letter he said, 'Saw Betsy the other night at the country club dance. Sorry to relay to you that she was with Billy Connor. I thought you should know. Sorry.'

"I was furious, but I should have expected it. Cables between us stopped. I would be damned if I was going to be the one to write an apologetic letter, and I'm sure she thought the same. We stopped writing altogether. Weeks went by without a word from Betsy. On my twenty-ninth birthday, I went downstairs to the Empty Mug, had a sandwich and a beer alone, went home, and went to sleep. On December 20, I received a Christmas card from Betsy. It was signed, 'Merry Christmas, Betsy.' Nothing more. No 'I love you' or 'I miss you.' Nothing personal. It could have been a card written to the milkman. That hurt even more."

CHAPTER FOURTEEN

"KRISTALLNACHT HAD CAUSED an enormous increase in visa applications. So many were trying to flee Germany. The German borders were closed to Jewish refugees, unless they could come up with a very steep exit tax, which amounted to everything they owned. And you had to prove it. And even then, it might not be enough."

"How did the Nazis know how much a refugee owned?" Karyn said.

"They took an inventory from every single Jew. Not Christians, just Jews. Bank accounts, real property, personal property, jewelry, you name it. Many of those who paid the tax and received permission to emigrate, or those who escaped, they would cross the border and go into Belgium, France, and of course, the Netherlands. Serving these people at the consulate was frustrating and exhausting. Many of them didn't have anywhere to go, and even if they could afford the passage, I couldn't give them a visa to get into the US. The quota was filled. Those days were long. I was very tired and very lonely and very depressed. I'd work those long hours and go back home to my apartment. It was the Christmas season, and the city was bright and cheerful, but you wouldn't know that by me. I'd pick up a sandwich on the way home, and spend the night trying to read a book, or listen to the radio. Ho, ho, ho, I spent Christmas alone.

"On December 27, 1938, the consulate seemed busier than usual. When we finally closed for the night, Julia came into my office, sat down, and slid a Coke across the desk. 'What are you doing New Year's Eve?' she asked. 'Do you have plans?' I immediately thought she was asking me to take her out, and to tell you the truth, I would have jumped at that, even if it would make me feel guilty.

"Anyway, I was wrong. Julia wasn't about to ask me out. She already had a boyfriend. His name was Willem. She knew my social life was zero, so anything she suggested would probably be accepted. She said, 'Teddy, one of my best girlfriends, her name is Sara Rosenbaum, doesn't have a date for New Year's Eve, which is very unusual for Sara, believe me. She's very popular, she's very nice, very pretty, and very smart. She's been my best friend since I came to Amsterdam. So when I heard she didn't have a date, I immediately thought of you. You and Sara are very much alike. She's scholarly, just like you, but fun.'

"'Does that mean I'm not fun?' I asked.

"She laughed. 'You'd like her, I'm sure. Really, I'm serious. So, if you don't have plans, I would strongly suggest that you let me fix you up with Sara. You won't be sorry. Why don't you and Sara come along with Willem and me? The four of us would have a blast. What do you think? Do you want to take Sara out for New Year's?' Julia had a big smile, and her eyebrows were raised high in anticipation. This was iffy, but Julia was cute, and maybe her best friend would be too. She continued, 'Amsterdam is a smash on New Year's Eve. We go from place to place and then celebrate the light show at midnight. So, what do you say, Teddy? Can I tell her?' I didn't need a lot of persuading; I was dying of boredom. 'That sounds like a great idea,' I said, 'if she'll go with me.' Julia responded, 'Oh, she'll go, Teddy, you can depend on that.' And I answered, 'Then yes. I'd love to. That's the best news I've had in a long time.'"

Karyn leaned back and said, "Yay! There's a pleasant twist to your story. I was getting pretty depressed listening to your sad social life."

"Imagine how I felt."

"Up to now, from what you've said, Betsy was the only girl you ever dated," Karyn said. "From Julia's description, I'm forming a picture of Sara in my mind, and I'm thinking she might be just right for you. What was she really like?"

"Oh, you have a picture in your mind, do you?" Teddy smiled and said, "What's your picture look like? Describe her for me?"

Karyn bit her bottom lip. "She's very smart, very scholarly, and she doesn't have a date. Hmm. Brown hair, pulled back in a bun, wire eyeglasses, long wool dress, laced shoes with a block heels, not too much makeup, you know, a bookworm."

Teddy closed his eyes, shook his head, and laughed. "Well, you got a couple things right. She had brown hair, but it was curled. She wore makeup, at least she did the night I met her. But I came to find out that she didn't always wear fancy makeup. She was a teacher. She did wear glasses. But they weren't wire-rimmed. They were stylish. And the night I met her, she wasn't dressed in any long wool thing. It was New Year's Eve and Sara was dressed to party."

"Ooh," Karyn said, and nodded her understanding. "What happened next?"

Teddy took a breath. "Things continued to be very busy at the consulate. Lines of refugees seemed to increase every day. German emigrants were doing anything they could to get out of Europe. It wasn't enough to get out of Germany. They knew what a warmonger their führer was. No place on the Continent was safe in their mind. As the winter months passed, newspapers continued to report on troop consolidation in southern Germany, and . . ."

Karyn held up a stop sign. She wagged her index finger back and forth. "Whoa, whoa, hold on," she said. "Wait a minute. What happened to *New Year's Eve?* What about your date with Sara Rosenbaum? C'mon, Teddy, you can't tease me like that."

Teddy rolled his eyes, twisted his lips, and grumbled, "Okay, all right. We assembled at Julia's apartment for cheese and crackers and a little wine about nine o'clock. Willem, Julia's date, was late. His family owned the Majestic Hotel, a very swank hotel in Amsterdam. Willem was the manager at the hotel. As you can imagine, on New Year's Eve there was a lot of work for Willem to do. He said he'd try to get away and catch up with us later. So the three of us, Julia, Sara, and I, went out for a bite and returned to her apartment around ten thirty. Soon a tall, muscular guy with a crew cut showed up. 'Sorry,' he said, 'the hotel was crazy tonight.' I thought he had a very confident look about him."

"Okay, that's Willem," Karyn said. "What about Sara? Personality? Talkative? Did you two hit it off?"

"Sara looked very attractive that night, I have to say. She was probably in her late twenties at the time. She was easy to talk to, except all she wanted to talk about was me. Where did I grow up, where did I go to school, what was life like in Washington, and how did I end up in Amsterdam?"

"Hmm," Karyn said, "nice move."

"Yes, a good opening. Of course, I'd like to know how I ended up in Amsterdam too, but that was another story. Sara thought her life was nice, but a little boring. She grew up in Utrecht and that's where her family still lived. She attended Utrecht University, where she received her education degree. Three years previously, she was offered a position at the Reformed Teacher Training College in Amsterdam, the one directly across the square from the consulate. It was a prestigious posting, and she took it right away. That caused her to move to Amsterdam."

"How was the date? The date?" Karyn asked impatiently.

"It was good."

"Good?"

"What do you want me to say? It was, I mean it was good. We hung out at Julia's for a while, until Willem arrived, as I said, at about ten thirty. Then Julia said, 'All right everyone, it's New Year's Eve, let's go!' I had never spent New Year's Eve anywhere outside of DC, let alone in Amsterdam, and I was not prepared for it. It was wild! We started off in Leidseplein Square, where there were numerous clubs, bars, pubs, whatever you want to call them, and the streets were packed. It was the Amsterdam Light Festival. The entertainment district was unlike anything I'd ever seen, and Julia knew the places to go. She also knew doormen at the exclusive clubs, who, for a few guilders in their palm, would get us in, no matter how long the line."

"How much was a guilder?"

"About two, three bucks."

"Wow. That's good money in 1939."

"Willem had a lot of money."

"Did you guys go dancing?" Karyn said.

Teddy rolled his eyes. "You sure are a nosy person," he said. Then he sat back, with a faraway look in his eyes. He took a deep breath. Karyn could tell it was a nostalgic moment for Teddy. No wonder he wanted to make this memoir, she thought. This was one of those moments he never wanted to forget.

"Julia was a great dancer," he said. "When it came to dancing, she was the leader. This was her scene. It was made for her."

"What about Sara?"

"She was a pretty good dancer too. Me, I felt a little out of my element, but after a few drinks, I did much better. I was a fast learner.

"At ten minutes to midnight, Julia pulled us out into the street. Everyone was gathering to watch Amsterdam's famous fireworks show. It took place on the waterfront, at Scheepvaart. I learned that it was an Amsterdam tradition for people to come out of their homes at midnight, and light off their own fireworks on their sidewalk."

Karyn had a mischievous smile. "Wasn't it also a custom in Amsterdam to kiss your girl at the stroke of midnight?"

"You mean, did I kiss Sara? You are so nosy."

Karyn chuckled. "Maybe I am. So what? It's your memoir, isn't it? Don't you want everything in there? Aren't you going to include kissing Sara at the stroke of twelve?"

Teddy nodded nostalgically. "It was also tradition in Amsterdam, and yes, I did kiss her, you're damn right. And she was a damn good kisser. So, what do you think of that, Miss Nosy? Are you going to ask me if I thought I was betraying Betsy, is that your next question?"

"Nope, not at all."

"Good, because I didn't. I was a million miles away from Betsy and all of her nasty accusations. It seemed evident that she didn't want anything more to do with me. My dad said she was dating other guys, and I was sure she was out kissing someone else on New Year's Eve. So that night, I was with Sara, and she liked me, and I liked her."

Karyn's mouth was open and her smile was giddy. She sang softly, "And a boy meets a girl."

"Yeah, yeah, yeah. So, the four of us went from club to club into the wee hours, and that was just fine. No regrets."

Karyn bit her lip again. "Then?"

"Then? How much more do you want? I walked Sara home. She lived close to the teachers' college, which was right next to the Schouwburg.

As I said before, it was just like a small town. I said good night, and went home to my apartment."

Karyn seemed disappointed. "That's it? That's all?"

Teddy shook his head. "Boy, no wonder you were a reporter for the *Jerusalem Times*. You are nosy. I know what you're looking for. But no, I wasn't that brave. I just went home."

Karyn scrunched her nose. "Did you work up the courage to call her again?"

Teddy chuckled. "Probably not on my own. I wasn't used to the dating scene, you know. I had gone with the same girl since I was four years old, and she always called the shots. But a few days later, Julia stopped into my office and said, 'Did you have a good time with Sara last Thursday?' I nodded. 'It was fun. Thanks for fixing me up. We had a great time, at least I did, and I hope she did too.'

"Julia wasn't done. 'Well, she did. So, have you called her since?'

"I blushed. 'No.'

"Julia smiled, nodded, and wagged a finger at me. 'Well, Sara called me. She told me she had a wonderful time on New Year's. She liked you a lot. She was a little disappointed that you hadn't called her, and she was hoping that you would call her again. In fact, Willem and I would like you two to join us for dinner Saturday. We're going to eat at the Majestic.'"

Karyn leaned forward. "And?"

"Well, I did. Saturday was Julia's birthday, and we had a ball. Willem had arranged a fancy dinner with Champagne. Actually, the more I was with Willem, the more I liked him too. From then on, Sara and I started seeing each other quite often."

Karyn clapped.

CHAPTER FIFTEEN

"A MONTH LATER, on January 30, 1939, I was working late at the consulate, as I often did. There were dozens of people crowding, trying to get an appointment before the consulate closed. The line, which stretched down the block, was unusually long. Then, I realized why. Hitler had delivered another one of his belligerent, hateful, anti-Semitic speeches at the Reichstag. It was being widely broadcasted. It was picked up in some offices on a console radio, and the word spread.

"The speech wasn't pointed at any particular country, it didn't threaten to start a war, and it didn't promise to take over any specific piece of land. No, it was worse, if you can imagine it. It was directed at the Jewish people as a whole, no matter where they lived. He started by reminding his listeners, 'When I prophesied that I would settle the Jewish problem, they all laughed at me. Then I promised that I would take over the country, and when I did, the Jews all laughed at me again.' Then Hitler delivered the deadly message: 'If the so-called Jewish financiers should succeed in bringing the nation into war, it will end in the annihilation of the entire Jewish race.' People were shocked. Never had the leader of a large nation delivered such a diatribe. It was even more astonishing given the fact that Germany had over half a million Jews, many of whom were legendary in medicine, science, music, and education."

Karyn looked at Teddy and her lips were tight. She covered her mouth. "Did it cause an uproar in the streets? Was the common man at all offended by this harangue? Even if they were afraid to speak up in Germany, what about in the adjoining countries, like the Netherlands? Was there a campaign of solidarity or were they scared to disagree? I would think it might cause many to rush to the consulate to get far away from Hitler."

Teddy quietly shook his head. "Oh, it did, mostly the refugees. In the streets of Amsterdam, the non-Jewish people responded by shaking their heads in disgust. What could they do, even if they wanted to? They shook their heads because it was just another diatribe directed against the Jews, wherever they may live. Dutch people could tolerate them because they were miles and borders away. Thankfully. They could toss aside his speeches as just more horse-babble from *der Führer*. They took pity on the German Jews, but again, Hitler was far away, and he never threatened Holland. But if you were a Jew, you knew better. You took it personally and it boiled your blood. So did the failure of the free world to silence him once and for all. Why did people put up with it? Unfortunately, history taught us that anti-Semitic campaigns could sometimes attract followers. It was up to decent honest people to put a stop to it.

"At the consulate, the Jews standing in line trying to schedule an appointment knew better. They were scared to death, and they would wait in that line if it took forever.

"Sara knew better. An hour after the broadcast, she burst into the consulate and ran up to Julia's desk. She waited by her side until the end of the business day, until the doors were closed, and then she ran upstairs to my office. Sara was Jewish. I don't think we had ever discussed that, but now I knew. Tears were flowing. I opened my arms for her, and held her tightly. She was shaking. Hitler's speeches were nothing to ignore, even if they were far away. He wasn't just talking hate, he was preaching annihilation. Sara knew what was happening to the Jewish people in Germany; her father had close contacts there.

"'He's not just threatening the Jews who live in Germany,' Sara said between gasps. 'If you listen to him, he's prophesying the total elimination of my people—my mother, my father, all my people—wherever they may live, and he has the world's largest military behind him. Teddy, who's going to stop him?'

"I continued to hold her tightly and brush away her tears. 'Other countries won't put up with his bullshit,' I said. 'He may have the world's largest army, but I wouldn't bet against the rest of the free world.' I said softly, 'I don't care how many goose-steppers he's got, the United States wouldn't put up with his shit. Right now, he's flapping his mouth in Berlin. Sooner or later, people will come to their senses and shut him up. In the meantime, Jews are smart to leave Germany, make applications for visas to whatever free country they can get into, or, like so many are doing right now, just walk over the border into Holland, or Belgium, or France, and make their home there. Many want to go to the United States, and who could blame them, but they can't do it right now. I'm processing more and more applications every day, aren't I?'

"Sara looked at me and smiled. She gave me a squeeze. 'You are, and I love you for it, but even though you're processing their applications, they're not all getting visas, are they?'

"'No, sadly, they're not. Not today, not all at once,' I answered. 'They're not being turned away, but the number of visas is limited. There's a quota. They're put on a list and when their number comes up they can enter. But things could change. Hopefully someday soon America will open her arms.'

"She looked at me with those beautiful brown eyes, and said, 'Teddy, I'm frightened. I don't want to go home alone. Would you mind if I stayed with you tonight?' And I answered, 'Of course you can. In fact, you can stay with me for as long as you want.' That was the first night of many. From that night on, she felt comfortable asking me to stay the night, and similarly, I felt comfortable asking her to stay."

Karyn said, "Were Hitler's speeches having a similar effect on you?"

"First of all, I didn't need Sara to alert me to the evils of Adolf Hitler. The State Department had been following that rat closely for years. Remember, I had been working in the Western European section. I was aware of each and every one of Hitler's speeches. They were catalogued and filed away. In the beginning, we believed that he was just blustering, trying to secure a political foothold among the disenfranchised. This was a financially depressed era, especially for Germany, which had just suffered an economically disastrous defeat in World War One. Hitler found a scapegoat. Though he could offer no proof, he blamed the Jews for Germany's sad economic state, and invited his followers to rally around. As time went on, Hitler's speeches became more aggressive. The European

Jewish community saw them for what they were, and took them seriously. The applications for visas increased dramatically after each one of them."

Karyn nodded. "I'm sure, but I think Sara made a good point when she said they weren't all getting visas, didn't she? All those people standing in line waiting to make application for a visa to the US, knowing that there was a huge backlog, seems like a futile effort to me. Why would applications increase dramatically when it was common knowledge that the immigration quotas were already filled?"

"Because people didn't give up hope; what else could they do? Quota limitations could change. America was the beacon of hope. After all, it was America that bailed Europe out of Germany's clutches in the First World War. That is why there were long lines. There was always hope that Congress would enact emergency measures and allow more refugees. And it did, but it took a long time. There was always talk about it in Congress. In fact, the following month, on February 9, 1939, Democratic Senator Robert Wagner and Republican Congresswoman Edith Nourse Rogers introduced legislation in Congress to admit twenty thousand German immigrant children under the age of fourteen, without regard to the current quotas. Ten thousand in 1939 and ten thousand in 1940. First Lady Eleanor Roosevelt supported the bill, the first time she ever endorsed any bill as First Lady. Sara was visiting me at the consulate when news of the bill was circulated, and she jumped up and down."

"Oh, my goodness, that must have boosted their faith in America."

"Damn right. Although it didn't need any boosting. European Jews regarded the US as their last and best hope, and that's why the lines were long every day."

"IN THE FOLLOWING year, Sara and I stayed together more often, and we grew closer and closer. Like a married couple, we would each leave for work in the morning and come home at the end of the day. We'd make dinner, or we'd go out. Remember, we were in Amsterdam, and there was no trouble finding a place to eat. Afterward, we'd come home, put on some music, or read a book, or just talk. The nights she stayed with me were heaven."

"Where did Sara work?" Karyn asked.

"Her principal job was at the Reformed Teacher Training College. Before that, Sara had worked for Henriëtte Pimentel at a very well-known primary school and day care center called Crèche Vereeniging Zuigelingen-Inrichting en Kinderhuis, or commonly known as the Crèche and Kindergarten Institute in Amsterdam. Sara still volunteered there in the afternoons after she finished at the teachers' college. She just loved being around the little children. Her sister Sylvia worked there full-time. She was seventeen years old and a teacher in training. Henriëtte had been there for ages, and she was a legend. She was born in Amsterdam to a well-to-do family. Her father was a well-known diamond cutter. They were Portuguese. Henriëtte graduated from education school and was also trained to be a nurse.

"The crèche was a large, three-story redbrick building, adjoining a large grassy area called the Plantage Middenlaan, which also adjoined the Reformed Teacher Training College. And on the other side, across the train tracks, was the Schouwburg. Henriëtte was a friend of Sara's father, who was a political science and history professor at Utrecht University. She knew everybody. When it came time for Sylvia to find a profession, Henriëtte offered to take her under her wing. And when Sylvia accepted the position, Sara volunteered to help Sylvia, but found that she enjoyed the volunteer work, so she would come every now and then."

Karyn looked quizzically at Teddy. "It was called 'the crèche'? Did it refer to where Jesus was born?"

Teddy chuckled. "The Amsterdam crèche did not resemble Bethlehem. No shepherds, no sheep or kings. 'Crèche' was a common term for nursery. It was a place where children were cared for during the day. Babies and young children were dropped off in the morning, as early as six o'clock, and picked up in the afternoon. The crèche closed at five. It cared for a hundred or more infants and toddlers every day. The little babies were well cared for, they had rooms with lines of cribs and play areas. And that is where Sylvia and Sara spent most of their time. There were also classrooms and playrooms and naptime rooms for the toddlers.

"The Amsterdam crèche was a beautiful building, well funded and well respected. The students were mostly Jewish, though not exclusively, and it was operated by Henriëtte and her staff, the majority of whom were Jewish. Henriëtte actually lived in the crèche building. It was owned by a Jewish charity, but Henriëtte operated it. It was her baby. She made sure that all of the childcare workers received thorough training before they were allowed to care for the infants, toddlers, and preschoolers.

"'Miss Pimentel' could often be seen standing out in the yard. She had a short gray haircut and dressed in a white jacket. She and her dog Brownie would play with the children in the yard. It was easy to see what a delightful and cheerful woman she was. She was a child among the children. That was her method. Sara said she was a follower of Friedrich Fröbel and Maria Montessori. Even by 1939, Maria Montessori was a well-known educator and doctor, who opened her first childcare center in Rome in 1907. Henriëtte spent a little time with Maria before opening the crèche."

"I've heard of Maria Montessori," Karyn said, "but until you mentioned her, I had not heard of Henriëtte Pimentel. Or the crèche, for that matter. I guess I have a lot to learn."

"Both Maria Montessori and Henriëtte Pimentel are well known in childhood education circles," Teddy said. "She was a remarkable woman, a legend in Holland. Even though Sara and her sister worked for Henriëtte, I had not made her acquaintance until she asked Sara to introduce me. Sara came home one night and said that Henriëtte urgently wanted to meet me. I was shocked. 'Me? Why would she want to meet me?' And then Sara said it was about the Wagner-Rogers Bill. Now the light bulb went on."

"You lost me," Karyn said. "What was the Wagner-Rogers Bill again?"

"American lawmakers were not unaware of the crisis facing European Jews. Between July 1, 1938, and June 30, 1939, the US State Department granted the maximum number of immigration visas allowable—27,370 to German-born individuals—filling the German quota for the first time during the era of Nazi rule. And I told you, 309,782 German-born applicants remained on the waiting list. In December 1938, prominent child psychologist Marion Kenworthy asked Clarence Pickett, the director of the American Friends Service Committee, a Quaker relief organization, to help lead an interfaith, nonsectarian effort to support legislation allowing refugee children from Europe to immigrate. Pickett immediately began to lobby for support, including First Lady Eleanor Roosevelt.

"On February 9, 1939, Democratic senator Robert Wagner of New York and Republican congresswoman Edith Nourse Rogers of Massachusetts sponsored identical bills in the US Senate and House of Representatives to admit twenty thousand German refugee children under the age of fourteen over a two-year period. That was known as the Wagner-Rogers Immigration Bill.

"One day, Sara and Henriëtte were chatting, and Sara mentioned the Wagner-Rogers Bill. Henriëtte was overjoyed. 'Twenty thousand German children to receive visas as additional refugees? What a miracle!' Henriëtte said. She then asked Sara if she would be able to schedule an appointment to meet with me to talk about the bill. That caused Sara to laugh. 'You won't need an appointment,' she said. 'I'm seeing him at lunchtime, and I'll bring him over. If I ask him to come meet you, he won't turn me down.'

"It was so busy at the consulate, but I always found time for a lunch date with Sara. You can guess which took precedence. When I met her, she told me she had mentioned the Wagner-Rogers Bill to Henriëtte, and she hoped I wouldn't mind talking with her about it."

"How did Henriëtte know about the bill?" Karyn said.

"It wasn't a secret. Hell, the bill was public knowledge. I must have mentioned it to Sara, but Henriëtte may have known about it on her own. I mean, it was in *The New York Times*."

"And Henriëtte read *The New York Times*? She had time for that? Seriously?"

"Okay, I mentioned it to Sara and she might have told Henriëtte. But it was just a bill, not a law. And given the disposition of the American people, it had little chance of passing. I mean, the newspapers took a poll, and it was twenty-six percent for and sixty-seven percent against. But Sara asked me to talk to Henriëtte anyway, and so I did. We walked across the Plantage Middenlaan, where lots of little children were outside playing.

"'Teddy, this is Henriëtte Pimentel,' Sara said. 'She has been the director of the crèche since 1926. It is my privilege to volunteer here as a member of her staff.'

"'We are the ones who are privileged,' said Henriëtte. 'The children love Sara and Sylvia.'

"That brought a smile to my face. 'Lovely to meet you, Miss Pimentel. What can the US consulate do for you?'

"'Oh, not for me, Mr. Hartigan; for the children. As you may know, many of our children are German refugees. I'd like to know what I can do to make sure they are included with other German children who apply for visas under the new Wagner-Rogers Immigration Bill.'

"I smiled. 'Did Sara tell you about the bill?'

"'I read the papers, Mr. Hartigan,' she said. 'Sometimes even *The New York Times*. I'd be very irresponsible if I wasn't aware of things that could affect the welfare of our children, not the least of which are the current US immigration quotas. Our parents also stay abreast of US immigration, as much as they can. The majority of our children at the crèche come from Jewish homes. Most of the German parents would do anything to get their children out of Europe, especially right now. So, if you don't think it too forward of me, what can you tell me about the Wagner-Rogers Immigration Bill, maybe the parts that aren't reported in *The New York Times*? When will it become law? What can our children do to be among the first to apply? I assume that a US consulate, an arm of the Department of State, will have authority to administer the act. Am I right? I mean, the visas will be issued through US consulates, like the one in Amsterdam? Right?'

"That set me back on my heels. Not only was she well informed, but she was bold enough to raise the topic with a US consular official. I took a deep breath. I glanced to the side at Sara, as if to say, *You brought me over to this woman, and you're getting me in trouble*. She smiled and shrugged. 'Miss Pimentel . . .' I said, but she broke in, 'Please, Mr. Hartigan, call me Henriëtte.'

"I smiled. 'Yes, of course, Henriëtte. And I'm Teddy. While we are normally not allowed to discuss inner workings of our congressional committees, in this matter, I'm afraid you know as much as I do. The Wagner-Rogers Bill is currently buried in committee.'

"Henriëtte raised her finger. 'I understand that it has the support of Eleanor Roosevelt, your First Lady. At such time as the bill becomes a law, as I'm sure it will with such powerful support, I assume that young German children who apply, like *my* young German children, will be in the front of the line, is that not so?'

"Yikes! Here she was lobbying me to put her kids at the front of the line. 'We would surely consider them, Miss Pim . . . I mean Henriëtte. *If* it becomes law. But I must tell you, despite the First Lady's support, the bill has substantial opposition. There are those congressmen who don't favor immigration at all.'

"'Hmm. Well, Teddy, I asked Sara to bring you over here so that we might make our mutual acquaintances. At such time as the bill does become law, as I'm sure it will now that it has Mrs. Roosevelt behind it, I would hope that you would promptly inform me, so that the women and I might assist the children of the crèche in making their applications.' Her smile went from ear to ear, and she gave a polite nod. 'Now, if you'll excuse me, please, I must attend to my children.' She and Sara turned to leave and Sara whispered, 'I'll see you later.'"

"Well, that was a marvelous story," Karyn said. "Twenty thousand little children. No wonder Henriëtte was advocating for her children. So, did it pass? Did it become law?"

Teddy shook his head. "It never had a chance, Karyn. The polls let the congressmen and senators know how the American people felt. Conservative congressmen maintained that the immigrant children would eventually take jobs away from American children. A rumor also spread that some of these German children might join the so-called Fifth Column of spies and saboteurs working on behalf of the Nazis."

"Oh for God's sake, Teddy. Eight-, nine-, and ten-year-old children?"

"And younger. Ridiculous as it sounds, the Wagner-Rogers Bill was never called up for a vote."

"From your perspective, did the failure to pass that bill affect Europeans' opinion of America?"

"It was a disappointment, that's for sure. When refugees visualized the United States, they saw the Statue of Liberty lifting her lamp beside the golden door. It was emblematic. I suppose it still is. Shutting that golden door was contrary to everything she stood for. For the parents who had German children in the crèche, it was a huge disappointment. When they came for their scheduled appointment at the consulate, I had to inform them that the bill had not yet been called for a vote, and as of now, their children would have to wait until their number on the waiting list was reached."

CHAPTER SIXTEEN

"EVERY DAY, MY work at the consulate was becoming more stressful and more time-consuming, which I regretted because it meant less time to spend with Sara. The more aggressive Hitler became, the busier we became. Quite often it was American citizens in line seeking information. What was happening? How were their rights affected? Were they at risk in Holland? How could they secure passage home? Oftentimes the ships sailing from the Netherlands were overbooked. Some lines had canceled altogether. We were recommending Portugal and Spain.

"Among those seeking appointments at the consulate, they weren't all Germans, Austrians, or Poles. Sometimes it was the Dutch. Some were seeking immigration. Some were seeking NIVs, the nonimmigrant temporary visas, to get out of Europe before something horrific happened. You could sense it in the air.

"Immigrant visas were available until the Netherlands met their yearly quota of 3,153. Now it was filled. There were still quotas open for citizens of other countries, Brazil for example, but we didn't have any Brazilian applicants. Thousands were open for Irish applicants, but they never showed up at our consulate either. Most of the applicants continued to be German, Czech, Austrian, and other middle European countries, and they were desperate. They were refugees; they had escaped from Germany and central European countries, made their way into the Netherlands, and now they stood in line at the consulate with their families, carrying bags of clothing and whatever else they could fit into cloth containers. Even the little ones carried a pillowcase full of belongings. At least an hour before sunrise they would be standing in line on the sidewalk, and after we closed, they would have to find somewhere to stay for the night. Some of them were sick. Some would beg for a visa trying every possible excuse. 'Can we apply for a nonimmigrant visa, you know, to visit the museums and return? We'd like to visit our mother's uncle in St. Louis. Can't we go stay with him?' Of course, they would have nothing to back up their request, none of the required documents, and we'd have to turn them down.

"The more territories Germany occupied, I should say conquered, the more refugees fled for freedom. And Germany was gobbling up territories left and right. In March 1939, Hitler put the pressure on the Slavic states, Czechoslovakia, Slovenia, Ukraine, and bending to the pressure the Slavs declared their so-called independence called the Slovak Republic, which was of course controlled by Germany. The Germans occupied more and more of Czechoslovakia and ultimately dismantled the whole of Czech lands, in violation of the Munich Agreement.

"On March 15, during a visit to Berlin, the Czechoslovak president, Emil Hácha, signed away his country's independence. On March 16, Hitler went to Prague Castle and proclaimed the 'Protectorate of Bohemia and Moravia.' He appointed Hácha as the head of state with the title of state president. However, Hácha was a puppet; real power was vested in the Reichsprotektor, who served as Hitler's personal representative. In each of these annexed territories, Hitler imposed his harsh laws and regulations. Jews lost their jobs, their property, their professional licenses, their right to send their children to school, and many times their lives. What other choice did these people have but to flee? Somehow, they'd make it across the German border and stand in line at consulates in Belgium, France, and the Netherlands, and they'd apply for visas. In Amsterdam, even if they brought each and every document required, all I could do was give them a number on the waiting list. And you wonder why I was stressed out?

"Working long hours prevented me from being with Sara and added to my stress level. We'd make plans for dinner at a neighborhood restaurant, she'd get a table, and then she'd sit there all alone until I could get there. When I finally got away from the consulate, I'd rush over to the restaurant, hopefully before it closed. We didn't have cell phones back then. After a time, if I was late, she'd nod her head, order a takeout dinner, and bring it home. She knew I'd get home as soon as I could. Whether it was at the restaurant or at my apartment, being with her was so peaceful. I would long for an opportunity to get away, and it finally came in April. Sara asked me if I would like to join her at her family's home in Utrecht. It was Passover time, if I wouldn't mind joining her family for Passover Seder.

"I told Consul General Lee that I needed to take a few days off in April. I hadn't taken any time off since I arrived the previous fall. He asked where I was going, and I told him Utrecht. I was going to visit my girlfriend's parents. I realized that was the first time I had publicly referred to Sara as my girlfriend. Lee gave me a three-day pass.

"I was anxious, to say the least. I had never been to a Seder, and I really didn't know much about Passover. So think about this: here I am, working on visa applications for thousands of refugees, most of whom are Jewish, and I really don't know anything about the tenets of their religion. I feared I would do something or say something stupid at the Seder. I expressed my anxiety to Sara, that maybe I would embarrass her, or myself, for sure myself, but she waved it off. 'My family is very understanding. You won't be the first guest we ever had that wasn't Jewish.' I came to learn that the Netherlands was a very tolerant country. There were several religions. Intermarriage was not uncommon. Our relationship had been going so well, I was worried that a trip to her parents' for a religious holiday might provide an opportunity for me to screw things up. But we packed our bags and off we went."

"UTRECHT IS THE fourth-largest city in the Netherlands, located about an hour away from Amsterdam. Nothing is very far in the Netherlands. As Sara had predicted, her family graciously welcomed me into their home. They were lovely people. Sara's father, Saul, was a professor emeritus at Utrecht University. The family lived in a house on the outskirts of Utrecht, almost in the woods.

"Sara showed me around the house, including her bedroom, where her girlhood possessions still sat on the shelves. Stuffed animals still lay on her bed; a large pink doggie was her favorite. I saw a picture of her third-grade class with little Sara sitting cross-legged on the floor in the first row. As we walked around her room, I could see that Sara was self-conscious, and she blushed. I thought she was adorable, and it made me love her even more. Of course, that night, Sara slept in her bedroom, and I slept on a couch in the study." Teddy smiled bashfully. "We weren't married, you know. We didn't sleep together at her parents'.

"Sara's sister, Sylvia, whom I knew well, greeted me warmly. I met her cousin Rivka and Rivka's husband, Jonah, and their seven-year-old daughter, Leah. They arrived just before dinner. Sara's father conducted the service. We sang songs, and everyone read a passage from the Haggadah. I didn't read or speak Hebrew, but I could read the portions written in Dutch. From the few Hebrew words I did understand, I could follow along. I loved the part where Leah went looking for the hidden matzah." Teddy stopped and looked at Karyn. "You're familiar with all of this, aren't you?"

"Of course," Karyn said. "I'm Jewish. The hidden matzah that the children search for and get a reward is called the afikomen. It was always my favorite part of the Seder too."

Teddy's eyes went glassy and he stared at the ceiling. He didn't say a word for a minute or so, and finally said, "I can see it, Karyn. I can see them all sitting here. I can hear the children, just like it was yesterday. I can smell the matzah ball soup. That's why we need to finish my memoir. I don't ever want to lose any of those precious feelings.

"The Seder concluded, and we stood and sang a song, which was a prayer for peace. It was called 'Oseh Shalom.' These were peace-loving people, Karyn. It made it even more impossible to understand how a soulless, insane person could advocate hating the entire Jewish people. It was even more incomprehensible that millions of German citizens would blindly follow him and espouse that hatred. Maybe, if each one of those followers was required to meet a Jewish family and sit down at a Seder, we'd do away with anti-Semitism in a second. Silly thought. I had been told that when a powerful autocrat incites or threatens violence upon a certain class of people, his timid followers had been taught to obey and be thankful that they didn't belong to that class.

"The next day, Sara showed me around Utrecht, known for its classic medieval buildings and monuments. It has beautiful canals winding through tree-lined walkways. There were gorgeous churches and Roman fortresses built in the first century. She told me that the Utrecht Jewish community dated back to Roman times.

"We met Sara's father at the university. His classroom was on the third floor, where he introduced us to a few of his students. They crowded around me, full of questions about US immigration policies. I got stuck answering questions for an hour. The biggest question, without a doubt, was when and why did the US start setting such tight limits on issuing visas? I explained that the first restrictive law was passed in 1917. In 1924, the Johnson-Reed Act amended the formulas for issuing visas, and that is what we still used in 1938. The next question, and the most difficult of all to answer, was 'How come a big country like Poland only gets a small number of visas, but a small country like England gets a lot more visas than it can use?'"

"Oh, I agree," said Karyn. "Makes no sense. How did you explain that one?"

"I told you it was the most difficult. The Johnson-Reed Act set the total number of visas for each country at two percent of the total number of people of each nationality in the United States as of the year 1890, as shown in the national census. This put the total number of visas available each year at three hundred and fifty thousand."

"What?"

"That's the same response the students had. How do you explain that? I said, 'For example, my great-great-grandparents came from England. So if I am applying for a visa, the act would set the limits on what percent of America was of English ancestry in the year 1890. We know that it's undoubtedly the largest, they founded the country, so it gets the largest percentage of visas. England's quota was set at 65,721 per year, because that was two percent of Americans who had British ancestors in 1890. But the immigration quota for the Netherlands was set at only 3,153. Germany was 27,370, while Poland was 6,524. All based upon how many citizens were of that nationality in 1890. Why did they pick that date, I don't know.'

"That night, before we turned the lights off, Sara asked me if the quotas could ever be expanded. Was there any hope that more than 3,153 visas would be issued for the Netherlands?

"I told Sara, 'The easy answer is: not until Congress amends the Johnson-Reed Act. Right now it's doubtful they will. Those born in the Depression, and those influenced by demagogues like the radio priest Charles Coughlin, they don't want any immigrants at all, especially Jewish immigrants. In 1939, pollsters found that fifty-three percent of those interviewed agreed with the statement "Jews are different and should be restricted."'"

Karyn shook her head. "I guess the Rosenbaum family didn't have to be told about anti-Semitism. They lived right next door to Nazi Germany, and they had friends in Germany. But the Rosenbaum family wasn't trying to immigrate to America, were they?"

"No, they weren't," Teddy said. "Before I went out to their house, I wondered if they would ask me to help them get a visa. I figured that since they were Jewish, they would want a visa to America. Most of our applicants were Jewish. That was ignorant on my part. Every Jew wasn't looking for a visa to America. The subject never came up during my visit.

"When Sara and I returned to Amsterdam, I asked her if her parents ever discussed applying for a visa, and she said no. To her knowledge, they never discussed immigration. Her family was content where they were. Her father had a prestigious teaching position, head of the history department, and they had a lot of friends, many of whom were Jewish. After all, they lived in what was called the Jerusalem of the West. As long as Germany stayed on their side of the border, like they did in the last war, the Rosenbaums were comfortable living in Utrecht."

"How did you feel about that?" Karyn asked.

"To tell you the truth, I thought they were naïve. Who could trust Hitler to stay on his side of the border? If he wanted to cross it, then he'd cross it. Then everything would change.

"Sara said to me, 'What difference would it make? Even if my parents wanted to leave, which they don't, the immigration quota for the Netherlands has been reached for this year, hasn't it?' To which I answered, 'Yes, it has, months ago. There are no visas available for this year. They'd have to apply to get on the waiting list.'

"Sara's next question was, 'Are there no exceptions?'"

Karyn raised her eyebrows. "Oh, there it is. Couldn't you see it? Couldn't you tell where she was headed? I mean, wasn't it the elephant in the room? Didn't she mean to ask you, 'Couldn't the *wife* of a US citizen, especially a State Department officer, get a visa if she was to accompany her husband back home?'"

"It may have been an elephant in the room, I'm sure it was in the back of both of our minds, but it wasn't spoken at that time. I didn't want to bring up how difficult immigrant visas were to obtain, even for spouses of US citizens. The fact was, the quota system was strict, and there were few exceptions. Sara did ask, 'Are the quotas reviewed from time to time? It doesn't seem to be a very fair policy to limit the number of visas to countries where great-grandparents came from.' To which I answered, 'No, it sure doesn't.' I wanted her to be more optimistic, but there were no indications that Congress would expand them. If anything, they were likely to limit them further.

"We dropped the subject. The rest of the evening was spent on small talk about unimportant topics like whether Walter was producing plays for the Schouwburg, how much we enjoyed New Year's Eve, or the fireworks show. Then one night, out of the blue, Sara burst out with, 'It's totally unfair, Teddy. And really dumb! If Congress is so concerned about how many immigrants are coming into the US in any given year, I can understand that. There are only so many that can be processed at one time. From what I understand, there are plenty of jobs available, the schools can absorb the children, cities have plenty of housing, it's a very large and wide-open country. But even so, what if a man applies who is a professional, maybe a doctor, and doctors are needed? He couldn't jump to the front of the line, could he? No, because it's all based on the dumb system of where ancestors came from in 1890. What if a talented foreign woman wants to immigrate because she has married a citizen?'"

"Uh-huh," Karyn said. "Did she mention anyone in particular? Like a State Department officer?"

"I put my arm around her. 'You're right,' I said. 'I agree. Last week, I interviewed several people from Hungary. Hungary is occupied by Germany and is subject to all the Nazis' nasty laws. The total yearly quota for US immigration visas for Hungarian citizens is 869, which was filled in the first few weeks. Even the waiting list has been filled for a long time. On the other hand, I don't believe I have interviewed anyone from Ireland. The quota for Ireland is almost 18,000 per year. Thousands of Irish visas will go unissued this year.'

"Sara nodded. 'What would Lady Liberty say about that? Didn't she say, "The wretched refuse of your teeming shore, send those to me?" Isn't that supposed to be the US motto? She didn't say, "Send the wretched refuse to me if they come from Ireland but not if they come from Hungary, or Belgium, or Holland," did she?'"

Karyn sat back and whistled. "Pretty smart girl, that Sara Rosenbaum."

"Oh, you have no idea. I was breathless. My Sara was a genius. How did she know about Emma Lazarus and Lady Liberty? And how in the world was I going to answer her? Should I say that our country abandoned Lady Liberty in 1924? Sara stood up with a smug look and said, 'The US doesn't want wretched refuse. Or German refuse, or Jewish refuse, or the persecuted refuse. Your quota system doesn't have a heart.' And she was right.

"Six weeks later the newspapers started running stories about the MS St. Louis, and that was a confirmation of Sara's criticism. Sara found the story in The New York Times and pointed it out to me. Of course, I already knew, and was hoping she didn't see it. Bulletins had been circulating in the office. I just didn't want to be the one to bring it up because it would fire up her anger again. It turned out to be a topic of conversation for a month, and not just for us.

"The steamship MS St. Louis left Hannover, Germany, on May 13, 1939, carrying 937 immigrants bound for Cuba. They had forfeited and handed over almost all of their belongings to Germany as a 'tax' in order to get permission to leave. They all carried Cuban transit visas, which gave them the right to live in Cuba. They tried, but they couldn't get US visas, they were way down the quota list. When they arrived in Havana on May 27, Cuba turned them away. They had decided to revoke the visas that they had issued. So then the boat was stuck in the Havana harbor.

Cordell Hull and Treasury Secretary Henry Morgenthau tried to persuade Cuba to honor the visas and let the people ashore, but Cuba said no. So, the ship sailed ninety miles north to Florida, but guess what? They weren't allowed to land. They sat offshore asking for permission to dock, but none of the passengers had a US visa. Some in the US government would have allowed it on humanitarian grounds. People said what about the Statue of Liberty?

"And then there were those, like Senator Gerald Nye and his group, who lobbied strongly against the boat. They favored sending the *St. Louis* back to Germany.

"As the days went by, Sara and I were rooting for them. But the State Department sent a telegram to the ship denying them entry, stating, 'Noncitizens must wait their turns on the waiting list and qualify for and obtain immigration visas before they may be admissible into the United States.' The coast guard was sent out to prevent them coming close to shore. They went north all along the coastline to Canada, where they begged Prime Minister Mackenzie King to allow them asylum. But Canada wasn't any more lenient, and it turned them down. So, the MS *St. Louis* with its 937 passengers, mostly Jews, headed back to Europe."

Karyn shook her head. "I didn't know about that. Did they all end up back in Germany?"

"No," Teddy said, "England took in 288. The ship was then allowed to dock in Antwerp, Belgium, where the ship's captain negotiated with various countries. He convinced Belgium to take 224, France to take 214, and the Netherlands to take in 181."

"That was generous on the part of those countries," Karyn said, "but the tragedy was that they were not welcome in the United States and were sent back to Europe."

"You are right. It was a topic of conversation wherever you went. Sara and I would go out to a bar and hear people talking about it. We went shopping for furniture and people in the store were talking about it."

Karyn was surprised. "What? You were shopping for furniture?"

Teddy looked at her sheepishly. "We had decided to get an apartment and move in together. We were staying together more or less all the time anyway, and my green-glow Heineken apartment was way too small. I had a generous living allowance from the State Department, and I put that allowance and some of my own money together, and we found a very nice rental unit a few blocks away."

CHAPTER SEVENTEEN

KARYN'S PHONE RANG at 8:00 A.M., and she reached over to answer it. She had been awake for a while thinking about Teddy and Sara, as she so often did, but the ring startled her. It was Burt. There was no reason for Burt to call so early in the morning unless something was wrong. "Is everything all right?" she asked. "Is Teddy okay?"

"I'm not sure," he said. "Apparently, Teddy had a bad night. He's with the doctors this morning. He can't make his interview session today. That's why he asked me to call you."

Karyn shook her head to clear her thoughts. "What does that mean, 'He had a bad night'?" she said. "What's wrong with him?"

"I don't know. He had a bad night, that's what he said. I'm not sure what that means. He doesn't share his private medical conditions with me. Anyway, he asked me to tell you that he wants to continue with the interviews, but not today. First, the doctors have to check him out and run some tests. He's pretty sure he'll be released in a few days."

"A few days? What's wrong with him that he needs a few days? What's going on, Burt?"

"I don't know, Karyn, I'm sorry to upset you. He said he'd call me later. Are you all right?"

"I'm fine, but I'm worried about Teddy. Is it serious, Burt? Are the sessions taking too much out of him? Tell me."

"I don't know. It could be anything. He sounded fine on the phone. He said that he wanted to continue the sessions. I know he's made some calls recently, seeking information about your sister Annie, but I don't know the result on that either."

"The sessions must be hard. If he wants to stop, of course—but I would keep going, if he wants. I think they're very interesting. I'm learning quite a bit about the Netherlands. I keep thinking it would make a good book, depending on how it all turns out. It seems like the Second World War is approaching and I'm worried about some of the characters and whether they'll make it. Other than that, my time is spent at the hotel. It's pretty quiet."

"Well then, do you want to join me for breakfast? How about ten o'clock?"

KARYN AND BURT sat in a booth at the Pancake House. "Thanks for inviting me out this morning. I don't know what I would have done today. Maybe I'd check out one of the Washington museums."

"They have plenty. I'd be happy to show you around, but I'm tied up today and I'm leaving town the day after tomorrow. Maybe when I get back."

"That would be nice," Karyn said. "But tell me, Burt, what's wrong with Teddy? I think you know more than you're telling me. Did he have an attack of something? How serious is he? He's always in a hurry to get his memoirs down on paper. Is he afraid that he won't have enough time to finish telling the whole story? Does he have some terminal condition, Burt?"

Burt shrugged. "Not that I know of. Hell, he's ninety-two. Doesn't everyone have something by the time they're ninety-two? But whatever's wrong with him right now, I don't think it's terminal. He sounded okay on the phone. Apparently, the nursing home called his doctor last night. He was taken to the hospital and they're checking him out. I think the nursing home wants to move him from the independent-living wing to the assisted-living wing, but you know Teddy. He doesn't want to do that."

"What happened at the nursing home last night? He was fine when I left him."

"He fell. Second time this month. He couldn't get to his phone, and he just lay there. It wasn't until his dinner was delivered that they discovered him. So, he's at the hospital and they're running all their tests;

you know, X-ray, MRI, heart and lung scans. He doesn't know exactly when he can come home. I know they want to keep him for a few days. He wants to resume as soon as he can, the stubborn old buzzard. The doctors will tell him this afternoon when he can come home. He hopes it's soon."

"Maybe the interview sessions are too hard on him."

"Maybe they are, but that should be his decision, don't you think? In his words, 'As long as my brain is still working, and my memories are still intact, I want to plug ahead.' By the way, I almost forgot, he wants you to get pictures of yourself when you were very young. And also pictures of your adopted parents, your *tante* and your *oom*. Do you still have them? He realizes that you wouldn't have any pictures of the time before you were adopted, but any pictures taken at the Leisners' would be very helpful. The younger, the better. He suggests you call your daughter and ask her to make a search for them. If she is successful, she should send them here by overnight mail."

Karyn nodded. "There is a framed picture of my *tante* and *oom* sitting on top of my bedroom dresser. I have a lot of pictures taken when I was growing up. Some are in old photo albums. Beth would know where to look. She would know what I looked like when I was very young, I've showed her the pictures."

A little later, Burt put down his coffee and said, "I have to go back to Tel Aviv the day after tomorrow. I'll be gone for at least a week. If your daughter can find the pictures Teddy has requested, I could airmail them back, although I don't know if that's such a good idea. I'd rather bring them back myself."

Karyn smiled and patted Burt's arm. "That's very kind of you, Burt. I'll call her this morning. I assume that Teddy wants these pictures to show to someone who is looking for information about Annie, isn't that right?"

"Yes. Teddy told me he has an old friend in the Netherlands. And when I say old, I mean old. But they have done this kind of thing before. You know, trying to put together people who were separated during the war. It's very likely that Annie resembles you, and assuming that's true, your pictures can be very helpful. Or somebody might say that looks like a girl in their third-grade class. Or maybe like a girl who lived down the street.

Or maybe your Annie got married and she had a daughter that looks just like your picture. I don't know, but that's how they put it all together."

Karyn wrote down her daughter's address and phone number in Tel Aviv. Burt said, "I'll be there in a couple of days. Tell her to give me a call."

"I sure appreciate all you're doing for me," Karyn said.

"It's my pleasure. And I appreciate all you're doing for Teddy. Maybe when I return, we could spend some time together. I enjoy your company very much."

"I'd like that," Karyn said. Just then, Burt's cell phone rang. He answered it, looked at Karyn, and mouthed *Teddy*. He nodded and mm-hmmed a few times and then handed the phone to Karyn. "He wants to talk to you."

Karyn took the phone. "Hello, Teddy, I'm so glad you called. How are you feeling? Are you okay?"

"Yeah, I'm okay. I fell," he grumbled. "That's all, but they won't let me come home for a few days."

Karyn smiled. She put her hand on the mouthpiece and whispered to Burt, "He's the toughest old man I ever met." Then she said to Teddy, "Well, I hope you get better soon and we can do a few more interviews."

"A few more?" Teddy said. "I'm better now. Let's get on with the memoir. I asked the doctors and they said it would be all right if you did your interviews right here."

"In the hospital?" Karyn responded. "Really, Teddy, I don't think that's a good idea."

"Why not? I'm not contagious. There's a big, comfortable chair right next to my bed. They bring tea and coffee and other stuff to the room." He paused. "Please, Karyn?"

Karyn looked at Burt, looked at the phone, and shrugged her shoulders. "Okay. If it's all right with your doctors then I'll come. I'll see you tomorrow."

CHAPTER EIGHTEEN

TEDDY WAS IN a sitting position when Karyn arrived at Georgetown University Medical Center. There was a large chair beside his bed. He smiled and said, "Welcome back."

Karyn bobbed a quick curtsy. "And the same thing to you, sir. You're looking pretty good."

Teddy chuckled. "Don't bullshit an old bullshitter. I look like the wrath of God. But I feel well enough to get on with our memoir."

"That's good. By the way, my daughter is looking for some pictures," Karyn mentioned, "and if she can find them, Burt will bring them with him when he returns next week. He decided he doesn't want to trust them to an overnight delivery service."

Teddy agreed. "That's fine, now let's stop the small talk, and get on with my memoir. I believe we were in the summer of 1939."

Karyn grabbed her pen and tablet, gave a firm nod, and said, "Let's do it."

"The summer of 1939. The weather was gorgeous, Amsterdam was beautiful, and I guess you already know; I was in love." Teddy closed his eyes and smiled. "If I could have only frozen that moment in time forever. Sara and I took advantage of every opportunity. We attended outdoor concerts, went on long walks through parks, and took weekend side trips to the Dutch countryside. You've seen them in books: windmills, canals, and rows and rows of tulips. The only break to our peaceful existence was the consulate, you know, my job, which was getting busier and busier every day. It wasn't just German refugees who were applying for visas, now there was a flood of Polish refugees. Unlike the German refugees, the Poles had money. Hitler took all the money and assets away from German refugees as some kind of a 'flight tax,' but Polish refugees could leave Poland and take their wealth with them. I could have been a very wealthy man if I accepted all the bribes that were offered to me under the table. Of course, I wouldn't do that, and the bribe wouldn't have done them any good anyway. The quota for US immigrant visas for Polish citizens was six thousand, five hundred. That for a country of thirty-five million. Washington would have never approved of the issuance of a visa in excess of the quota."

"Why the sudden influx of Poles?" Karyn asked.

"Well, you know what was coming and they knew what was coming. It was getting hotter every day. In 1939, Hitler continued ranting and railing about one thing or another, but as the summer passed, he had turned all his attention to the city of Danzig, the peninsula on the top of Poland that extended out into the Baltic Sea, and from there, to the Atlantic Ocean. Through the centuries, that parcel of land has belonged to Poland, then to Germany, to Prussia, to Poland again, and at the end of World War One, the victorious Allies created the 'Free State of Danzig.' It was a free state, meaning anyone could use it, but Poland's rights included free use of the harbor, a Polish post office, a Polish garrison in the Westerplatte district, and Poland was given the right of administering Danzig. For almost twenty years, Danzig was part of Poland, with which it shared economic interests. It flourished and enjoyed wide autonomy.

"Hitler wanted it, and he was demanding it for Germany. As in the Sudeten Mountains of Czechoslovakia, there were more Germans in Danzig than any other ancestry. Out of Danzig's four hundred thousand citizens, ninety percent spoke German. Hitler wanted Danzig for the Germans like he had wanted the Sudeten Mountains. He said he only wanted Danzig and nothing more. Of course, he couldn't be trusted. He had also claimed he only wanted the Sudetens, and nothing more, after which he attacked and conquered all the rest of Czechoslovakia. Now he was saying all he wanted was Danzig, and the rest of Poland didn't believe him. And at the US consulate, we were flooded with Polish applications.

"But," Teddy said with a smile, "it was summer, and it was gorgeous, and we were in love. One evening, Sara said, 'You have to leave work early on Monday.'

"'That won't be easy,' I said. 'What's the occasion?'

"'It's Julia's birthday and Willem has managed to get the Majestic Hotel's boat to take us all out on a cruise on the canals. But don't say anything, it's a secret. Be ready at five p.m.'"

Karyn looked surprised. "Willem could get one of those giant boats for his girlfriend's birthday? I've seen pictures of them. They were large wooden boats with the open windows, made to carry dozens of people. Willem was going to get it for just the four of you?"

Teddy chuckled. "His parents owned the hotel and he was a general manager, so he could get anything he wanted. But he didn't want the big boat. There was a smaller boat. We took it on a cruise earlier in the summer. Willem had been navigating the canals since he was a teenager. He had even taken boats through the locks and out into the inland sea. He told me that he planned to sail all the way around the top of the Netherlands and out into the North Sea to England someday. Anyway, we were all set to go, but it didn't happen. Not for me, anyway."

"Why not?"

"Julia's birthday was on July 10. That afternoon an alert went out in the embassy and in the three consulates that put an end to my celebration. I remember it clearly. We were advised, on an emergency basis, that British prime minister Neville Chamberlain was going to address Parliament on matters concerning Central Europe. The consulate staff were all required to gather in Consul General Lee's office to listen to the broadcast on shortwave radio. Julia, Willem, and Sara went on the boat without me. When the broadcast began, Chamberlain, speaking in his dignified, sonorous tones, stated, 'His Majesty's government are maintaining close contact with the Polish and French governments on the question of Danzig.'"

Karyn's eyes widened and her lips formed a circle as if to say *Ohh*. It was clear that Karyn understood the severity of the moment.

"Chamberlain acknowledged that Danzig was almost a German city, but the prosperity of its inhabitants depended upon Polish trade. He pointed out that the Vistula River was Poland's only waterway to the

Baltic, and the port at the mouth of the river, the tip of Danzig, was of vital, strategic, and economic importance to Poland. If a country occupied Danzig, it could block Poland's access to the sea and exert an economic and military stranglehold upon her.

"He reminded everyone that the maintenance of the status quo was guaranteed by Hitler himself by the ten-year treaty that Hitler had concluded with Poland's Marshal Pilsudski. Chamberlain went over a list of the threats that Hitler had recently made against Danzig and Poland. Then he delivered the shocking statement: 'We have guaranteed to give our assistance to Poland in the case of a threat to her independence, when she considers it vital to resist with her national forces, and we are firmly resolved to carry out this undertaking.'"

Teddy looked at Karyn and said, "In simple English, that meant that Great Britain would defend Poland if Germany attacked her. Consul General Lee reached over and turned off the radio. His face was ashen. He swallowed hard and told us that Chamberlain's speech took great courage. Coupled with France's similar declaration, it was a crystal-clear promise to militarily defend Poland. The hopes were that Chancellor Hitler would think twice before taking any rash move against Danzig or Poland itself. And then Lee cautioned us all to be ready for anything. 'We will get our instructions from Washington,' he said. We all left the office muttering to each other that a world war was a distinct possibility. It all depended on Hitler.

"Sara came home that night and told me what a fun time I missed. Willem had navigated up and down the canals, stopping at the Redhead for cocktails and at Marie Ladue for birthday cake. Everyone was sorry that I couldn't make it, and Sara brought home a piece of cake for me. She asked what was so important at the consulate that I couldn't come to Julia's birthday party, and I shrugged it off. Why should I put a black cloud on such a nice day? 'Nothing,' I said. 'Just a policy meeting. I wish I had been on the boat.'

"Sara's face was animated, and she talked at length about their boat trip. Then she noticed I had no color in my cheeks, and I really wasn't listening, and she asked me again to tell her what happened at the consulate meeting."

"So, did she talk you into telling her?" Karyn said.

"Yeah, she did. 'Don't you see what all these heads of state are doing?' I said to her. 'It's a case of whose dog has the loudest bark. Hitler threatens Poland because he wants the Free State that by the Treaty of Versailles belongs to everyone, not just Germany. And that riles Hitler. Unless Poland allows Germany to have Danzig, if such a unilateral act was lawful, then Hitler threatens to take it by force. This is typical Hitler diplomacy. Give me what I want, or I'll take it anyway.

"'The hope is that Hitler sees the mutual defense pact that has now been formed between Poland, Britain, and France, and recognizes that they would be a formidable opponent. On the other side, we hear that Russia has formed an alliance with Germany, and they are formidable as well. Now what? Who blinks first?'

"Sara nodded and told me she understood. 'So, the democracies have aligned, and the dictatorships have aligned. The difference is the democracies play fair. They keep their word. They honor borders. They honor mutual treaties. Am I right? The Treaty of Versailles is a treaty that all have signed, and the democracies intend to honor it. The signatories will defend it against an enemy, won't they?'

"'They're supposed to. The question is, what country will stand up to Hitler and prevent him from breaking the treaty?' I shrugged my shoulders. 'The question is also, does Hitler really want to take on all the democratic countries that signed the treaty because of a small free territory called Danzig? Or will he occupy it just to show how tough he is? That is what he did with Austria and Czechoslovakia, and no one stood up to him. Remember Neville Chamberlain and 'Peace in our time'? What will happen to the rest of Europe if he wants it? Does it all become a battleground? And if push comes to shove, what about the neutral countries? The Netherlands, Belgium, and Denmark are politically similar. They are geographically similar, they all border the ocean, and they all pose no threat. What would Hitler have to gain from attacking any one of those countries? They all have a tradition of staying out of conflicts. And that's what we're counting on.'

"Sara reached over and held my hand. 'Teddy, you should go back to Washington before it's too late.'

"'Sara, right now it's all talk. All bluster. Nothing is certain. Threats have been made and now it's time for diplomacy to take place. That's what happened with Czechoslovakia. Maybe they'll talk for months and months, during which time there will be new threats and shouts and bartering. Danzig is not so important that Germany needs sole ownership. The treaty provides that they have the right to use it. So, ultimately an accord will be reached, we hope. And if it isn't, then Hitler, the aggressive bastard that he is, will start a military conflict. In the four years of the last world war, thirty-seven million people were killed, wounded, or missing. Is Germany prepared to initiate that again? Maybe Hitler is, he's that insane.'

"Sara sat frozen, and tears were flowing down her cheeks. I was so sorry that I had rattled off all that statistical horror, and I held her tightly. 'But,' I said, 'it hasn't happened and may never happen. These are just wild projections. And remember, the Netherlands has not promised allegiance to any side and will remain neutral, just like she did in the last war, and she didn't lose a single soul. So, if you're in the Netherlands, you're safe.'

"But that didn't calm her down. Sara was still shaking. 'What if Germany or other countries don't honor the Netherlands' statement of neutrality?'

"'Sara, there is a history here. They honored it before. What would other countries have to gain by attacking the Netherlands? What would be the benefit? The Netherlands are at peace with everybody. They do business with everyone. Even Germany, so far. Germany does substantial business with the Netherlands. They enjoy a mutual trade balance. Why would they want to upset it?'

"'Does Hitler have to have a reason?' Sara said. 'What if Hitler wants to own us, like he wanted to own Austria, Czechoslovakia, and now Danzig. He wants to own the world, Teddy. And I repeat, you should think about going home. You have a safe place to go. Far away from Hitler.'"

"Was that at all on your mind?" Karyn asked.

Teddy shook his head. "Even if all that was so, I could never leave Sara. I tried to make light of the situation, even though I thought the same things that Sara did. So I said, 'Sara, sweetheart, I have a job here, and responsibilities. I work for the United States of America. I am an officer in the US State Department. That's a pretty safe place to work. Do you think that loudmouth paperhanger wants to take on the United States? I don't think so.'

"Sara's lips were tight, and she was on the edge of crying. 'You just said America is far away, Teddy. And you've told me about people like Senator Nye and his isolationist friends, who don't want the US anywhere near a battleground. Europe could be on fire, and they would vote to stay away and be safe. They're not going to protect you. You should think about going home. You are an American.'

"'I don't care,' I said firmly, staring directly into her eyes. 'You want me to go back to Washington and leave you here? I would never, ever do that, Sara. I will never leave you, and I will never break that promise. How do you say 'I love you' in Dutch?'

"She blushed. *Ik heb je lief.*'

"'Then *Ik heb je lief,* my Sara Rosenbaum. I'll stay as long as you'll have me.'"

CHAPTER NINETEEN

AFTER A THIRTY-MINUTE hospital break, during which time Teddy was administered to by a team of doctors and nurses, a nurse came out into the lobby where Karyn sat. "We told him he should rest now," the nurse said, shaking her head, "but Mr. Hartigan has a thick skull, if you know what I mean."

"As thick as they make them," Karyn answered. She was allowed to enter the room. Teddy was propped up in his bed. He had Band-Aids on his arm and who knows where else. She took her seat.

"You ready?" Teddy said.

"Ready, Teddy," Karyn said with a smile.

"It was in late August that I received a call from Walter Süskind," Teddy said. "He asked if I could come over to the Schouwburg after work. That excited me. He must be getting his new production under way, and maybe Sara and I could participate. Not Betsy! It takes a lot of people to staff a theater production. You need more than just the actors and actresses, even if it is a small amateur production: lighting, stage-hands, costume design, programs, publicity, you name it.

"I called Sara, who was working at the Reformed Teacher Training College that afternoon, and I asked her if she wanted to join me, which she did. On one side of Schouwburg was a row of hedges and field of grass, and on the other side was the crèche. It was a beautiful summer afternoon, and there were children playing outside the crèche in the grass. A ball came rolling toward the sidewalk, and Sara bent down to pick it up. A cute little girl came running to Sara. She had to be about three years old. Sara handed her the ball, gave her a warm smile. Then she looked up at me and said, 'Teddy, this is Katy, one of my very best friends.' Katy blushed and covered her face. Sara whispered, 'She's all alone. Someone dropped her off here a few weeks ago. It's quite a story. Sylvia's been caring for her. Can we take her for a walk this afternoon, is that okay?'

"I was confused. I had never heard her speak about Katy. But what did I care? She was an adorable little girl, and very well behaved. 'Of course we can,' I said. 'I'm glad to meet you, Katy.' She ducked her head behind Sara's arm. The three of us walked across the lawn into the Schouwburg and Walter greeted us. I looked around the theater, a large theater that would probably seat between fifteen hundred and two thousand. I noticed a bill on the wall that advertised a string quartet on Saturday night. Walter said he was reading over some scripts, but he hadn't made any decision yet. He was considering a musical. 'With all that's going on in the world,' he said, 'wouldn't a musical lift everyone's spirits?'

"'I think that's a grand idea,' I answered. 'How can we help you?'

"He twisted his lips back and forth, thought for a moment, and said, 'Oh, I don't know. We'll have to think about that. When I get around to choosing a musical, I'll give you a call.'

"Now I was bewildered. Why did he ask us to come over? He didn't need us for a production. He didn't even have a production in mind. I shook my head and said, 'Is there something else I can help you with?'

"He looked at me with a cautious eye, and said quietly, 'Would it be all right if you and I stepped aside for a minute?' He motioned at some props and said to Sara, 'There are some fun props and costumes that the little girl can play with.'

"Walter and I walked to the back of the theater. 'Let me get to the bottom line. Is there anything you can do to move my family up the waiting list? We speak English fluently, I'm a talented artistic director.'

"I shook my head. I was peeved that he would do this. 'No, I'm afraid not. As talented a theater director as you are, the quota is filled. Your application would not be approved, no matter where you were on the list. The best thing you can do is to put your name on the list and hope that it gets to you soon.'

"'Hmm,' he said. 'I thought you'd say that if it was just me alone. But, successful musicals travel from country to country, don't they? What if we put together a very great musical, one that we could take on the road. If I came to see you then, could I get a temporary visa to take our troupe to America? If your girlfriend was in the cast, she could get one too.'

"As angry as it made me, it was definitely something to think about. It sounded like Walter was trying to find a way to circumvent the immigration rules. What if we could do that? I could take Sara to America. Maybe he felt he could do that because a year ago I was talking to him about putting Betsy in one of his plays. Musicals do travel. A French musical had just finished a two-week run in Amsterdam.

"'Walter,' I said, "no one knows the future, do they? I think at this particular time it might be very difficult for a theater troupe to travel from Europe to America. Maybe one of the larger ocean liners would consider your musical if it were all finished and ready for performance. The *Queen Mary* goes to New York. How hard would it be to put together a quality musical? It would have to be very good.'

"'It might take a while,' he said. 'But I know people who have the money to do it. We just have to get the talent.'

"'The play would have to be fully cast and already have a successful run here at the Schouwburg, and get a booking . I'll help you all I'm able. Within the regulations, of course.'

"He understood. We shook hands and Sara, Katy, and I left. When we were outside, Sara gave me a kiss and said, 'Why don't we take a little walk with Katy, and when we're done, we can go over to the Majestic. Just before you picked me up, Julia called and invited us all to join her and Willem for a quick dinner. When we drop Katy off you can tell me what Walter had in mind.' We took our walk and dropped Katy off at the crèche, where we handed her over to Sylvia. Sylvia had a smile on her face, looked at me, and said, 'She seems to like you, Teddy. She's very shy and doesn't warm up to very many people.' I was flattered."

"ON THE WAY over to the Majestic on this gorgeous night, I wondered why we were going to dinner at this fancy hotel. I wasn't dressed for it, the dinners were expensive, and I'd just as soon eat outdoors, have a beer and a sandwich. Little did I know, the Majestic had an outdoor beer garden, and Willem and Julia were already there waiting for us.

"We were having a delightful evening, watching the boats down the canal, sipping our beers, eating croissant sandwiches, and all I could think about was if Walter would really produce *Anything Goes*. I knew that play backward and forward. After all, wasn't I going to be Billy Crocker? We could definitely do it! And wouldn't Betsy be surprised? Maybe she'd even want to come over and . . . Nah! Sara leaned over and said, 'What in the world are you thinking about?' I smiled. 'Tell you later. The world sure moves in funny directions.'

"Just then, just when that thought was running through my mind, the world crashed. One of the hotel employees ran over and whispered something in Willem's ear. 'Shit!' he said. 'Hitler has threatened to invade Poland. Mussolini said he'll back him. I think this is for real.'

"Poland did not respond to Hitler's threat to hand over Danzig. They'd heard that threat before. In Poland's judgment it was wisest to do nothing and depend on the diplomacy of England, France, and the League of Nations. Surely they would work it out. That threat and our dinner was on August 30, 1939.

"In the early morning hours of September 1, 1939, the German battleship *Schleswig-Holstein* sailed silently through the fog of the Baltic Sea toward the port of Westerplatte. At four forty-five A.M. it unleashed its guns upon Danzig's major port. Westerplatte, well fortified, fired back and repulsed the attack. At the same time, thousands of Luftwaffe planes took off to bomb their targets all over Poland. Shortly after sunrise, one million German troops crossed the Polish border and begin their assault on several Polish cities.

"On September 2, we were on full alert at the consulate. Who knew what Hitler would do next? In the morning of September 3, we were given notice that shortly after eleven A.M., British Prime Minister Neville Chamberlain would broadcast a very important message to his nation. We all gathered in Frank Lee's office. At precisely eleven, the BBC introduced the prime minister. Teddy reached into his folder and handed a newspaper clipping to Karyn.

This morning the British ambassador in Berlin handed the German government a final note stating that, unless we heard from them by eleven
o'clock that they were prepared at once to withdraw their troops from
Poland, a state of war would exist between us. I have to tell you now
that no such undertaking has been received, and that consequently this
country is at war with Germany. You can imagine what a bitter blow it
is to me that all my long struggle to win peace has failed. . . . Up to the
very last it would have been quite possible to have arranged a peaceful
and honorable settlement between Germany and Poland, but Hitler
would not have it; he had evidently made up his mind to attack Poland
whatever happened. . . . His action shows convincingly that there is no
chance of expecting that this man will ever give up his practice of using force to gain his will. He can only be stopped by force, and we and
France are today, in fulfillment of our obligations, going to the aid of
Poland who is so bravely resisting this wicked and unprovoked attack
upon her people. We have a clear conscience, we have done all that any
country could do to establish peace, but a situation in which no word
given by Germany's ruler could be trusted, and no people or country
could feel itself safe, had become intolerable.

"And you, Mr. Hartigan, must call it a day," declared the nurse, in
her white uniform, wheeling in her cart loaded with medications and
medical equipment.

"But Gertrude," protested Teddy, but before he could say another
word, the nurse held up her index finger. "Good night, Ms. Sachnoff," she
said to Karyn in her straightforward manner. "We'll see you tomorrow."

CHAPTER TWENTY

KARYN WAS GETTING ready to leave for the hospital the next morning when she received a call from Burt. He said he had a satchel full of photographs. Beth had gone on a treasure hunt and had located pictures of her mother and whole family, some taken when Karyn was quite young. "Do you remember that you had red hair?" Burt said, and Karyn laughed. "I do." Burt continued, "And you wore your hair in pigtails?"

"Of course I remember," Karyn said. "I loved those pigtails, but some of the boys would pull on them."

"And Beth showed me pictures of her wearing them as well when she was a child," said Burt softly, knowing that pictures of Beth along with Karyn and her deceased husband might strike a nostalgic chord. "Beth pulled out several pictures of the family."

"I know those pictures. I look at them often."

"There's a remarkable resemblance between you and Beth," Burt says. "Beth also sent me pictures of her daughter Grace with her red hair in pigtails. Red hair seems to be a dominant gene among the Sachnoffs."

"And you're going to tell me that all three of us look alike?"

"It's uncanny," Burt said. "You know what else? You all have the same dimple, same hairline, same cheek structure, and same smile. I think this is just what Teddy is looking for. If those characteristics are so dominant in your family, what is the possibility that your sister Annie has them as well? Tell Teddy that I will bring the pictures in three days, and he should notify his contact. By the way, how is he doing?"

"He's holding his own, Burt. Cranky as hell, but lovable as ever. In fact, I'm going to visit him now. I'll see you in three days."

* * *

KARYN WAS MET by Nurse Gertrude at the nurses' station. "Teddy had a good night's sleep," she said.

A thought ran through Karyn's mind. *He must be behaving if Gertrude is calling him "Teddy."* "Can I go in there now?" Karyn asked, and Gertrude nodded. "Tell him to finish his breakfast," Gertrude said sternly. "He needs his nourishment. He won't listen to me."

Teddy's breakfast was sitting on the tray, barely touched. "Good morning, Teddy," Karyn said, "and finish your breakfast."

"And who are you? Nurse Griselda, the Bad Witch?" he said loudly, projecting his comment toward the hallway. Then he turned and softly said, "She's really nice, but the food stinks."

"Burt has the pictures," Karyn said with a glint. "He'll be here in three days."

"Hmm, good. Write this down in case this hospital poisons me to death: Nicholas Grescher, 10322 Elsinoor, Utrecht, Netherlands."

"Is that where the pictures are to be sent? Is he going to help us look for Annie?"

"Yep. He'll know what to do. Now can we get started, or I'll wither away to nothing."

Karyn lifted her pencil and her pad and said, "Full speed ahead."

"Where did we leave off?"

"Like you don't know," Karyn answered. "Germany attacked Poland, and the European countries had chosen sides, and right about then, General Gertrude ordered you to call it a day."

Teddy nodded. "Right you are. In the first week of September 1939, there were a half dozen countries that declared they were at war. That was their position, they said so, but then, talk is cheap. The only actual fighting taking place was in Poland, and it was brutal. Poland was attacked on September 1 with one and a half million men, twenty thousand tanks, nine hundred bombers, and four hundred fighters. They never had a chance. They fought bravely, but it was over before it started. Poland surrendered to Germany on September 17 and Germany commenced its bloodthirsty occupation.

"At the Amsterdam consulate, we were given a daily alert. We knew that almost anything could happen in Europe, but for the time being, the fighting was on the other side of Germany, on the east side of the continent, and we were advised to maintain consular operations 'as usual.' Day-to-day operations did not change. That didn't mean that the operations were calm. The number of people waiting in line increased dramatically. Some of those seeking interviews held American passports. Many already held valid visas and were trying to book passage. We published daily bulletins that contained information about scheduled passages on ocean liners. We also published alerts to ocean liner companies containing the latest information about attacks at sea, those directed at military vessels, but equally dangerous to civilian vessels leaving from Belgium, France, the Netherlands, and Denmark. The lines at the consulate were long, and we stayed open for longer hours. People had so many questions.

"But in the streets outside the consulate, it was relatively calm. Life carried on as usual. We were neutral, we were safe. Same for Belgium and Denmark. The Dutch were assured by Queen Wilhelmina that we were not at war and that we had not taken sides. We were a neutral country and we had nothing to worry about. In fact, we had received a guarantee of neutrality from Hitler himself. That's what we expected to receive.

"The Netherlands business community was booming in the fall of 1939. Germany needed Dutch oil, armaments, manufactured goods, and most important, Fokker aircraft. Ever since the Dutch East Indies had imported oil, the Netherlands was a primary source. Trade with German companies was energetic. There was money to be made, and Germany wanted to spend it. Even tourism from Germany to the Netherlands increased. On the one hand, it was great for the Dutch economy, but on the other, we were supporting the German military machine. We asked Willem how he felt about that, and he shrugged his shoulders. 'The Majestic is booked solid. Being neutral is good for business. We're making a nice profit, but it doesn't make me feel good.'

"On another night, the four of us went out to dinner with Dietrich Schultz and his girlfriend, Marta. Dietrich was Willem's close friend and business associate, and he worked in the Majestic business office. Being a German citizen, Dietrich coordinated marketing with German travel agencies. To Julia, playing ball with Germany left a bad taste in her mouth. When Julia questioned the moral implications, Dietrich shook his index finger back and forth. He didn't want to discuss it at all, especially not in public. 'Not good for business,' he said. 'It's too easy to let a comment slip out and offend the wrong person. That man could be the fountainhead of contracts that bring in millions. Just let it be.'"

"ON SEPTEMBER 20, Undersecretary of State Sumner Welles called a meeting at the US embassy in The Hague and I was present. All officers of the US consulates in Rotterdam, Amsterdam, and The Hague were required to be in attendance. The US ambassador to the Netherlands, George A. Gordon, was present and would address us."

"What about Julia, did she go with you?" Karyn asked.

Teddy shook his head. "Only officers. Sumner Welles began by discussing the present state of the war. The realization that major countries had formally declared war, and weren't just posturing anymore, was frightening. The Netherlands had a signed contract of neutrality. No one expected Nazi Messerschmitts to fly through Dutch air. In fact, warplanes were only flying through Polish air. The conservative members at the meeting felt that the war would be short, and France and England would sign a peace treaty, now that Poland was conquered.

"Was it over that fast?" Karyn said. "You said that the fighting in Poland was brutal. Tens of thousands were killed."

"That's true. Poland fought bravely, but they were no match for Germany. No single country was in 1939. Within a month, the government in Warsaw had surrendered. Germany and the Soviet Union had signed a secret protocol in their nonaggression pact on September 29, 1939, that partitioned Poland between the two of them. To all intents and purposes, the war was over. But the Allied forces still had an active declaration of war against Germany, and they hadn't retracted it. Hitler made an offer of peace that would formally end the war with all concerned, but Chamberlain and Daladier turned it down. They had made an agreement with Poland, and although the physical fighting had ceased, they respected their agreement. In fact, there were no military actions for several months, and it was referred to as 'the Phony War,' although Winston Churchill referred to it as 'the Twilight War.'

"The four of us were having an early dinner; Julia and Willem, Sara and I, and that was all we could talk about. What would become of Poland now that it was vanquished? Would it be annexed into Germany like Austria was? Like Czechoslovakia was? I don't think any of us ever thought that Poland could defeat Germany alone, but what if it had the assistance of England and France? They had given their word. They had declared war. Would they fight? There were a few squabbles at sea, but no armies were coming to Poland's aid. Still, in the event the war continued, and other countries became involved, preparations were being made by the US consulates, and we were told to attend another meeting the next morning.

"I left the apartment early, before Sara awoke. This meeting had also been called by Gordon, who had been the US ambassador to the Netherlands since his appointment in 1937. Because of the meeting, the consulate was closed to the public. All staff members were required to be in the building at nine A.M. I sat next to Julia and asked her if she knew what this was all about. 'New regulations for issuing visas, updating passports, and evacuating American citizens now that Europe was at war,' she said. She always seemed to know everything that was going on.

"Ambassador Gordon passed around the new regulations for both the embassy and all the consulates. All new applications for visas to the US were to be put on hold. Visa renewals were to be strictly limited. Why did the holders allow them to expire, and why were they seeking renewal at this time? The same for reissuing supposedly 'lost' visas. People holding valid passports and visas, who were now seeking entry to America, were in a class of close scrutiny, mandated in order to detect those who might be Nazi agents. Gordon passed around Departmental Order 810, establishing the State Department's 'Special Division,' which arranged for the repatriation of American citizens from war zones in Europe, and set rules on how to handle inquiries about their welfare and whereabouts. Departmental Order 813, announcing the appointment of Breckinridge Long as special assistant in charge of the Special Division. There were bound to be numerous inquiries by American citizens in the Netherlands, who were desperate to return home. We were given instructions how to deal with them. 'Patience is the key!'

"It was a long meeting, but the bottom line was, hardly anyone except US citizens would be allowed entry into America from Europe, and even US citizens were to be 'closely scrutinized.' Lastly, we went through the updated procedures for evacuating US citizens from the Netherlands, should it become embroiled in the war.

"We were on edge; we had our orders, but out on the streets, it was as if nothing had changed. Everything continued as before. Sara would tell me of activities at the school and at the crèche. They were planning for the holidays, busier than ever. In fact, there was a waiting list to enroll at both institutions. November came and went, we prayed that negotiations would succeed, but unfortunately, no progress was made. December, normally a joyous month, put on a happy mask, but we all found it difficult to celebrate. Who knew what tomorrow would bring? What would Hitler do next? 'He's quiet now, but what about tomorrow?'

"Amsterdam's famous New Year's Day fireworks display went off as before, and the revelers filled the streets, but the day after, it was quiet. Maybe 1940 would be the year we would turn the corner and peace would come to the continent."

CHAPTER TWENTY-ONE

"IT WAS MID-FEBRUARY, and after the consulate's weekly meeting, we broke for lunch. Julia and I grabbed a sandwich at the Café Amsterdam. After a few minutes, she said, 'What's on your mind, Teddy? It's like you're somewhere else. Is something wrong? Are you okay?'

"'Oh, I'm fine,' I said, 'but I'm concerned about Sara and Sylvia. Sylvia usually leaves the crèche every day at five, but lately she's been staying later, sometimes till six or seven. Recently, Sara has been staying with her, and coming home late. When she does come home, she is extremely upset. I tried to get her to tell me what was wrong, but she didn't want to talk about it.'

"'That's not like her. I don't blame you for getting upset. Do you want me to find out what's wrong?'

"I shook my head. 'I know that she'll tell me eventually. It may have something to do with the little girl that Sylvia has been watching in the crèche. I met her myself a few weeks ago. She was a very clingy, shy little girl, hanging on to Sylvia. I get the feeling that Sara's gotten herself involved with this little girl too, and she and Sylvia are trying to do something to help her.'

"'I think I know,' said Julia. 'Is that the little girl named Katy?'"

"Katy?" Karyn interrupted. "Katy, not Karyn, like yours truly? What a coincidence."

Teddy nodded. "It is a coincidence, but her name was Katy. At first, the teachers at the crèche didn't understand what Katy was saying when she said her name or what she wanted. After a while, they just gave her the name of Katy, and she seemed to like it. I told Julia that I thought maybe Sylvia and Sara had spending too much time with Katy and keeping her from the crèche activities. Julia smiled. 'What's wrong with that?' she said. 'Are you jealous?'

"'No,' I answered. 'Sara has taken Sylvia and Katy to dinner with us twice. She seems to enjoy our company, although she doesn't speak very freely. I just wonder how this whole thing came about. I mean, we had a nice time, but maybe taking her away from the other children at the crèche was not a good idea. I don't know. It seems to me that the child is in need of something more than going to a day care center.'

"'What do you mean?' Julia said.

"'When it's time for Sylvia to leave the crèche and go home for the night, Katy doesn't want to let her go. They have to get the crèche president Henriëtte Pimentel to come and walk her back into the building. And then she cries, oh mercy how she cries. And I'm sure you can imagine how that upsets Sylvia and Sara. Henriëtte told them that she can't stay there permanently, they either have to find her parents or make arrangements with an orphanage. How can that be a good thing for this sweet little child? Or for Sylvia and Sara? By the time Sara and I get home, Sara's the one who's full of tears. Like I said, Sara doesn't want to talk about it. So, what am I supposed to do? You're her best friend, Julia. What do you think?'

"Julia thought for a minute. 'You've been with the child, what do you think of her?'

"'She's a sweet little girl. Seems intelligent, but unwilling to talk to anyone but Sylvia or Sara. I don't understand.'

"'You're right,' Julia said. 'Sara told me that she's put herself into a situation. I know a little bit of the story. A month ago, an older woman, maybe a German refugee, came by when the children were out playing in the yard. Sylvia saw them. She brought Katy into the middle of the yard and motioned for Sylvia to come over. She did, and the woman handed Katy to Sylvia and walked away. Sylvia called after her, not knowing whether Katy was already registered or not, but she wouldn't stop or turn around. Sylvia took Katy into the yard to play with the other children, but she was afraid. When Henriëtte rang her bell, all the children went inside. But there was little Katy, not knowing where to go or what to do. No one knew what group she was with. No one even knew her name. She just came in with the children, walked into a corner, and sat alone, all by herself. Henriëtte tried to talk to her, but Katy wouldn't speak. Or maybe didn't understand the language, although Henriëtte tried a few different ones, including Hebrew. Henriëtte asked the police if there were any reports of a missing child, but there weren't. At the end of the day, no one came to pick up Katy. They didn't know what to do with her. There are a few children, mostly the children of the staff, that stay the night at the crèche. So, they gave Katy dinner and put her in a bed. Maybe in the morning, her parents would show up.'

"'But they didn't, did they?'

"'Obviously,' Julia said. 'Henriëtte asked around, but the woman who dropped Katy off had vanished. Some speculated that she wasn't Katy's mother, that she had rescued her and brought her to safety. In the meantime, Katy would sit all by herself at a corner table, that is until Sylvia would come to her. Sara came in one afternoon, saw Katy sitting with Sylvia, and asked the staff about her. One member said that she wouldn't talk to anyone but Sylvia. She talks to Sylvia, but Sylvia doesn't really understand her language and tries to teach her Dutch. It's working a little. Sara came the next day, and when Sylvia left, Katy was hysterical. Sara stayed with Katy for the rest of the day. She took her on a walk, and during the walk she thought Katy was speaking Yiddish. The next day, Sara mentioned this to Sylvia, and they tried a few Yiddish words and expressions. She reacted to a few. So, they concluded that Yiddish is her mother tongue, but only the Rosenbaum family knew Yiddish.'

"'When I met her,' I said to Julia, 'Katy said a few basic words in Dutch.'

"'By then she had been spending time with Sylvia and Sara and had been learning basic Dutch. Did you notice anything when Katy spoke her few words in Dutch?'

"I shook my head. 'No, I wouldn't know.'

"'German. Strong German accent.'

"Now I got it. 'So, Katy is a German child who was rescued by some family, taken out of Germany, or maybe when they escaped, and dropped off at the crèche. She is Jewish and maybe her parents were persecuted, tortured, or sent away to some detention camp, and Katy was incapable of talking about it, or even telling anyone her name.'

"'I think so,' said Julia. 'That may very well be correct. And Katy is too young to give us her history. I'm sure whatever it was, it was traumatic.'

"I nodded my head. 'And the crèche is caring for her now? It's her new home?'

"'That's the problem,' said Julia. 'The crèche is not set up to be her foster home. It's a day care center. It's a preschool for babies and young children. A few of the staff have been watching Katy at night, but it's not their responsibility. They are not her parents. Katy treats Sylvia and Sara like they are family. Henriëtte is trying to find a new home for Katy, but so far she's unsuccessful. Sara and Sylvia are the only ones caring for her, but it's only until Henriëtte can find an orphanage that will take her.'

"'Sara and Sylvia have thought of taking her to their parents in Utrecht, but every time they try to leave her there, Katy becomes hysterical, and Sara's mother can't handle it. Katy didn't want them to leave her, maybe like her own mother left her. On the weekend, Sylvia would take Katy out to her parents', but they would have to leave very early Sunday because she had to be at work at six thirty on Monday. I'm sure that Sylvia was thinking about adopting Katy, but Sylvia is seventeen years old, and she lives with two other girls. That leaves it up to Sara. Sylvia has suggested that they co-parent her. But she wonders what I have to say about all that. She wants to protect Katy, but she doesn't want to lose me. Am I doing the right thing, Julia?'"

As she listened to Teddy's story, Karyn had a big smile on her face. "I saw this one coming, Teddy. The other day when you told me that Sara met this cute little girl in the yard beside the crèche, and she was all alone, and that Sylvia and Sara were caring for her, I suspected what was going through their minds. Maybe Sara was checking you out. Katy had nowhere to go. She couldn't stay at the crèche. Either Sylvia and Sara would agree to take her in, or she would have to be placed in an orphanage. It was Sylvia and Sara or no one. And they wondered what you would think about that? Could Sara take in this little girl? What would that do to your relationship?"

"That's right," Teddy replied. "You hit the nail on the head. But that wasn't the only problem. While I was talking to Julia, she said, 'What if you agreed to take Katy in, and adopt her and become a family? You're not married, Teddy. You two did not plan for this. Can you handle that? Now do you understand why Sara is so troubled? She needs to talk to you about this, but she doesn't have the nerve. She doesn't know how it will affect the two of you going forward.'

"'We can get married; we've talked about it,' I said to Julia. 'We can get married, adopt the little girl, and become a family.'

"'Well, that's one thing,' Julia said. 'There are other problems that you're not thinking about. Problems that might be more troublesome. You and Sara can get married tomorrow, that's a snap. Where are you going to live? Oh, I know that right now you live here in Amsterdam in a nice apartment, but what if the State Department wants to transfer you somewhere else, maybe back to Washington? Or what if you want to return home after your three-year term? What if the war becomes worse here, and you are ordered to return home? If the US becomes involved in the war, you might lose your diplomatic immunity. And I don't know if your diplomatic immunity extends to your family? I think it does, but this is a family put together here in the Netherlands. One American and two non-Americans.'

"Julia continued, 'Then there's the matter of repatriation. Right now, you have the legal right to go home—you're a US citizen and an officer in the State Department. You have a passport, and you can leave tomorrow, but what about Sara? What about Katy? They don't have an American passport, or even a visa. You know the regulations concerning an immigrant visa for the spouse of a US citizen. They are not even issuing visas at all right now. There is a hold on issuing nonimmigrant visas, you know that. You could submit their applications and supporting documents right here and we could do whatever we can to rush them along, but the doors are shut right now.'

"'I'm a citizen and I work for the State Department. This isn't an application for any old person, it's for my wife and my child. I mean my would-be wife and child.'

"Julia rolled her eyes. 'And that's another thing. You're going to have to adopt Katy. How long will that take? Can you prove that she is abandoned? How long will the adoption procedure take under Dutch law? Hell, I don't know.'

"'Julia, if I had to pull a few strings or fudge a few documents, I'd do it.'

"'I won't tell Secretary Lee you said that. You've been watching too many movies. But let's set aside the immigration issues. Then there're the personal issues that face the two of you. You are a Lutheran, as I understand it. You grew up a Lutheran in Washington, DC, and your family is Lutheran, right?' I nodded. 'Going back how many generations?'

"I raised my eyes to think about that, and then said, 'I know my father, my grandfather, and my great-grandfather Charles were all Lutheran.'

"'Exactly. Sara's family is Jewish. Traditional Jewish, and I don't know how many generations back. I think it's a reasonable assumption that Katy is also Jewish—she came over from Germany and was dropped off at the crèche where the children are mostly Jewish. How are you going to work through that with your families? What's Sara's father going to say? And, by the way, what's *your* father going to say, the eminent conservative statesman Broderick Hartigan? How are you going to work through all that?'

"I nodded. 'I know those are problems, but they're not insurmountable. I would call them bumps in the road. Don't people face those situations all the time? Isn't Holland a liberal society? Isn't intermarriage common here?'

"'It depends on what you mean by "common." Mixed marriages are more accepted in this society than in other countries. That may be how society as a whole feels about it, but that isn't necessarily the feeling of the individual, is it? How will Mr. Rosenbaum feel about his little daughter marrying a Lutheran? Would Broderick Hartigan warmly welcome Sara, and maybe Katy, and take the three of you to dinner at his Gentile country club?'

"'I think Mr. Rosenbaum would be more accepting than my father, but none of their prejudices are going to stand in the way of what Sara and I want to do. That will *not* be a problem. We'll get through it together.'

"Julia let out a soft whistle. 'I hope you're right. I don't think it will be easy, but you'll get through it if your love is strong enough. Sara and I have spoken about this as well, and I think you should have a talk with

Sara now. Assure her that you would accept Katy, if Sara intends to adopt her. She'll want to be certain that you can be a loving father to Katy.'

"'To be honest, that's a tough question. I don't know Katy as well as Sara. Would Katy accept me? Would she love me as a father? If she would, I would try like hell to make it work. That's the best I can say.'

"'Those are exactly the words that Sara is hoping to hear. You're a good man, Teddy Hartigan.'

"I took a deep breath. I stood up and put my hands on my head. 'And now Sara's going to have a baby, sort of. We're going to have a child. Oh, my goodness, I can't believe how all this is all coming together. Julia, I need a bit of expert advice. What am I supposed to do now?'

"Julia looked at me like I was lost in space. She rolled her eyes and said, 'You ask me what you should do? Do you love Sara?'

"'More than anything in the world.'

"'Then that's the answer, Teddy. Ask her to marry you. She loves you as much as you love her. I've known that for a long time. Go over to Wiesenthal Jewelry, buy a ring, get down on your knee, and ask her to marry you. I think I know what her answer will be.'"

Karyn was enjoying this. "So, Mr. Confidence, did you go that afternoon and buy the ring?"

"Well, not that afternoon. I bought the ring at Wiesenthal's a couple of days later, like Julia told me to. But my nerves were on edge. What about a marriage between two people of two different religions, and two different countries, and two different upbringings, and now add Katy, will that work? Was this all too much for Sara to handle? What if she said let's wait? But then, Julia said she wouldn't. So, I decided to do the manly, confident thing. I went over to Julia and asked her if she and Willem would go with me when I asked Sara to marry me. You know, give me a little backbone. What if I screwed it up? Julia put her hand on her forehead. She firmly said, 'No, Teddy, this is your night to shine, a private moment, just for the two of you. Don't chicken out.' So, I contacted Willem, told him what I was doing, and asked him to reserve a table for Sara and me, and maybe a little girl, at the small restaurant at the Majestic. "About time,' Willem said. But he reserved a table for us in the fancy King Wilhelm Dining Room, no less."

"Good guts," Karyn said. "How did it go?"

"I asked Sara if she would like to go out to dinner at the Majestic, and I think, because of the cost of the Majestic, she might have turned me down, had it not been that she and Julia had been talking, and Sara figured that I was going to propose. She was dressed to kill. The King Wilhelm Room was the nicest dining room in Amsterdam. Tablecloths and flowers on every table. Candles everywhere. It was hard to get a reservation there. I was lucky I knew Willem. All was perfect except for a table of loud, obnoxious uniformed German soldiers a few tables away."

Karyn was surprised. "Was that common, to have uniformed German soldiers in fancy dining rooms in Amsterdam? That surely would give me a chill if I was eating there."

"More common than you think. After all, we were right next door to Germany. For many years, trade between the two countries had been robust. The sale of Dutch petroleum and other minerals to Germany was substantial, and no doubt these three had been at a meeting at one of the petroleum companies that afternoon.

"Willem, my co-conspirator, showed us to a very nice table, and gave me a wink. I ordered a bottle of Champagne, and we had a few sips. When I had finally built up enough courage, I got down on my right knee, held out the ring, cleared my throat, and said, 'Sara, my one and only love, would you please marry me and make me the happiest man on earth?' At that, the whole room clapped. The whole room except for the table of uniformed Germans. They mocked me. Other people told them to shut up, but the Germans laughed at me."

"Forget about the Germans," Karyn said. "I don't care if they were jerks, what did Sara say?"

"She told me that she would be 'the happiest girl on earth.' All in all, it was very lovely, picture perfect. In fact, Willem took a few pictures. It was perfect until one of the Germans, a large, blond, barrel-chested man with a grin from ear to ear, elbowed his buddy, pointed at us, and gestured for his table to stand up. The Germans, who'd had far too much to drink, all stood up and started singing the German national anthem as loud as they could. A few others in the room stood up as well, but not many, and definitely not Sara and me. The big German, his name was

Hans, looked straight at me, and with a pointed finger, ordered me to stand in deference to the anthem. I looked the other way. He walked over.

"'Why do you insult the German people?' he said. 'Get up.'

"'I insulted no one,' I said, 'but I stand for no country's anthem except mine, the United States of America. Now go! Leave us alone.' Them was fightin' words to him.

"He came up to my chair and repeated his demand for me to stand up. I had a few drinks in me, and I wasn't going to back down to this slob, not in front of my girl, and I said, 'And if I don't want to, what the hell are you going to do about it?'

"The German laughed from deep down in his belly, took his jacket off, rubbed his hands together, took a prizefighter's stance, and jerked his fists in the air. *'Aufstehen!! Steh auf, du pussy!'* he commanded. *'Komm schon, jetzt!'*

"I was in a fix. This was not going to end well. He was twice my size. But screw him. I took off my coat and threw back my chair. I started at him. Hell, he had too much to drink, maybe I could take him, but I wasn't going to back down. Maybe I would end up with a broken nose, so be it.

"Suddenly, a voice behind the man stated, *'Halte jetzt an!'* It was Willem and Dietrich, who were quickly approaching the table. 'You can get your things and leave,' Willem said sternly to the German. 'Now! Or do I need to call Major Steiner?' That did the trick. Major Steiner was his commanding officer, and a friend of Dietrich's. The Germans quickly picked up their things, turned, and made for the exit. Hans stopped on his way out, pointed at me, and said, 'I will not forget you. There will come another time. You hear me? You don't know, but *I know,* and the time will be soon.' He gave me a big smile, with a missing tooth.

"When they were gone, Willem came to our table and apologized. He then instructed the musicians to play a waltz, 'appropriate for an engagement,' and they played 'Blue Danube.' A cake was brought over with the Majestic's compliments. I raised my Champagne glass and said, 'Here's to you and me and Katy.' That did the trick. It brought tears to Sara's eyes. It was quite an evening."

CHAPTER TWENTY-TWO

"I HAD PASSED my first hurdle. Now to deal with next dilemma, our wedding. Where and when? Resolving those dilemmas might be harder than squaring off against Hans."

Karyn laughed, but agreed. "I suppose in your situation, that's true. But the sooner the better, right? Not only did you two have to decide where you were going to get married, but weren't you going to have to talk with your parents, at least as a courtesy?"

"That was the plan. Since we were going to be a mixed-faith couple, I figured on a civil ceremony at the Amsterdam city hall, which was in the Royal Palace. The Lutheran church and the Jewish synagogue were out of the question. Back where I came from, churches wouldn't marry interfaith couples. But Sara surprised me. She wanted to talk to her father first. She thought it might be possible to be married by her rabbi at their synagogue; that is, if I would go along with it. I knew it was important to Sara, and it didn't matter to me, but I was wary of what her father would think about it. As far as I knew, he wasn't even aware of our engagement. Or the fact that we were thinking of adopting Katy. Sara later conceded she hadn't spoken to her folks about that yet. She thought her father might be more open to our marriage if we were to get married in a temple."

Karyn leaned back and scratched her head. "Well, I sure wouldn't want to be in your shoes."

"My thoughts exactly. There's more to this romance stuff than just agreeing to get married, adopt a child, and live together. You have to make peace with the families. So, we made plans to go out to Utrecht and face her parents. Katy was going to stay with Sylvia at the crèche. It was March, seven months after Germany attacked Poland, and the major European countries—Germany, Poland, France, England—though technically at war, were not fighting. Not much was happening. No troops were on the move, no planes were in the air. There were reports of occasional tussles at sea. I think most of us thought it would come to a resolution, sooner or later. A negotiated compromise, a peace treaty, was bound to be reached. But the world was still at war.

"As we walked from the car to her parents' front door, Sara asked me if I knew it was Passover again. We would be eating the traditional Passover foods. I stopped in my tracks and looked at her. 'Will this be another four-hour meal?' I remembered last year's Seder. 'I'm starving. Does Passover come very frequently?' Sara laughed. 'Once a year. And relax, it's Passover, but there won't be a long Seder tonight, we're in the middle of the week.'

"Her father greeted us warmly at the door. 'Hello, Mr. Rosenbaum,' I said, 'it's so nice to see you.'

"'You, as well,' he said. 'You must love charoset. You've become an annual Pesach guest.' I didn't really know what he was talking about.

"Sara's mother, Deborah, was standing at the door as well, and she gave me a warm hug. She was such a lovely person. Then she went to embrace Sara, and asked how plans were coming along for Katy. I froze in my tracks. How did she know about that? Daughters must talk to their mothers a lot more than sons talk to their fathers. Especially when their fathers are Hartigans.

"Sara and I had talked about how and when we were going to reveal the news about our engagement to her parents. 'Not at the front door, please,' Sara said. I agreed. I didn't want any shocks or bad feelings before I could eat dinner."

"Oh, come on, Teddy," Karyn said. "Did you think that when they learned about your engagement, they would turn their backs on you? They weren't those kind of people, were they? You described them as nice folks."

"Her mother was very nice, but I was a little wary of her father. I didn't know him very well. He was the quintessential history professor: gray hair, goatee, wool vest with a pocket watch, and a no-nonsense way about him. How would he feel about an American Christian man taking away his sweet little Jewish daughter? Really, how does any father feel about a prospective son-in-law? Knowing Sara, I could certainly understand if he felt that I wasn't good enough for her. Because, in my opinion, I wasn't. We were going to wait until after dinner to broach the subject, maybe over coffee and dessert."

"Sounds like a good idea."

"Well, it didn't work out that way. We sat down for dinner, went through some prayers, and were having our chicken, when Sara blurted out, 'Mom and Dad, we have a surprise for you.' To Deborah, this was no surprise. Her lips were closed, and her tongue pushed hard against the inside of her cheek. Saul might have had an inkling, but he waited patiently to hear the news. Sara continued, 'Teddy and I are going to be married, and it's very likely we're going to have a child.'

"Saul was shocked. He instantly looked at Sara's tummy. I added, 'And we would like your blessings, sir.' And he said, 'Of course you would, and I'm going to give them to you . . . on conditions.'

"I was stunned. What father would say that? What conditions? What hoops would I have to jump through to get his approval? What would we have to do? I said, 'Conditions, sir, what does that mean?'

"He smiled. 'You and me, we'll talk about it after dinner, but Deborah and I wish you both the very best, especially if the baby's a boy, and then you should name him Joseph, after my great-grandfather.'

"I clenched my teeth. This night was not going as planned. 'I'm afraid we can't name our child Joseph, she's a girl.'

"'A girl? How the hell would you know that?' But I didn't have to answer, Deborah answered for me. 'They are thinking of adopting a little girl named Katy.'

"'Oh, well then, the next one should be Joseph,' he said with a smile.

"The rest of the meal was joyful, but I was nervous. What conditions was he talking about when he said we'd discuss it after dinner? Why was he holding back? The best I could figure, it was about the marriage ceremony.

"Sara brought that subject up as well, right after dinner was over. No sense waiting. She said, 'Do you think Rabbi Becker would marry us at the temple?'

"Saul immediately shook his head. 'Definitely not. Not at the temple. The Netherlands is becoming very liberal these days, but you'd both have to be Jewish before you could have the ceremony at the temple.' He looked at me. 'Teddy, are you planning on converting to Judaism?'

"This evening was spinning out of control. That question put me on the spot. I hadn't given any thought to converting. In fact, other than a Passover Seder, I didn't know anything about Judaism, or what a person would have to do to be a convert. Maybe I could be part Lutheran and part Jewish. Like our marriage. Sara came to my rescue. 'Dad, that's not appropriate. Teddy's religious beliefs are his business, and they are not a precondition to our getting married.'

"Saul nodded. 'Well, if you are planning on a Jewish wedding, Victor will probably perform the ceremony, but not at the temple. Talk to him, I'm sure he would officiate if it was a Jewish ceremony at a hotel.'

"Sara and I had the same thought. 'What about the Majestic?' she said. 'Would Rabbi Becker travel to Amsterdam? It's only an hour away.' Saul said he would reach out to him, they were good friends, and he would let us know. Then, Saul stood up and asked if I would accompany him to his study, so that we could talk about important matters he had in mind. Uh-oh. So, it wasn't about the location of the wedding. Maybe it was about how we were going to raise Katy, and I expected him to be pleasantly surprised because she was Jewish and spoke Yiddish and I wasn't going to change that. But that wasn't the subject either.

"We went into the study and Saul closed the door. 'Katy comes from a Jewish family, and we intend to raise her Jewish,' I said before we even sat down. 'That's good,' he said, 'but that's not why I called you in here. I want my daughter and my adopted grandchild to be safe. Do you understand?'

"'Of course, so do I. We intend to give her a safe home. We believe that Katy came from a very unsafe place. She speaks Yiddish but with a strong German accent. She was abandoned at the crèche, the day care center, several weeks ago.'

"Saul's face turned solemn. 'Do you know what Hitler and the Germans are doing to the Jews in the German-occupied lands? Especially to the Jewish babies? I am a history professor and I have contacts in Germany, men I have known for years. You, of all people, an officer in the United States Department of State, you should have that information, as well.'

"I nodded. 'We have plenty of information about Hitler. Most of the applicants for visas are German, Austrian, or Czech. Most of them Jewish. It's sad, but at this time we have to turn almost all of them away. They're no better off now than they were in Germany.'

"His face turned red and he shook his head in disbelief. 'Oh my God,' he said under his breath. 'How can you say that? They're trying to flee Germany.'"

"I'm sorry, sir. I meant they're no closer to getting a US visa than they were in Germany. They are much better off in the Netherlands"

"They were persecuted in Germany, do you understand? They're facing poverty, brutalization, death in Germany. They'd do anything to get out. Hitler commenced his pogroms against the Jewish people right after he took power in 1933. Each year he has become more demonic. He took away professional licenses, like mine, and dismissed people from their teaching professions and medical professions. Then he banned their children, our Jewish children, from attending the public schools. He forced Jews to wear distinctive armbands so they would stand out, all the easier to enforce their restrictions. In magazines, newspapers, and periodicals, Jewish individuals are displayed in foul and repulsive images. It was easy for Hitler to do, he controlled all of the newspapers and periodicals. His Brownshirts confiscated automobiles, radios, and all sorts of property from Jewish families. He did it in Czechoslovakia, Austria, Hungary, and now he is doing the same thing in Poland. Someone brought this child out of that hellish environment. And there is no doubt she carries the scars. Do you understand me?'

"'Yes, sir, I understand. As you know, I work for the US Department of State. We're not unaware. We keep close watch on Germany. Because of the historical precedence between the Netherlands and Germany, and the strong trade relationship, we currently believe that the Netherlands will not be a target. Taking into consideration all of our sources, I'm aware of no plans that Germany has to expand into the Netherlands. Really, sir,

Germany has its hands full right now. As you know, England, France, Ireland, and other smaller countries have declared war on Germany.'

"'But they haven't done a damn thing, have they, Theodore? They declared war seven months ago and they haven't made the slightest move against Germany. Last July they entered into a mutual defense pact with England to defend Poland, didn't they? But they haven't fired a shot, have they? So far, it's all just a war of words, and that's probably all it's ever going to be until they decide otherwise. If you want my judgment, England and France are waiting to sit at a negotiated global peace treaty.'

"'You might be right, Mr. Rosenbaum, they might be anticipating a peace treaty, but that doesn't mean that they will stand by if Germany advances into countries like Denmark, Belgium, or Holland. I believe they would see a lot more than a war of words.'

"Saul shook his head at what a naïve fool I was. 'You think Hitler's shaking in his boots? Germany's army is twice as strong and twice as powerful as any of those countries that have declared war.' He leaned forward to make a point. 'You work for the US Department of State, don't you?' He shook his finger to make his point even more emphatic. 'Listen to me, son. This is precisely why I called you back here. I want you to take Sara and your child and leave the Netherlands immediately. You can do it. You can move your family far away, back to America. You're in a position to make it happen. You're in charge of immigration at the consulate. Fill out the necessary papers, issue visas, and get your family out of Europe, far away from Hitler, as fast as you can.'

"I took a deep breath. How was I supposed to respond to Sara's father without starting a battle? I couldn't do what he asked. I had a position as an officer at the consulate, that's true, I was placed there by Secretary of State Cordell Hull, but I didn't make the rules, and I didn't have the right to break them. I didn't issue visas, they came from Washington. 'Listen, Mr. Rosenbaum, I'm not going to try to break the rules, please don't ask me to do that,' I said as respectfully as I could. 'I appreciate your concern, I understand your love for Sara, but that's not something I can do anything about. Thankfully, the Nazi army is far to the west of us, hundreds of miles, marching through Poland, and they're not making any advances in our direction. Really, Mr. Rosenbaum, why would they want to do that? They're not in any of the Atlantic coast countries, and—'

"Saul interrupted, 'That's exactly why! He needs to protect his left flank. All those countries'—he counted them off on fingers—'Denmark, the Netherlands, Belgium, France, they all share borders with Germany and they are the Third Reich's soft spots. If Britain and France were ever to keep their word and defend Poland, that's the direction they'd go.'

"I wasn't getting anywhere with my argument. 'But sir, we see no indication that Hitler plans to move there. Surely such a move would provoke France and England, and at the moment they're standing still. Why kick a sleeping lion? That would be stupid. We follow these things very closely at the State Department. The Netherlands is a neutral country, and it will remain that way. So will Denmark and Belgium. Germany has traditionally respected their neutrality.'

"Saul closed his eyes, folded his arms across his chest, and slowly shook his head. How could he get through the boy's thick skull? 'You are wrong, son, as wrong as a man can be. Hitler is coming, he's far more aggressive than Bismarck ever was. He wants the Atlantic coast. It's the only way to protect Germany and her occupied countries from an attack from the west. He will want the entire coastline: Belgium, the Netherlands, Denmark. And he won't stop there, he'll want France too. And he won't go after just one, he'll go after them all. Probably all at once. If he owns the coast, countries like England, Ireland, even the United States or Canada will be unable to come ashore and attack Germany.'

"I shook my head. 'Well, if he's building a coastline defense to form a barrier against attacks from the United States, he's wasting his time. The United States doesn't want to defend any part of the European continent. They want no part of a European war, and they make that clear every day in Congress. Believe me, I grew up among all those isolationist politicians; Senators Nye and LaFollette, Charles Lindbergh, and even my own father, Broderick Hartigan. It takes the vote of Congress to declare war, and it's never going to happen, you have my word. The isolationists are dead set against going to war to protect anyone else, especially Europe. The whole continent could fall, and the US would stay out of it. That's why our embassy, our consulates, and our properties are all so secure. Why would Hitler do something so foolish as to provoke America to change those isolationist minds? Germany's not stupid. Evil, yes, but not stupid.'

"'Well. I hope you're wrong, son, because we're going to need you,' Saul said. 'Mark my words, Germany is coming, and it won't be long. So, take my daughter and my grandchild and get the hell off the continent.'"

Karyn sat listening to Teddy's narrative, raising her eyebrows, and nodding her head. "He was a pretty smart man, Sara's father. He predicted Hitler's moves, and that's just what Germany did."

"Yep. But I was too dumb to believe him. I believed my superiors, those who said that the Netherlands would always be neutral and had nothing to fear from Germany. Sara and I were considering living in Amsterdam permanently.

"After dinner, we took the bus back to our apartment. The next day I went back to the consulate and Sara returned to her position at the teachers' college. She planned to talk to the superintendent, Dr. van Hulst, about taking a short leave after the adoption so that she and Katy might get better acquainted. Two more tasks were on our mind: making wedding plans and finding a larger apartment for the three of us. We made an appointment with the Majestic on Monday. There was a three-bedroom apartment available four blocks away. Sara was going to look at it in the afternoon, right after school. With any luck, we'd move right in."

CHAPTER TWENTY-THREE

"ON MONDAY, APRIL 1, 1940, Sara and I met with Willem at the Majestic Hotel. Willem introduced us to Gwendolyn, the party-and-events planner. How many guests did we anticipate, would there be an orchestra, how large a stage would we need, would we need a dance floor? How many rooms should the Majestic set aside for guests' overnight accommodations? As I stood there talking to her, I wondered who she thought we were: John and Laura Rockefeller? But Sara was in charge. I was nothing but a spectator. I left all the arrangements to Sara. She and her mother would know how many guests we should expect. We had friends in town, and there could be a nice crowd. Sara finally estimated attendance to be about seventy-five."

"Did you tell your family that you and Sara were engaged and about to be married?" Karyn said. "Surely you weren't going to keep them in the dark."

"No, as soon as Sara and I had set a date for the wedding, we were going to write to my mom and dad. From my work in the consulate, I knew how impossible it would be for them to make travel arrangements to Amsterdam, even if they wanted to come. Transatlantic travel was difficult. For example, the *Queen Mary* made her last round trip to New York on August 30, 1939, and stayed drydocked until after the war. I suppose it would have been possible for my father to charter a four-seater and fly to London, but it would be too dangerous and cost a fortune. As impossible as it was to travel to Europe in 1940, I know my mother would have been hurt if we didn't include her in some way, and I asked Sara to find a way, even if she would only be designing invitations. Sara was going to write a long letter to my mother, introducing herself and requesting my mother to assist in the wedding plans, if she were able. I knew my mom would appreciate it.

"We told Willem we needed a hall to accommodate seventy-five guests, almost all of whom were Sara's family and friends. We told him that Rabbi Victor Becker would officiate. I asked him if they'd hosted Jewish weddings before, and Willem answered, 'Many times. There are a hundred and fifty thousand Jews in the Netherlands, mostly right here in Amsterdam. They get married too. I even have a recommendation for a klezmer band.' We passed on that.

"We finished the arrangements and Sara was delighted. The only thing left was to choose a date. We wanted to arrange it as soon as reasonably possible so that we and Katy could be a family. We chose a Sunday in mid-August. Hopefully the adoption would be completed by then. Katy could be a ring bearer or a flower girl. Willem showed us a party room that seemed just perfect. Sara was given several menus to choose from, and some were kosher. The sun was shining, we were moving into our new apartment, everything was working out so smoothly, and I had never seen Sara so happy. Eight days later everything changed."

"THERE WERE NO preliminary negotiations, there were no demands from Hitler. Early in the morning of April 9, 1940, without a bit of warning, hundreds of German bombers took off from Germany and filled the skies over neutral Denmark. They didn't drop bombs, they dropped thousands of leaflets warning the Danish people not to resist, to lay down their arms. Simultaneously thousands of German soldiers landed in the Copenhagen harbor. No shots were fired. The German emissary handed a document to Denmark's parliament. It was entitled 'Cooperation Agreement.' Germany proposed that Denmark would become a German 'protectorate.' Germany promised to protect Denmark against all foreign invaders. In exchange, Denmark would allow Germany to freely occupy the country, keep military bases there, and prevent Denmark from aligning itself with any enemy of Germany. The conditions of the protectorate were surprisingly liberal. Denmark would remain totally in charge of its country internally. Externally, Germany would call the shots. Within Denmark, Danes would be allowed to go about their business as they had before. No shops were closed, no professional licenses were confiscated. Although Denmark had a relatively small Jewish population, Germany promised not to interfere. No laws or restrictions would be imposed upon the Danish Jews. Having no choice, the Danish parliament surrendered at 7:09 A.M.

"Two things seemed to be somewhat promising. First was the fact that Germany had respected Denmark's declaration of neutrality and only asked for a cooperation agreement. It did not change their government or any of their laws. It did not formally occupy or conquer Denmark, although soldiers were allowed to traverse and bivouac in camps on Danish soil. Clearly, it was not like Austria or Czechoslovakia.

"For Holland, it was frightening to have Germany on their northern border. Who knew what they would do next? They didn't need a reason. Queen Wilhelmina and her government took preventative steps to fortify the country. Once again, as they did eight months previously, when Germany attacked Poland, defensive measures were instituted. Sandbags were placed at the base of important buildings. Holland's soldiers were put on full alert. Steps were also taken to fortify and arm the concrete trenches and Grebbe Line and the New Dutch Waterline."

Karyn held up her hands. "Wait a minute. What were they?"

"Fair question. You know Holland is one of the 'low countries.' That means that a great deal of the country is below sea level and floods are common. But the floods can be controlled and can be a useful part of defensive tactics. In the 1600s, the Dutch Republic developed a defensive scheme to protect the cities from attack. It was called the Dutch Waterline. Basically, it was possible to direct the water to flood the countryside, keeping attackers away from the cities. Cities were like islands. Sluices were constructed in dikes and barriers. They could be opened and shut. Thus, the water level could be manipulated. The flooded areas were carefully maintained at a depth of three to four feet, just deep enough to thwart an advance on foot, but shallow enough to prevent the passage of enemy boats. It was very effective during the Franco-Dutch War in 1679.

"In the early nineteenth century the Dutch Waterline was shifted east, just beyond Utrecht, and referred to as the New Dutch Waterline. A second line was constructed called the Grebbe Line, and it was modernized with fortresses and gun towers along the bridges. It was located farther to the east and closer to Germany. A third line was constructed even farther to the east, called IJssel Line. It went as far east as it could without running into the high ground on the eastern edge of the Netherlands. The idea was to flood the fields, leaving the cities dry, as though they were islands. Following April 10, the lines were manned twenty-four/seven with Dutch soldiers.

"The Dutch had every right to believe that Germany would honor neutrality like it did with Denmark, and respect their independence. But on the same date that Germany attacked Denmark, it attacked Norway, another country that had previously declared its neutrality, like it did in the First World War. Germany delivered a similar ultimatum to King Haakon to lay down his arms and surrender, but King Haakon refused. Norway would never succumb to Hitler's threats. It would not become Hitler's puppet. This time the German planes didn't drop leaflets, they dropped bombs, and German ships entered the Oslo harbor. A bitter war ensued between the Norwegians and the Nazis.

"Back in the Netherlands, on April 9, 1940, an immediate meeting was called in the consulate by Consul General Frank Lee. At two o'clock he closed the consulate for the rest of the day. All staff members, all consular officers, were required to be present at four P.M. Ambassador Gordon was also present. Frank Lee's face was set in steel. 'I have received orders from Washington. They have compiled all the recommendations that Allied intelligence has been able to put together. Washington believes that when it comes to Germany, the declarations of neutrality are henceforth meaningless. Prepare for invasion.'

"That was a total shock to me. I didn't get it. I was under the foolish impression that international promises would be honored. I had to raise the question. 'Consul General Lee,' I said, 'Germany has promised to honor Denmark's neutrality, and they both signed a cooperation agreement. Germany has offered the same arrangement to Norway. Why wouldn't they make the same offer to the Netherlands? They signed the written declaration of neutrality with us eight months ago. Holland hasn't violated it. Why should we fear an attack from Germany? What do they have to gain from attacking us?'

"Ambassador Gordon sighed. 'Are you looking for logic, Mr. Hartigan? Honesty, perhaps? Hitler gives no reasons, and doesn't play by any rules. Fighter planes in the sky are his statements.'

"'If there are any reasons for his attacking Norway,' Consul General Lee said, 'Washington believes it's to control the Norwegian coastline. Sweden ships its priceless iron ore, minerals, oil, and manufactured goods to northern Germany along the western Norwegian coastline. Germany needs to protect those shipping channels. Norway also does substantial business with Britain and France, and Germany intends to cancel it.'

"'Why attack Denmark? They're not in the way of any shipping channels.'

"'Germany can't attack Norway without going through Denmark,' Lee said. 'It is a stepping stone. It is a passageway. They will maintain bases in northern Denmark from which to attack Norway and anyone else who might consider coming through that area. And who knows what Germany's plans are for the North Atlantic Sea? If you ask me, it's the same. They want to control it.'

"Lee continued, 'Denmark capitulated this morning, but as of yet, Norway has refused. It was prepared for an attack. They realize the value of their coastline. There was no passive surrender there. According to intelligence, the Norwegians have launched a strong counterattack. Last night, the German steamship *Blücher* led a flotilla of warships into the Oslo harbor to seize the capital of Norway. But Norway was ready and sank the *Blücher* and a thousand Nazi soldiers. They also sank and destroyed several other Nazi ships in the flotilla.'

"Lee continued, 'Washington understands that discussions have taken place between the Netherlands and German diplomats in The Hague. There was a formal request for assurance, and the Netherlands was advised by Germany that it has nothing but peaceful intentions for the Netherlands. At the present time, please continue operations normally.'

"One of the older officers stood up, looked around the room, and said, 'And you believe that? You take the word of that Nazi criminal?'

"'No, Mitchell. That was what Washington is informed, not what it believes. As far as I'm concerned, it's just as likely that German troops will continue their march south along the coastline. I want you to take steps to secure all of your confidential and highly classified documents.'

"Mitchell stood up. You could see he was shaky. 'What are Secretary Hull's plans for evacuating us, protecting us, and bringing us home?' He said, 'I don't want to be caught up in anybody's war, and I don't want to be looking up the south end of a Nazi rifle.'

"'Calm down, Mitchell. No one's attacked our host country. Until you hear otherwise, we follow regulations. Cordell hasn't issued any specific change in protocols or procedures. We're certainly not closing our embassy or our consulates without State Department orders.' Consul General Lee was firm. 'Tight scrutiny is still the rule regarding all immigrant and nonimmigrant applications. You can take them in, but there's a temporary hold on issuing visas. Period. Cordell's orders dictate that all of our European embassies are to remain open pending further order. So, you're not going anywhere soon, Mitchell. You're safer in here than you would be anywhere else. Germany has always respected diplomatic immunity, and has never posed a threat to any US embassy. They'd be stupid to do that.'

"Lee concluded by saying, 'We don't know what Hitler plans next. No one does. Remember, Britain and France are in a technical state of war with Germany. Where does that put the Netherlands? On a map, it puts us in the middle of the coastline. But we're neutral. Will Germany seek to occupy the Netherlands to continue building its physical barrier from the ocean?' Lee shrugged. 'Washington says no. I say he might. Stay cautious, be on guard. Report anything unusual. Until we are notified otherwise, our embassy and our consulates will remain open and doing business.'"

"I LEFT THE meeting and went straight home. Sara would be anxious to know why a special emergency meeting had been called. She had made plans to go shopping with Julia, but Julia had to attend the meeting and was forced to cancel. No doubt Julia left the meeting to talk to Willem. As I related the content of our meeting to Sara, she sat as still as a statue. She was unaware what had happened to Denmark and Norway. It wasn't generally well known yet.

"The more I told her about the meeting, the more her eyes filled with tears and the more her jaw quivered. I expected her to say something like, *How does this affect our wedding date?* That was on my mind, but all Sara said was, 'Those poor, poor Danes, they haven't done anything to deserve this.' And then she added, 'I have a cousin in Denmark.'"

CHAPTER TWENTY-FOUR

"BY THE NEXT day, April 10, 1940, Germany's military advances into Denmark and Norway became widely known. Despite all of Germany's assurances broadcast on Dutch radio, everyone was a bundle of nerves, Sara included. She looked at me and said, 'What about poor Katy! She's seen public hysteria before; she's encountered mass catastrophe back in Germany. She knows what the Nazis can do. It tore apart her family. Now here it is again. Damn, Teddy, she was making such nice progress.'

"'Where is she, Sara? Did you take her back to Sylvia's?'

"'I was waiting for you to come home from the consulate. I fed her dinner and thought about returning her to Sylvia. That's where her things are. But she's seventeen and lives with two other young girls. I didn't think that was a good environment for Katy. What am I supposed to do? I didn't know any differently.'

"'Don't worry, she'll be all right. Until we can file an application for adoption, and get an order for temporary custody, we can rely on Henriëtte and the crèche. She's at the crèche during the day every day anyway.'

"Sara stared at me. Her lower lip was quivering. She gave a quick shake of her head, grabbed her jacket and her purse, and headed for the door. 'They have their own kids to take care of,' she said. 'Katy is an island. No one is as close to Katy as Sylvia and me. I want to keep her here at our apartment. That poor child is in no shape to play musical apartments or handle the current state of lunacy all on her own. I want her to be with us.'

"I looked at her in awe. What a powerful woman. What a lucky man I was. 'I'll go along with that,' I said. 'What can I do to help?' Sara threw her arms around me and cried on my shoulder. 'I love you,' she said. 'If you want to help, you can go out and get something for Katy to sleep on, extra bedding and a pillow. Thank God we have this new apartment, but we don't have any food for her. See if you can stop by the grocery.' She thought for a moment and said, 'I love you, Teddy.' She stopped again and said, 'She needs clothes. She only has a couple old hand-me-downs she was given at the crèche. If you pass a shop that sells girls' clothes, pick up some things. Three-year-old girls' things, but not too big. On the small side. Use your imagination. The saleswoman will help you.' She smiled and kissed me goodbye.

"I watched her walk out the door. 'Oh, jeez. I'm out of my league.'"

"So, I have a question," Karyn said. "How in the world were you supposed to run out and buy a bed, all kinds of bedding, children's clothes, and go to the grocery store on a Wednesday night in the middle of chaos, and then get all that stuff home? Did you have a truck?"

Teddy took a slight bow. "It wasn't easy. Thankfully, our new apartment was furnished. There were beds in two of the bedrooms. I found a store that sold sheets and pillows, that was easy. The food, that was a little tougher. All the grocery stores were packed. I was lucky there was any food left on the shelves when I got in. I had to go to three different stores just to get milk and cereal and fruits and vegetables. People were panicking. Some would say, 'Don't worry, the Krauts aren't bringing their troops here. We have an agreement,' while others would say, 'The war is coming, I saw the same thing in Czechoslovakia, get your supplies.' People were loading up their grocery carts to the top. They didn't know what they would be able to buy tomorrow. What if the Germans attacked and there were air raid sirens and all the stores closed?

"As I walked back to the apartment, both arms loaded, I saw a children's store. The owner was locking the door. I rapped on the door and begged her to open. She opened the door a crack and said, 'The store is closed, what do you need? Make it quick.' Of course, I didn't have a clue. 'What do you buy for a three-year-old girl?' I said. 'I think she's three. She's small.' The woman asked me what she needed. Good question. What did I know? I said a little of everything, she's an orphan. She asked me what size she was, and I held my hand about thirty inches off the floor. Then she shook her head and told me to sit down. The woman turned out to be a godsend. She went around her store picking things from here and there, and loaded up her cart with all sorts of girls' clothes, shoes, undies, jackets. And she said, 'Where are you headed? I'll go with you.'

"What a nice lady," said Karyn. "I'll bet you probably spent a fortune."

"I don't know. She said she gave me a discount. Anyway, when we arrived at the apartment, there were Katy and Sara sitting on the couch. 'Hi, Teddy,' Katy said with a smile. 'She would like to stay here,' Sara said. 'Isn't that right?' And Katy nodded her head. 'Yes,' she said shyly.

"I walked over, lifted her off the couch, and hugged her and twirled her around. 'You can stay as long as you want. I hope forever, and I brought you some things.' Sara stood and looked at the collection of clothes, and thanked the saleswoman. Then she closed the door, came to me, and she cried. Why do women always cry when they get a happy surprise? Anyway, the clothes were perfect."

Karyn held her hand to her chest, took a deep breath, looked at Teddy, and said, "My heart is palpitating. Can we finish the story tonight? At least tell me how everything turns out."

"Hm, that's a big order. We'll see. When we had finished dinner, and Sara had put Katy to bed, we sat down to relax and drink a glass of wine. 'We didn't bring any of the clothes they gave her at the crèche,' Sara said. 'She only has what she has on. You're a lifesaver.'

"As we sat there, we decided there were two matters that deserved our immediate attention. One was the adoption. I would try to research Dutch adoption requirements, and obtain the necessary documents, to the extent they were even available. I knew we didn't have a birth certificate or even the names of her parents. Truth be told, we didn't even know exactly how old she was. We said she was three, but she could have been four. She was small. From the many petitions that were presented at the consulate, I had made the acquaintances of several counselors that I respected. I would ask one to help us.

"The second matter was our marriage. As far as I was concerned, we could do that in a civil ceremony: walk over to the Royal Palace, pay the fee, say our vows, and kiss the bride. That's the only way to get legally married in the Netherlands anyway. If you want a religious wedding in addition, you may have one, but to be legally married, it has to be done before a civil administrator in the civil building, and that's the Royal Palace. Sara felt just the opposite, of course. Unless you are married in a temple by a rabbi in a ceremony before God, you are not truly married. Sara deserved to be a bride in a real wedding, so we would have two ceremonies.

"Sara contacted her father to find out if Rabbi Becker was still able to officiate our ceremony and could he do so in August like we planned? Naturally, her father asked us to come up to Utrecht to talk with him about it. I thought to myself, *I hope we don't have go through the issue of living in Amsterdam again.* It was very trying. We said we would come up there and, naturally, we would bring Katy. She was ours. Sara had a small talk with Katy and asked her if she would approve of our getting married. We were a little worried that all these changes might be too much, too soon. Everything was happening so fast, was she able to cope with it? She'd just left the crèche that day with Sara promising that she could live with us forever. Would it be too much for her to meet Sara's parents and hear plans about getting married? Would she even understand that? With Nazis invading half the world, and Amsterdam in a frenzy, I think a lot of psychiatrists would caution 'One thing at a time.' But Sara sat down with Katy in private, and talked it all over. Katy's reaction? She just clapped. She was all for it.

"Sara and I traveled out to Utrecht with Katy in her new dress. She had quite a few by that time, thanks to my shopping trip. They were glad to see us, and their reaction on meeting Katy was even better than I could have expected. Deborah couldn't have been happier. She was absolutely giddy. Saul was delighted to be a grandfather, but you could see in his eyes that he was calculating things that needed to be done. Sylvia had traveled from Amsterdam for the occasion and was also delighted to see Katy, and the two of them reconnected. After all, it was Sylvia who had first seen her being dropped off at the crèche.

"After a pleasant dinner, Sara, her mother, Sylvia, and Katy sat at the table talking up a storm. 'Tell me all about the new apartment.' 'Do you need anything for Katy's room?' 'I know that Miriam has extra girls' outfits, her girls are growing so fast.' 'How are the plans coming along for the wedding?'

"Saul and I sat there listening, until finally, Saul quietly said to me, 'That's enough girl talk. Let's go in the other room,' and he invited me to join him in his study. I knew what was coming. He offered me a glass of wine, said 'L'Chaim,' and we talked. I couldn't be mad at him, he was a very well-learned man, as nice as could be, and he was only looking after our welfare. After a while, as was typical of Saul, his face turned serious. 'The bastards are now in Denmark, right down the road. Copenhagen is barely three hundred miles away from us. They took over the country in less than a minute, and they promised that they won't disturb how the Danes run their country. Well, between you and me, that's bullshit! They also said they won't bother the Jews, and that's bullshit too. They'll do what they want, when they want.'

"'I know, Saul, but we've talked about this before. We're not leaving the country and going to America. I can't get us there.'

"Saul shook his head. 'That's not what I want to talk about. You made yourself very clear last time. I want to talk about something else. First, I want to ask you if you know what happened during the last seven years in Germany?'

"I didn't know where he was going with this. I just said, 'No.'

"Well, I'll tell you,' he said. 'German President von Hindenburg formally appointed Adolf Hitler as chancellor in 1933. Within a year they forced everybody to register their names, addresses, and of course, their religions. They want to know everyone's religion, even though the Nazis don't believe in religion. But Hitler does. He hates the Jewish religion and all the Jewish people. They went into Denmark and it wasn't hard to find out. People are already registered in Denmark at the census bureau, and their religion is one of the categories in the census. And, in case you didn't know, census records have the same information here in the Netherlands. So it won't be hard for the Nazis to tell in a minute who and where the Jews are.'

"I stopped him. I held my hand up. 'Saul, there are no Nazis in Amsterdam or in Utrecht or anywhere in the Netherlands. You have to stop these lectures.'

"'No Nazis yet,' he said. 'Not yet.' He leaned over and pointed. 'Son, once they get here, the first thing they'll do is find out who's Jewish.

They did that in Poland and Austria. Once they find out who's Jewish, it's only a matter of time until they issue their edicts against us. Believe me, I know, I am an expert on European history.'

"'I know,' I said, 'and I don't mean to be rude, but we can't move to America. We've already been through that.'

"Saul smiled. 'I want to talk about something different.'

"'It just doesn't seem different.'

"'Hear me out and then I won't say it again.'

"I didn't believe him, but he was about to be my father-in-law and he was a nice man. And smart. So I nodded. 'Okay.'

"'Thank you,' he said. 'Within a year after coming to power, or by 1934, Hitler ordered all Jews removed from public service. By the next year, Germany had passed the Nuremberg laws, the most violent anti-Semitic laws ever passed. Citizenship rights were restricted to those of German blood. Marriages, and even relationships, between Jews and non-Jews were now prohibited, even criminalized. See, you couldn't get married to Sara. You couldn't even date her. Some municipalities ruled that Jews could only live in certain areas, or not in their town at all. They took away Jewish licenses and did not let Jewish doctors practice on anyone but Jews. Jewish children were banned from public schools. Jewish stores were boycotted and vandalized. Some towns enacted restrictions governing where Jews could do business and where they couldn't.'

"'Saul, I know some of these things. At the consulate, I talk to German refugees every day.'

"'Well then, what makes you think that they won't do the same thing in Denmark? Or, God forbid, here in the Netherlands?'

"I took a breath. He was wearing me out. 'There is a difference, Saul,' I said confidently. 'You are talking about Germany and those countries that are ruled by Germany. The Netherlands is independent and not governed at all by Germany. We are neutral. Just like Denmark, where Germany has promised to let them run their country as they see fit. No restrictions against Jews in Denmark. And the Netherlands are neutral as well.'

"'And how will you enforce that neutrality and independence?' he said. 'Tell me that, Teddy. If Germany wants to occupy the Netherlands, can we stop them? Can anyone stop them? And what will become of the one hundred and fifty thousand Jews who live here? Will they stand in line at the consulate and apply for visas like the three hundred thousand Germans did applying for their visas?'

"'Well, they won't line up today, Saul. We've temporarily stopped issuing visas. But, Saul, you promised we wouldn't talk about this again.'

"'It's not about standing in line, or waiting too long. Hell. Jews have been guilty of that for thousands of years. But there is something you must do before it is too late. And that is why I asked you back into the study. Do you hear me? You have to promise me something before it's too late.'

"'Promise what, Saul? What is it you want me to promise?'

"He leaned over and spoke softly, but firmly. 'Sara and the child. You must take all steps possible to hide their identities.'

"I wondered what in the world he was talking about. 'Saul, how am I supposed to do that? Do you want them to wear costumes with masks?'

"His expression told me that was not a good joke. Was I that much of a simpleton? 'Costumes?' he said incredulously. 'Masks? Have you lost your senses? I'm not talking about hiding the way they look. You have to hide who they are. If the Nazis find out that Sara and Katy are Jewish, they will be subject to their vicious edicts. They'll be wearing armbands within days. They'll know who's Jewish and who's not on the streets of Amsterdam. The Jews will be forced down on their hands and knees to scrub those sidewalks like they did in Austria. You know what I'm talking about, don't you? You hear it every day in the immigration lines, don't you? So, Teddy, we don't want them to know Sara and Katy are Jewish. Hide their religious identity. When the Nazis come to Amsterdam, and they will, they'll want to register all the Jews, but they won't know about Sara and Katy, because you won't tell them. Sara will become Sara Hartigan. She'll no longer be a Rosenbaum, she will be a Hartigan. And Katy will become Katy Hartigan, not whoever she is.'

"I threw up my hands. 'That's it? Okay. I can promise that. You're right! Sara Rosenbaum will become Sara Hartigan, my wife. The wife of an officer of the US consulate. And Katy will be Katy Hartigan, our child. It's not that tough. As a matter of fact, Sara and I are going to the Royal Palace as soon as possible, maybe tomorrow, and we'll be married under Dutch law. We'll take Katy with us. We need to start adoption proceedings for her as soon as possible. There you go, Saul, no problem. All solved.'

"His reaction was not at all what I expected. He put his palm to his forehead and hung his head. '*Oy Gotenyu,*' he said. 'What am I going to do with you? Do you not understand anything? No! No, you can't go to the Royal Palace to get married! The minute you register at the Royal Palace, they will have a record that Sara Rosenbaum has married Theodore Hartigan and has changed her name from Rosenbaum to Hartigan.'

"He continued. 'If the Nazis want accurate records identifying each and every person in the Netherlands, they need look no further than the census records, birth records, or marital records. Or in this case, adoption records. Who is the individual, where does he live, and what is his religion? And they'll come visit you tomorrow. So, you see,' said Saul, 'you cannot get married at the Royal Palace.'

"What about if we get just married at the Majestic. The rabbi could marry us and he wouldn't have to fill out any records at the Royal Palace?'

"Saul shook his head. 'There would be records of the wedding and the rabbi's officiating at the temple, and those records will be the first place the Nazis look.'

"I sighed. 'I suppose we could wait until we get back to the United States, but there are problems with that. One, we are planning to adopt a child. That will have to be registered, presumably at the Royal Palace. We need to be married for the adoption to be legal. Two, for any number of reasons, we need to officially be husband and wife. What if one of us was ill or injured and needed medical care? Who could authorize it? And most importantly, Sara wants a religious wedding. She also wants a religious adoption ceremony. So, we not only want our union to be legal in the eyes of society, but also in the eyes of God. Sara is firm on that. You brought her up with those principles. What are we supposed to do, Saul?'

"'Simple. Don't get married! Sara can live with you as your wife. Mr. and Mrs. Theodore Hartigan. Who would know the difference? But you cannot get a marriage license here in the Netherlands. You can tell people that you eloped. She lives with you, she shares your name, you have a three-year-old child who shares your name as well. You all live together, you're a family. Does a piece of paper make you a family, or does living together and loving each other? How would the Nazis know that you didn't all come here together from America? They're not going to check official US State Department records, are they?'

"'No. of course not.'

"'Right. So just tell everyone you're married, and no one will know the difference.'

"I didn't know how to answer that. Who would know the difference? Only everyone who knew us. And all that would have to happen is for one person to say so. Loose lips sink ships. But Saul was right, we couldn't have a wedding without disclosing Sara's birth identity, and if you traced that, the census would show she was Jewish. But it would break Sara's heart. A girl deserves to be a bride, to have a wedding. My initial reaction was *The hell with it, our lives will not be dictated by a bunch of soulless Nazis. We'll do what the hell we please.* But I knew that Sara wanted to be a bride so badly. I stood up. 'I'll think about it,' I said, 'and I'll talk it over with Sara. I know you're right, Saul. Right now, there are no Nazis here, and there may never be, and right now, no one's checking any records to see who's Jewish. The Nazis are three hundred miles away.'

"We walked back into the living room where Sara, Deborah, and Katy were having a snack and laughing it up. 'August 17,' Sara said. 'That will be the date for our wedding. Mom called Rabbi Becker and he is available on that date, and he penciled us in. We called Willem. The Menorah Room is available for the event, and the caterer is checking his calendar. I know the world is going nuts, but I am so happy.' Deborah stepped forward. 'And so am I. I couldn't be happier that my daughter is getting married to such a fine man, and we have the world's nicest little girl,' she said with her arm around Katy. I looked at Saul and shrugged my shoulders. He shut his eyes.

"That night we put Katy to bed, and Sara and I lay together in each other's arms. Sara was as calm and as happy as I had ever seen her. She asked me what her father and I had talked about, but I didn't have the heart to tell her. Maybe another day."

CHAPTER TWENTY-FIVE

"ONE WEEK PASSED, and then two weeks, and then three, and there were no signs that the Nazis were massing to move south. They had captured Denmark and secured the Danish seashore. It was what they needed to defend an attack from England over the North Sea. Should Germany be attacked by any of the powers that had declared war against it many months ago, it was also a launching pad for German aircraft to attack England. And just as quickly it was a port for German warships to guard and manage the western front. So, as the thinking goes, why move south to capture the Netherlands? We were certainly no threat to Germany, and we provided nothing more in defensive strategy.

"One week passed, and then two weeks, and then three, and the man on the street stopped looking east. Fears subsided. Conversations turned to something other than defensive strategies or stocking up on groceries.

"But Queen Wilhelmina's government did not look the other way. It continued to focus east. It continued the military readiness it had begun the previous September. Closed-door debates considered what the response should be if Germany were to demand their surrender. Would they sign a cooperation agreement or stand their ground? Could they count on the Allies, those countries that had already declared war on Germany eight months ago: France, England, Belgium? Would they come to the Netherlands' aid?

"The US embassy and consulates were put on alert. The secret intelligence reports that Washington received continued to show German military activity. Specifically, what positions the consulate should take relative to American citizens in Holland. What assistance it should provide in the event visas and travel documents were needed."

"I HAD LUNCH almost every day with the same group. All were consulate staffers: Julia, Mitchell, Michelle, and me. Julia was the most talkative. Like the rest of us, she would receive the daily alerts, which most of us found unnerving. But Julia didn't seem rattled. 'Suppose the Germans did decide to occupy Holland?' she said. 'Of course, there isn't a thing we could do about it, but why would they treat Holland any different than they treat Denmark? When the Germans occupied them, they decided not to antagonize the populace. That's smart. It's much easier to govern a country if the citizens are cooperative. The Nazis haven't even interfered with Denmark's Jewish citizens. They weren't forced to wear armbands or give up their licenses. Things are peaceful in Denmark. Why would it be any different if they occupied Holland? Why antagonize the Dutch? Just rule peacefully until this damn thing is over. You know this so-called war will be over in a matter of months.'

"'You're a fool,' Mitchell said. 'Why would they antagonize? Because they're jackboots, that's why, warmongers, led by an insane dictator who wants to rule the world and have everyone bow down to him. Forget about what they're doing in Denmark, they've only been there for three weeks. Take a look at Poland, Austria. See the murdered thousands. If things don't change, I'm going to get the hell out of here.'"

"LATER THAT AFTERNOON, Julia came into my office. 'I have good news and bad news,' she said.

"'Okay, give me the bad news first,' I said. 'It's been that kind of week.'

"'Okay, bad news: Mitchell just handed in his resignation. He quit. He's traveling to Paris and taking a steamship home. No more Mitchell. And guess who's going to get all of his work?'

"'Great. Then it is impossible for you to give me any good news, because all Mitchell's work is going to end up on my desk.'

"'Probably. But here is the good news.' And she pulled four tickets out of her pocket, and waved them in the air. 'William James Basie, the Count himself, his orchestra, and Billie Holiday, "What a Little Sunshine Can Do?" are concluding their European tour tonight. Guess where?'

"'I don't know. Paris?'

"'Nope. Amsterdam. At the Schouwburg. And little Julia has four tickets. It's a sellout, naturally.'

"I grimaced a little. 'I don't know if we can make it. I'm not sure if Sara is up to going out tonight. And besides, what are we going to do with Katy?'

"'Sara has already arranged for Sylvia to babysit. Sara's polishing her nails, and putting on her killer dress, and she's ready to go.'"

"Oh my!" Karyn said. "I would have loved to see Count Basie. And Billie Holliday. How did Julia get those tickets?"

"Who knows? Julia could work magic. Wasn't that the first thing that Frank Lee said to me when I arrived at the consulate?"

"I think you told me that. How was the show?"

"Amazing. Walter had rearranged the chairs so there was a large dance floor in the middle. Count Basie's orchestra was up on the stage. Drinks were served. Never had a finer night. I mean other than with my family."

"QUEEN WILHELMINA'S GOVERNMENT was listening to the same intelligence reports as Frank Lee. She was solidifying her defenses as best she could. But she had a long way to go. The Royal Netherlands Army was ill-equipped. Their weapons and military equipment were outdated and in poor condition. The Dutch government was placing its faith in the defense of 'neutrality.' It worked in World War One. There was also the remote possibility of support from France or England should it become necessary, but that was certainly no sure thing."

"And what about Teddy and Sara? What were you doing to prepare?"

"Shopping. Actually, Sara was, not me. She was trying on gowns, she was meeting with the caterers at the Majestic, she was even taking Katy to try on dresses so that she could be in the wedding too."

Karyn started laughing. "That is so incongruous. The world is falling apart, and Sara is out shopping for her wedding. She is a typical bride! There is only one thing on her mind. I love it!"

"It's true, but this time it got us into trouble."

"Oh, I'm sorry. How did that happen?"

Teddy let his eyes gaze around the room. His lips were shut, though they quivered. He swallowed a couple of times. Karyn could feel that this part was going to be tough. He took a breath and commenced. "It was Wednesday, May 8, and Sara and Sylvia had decided to take the rest of the week off and go shopping in Utrecht. They would stay with Deborah and Saul. Naturally they brought Katy. I couldn't get away. Things were nuts at the consulate. We had shortened the number of hours that we were open to the public. Mornings were dedicated to consular meetings. Correspondence between and among our embassies and consulates was frequent. 'What have you learned? What have your intelligence agents discovered? How much support can we count on from Washington?' The answer, of course, was very little.

"On Thursday, May 9, we received reports from more than one agent that the Germans were mobilizing. Our French embassy shared a report that German troops were massing on the western border. We were also advised that all Dutch troops were called to active duty and all military leaves had been canceled. The three water lines were tested, armed, and monitored.

"It made me sick to my stomach. I was scared to death for Sara and the girls, and I tried to contact her, but Saul answered the phone. He told me that the girls were out shopping. I should have figured; after all, that's why she went to Utrecht. I told Saul that our collective judgment led us to believe that an invasion in the near future was possible. No, more than possible. Likely.

"'I knew it,' Saul said. 'I told you this could happen.'

"'I should have listened, although what difference would it have made?'

"'What do you want me to do?' he asked. 'If there is an invasion, I don't know where they would be the safest, here or with you. I am inclined to think that Sara should be in Amsterdam with you, as Mr. and Mrs. Hartigan. I also think that Sylvia would be safest at the crèche. No army would attack a childcare center.' I agreed and asked him if he could send them right home. 'Remember, they are out shopping for wedding dresses today, Teddy, and I don't know when they will be home. I'm sure I won't see them until tonight.'

"'Okay. Can you send them to Amsterdam tomorrow?'

"'Absolutely. I'll reserve a car for them tomorrow at noon.'

"'Thanks, Saul. I feel bad I ever doubted you, and I'll look for them tomorrow.'

"'You don't need to apologize, but tomorrow is Shabbat. Let's all pray for peace and that a war with Germany never happens.'"

CHAPTER TWENTY-SIX

"DESPITE HOLLAND'S FIRM policy of neutrality, despite Germany's guarantee of Holland's independence and neutrality, Holland was invaded by Germany early the next morning, May 10, 1940. Despite the defensive preparations that were being made, it was still a total shock. It was not preceded by Hitler ranting on the radio, there were no demands or formal declarations of war. There were no leaflets dropped from the sky, there were no messages sent to the Royal Palace insisting on surrender. There was no offer of a 'cooperation agreement' tendered to the Dutch government. That morning, German forces moved simultaneously into the Netherlands, Belgium, France, and Luxembourg under the German operational plan called Fall Gelb (Case Yellow).

"They had been doing maneuvers for months, but the Royal Netherlands Army was not mentally, physically, or militarily prepared for the German onslaught. The Dutch military's arms and equipment were old and in poor shape. In fact, they could only mount a limited number of armored cars and tankettes. The air force had only one hundred and forty aircraft, seventy percent of which were outdated biplanes. They had thirty-nine armored vehicles and four tankettes. As a result, sixty-five of the Dutch aircraft were destroyed on the first day of the campaign.

"Yet, despite all that, the Dutch military mounted a gallant defense and in many areas pinned the Germans down and prevented their advance."

"What about the water lines?" Karyn asked. "Did they work? Were the Dutch able to flood the fields and prevent the German army from moving in?"

Teddy smiled and shrugged his shoulders. "It depends on what you mean by 'work.' Did they do what they were designed to do? Yes, they flooded. Are you asking whether they stopped the German army? Well, it slowed their foot traffic down a little. The Germans were prevented from exercising a rapid land advance because of the trenches and the armed water lines. But this was not 1769. The Germans were prepared for the water lines. They had carefully studied the battlegrounds they were planning to cross. A month ahead of the actual invasion, a group of German army officers, dressed in civilian clothes, crossed into the countryside and studied the Grebbe Line. They carefully measured the actual depths, and noted the best areas to breach the lines. They paid special attention to the Rhenen area, close to the Rhine River. The German spies were able to map the weak spots in the Grebbe defense line. Besides, while the flooded fields were ingenious defenses in the seventeenth and eighteenth centuries, this time the Germans had airplanes. German paratroopers met on the ground in The Hague, huddled together, and advanced up toward the Royal Palace.

"The Amsterdam citizens were alerted to the attack early as the plane motors roared overhead. I was alone in the apartment, sound asleep. Remember, Sara had taken Katy and was staying at her parents' in Utrecht. The noise woke me up, and the first thing to pop into my mind was Sara and Katy. If the planes were here, what was happening in Utrecht? Were they under attack? I immediately called the Rosenbaums, but the phone service was jammed. I couldn't get an operator for the intercity call. Everyone must have been using the phone at the same time. I dressed as quickly as I could and raced over to the consulate. I didn't see any planes or German land forces. But I could hear the sounds of Fokkers and mortar fire in the distance.

"When I arrived at the consulate, it was on lockdown. I banged on the door to be admitted. Some of the staff were assembling in the conference room. Consul General Lee, who lived in the consulate, was setting up at the front of the room. Members of the staff were rushing in and out with messages. Lee said that he would give us all a briefing in thirty minutes. That was enough time for me to run to my office and try again to call Sara. Miraculously, the call went through. Saul answered.

'We're under attack,' he said in a shaky voice. 'I haven't seen any enemy soldiers, but I can hear the gunshots. As far as I can tell, the shooting is out at the airfields. Nothing in the city yet.'

"'It's the same for us,' I responded. 'How is Sara? How is Katy?'

"'Sara and Katy are fine, but Katy is frightened to death. This must bring to mind some awful memories for her. Here,' he said, and he handed the phone to Sara. 'Teddy. Teddy, I'm so scared. I need you. Dad tells me I can't leave the house. And he says it's too dangerous for you to come here. We are all huddled up in a back room where there are no windows.'

"'Your dad is right. Stay out of sight and don't even think about coming to Amsterdam. It's no better here than it is in Utrecht. I'll came to you as soon as it's safe to travel. I'm fine, but I'm so worried about you and Katy,' I said. 'And how is Sylvia?'

"'We're all fine, except that we are shaking. There is a lot of fighting going on near here. We can hear the noise.'

"'The US consulates are probably the safest places in Holland,' I responded. 'I'll get to you as soon as it's safe.'

"I returned to the conference room. Julia, Michelle, and all the staff were present. Consul General Lee slammed a gavel, and everyone settled down. 'This is the latest we have: Germany has started a full-scale attack on the Netherlands. They've landed in all the major cities, but they seem to be concentrating their forces on The Hague to capture Queen Wilhelmina and her government. But you have to applaud the Dutch, they are battling back and holding their own. In Rotterdam, General Winkleman is directing a fierce defense. Surprisingly, there is no word yet from England or France. My advice to all of you is to stay here in the building as long as you can. For those of you that have families, we are trying to make arrangements to open space in the building for them should it become necessary.'

"I stood up. 'What about help from our neighbors. Don't we have a mutual defense treaty with Belgium, England, and France? Why is there no word yet? When should we expect them to come to our aid?'

"Lee shook his head. 'They have their own problems. They were attacked this morning at the same time, along with Luxembourg. It appears that Hitler wants nothing standing in his way between Germany and the Atlantic Ocean. He wants to own the continent.'

"When the meeting was over, I rushed to the phone and called Sara, but this time I couldn't get through. There was another staff meeting scheduled for two o'clock and I would try to call her afterward. I knew it was crazy to call her every few hours, but I was worried to death. The Dutch were brave fighters, but Germany was much bigger and too powerful. It was only a matter of time. The best we could hope for was a quick peace treaty like they had in Denmark.

"I walked out into the hallway and Julia was standing there. She looked at me, and she could instantly see what a bundle of nerves I was. She took my arm and we walked into an office. 'Did you get through to Sara?' she said. 'I'm so worried about her.'

"'Not recently. I couldn't get through. Utrecht is under attack. I need to get up there. I have to bring Sara back home. We'll be safe here at the consulate.'

"'You can't get up there, Teddy. There's no way. You think the trains are running on schedule, or at all? It's a battlefield out there.'

"'Well, what am I supposed to do? I can't leave her there alone.'

"'She's not alone, she's with her parents. They'll protect her as best they can. Even if you were there, what more you can do? We all just have to wait until the fighting is over.'

"'With France and England in the war, that might be months or years. I can't leave her there. What about Willem? He has a car, doesn't he? Doesn't the Majestic have a bus?'

"'Are you crazy? You're going to drive a bus through a battlefield?'

"'I will, if I have to.'

"At two o'clock, the meeting with Consul General Lee was reconvened. Lee went over the most recent information. The cables were coming in one after another. It was like a ticker tape. 'When the bombers flew over the country,' he said, 'it was first believed that they were headed out to the North Sea to attack England, but they turned around and headed straight for The Hague. Their intent was to capture Queen Wilhelmina and take the Dutch government. But they failed. German paratroopers were either shot down or captured. The Dutch took over the bridges, surrounded pockets of German troops, and stopped the air attack. It is estimated that the Nazis have lost over one thousand soldiers. Having lost, they returned to Germany.'"

"That's unbelievable," Karyn said. "How could little Holland do that?"

"Historians call it the Battle for The Hague, and it became the first failed paratrooper attack in history. The fighting that day seemed centered up and down the Holland coastline. The Luftwaffe aimed to take over the Dutch airfields on the Dutch coast in order to launch air raids against the United Kingdom. At least on this day there seemed to be little or no fighting in the center of Amsterdam. It was relatively quiet. Thus, when our consulate meetings were over, most staffers either went back to their apartments, or went to get something to eat. Julia and I walked to the Majestic. She warned me, 'Don't bother Willem, he has his hands full. And for sure, don't ask him about borrowing his bus.'

"The Majestic was also quiet. Thankfully the kitchen was functioning. After all, there were still residents and guests at the hotel, but thankfully, no German soldiers that I could see. Willem said it was his intent to keep the hotel operating as long as the fighting was west of us. He agreed that the Nazis were trying to establish airfields along the coastline. Then they would have bases from which to attack England. He said they cared more about the strategic positioning than they did about conquering the Netherlands.

"Before we left, I tried again to reach Sara, but either the lines were down or the operators weren't working. And all that made me even more nervous. I did ask Willem if the Majestic's limo or bus were operating. He said they were locked up tight. He didn't want the Germans to have additional motorized equipment. After dinner, I went back to the apartment, but I couldn't sleep more than half an hour at a time."

CHAPTER TWENTY-SEVEN

"WILHELMINA HELENA PAULINE MARIA, Queen of the Netherlands, was beloved by her people. She ascended to the throne in 1890 at the age of ten years old."

"Wow!" said Karyn, biting her lower lip. "Ten years old!"

"Her father, King Wilhelm, died and she was his heir. Her mother became regent. Her family was very wealthy and Queen Wilhelmina, who was brilliant and well educated, invested her funds and became the richest woman in the world. She used her wealth to help build the Netherlands into an industrial power.

"She wasn't just a functionary. She firmly instituted Holland's policy of neutrality. Though coaxed in World War One to join with either the Central Powers or the Allies, she was steadfast, and because of that independence, the Netherlands prospered during the war, and its citizens remained safe. In 1933, when Hitler came to power, she refused to align with Germany. It was her intent to remain neutral. She would allow trade and commerce with Germany as well as anyone else, including the Allied powers. Personally, she detested Hitler and the policies of the Third Reich.

"In that year, 1933, in response to Hitler's anti-Semitic policies, a tide of refugees started crossing the border and flooded into the Netherlands. Professor David Cohen and businessman Abraham Asscher formed the Committee for Jewish Refugees. It was located initially in Amsterdam, which already had a large Jewish community. The committee assisted Jewish refugees by providing housing, expenses, and employment. Queen Wilhelmina was sensitive to refugees fleeing the Nazi persecution. She helped establish a camp for the Jewish refugees in the village of West-erbork."

"ON MAY 10, 1940, when the Nazis invaded Holland, their principal objective was The Hague, the seat of Dutch government. The attack was fierce, but the closer the Nazis came, the harder the Dutch army dug in. Though ten thousand Dutch soldiers were battling the Nazis, they were still greatly outnumbered and were relying on outdated and cap-tured ammunition. At the Royal Palace, the Dutch Grenadier Guards fought their way into a position where they could launch artillery attacks against the airstrip and the Nazi aircraft, damaging it, and forcing the Nazis to evacuate the burning airstrip and retreat. The Grenadiers man-aged to recapture the airstrip and to capture dozens of German soldiers.

"During a temporary lull, Queen Wilhelmina, the royal family, and the key members of her government found an opportunity to escape. She contacted England's King George VI, who sent the British destroyer HMS *Hereward* to The Hague. Queen Wilhelmina and her family—Princess Juliana, Prince Bernhard, and their daughters Princess Beatrix and Princess Irene—were all guests at Buckingham Palace. Queen Wil-helmina established the Dutch government-in-exile, which remained in place until the war was over. She set up a radio channel and addressed her people every night, urging them to resist."

"ON MAY 11 I arrived at the consulate before the sun came up. I'd had little or no sleep. I knew that if I called Sara at this hour, I'd stand a good chance of getting through to her, but I didn't have the heart to wake them up. The streets were pretty quiet. I didn't hear any gunfire, nor did I see any German aircraft. Julia arrived at the consulate a little after I did. She told me that she didn't sleep well either, but she awoke early enough to bring us a couple of sweet rolls for breakfast.

"It was time for the morning briefing. Consul General Lee took the stand and advised us of the latest information he had received. 'First of all, you may all be happy to know that Queen Wilhelmina has reached England safe and sound, and will continue to operate the government in exile until this invasion is over. Second, the Nazi attack on The Hague has thus far been repulsed, and the Nazis have retreated. Third, the Dutch army is holding back the Nazis from entering Rotterdam. Finally, and unfortunately, things don't look so good in Utrecht. The Dutch forces are struggling but the Nazis are on the verge of taking the city.'

"When I heard that, my stomach immediately tied itself into knots. I wanted to jump out of my seat and run to rescue Sara. Julia saw me, placed her hand on my arm, and said, 'Settle down, Teddy. The armies are fighting each other. That doesn't mean that the residents are in danger. They're not aiming for residential areas.' I didn't much buy into that, but I appreciated her concern.

"One of the staffers stood up and asked Lee, 'What happened to France and England? Are they blind and deaf? Why aren't they helping out here? Are they just going to stand by and do nothing like they did with Poland, who they swore to protect? Maybe their prime minister will say that there is "peace in the land" like he did last time. So tell me, where are they? They were supposed to be our allies.'

"Consul General Lee leaned over and spoke privately to one of his adjutants. Then he returned to the microphone and said, 'I am informed that France has her main force on the Belgian border and a lesser force in the Ardennes. France has her hands full battling the Nazi attack there. They won't be coming to Holland's aid. I do not have current information on British forces.'

"The morning meeting adjourned and I sat up in my office, more or less in a trance. I couldn't reach Sara and that was driving me nuts. I studied a map. It was thirty-one miles from Amsterdam to Utrecht. I could do that. It might take me a couple of days, but maybe I should give it a try.

"Julia walked into the office, and I shared my thoughts. I would walk to Utrecht, staying out of sight, and rescue Sara. Or maybe I could borrow a bike.

"'What about little Katy, your adopted daughter?' she said. 'Do you think she can walk thirty-one miles? Or maybe you could carry her.'

She shook her head. 'Get serious, Teddy, you can't walk thirty-one miles through a war zone, and it's insane to try to ride a bike. Hell, the Nazis are probably all over those roads.'"

"THE DUTCH ARMY was waging a gallant defense. Ten thousand Dutch soldiers were holding off the German onslaught in Rotterdam. Utrecht was still at a standstill, thankfully, and Dutch soldiers were holding firm. The Nazis had not been able to make progress in The Hague. We were trying to follow all the operations from our communications center in the consulate. In fact, I was such an emotional wreck, I had decided not to go home at night. On the evenings of May 12 and 13, I spent the night in the consulate. Julia saw me in my frazzled condition, and said she would stay the night with me. I don't know what I would have done without her. I'd have lost my mind.

"I was hoping that good sense would prevail, and the Nazis would weigh the cost of the Netherlands war, and strike a peace agreement with the queen. They had lost over a thousand German soldiers. If I were a Nazi general, I would think that the Netherlands was not worth it. It was not in a position to pose any threat to Germany, and it wasn't worth the loss of my men, right?"

"That makes sense to me," answered Karyn, "but we know that good sense was not a Nazi attribute. They didn't do that, did they? Meanwhile, what was the story with Sara and Katy? Did you make any further efforts to rescue them?"

"No, that would have been foolish. They were unharmed, and Julia talked me out of it. But then came one of the stupidest moves in the war, and the cost was catastrophic. In the city of Rotterdam, the Dutch soldiers were fighting bravely and holding off the Nazis. It was a stalemate. But on May 13, the Nazi general planned an attack on Rotterdam using tanks and precision bombs dropped from Luftwaffe planes. That attack was delayed for a day because of low clouds, but on the next day, May 14, the skies cleared and it was a go-ahead. Before the attack, the German general delivered a written ultimatum to the Dutch commander, Colonel Scharroo. I remember the ultimatum almost word for word. There is a copy of it in the museum, and I have a printed copy." He handed it to Karyn, who read:

> To the Mayor and aldermen and the Governmental Authorities of Rotterdam
>
> The continuing opposition to the offensive of German troops in the open city of Rotterdam forces me to take appropriate measures should this resistance not be ceased immediately. This may well result in the complete destruction of the city. I petition you—as a man of responsibility—to endeavor everything within your powers to prevent the town of having to bear such a huge price. As a token of agreement, I request you to send us an authorized negotiator by return.

Karyn held her hand over her mouth. "I can't imagine. I can't imagine someone telling me to do something or my entire town will be destroyed. What happened? Why do you say this was one of the stupidest moves of the war? Did Colonel Scharroo refuse to meet?"

"The letter gave Scharroo two hours to comply. Rotterdam's mayor pleaded with Scharroo to just surrender, but Scharroo thought the letter was a fake. He sent back a letter stating that the demand letter was not duly signed and therefore it might not be authentic. He demanded a signed letter. But the German planes were already in the air, headed to Rotterdam. The Germans had arranged that if the attack was called off, they would launch red flares into the sky and their planes would turn back. While the German general was signing a duplicate letter to be delivered to Scharroo, he could hear the sound of planes in the distance. The general quickly sent a telegraph to each of the two bomber squadrons to halt the bombing. He ordered flares to be launched into the sky. The southern air squadron saw the flares and turned back. The northern squadron received the telegraph, but Nazi General Kesselring told them to ignore it. He was intent on going through with the bombing. The pilots later said they didn't see the flares because it was cloudy. What happened was one of the most devastating bombings in history.

"The ancient and beautiful city of Rotterdam was carpet-bombed. It was totally destroyed. Twenty-five thousand homes were destroyed and almost one thousand residents were killed. It was revealed that a similar bombing order was in effect to bomb Utrecht. It was time for the Netherlands to surrender. Dutch General Winkleman sent out notice to the German general that he had ordered all Dutch forces to suspend operations. The next day, the Netherlands signed a document of surrender with Germany and the fighting ceased."

CHAPTER TWENTY-EIGHT

AS SHE WAS getting ready to leave for the hospital and her daily visit, Karyn received a call informing her that Teddy was being moved to the Silver Spring Home, an assisted-living facility. "He'll give you a call when he is settled in," the nurse said. Karyn knew that this was in the works, and it would be a good sign, but she didn't know exactly when it would occur, so she had a free day. On the off chance that he was in town, Karyn texted Burt. The return text informed her that he was in Washington, but he was in a meeting at the moment, and he'd give her a call when he could.

Karyn took advantage of her time off and took a walk down to the National Mall. It was a picture-perfect day. The United States Capitol sat to the east and the Washington Monument to the west. People were strolling, children were playing. She decided to take a guided tour at the National Gallery of Art. There was one leaving in an hour. It was so pleasant to have someone direct her thoughts to something other than wartime Holland.

She met Burt for dinner. He didn't know anything about Teddy's condition other than he had been released from the hospital and moved to the nursing facility. He asked Karyn how her story was coming along, and Karyn said, "I have reams of notes, I can't write as fast as he talks. It's exhausting, and I'm sure there's more to come."

Burt had an apologetic look on his face, but it didn't hide the smile. "I'm sorry for getting you involved with Teddy and mixed up in such an arduous assignment. I don't suppose he's shared any information about your sister Annie, has he? Has he said anything?"

She shook her head. "Not a word."

"I know he tried to contact a few people he used to know. I helped him send emails to two or three, but I believe they haven't been answered. Listen, you're not contractually bound to this project or to Teddy. You can leave any time you want."

Karyn wagged her finger back and forth. "Nope, nope, I gave my word that I would write his life story, his biography. I'll see it through. It's not like it's uninteresting. You know, Burt, it's a funny thing. In many ways, I can see myself in this story. At the crèche. I'm sure I must have been there. After all, I'm the right age, and I too was adopted in Amsterdam in the early '40s. I want to finish his story. It may reveal something about my life. Who knows?"

TEDDY WAS GLAD to see her and glad to speak in a sitting position in a chair, rather than being propped up in a bed. "Where did we leave off?" he said. "I believe it was on May 15."

Karyn nodded. "The surrender agreement had been signed."

"Right. It was broadcasted over the radio that the Netherlands had surrendered to the Germans and the war was over. It was now safe for people to come out of their homes. It took a while for the news to sink in, and for people to realize that they could come outside, but in a while, people took to the streets to celebrate. They weren't celebrating a victory, but an end to the fighting. People realized that barring some other countries coming to our rescue, there was no way we could have defeated Germany. A surrender was the only possible outcome that would have spared the lives of the Dutch populace. Now, in addition to our citizens, there were German soldiers walking the streets, but none of them were firing. No bombs were being dropped. In a few days, the intercity buses would once again be operating. I called Sara and told her I would be out there as soon as the buses or the trains started running. And in a few days they did, and I was on my way to Utrecht.

"I rang the bell, and guess who opened the door? You're right. Sara threw herself into my arms and hugged me so strongly I thought she'd break my bones. I think we stayed locked in that position for some time, until Saul loudly cleared his throat. 'Welcome!' he said in front of his family. I spun around, lifted Katy into the air, and gave her a kiss. I gave a hug and a kiss to Deborah, one to Sylvia, and a strong handshake to Saul. I was so happy to see them all. Of all the ways to be separated, this last week was worst. We were separated and worried about each other, and even though we were only an hour apart, it could have been oceans.

"We sat in the living room exchanging stories about what we did during the invasion. Most of all, we were grateful we were able to survive and exchange those stories. The Rosenbaums had no access to the intelligence that we were receiving every day in the consulate. They were in the dark. Saul's predictions of Germany's takeover had come true. He knew there would be battles, but he had no way of knowing how close they were to suffering the same fate as Rotterdam. 'What happens now?' Sara asked me, and my answer was, 'I don't know. Maybe we will become another Denmark. The Nazis will appoint someone to run the country and then we'll see.'

"'Heaven help us all when that happens,' Saul said. 'If we are a Nazi-run country, we will have Nazi laws.' He pointed at me and said, 'Now you must remember what I told you. No marriage ceremonies at the Royal Palace or at the Majestic, or anywhere else. You are Mr. and Mrs. Hartigan. And no formal adoptions. You are all Hartigans. From day one. Next, you must get out of here and go home to America as soon as you can arrange it.' I just nodded, knowing that would be impossible right now.

"Deborah, and her two daughters, Sylvia and Sara, and little Katy left the room to prepare a liberation feast. Naturally, Saul and I left to have a cocktail in his study. I could complain *Here comes another set of lectures from the world's most brilliant history professor,* but I was just delighted to be sitting with Sara's family. And give the man credit where credit's due, Saul had been right on the money.

"'Isn't it possible for the Netherlands to become another Denmark until this whole thing is over?' I said. 'Denmark is operating just as it was before it was conquered last month, with no interference from Berlin. And there is no religious persecution. Why shouldn't we expect the same thing?'

"Saul shook his head. 'You are asking me to predict the future. Will the Yankees win the World Series in your country this year? Or will it be the last-place Tigers? We make our predictions based upon empirical evidence. Look at the standings. Holland was violently attacked and we waged a brutal defensive war, but before it was over, thousands of soldiers were killed on both sides. Denmark was offered a peaceful agreement and there was no fighting. The Nazis trust the leaders of Denmark, while our queen is an enemy. There are one hundred and fifty thousand Jews in the Netherlands, people who Hitler has sworn to obliterate. Holland is strategically placed for attacking Belgium, France, and the British Isles. Now you tell me, Teddy, do you put your money on the Yankees or the Tigers?'"

Karyn's forehead wrinkled. "That's an odd analogy for a Dutchman to make, isn't it, Teddy? Holland's three thousand miles away from American baseball. How would Saul know about such a comparison?"

"Well, he was in New York in 1935 and he went to a game. He enjoyed it and he followed baseball in the papers. He knew that the Yankees won the 1939 World Series, for the fourth time in a row, and that the Tigers finished in last. I understood the analogy. Saul was a smart guy."

"IT WAS HITLER'S plan to install a puppet government to operate the Netherlands at his command. They knew that Queen Wilhelmina was a declared enemy of the Reich, so they reached out to Holland's prime minister, Dirk Jan de Geer, to return to the country and form a pro-German puppet government, similar to the Vichy government in southern France. De Geer was prepared to accept the invitation, but Queen Wilhelmina vetoed it, and then dismissed de Geer as prime minister. It turned out that might have been a mistake on her part. Hitler brought in Arthur Seyss-Inquart, an Austrian Nazi, to run the Netherlands. He was a vehement anti-Semite, and had been second-in-command to the vicious Hans Frank in Poland. Seyss-Inquart observed what Frank had done in Poland and how brutally to treat the Jews."

* * *

"SARA AND I returned to Amsterdam right before Seyss-Inquart was appointed. Until then, the country was being operated by the German military. We observed that things were relatively calm when we returned. Stores had reopened, as were the schools, including the Reformed Teacher Training College. Mr. van Hulst had asked Sara if she would return to her position as teacher. Sara advised him that her name was now Sara Hartigan, and she didn't wish to be referred to as Sara Rosenbaum. If there were any references to her in the records, she wished that they would only reflect the name Hartigan. Mr. van Hulst seemed to catch on and agreed.

"Henriëtte Pimentel reopened the crèche. Actually, it never closed. Those staff members and children who lived in the crèche remained there throughout the invasion. We stopped by the crèche to see if the day care was going to reopen on its same schedule. Henriëtte was happy to see us and gave a warm welcome to Katy. Sara quietly told Henriëtte that she and I had married in Utrecht in a private ceremony. Henriëtte looked at me and smiled. She totally understood. 'Congratulations, Mr. and Mrs. Hartigan.'

"Sara nodded and added, 'And it's Katy Hartigan, if you please.' Henriëtte smiled. 'Of course,' she said. 'We're happy to welcome her back, and I'll make sure the records conform.'

"So, Sara would go to work each morning. On her way to the school, she'd drop Katy off at the crèche, and walk across the lawn to the college. Sara would pick up Katy after school at about three P.M. each day and bring her back to the apartment. I went to the consulate every day, as it was now open full-time. On rare occasions, Julia and I would meet Sara for lunch. On those occasions, we would take a walk through the Rijksmuseum, Amsterdam's gorgeous art museum. Sara could spend hours there, and sometimes she did in the evening. She loved the impressionists. Katy loved the brilliant colors.

"In our communications center, staffers monitored the radio and the cables. The war was over in the Netherlands, but it was still going on with England and France. The staffers kept close watch on the reactions in Washington. Could we count on any aid at all from the US? Four days after the Netherlands surrendered, Charles Lindbergh, the popular

American aviator who flew nonstop across the ocean, took to the airwaves and gave a speech on behalf of the isolationists. He said that the United States was not in any danger unless they put themselves there by meddling in the affairs of foreign countries.

"In response, President Roosevelt delivered one of his fireside chats about the dire events occurring in Europe. He said our sympathies lie with those giving their life and blood to combat tyranny. He criticized the isolationists and said his administration would support our friends the best we could. Of course, I knew whose side my father was on. I had spent enough time with him and his friend Gerald Nye to know their devotion to isolationism.

"Now that the doors were once again open to the public, the question was for how long? Consul General Lee did not know. 'We will stay here and operate as an official arm of the United States government until Secretary of State Cordell Hull and the State Department tell us otherwise.' Wartime activities had ceased in Holland. It was safe to walk up and down the streets. Seyss-Inquart stated that he intended to govern the Netherlands with a 'velvet glove,' and for a while he did. But it was only for a short while.

"There were even some who traveled from Denmark to Holland to visit the consulate. The minister had left the US embassy in Copenhagen a month after the Nazis took over. But at the consulate, we were busier than ever. We were now the only US consulate in the Netherlands. When the Germans carpet-bombed Rotterdam, they destroyed the US consulate along with most of the buildings in the city.

"When the Rotterdam consulate was destroyed, so were all the records. All the applications for visas, along with all the records submitted by each of the applicants, went up in smoke. Those people had to start all over, and they came to Amsterdam to do it. We had to try to resurrect their applications. Some of them had copies of documents, but many had submitted their originals, and they had no way of getting more copies.

"There was a high level of tension inside our consulate. Those who were in line and had appointments did not want to give way to people who had been in line with appointments in Rotterdam. And these people were desperate. Each person had a hardship story to tell. Each person had an 'urgent' personal reason to have their papers processed. When we couldn't grant their request, some of the visitors lost control and created a scene. It was necessary to hire additional security guards.

"Maybe the decision to hire two more security guards was partially due to the incident I had with a man from Iowa. I was in my office, and I heard this man hollering and slamming his hand against a table. I ran downstairs to find that he was in Julia's face. 'I want a damn passport,' he screamed. 'I'm a goddamn United States citizen, lady, so gimme my passport or else! I'm entitled to it, I know my rights, and I ain't leaving till I get it.' I quickly moved in front of him and said, 'It's time to go, fellow. Calm down.' He threw me aside and then he took a swing at me. I had no choice but to hit him. I decked him, he hit the floor hard, and I held him there until our security guards came and took him away. I hadn't done that kind of thing in a long time, but the man was out of control."

"You punched the man?" Karyn said. Teddy nodded. "Good for you, the guy had it coming."

Teddy smiled. "Julia thought so too. She called me her hero. And I got a reward. Willem and Julia bought us dinner at the Majestic that night."

"So, you're saying it was getting tense inside the consulate?"

He nodded. "Very tense. That's why we needed extra security. These people were caught in the middle of a war, and they wanted to go home. Enough of the windmills and tulips. They wanted to go back to Nebraska or Vermont or whatever state they came from, and they wanted their government to get them there. Some of the people who entered the consulate were in need of medical attention, and all we could do was refer them to Dutch hospitals. Some were American travelers who were requesting that we help them find passage back to America. I wished we could. We weren't set up to do that, and travel to and from Europe had become almost impossible. If you were stuck in the Netherlands, there was nowhere else you could go. To the north, the Germans occupied Denmark. To the south they occupied Belgium and France. Germany was to the east, and on the west was the North Sea, patrolled by German warships.

"Later that afternoon, Frank Lee asked me into his office. He told me he'd received a cable from Undersecretary of State Sumner Welles.

Arrangements had been made for me to talk to my father, who was scheduled to place an overseas call to Consul General Lee at four o'clock in the afternoon. Frank said that I could use his office when the call came in. The first thing I thought was that my mother had died. I was so upset; it was hard to wait until four o'clock. I went into his office at four, and Frank stepped out to give me privacy.

"'Theodore, it's your dad.'

"I quickly said, 'How's Mom?'

"'How's Mom? That's the first thing out of your mouth? She's fine. And so am I, thank you very much.'

"'Oh, I'm sorry, Dad, I didn't mean anything by that. I just thought that maybe the call was placed because Mom had taken ill or something, you know. It's kinda crazy here. Things are real tense.'

"'I'm aware. There's a war going on over there and you're in the middle it. Those goddamm Nazis are taking over the whole eastern hemisphere. You have to get your ass out of there right away. I talked to Sumner, and he thinks he can arrange it. There's a military flight scheduled to take off tomorrow. There's one extra seat and I convinced Sumner to let you on. Believe me, that will cost me a dinner or two.'

"The things my dad could accomplish never stopped amazing me. The Nazis were in control of the Amsterdam airport, and my dad could get me on a plane to America? 'Dad, are you talking about Schiphol Airport, the one I flew into? It's held by the Nazis.'

"'Skipples. Yeah, that's the one. Don't worry, you have diplomatic immunity. The Krauts are just as happy to get Americans out of there. A military plane is leaving from there tomorrow, bringing several US government employees home. Including you. You can thank Undersecretary Welles when you get here.'

"There was a long silence. Then he said, 'Son, are you listening to me?'

"'Dad, I can't go. I can't leave Amsterdam right now.'

"'Are you nuts? You get your ass on that plane, do you hear me?'

"'I can't, Dad. There's lots of reasons. I have an important job here, and I—'

"He quickly interrupted me. 'Don't worry about the dumb consulate. You want to worry about that job? Your mom's been screaming at me twenty-four/seven because I was the one who put you in Amsterdam in the first place.'

"'And I'm very appreciative, Dad, but I can't go. There's someone else. I'm in a serious relationship with a woman and her child. She's Dutch.'

"Now there was another long pause. Then he said, 'Oh, Christ. This sounds like another Betsy McCutcheon. How do you let all these girls get you in trouble? I guess you should have listened to the first one. The McCutcheons would have placed you in a job in Washington.'

"'No, Dad, this one is special. I love Sara very much, and I love little Katy, and I can't leave them here. I'm sorry.'

"'I understand,' he said softly, 'and I respect you for it. I'll deal with your mother. Take care of yourselves, please. Those Nazis are for real. Come home whenever you can.'

"'Thank you, Dad. I love you.'"

CHAPTER TWENTY-NINE

"I THOUGHT LONG and hard about the call with my father and his statement, 'Nazis are for real.' Denmark surrendered on April 10, the Netherlands surrendered on May 15, Belgium surrendered on May 28, and France surrendered and signed an armistice on June 25. Four countries in just eighty days, and Hitler now owned the continent. My father's offer to get me a plane ride out of there was a gift that I hadn't been able to accept. Who knew when that opportunity would come again?

"On the other hand, it was summertime, and the Dutch were doing the best they could to enjoy Amsterdam and all of its charm. If you didn't know any better, you'd think the situation hadn't changed. We would take Katy for rides in her stroller almost every evening, or I would walk with her on my shoulders, both with a mandatory stop at Koco's, her favorite ice-cream shop. It was owned by two Jews who escaped Nazi Germany, Ernst Kahn and Alfred Cohn. It was immensely popular and sometimes we had to wait for a long time, but Katy loved it so much, it was worth it.

"On occasion, Sylvia would come with us on our walks. She still worked at the crèche and now had a boyfriend named Avram. The Dutch economy was picking up. German companies and the German government itself were placing large orders with Dutch companies. Avram had a job in the petroleum industry and he was doing well. Unless you worked for the consulate, it might be possible for you to stay in your little innocent world and put all the politics out of your mind. That was not possible for me.

"Seyss-Inquart was promoting a false complacency. He gave a speech on May 29. He said that the new Dutch government would respect the Dutch institutions and the rights of the Dutch people. Saul was a political science professor, a lifetime Dutchman, and he knew better. He knew what the Nazis had done in the countries that they conquered, and how they imposed their racist laws. He predicted similar treatment and warned that the Nazis would chip away at our liberties, little by little. He was convinced that they would try to turn a Dutch country into a German satellite. In the consulate, to the extent we could intercept them, we kept track of Berlin's orders to its commanders in its occupied countries. Seyss-Inquart was following orders and he was only too happy to do so. For example, right from the start, he banned organizations like socialism and communism. In June, he laid down the first of the official anti-Semitic orders. All Jews must be removed from their positions as civil defense workers. I couldn't help but fear that this was step number one and exactly the type of progressive persecution that Saul had talked about. One repressive act would lead to another.

"In mid-July we had dinner with Saul and Deborah at their home. It was nice to have an occasion to leave the apartment and travel to Utrecht. We arrived early in the afternoon and Saul was in the middle of a meeting with some of his students in his study. On their way out he introduced me to them, including David Cohen, who I would contact again at a later time. The introduction was strange. Saul said, 'David, I'd like you to meet Mr. and Mrs. Hartigan. Theodore is an officer at the United States consulate in Amsterdam, should you ever need their services.' I thought, *What an odd introduction. He didn't say 'My daughter and her fiancé.'* Then I realized that Saul did not want Sara and me to be identified as Jews or even members of his family to any outsiders. It was a precaution, and I thought it was overboard, but Saul was educated in European history, and his studies had covered the come and go of European despots. I would honor his wishes.

"He told me that he and his students had been discussing steps to protect organizations, including Jewish organizations, that the Nazis were trying to eliminate. The German occupiers had implemented a policy of *Gleichschaltung*, which you can translate as 'enforced conformity or coordination.' They were systematically eliminating any non-Nazi organizations. The Germans had already taken steps to outlaw socialist and communist parties. The Jewish organizations would be next. And of course, he was right. Six months later they would expand *Gleichschaltung* to forbid all political or religious organizations except for the NSB, the National Socialist Movement in the Netherlands. Saul knew about the NSB, that fascist organization, because it was formed in Utrecht in the 1930s. They were staunch allies of the Nazis.

"*Gleichschaltung* was an enormous shock to the Dutch, who traditionally had separate institutions for all main religious groups. The Dutch called it *verzuiling,* which meant 'pillarization,' the vertical separation of groups by religion and associated political beliefs. The Nazis' policy of *Gleichschaltung* was contrary to Dutch pillarization and was particularly offensive to Catholics and Protestants, Holland's major religions. Roman Catholics were urged by their Dutch bishops to stay away from any associations that had been Nazified. But according to the Nazis, it was NSB or nothing.

"After the young men had left Saul's house, he explained to me that those students were forming a secret resistance group. They were soliciting members and they wanted Saul's advice. They intended to take whatever measures they could to combat the Nazi exclusion orders. As I sat there in his study sipping on my glass of brandy, I expected that he and I would talk political science all night long, but I was wrong. Saul informed me that Deborah was preparing a very special dinner and that was why the girls were taking so long in the kitchen. Since it was to be a surprise, we were not allowed to come out of the study.

"While we waited, Saul had lots of questions about my life growing up in Washington. He wanted to know about my father. I could tell him lots of things, but I wasn't about to bring up his politics or the America First Committee. Saul saw me hesitate, and politely switched over to baseball. Was I a Washington Senators fan? Of course. Who was my favorite player? Why, Buddy Lewis, who batted .320 and led the team with ten home runs! 'Hmm,' Saul said, 'I guess that's pretty good, but didn't Hank Greenberg hit thirty-three homers last year?' I laughed. 'Keeping track of the Jewish players?' I said. He laughed as well. Just then there was a knock at the door.

"I was startled, but he wasn't. We walked upstairs and opened the door for Rabbi Becker. 'Aren't we doing this outside?' the rabbi said. Saul shook his head. 'No, inside.' Then he looked at me and he said, 'Congratulations, you're about to get married.'

"As Saul would later tell me, I looked like I was going to pass out. He and Deborah had arranged the whole thing. Neither Sara nor I had any inclination. Saul had hurriedly arranged it because he didn't want us getting married in a civil ceremony, and he didn't want us getting married at the Majestic Hotel, or anywhere there might be a record, or even anywhere people might see us. This was to be a private wedding, and the rabbi, Saul, Deborah, Sylvia, and Katy were the only witnesses. There would be no basis for the Nazis to claim that a Jewish Dutch girl married a Protestant American man. When we walked out the door at the end of the evening, we would be Mr. and Mrs. Hartigan, American citizens, for real, and there was no way for the Nazis to know otherwise.

"'But we're not both American citizens,' I said to Saul.

"Saul nodded. 'I can't do that part. You'll take care of it. I'm sure you'll figure out a way.'

"We walked into Saul's living room, where he had constructed a chuppah, made of four posts holding up a sheet and decorated with flowers from his garden. Saul and I walked in first and stood with the rabbi under the chuppah. I wore a yarmulke. My first time. Deborah and Sylvia joined us. Sara walked in from the other room, looking more gorgeous than ever, and circled around me seven times, a custom I had never witnessed before. We shared a sip from the first cup of wine. The service was short and sweet. Katy carried in a ring that Saul had supplied. We said our vows, I stomped on a glass, gave my bride a kiss, and now when we said we were Mr. and Mrs. Hartigan, it was the truth. *Emeth*."

"Beautiful!" Karyn said. "Now you were officially married."

"Well, not officially in Amsterdam, but in America a clergyman has the legal power to marry you, so as far as I was concerned, we were officially married. And, by the way, Holland recognizes foreign marriages. So there."

"Too bad you didn't have the opportunity to go on a honeymoon. What did you do? Could you at least go to the movies?"

"Absolutely not. Immediately following the Nazi invasion, Seyss-Inquart banned all American and British films from all Dutch movie theaters. They were replaced with German newsreels and German films. You could see a film starring Marlene Dietrich but not Janet Gaynor. Some Dutch who attended a movie theater hoping to see *The Wizard of Oz* were shocked to see Wehrmacht soldiers marching down Unter den Linden to military music, and a movie called *Yud Sus,* a filthy racist propaganda film with vicious lies about Jews. So despicable, I won't even describe it to you. Patrons walked out booing. So what did Seyss-Inquart do? He passed a law making it illegal to boo. As you might imagine, people stopped going to the movies altogether."

"Good for them," Karyn said. "It must have made you proud that the Dutch behaved in that way. Were there other ways that the Dutch refused to become assimilated into German culture?"

"The Dutch considered themselves Dutch, not German. In many ways they were looking forward to the day that the Germans would go away, and things would return to normal. The Dutch were proud of their culture and would show it whenever they could. For example, on Prince Bernhard's birthday, many Dutch wore orange carnations. Orange was the symbol of Queen Wilhelmina's royal family. And the Dutch were proud of Prince Bernhard. When the Nazis invaded, Prince Bernhard stood outside the Royal Castle shooting at the Germans. When Queen Wilhelmina and her family left for England to form a government in exile, Prince Bernhard wanted to stay and fight, but the queen ordered him to go, and he helped her rule from England. The Dutch loved him for that. When the Dutch mailed their letters, they put their stamps on the upper left-hand corner because the upper right-hand corner was reserved solely for the stamp of Queen Wilhelmina.

"These were the quiet, subtle gestures that showed the solidarity of the Dutch people and that they stood uniformly behind the royal family. Symbolic gestures showed that their hearts remained true to the Netherlands. Symbolic gestures showed they didn't believe in Nazism, and they believed that the occupation would end, and they would return to their Dutch way of life. They listened to radio broadcasts of Queen Wilhelmina from London until they were jammed and until radios were taken away. As proof of Dutch loyalty, when the Nazi Party openly solicited new

members in Holland, only one and a half percent of the Dutch population joined the Dutch Nazi Party. In 1943, when university students were
required to sign an oath of loyalty to the occupying forces, over eighty-
five percent refused to sign."

CHAPTER THIRTY

"I BROUGHT YOU some doughnuts and a cup of coffee," Karyn said to Teddy as they began a brand-new day. "You look all perky this morning."

"Yeah. I'm feeling better, thank you. I had a good night's sleep, but it was filled with wild dreams, like I was still there."

"Good dreams or bad dreams?"

"A little of both."

"Before we start the next chapter in the life story of Theodore Hartigan and his wife and child, I have a personal question, if you don't mind," Karyn said.

"I don't mind, but I know where you're going. And the answer is: I don't have any answers. I'm still trying, but none of my contacts have been able to come up with any information about your sister Annie. I'm sorry. Maybe this whole thing has been a waste of your time."

"Not at all. I gave you my word that I would write your story. This is your history, but it's also my history, and it's much more than I ever knew about what happened to my people when I was a baby. You know, when you tell me about Katy, I think that could be my story too."

"I know. I also see the similarities. Anyway, don't give up hope. I haven't given up. I'm still trying. So, if you're ready, shall we plow ahead?"

"By all means."

"You remember that Seyss-Inquart promised to rule Holland with a velvet glove. He promised he wouldn't make any significant changes in the way the Dutch ran their lives. He was a liar, but he suckered the citizens into believing he was telling the truth. For example, in the months following the Nazi invasion, Dutch Jewry continued to enjoy the benefit of 'equal citizenship under Dutch law.' That's what he promised, and at the beginning, the Dutch Jews were suckered in. But inch by inch, their rights were taken from them. First in small steps, then in big steps and then giant steps.

"In September 1940, it was decreed that Jews could no longer be hired as civil service workers, but those who were already serving in civil service positions could keep their jobs. The Dutch felt that was unfair, but no Dutch workers were dismissed. So it was a little step. However, just two months later, all Jews were dismissed from civil service including the chief justice of the Dutch Supreme Court and forty-one university professors. A giant step."

"What about Saul? Did they order the university to dismiss Saul?"

"They did not, not at that time. I don't know how the Nazis made their selections. Students and fellow professors protested. Between September and November 1940, Jewish newspapers were shut down, and the assets of all Jewish businesses had to be registered.

"Professor Rudolph Cleveringa, Saul's good friend, was a professor of law at Leiden University. On November 26, 1940, he delivered a speech in which he protested against the dismissal of his colleagues at Leiden University. The speech was so impressive that within a few days, a copy was secretly distributed throughout the Netherlands. He inspired many students to commit acts of resistance, but the firings were not reversed. The Leiden students decided to strike and then the Nazis closed the university. It didn't reopen until after the war. Cleveringa himself was arrested and imprisoned in the summer of 1941 in the prison of Scheveningen, used for members of the Dutch resistance and nicknamed 'the Orange Hotel.'"

"IT WAS IN late January 1941 when the true Nazi intentions were revealed. Saul's predictions were on the money. One hundred percent.

"We did receive information that the Nazis were planning to order the registration of all the Jews in the entire country. Jews were going to be ordered to register in the municipality where they lived. That would mean Saul, Deborah, Sylvia, and her boyfriend Avram would all have to register at the Utrecht city hall. We were at Saul's home when we found out.

"'Why,' Sara asked in a plaintive tone. 'Why should we have to register at city hall or anywhere else? No one else has to register.'

"I looked at Saul and I feared what he was going to say. He knew the history of the Jews in Poland, Austria, and Czechoslovakia. 'Register, separate, and persecute,' Saul said. 'That is their way. But not you, my darling Sara. You're not a Jew. You're a Christian from Washington, DC, named Sara Hartigan, isn't that right, Teddy?'

"I nodded, hoping our charade would work. 'She's my wife and won't have to register,' I said. 'I'll make it right.' But now I was stumped. How could make it right? How could I prove that she was my wife and lived in the US? She didn't have a US passport or any other documents showing her residence in America. And how could I prove that she was a Protestant? Just because her husband was doesn't mean that she was. The only solution that came to mind was my father. Maybe he could contact Pastor Groves at St. Patrick's Church and ask him to give me something in writing which said that Sara, Mrs. Theodore Hartigan, was a member of the church. Could my father accomplish that for me? Would he? I cabled him that night with the strange request. I had no way of knowing if it would be granted.

"What if Pastor Groves asked my father if Sara was a convert? But I couldn't ask Sara to convert to Protestantism in Utrecht for any number of reasons. One, there would be a record for the Nazis to discover. Two, she wouldn't believe in a conversion and it would be under false pretenses. And three, she wouldn't do it anyway.

"As we worried about whether my father could get a church identification, the Nazis turned up the heat. On February 2, 1941, on the order of Arthur Seyss-Inquart, so-called governor of the Netherlands, formally announced that all Jewish people within the borders of the Netherlands must immediately register with their municipality as Jews. From that information, the government intended to construct maps identifying the name, age, gender, marital status, and location of all Jews living in each city and town.

"'You're not going to obey that order and register, are you?' I said to

Saul. 'What if all the Jews refuse? Just not show up? What could they do about that?' Saul gave me a shrug and said, 'What's the difference? If we don't comply, they'll consider that disobedience and grounds for punishment. Then they'll get the information some other way. Religion is already in the nationwide census records. Or they could go to the synagogues and get their records of their members, like they did in Poland. Utrecht University has my information on file, and it has my religion. If we hand over the information willingly, they may accept that as complete, and further orders would be unnecessary.'

"Now Saul's previous warnings made perfect sense. That's why the wedding had to be so secret. I was sorry that my bride did not get the fancy wedding she dreamed of, but she wasn't disappointed. She said that her wedding was the prettiest wedding she had ever attended. And the safest. If an order came in the future to have all the Jews line up at some specific place or time, they would check them all off according to the registration. They wouldn't see Sara's name. She'd be with me in Amsterdam as Mrs. Hartigan.

"As it happened, the Dutch Jews had no idea why they were being asked to register, but they had already done it once, so almost all of them did what they were told to do. By August 1941, the numbers were added up: 140,552 Jews, 14,549 half Jews, and 5,719 quarter Jews. 160,820 registrations in all. In April 1941, the Zentralstelle für Jüdische Auswanderung (Central Office for Jewish Emigration) was established to keep track of the Jews. Little did the people know the Central Office for Jewish Emigration was established for the purpose of deporting Jews from the Netherlands."

CHAPTER THIRTY-ONE

"AS I SAID, the registration of all Jews was first ordered on February 2, 1941. A week after that, nine months after the German occupation, the first organized anti-Jewish riots began. Groups of punks from the NSB roamed the streets looking for trouble. They sought confrontations with young Jewish groups. This resulted in numerous fights.

"On several occasions, Sara and I were awakened by street noise. Shouts, broken glass, police sirens, sounds of a riot, all made it impossible to stay calm. Katy was especially agitated. It must have brought to mind the same noise, the same screams, the same scenes that she witnessed before coming to Holland. On those riot nights, she would spend the rest of the night in our bed, shaking and weeping. Who knew what horrors she'd experienced before coming to us.

"First it only happened in the middle of the night, then more openly, at any time. These NSB rioters would walk through the Jewish neighborhoods, shouting insults and causing damage. They knocked over garbage cans, tore down mailboxes, pushed sculptures and statues into the streets and the canals. These racist acts did not go uncontested, however. Members of the Jewish communities formed their own defense groups to stand up to the attacks. But that would result in even more violent street battles.

"On February 11, an NSB member was badly injured in one of the street battles and he died a few days later. The anti-Semitic press blamed it all on the Jews. The street fights were out of control and lasted for days. The Amsterdam police were called in to calm down one area, but then the NSB moved to a different area. Nazi Party members posted signs in shop and café windows throughout Amsterdam and Utrecht that read 'Jews Not Wanted' or 'Jews Stay Out!'

"There were arrests, there were more fights, and there were more casualties. One night during a violent clash, the Dutch Nazi Hendrik Koot was badly injured, and he later died. In retaliation for Koot's death, Nazi officers in long green coats and high boots, called the Green Police, randomly grabbed four hundred Jewish men off the streets during a two-day sweep. They forced them into trucks and drove them away.

"The next morning, Julia knocked at my office door. Consul General Lee was out of town, presumably at the embassy, and I was in charge. Julia walked in with a middle-aged woman who was so distraught, she could barely stand up straight. Julia said she had come into the consulate crying. I pulled out a chair for her and said, 'What can I do for you, ma'am?'

"'Please, please help me,' she said. 'They're after me. The Nazis. They're going to kill me or send me away.'

"I tried to calm her down and gave her a glass of water. She said her name was Francine Anderson, wife of Dennis Anderson, a vice president of Western Oil Company, and they were both American citizens. Western was an American company with manufacturing and drilling facilities in the Netherlands. They had come here several years ago. 'In the midst of the street battles,' she said, 'members of the NSB came by and wanted the keys to Western's offices. No one on the premises had the authority or the codes to let them in. They took four of the workers and were obviously torturing them. They finally gave in and said that Dennis had the codes.'

"She stood up and held on to the corner of my desk. She leaned over and shouted, 'You have to help us! You are the United States embassy, aren't you?'

"'Sort of,' I said, 'but please sit down, and calmly tell me what happened to Dennis.'

"She took a sip of water, and a deep breath, and nodded. 'They came to the house, the same house we've lived in for twelve years, and hammered on the door. Dennis came out and they instantly grabbed him. Before they left, one of them said, 'Take his wife with us. Then he'll tell us what we need to know.' I knew that voice. It was one of the teenagers in our neighborhood. Dennis said I wasn't home. They searched the house for a while, but I was hiding in a closet. They said they would come back for me later.'

"With that she broke down. 'I can't go home,' she said. 'They'll kill me. You have to get me back to Houston.'

"Now I was in a fix. I didn't know what I could do. I didn't even know what Frank Lee could do. All I could do was say, 'You're safe here. You can stay here until we figure something out.'"

Karyn wrinkled her forehead. "Did you have the right to do that; to let a stranger, without credentials, stay in the consulate?"

Teddy gave one of Julia's tilted shrugs and said, "Probably not. But what was I going to do?"

"THE STREET VIOLENCE kept up. Shortly thereafter, unknown thugs smashed the windows of the Koco ice-cream shop. It's a good thing that Katy and I weren't planning on going that day. Koco was such a well-loved parlor that Jewish and non-Jewish customers formed their own assault team to protect the store. When the punks, which included German officers, raided the shop on February 19, the defense team sprayed their faces with ammonia. The German authorities were not about to put up with an attack on their officers. To put an end to the unrest, they decided to hold a roundup of Jews during the weekend of February 22 and 23.

"At the consulate, all Jewish staffers were advised to stay inside until the riots were over. That meant, stay the night! All staffers, Jewish and non-Jewish, were given that opportunity. The rioters were violently anti-Jewish, but they weren't fond of the United States either. That evening, Sara, Katy, and I all slept in my office at the consulate. We rolled out some bedding on the floor and did not go home until daylight. Julia, who felt safer staying with Willem in his residence at the Majestic than at her desk on the first floor, brought us some breakfast."

"I can understand why the consulate was a lot safer, with its armed guards, but why would it be safer at the Majestic?" Karyn asked.

"Well, for one thing, the Majestic was a famous, well-respected hotel that was frequented by German hotel guests, including German officers.

The director of marketing was Dietrich Schultz, a German national, re-member? You remember the confrontation I had with the German army officers the night we announced our engagement? Additionally, the Majestic had beefed up its own security force. The people of Amsterdam were shocked and angered that the ruling Nazi authorities would permit these roaming rioters to commit such crimes. 'Permit' is really not an accurate term. We knew at the consulate that the rioters were equipped, supported, and encouraged by the Nazis.

"We learned that night that the Jews who were arrested were taken to Camp Schoorl. From there, many were deported to the Buchenwald camp in Germany, and from there they were sent to the Mauthausen concentration camp in Austria. Only two of them survived. The Jewish owners of Koco ice-cream shop were severely dealt with. Ernst Cahn was executed by the Germans near The Hague on March 3, 1941. We also later found out that Alfred Cohn died in Auschwitz. Sara and I, who had spent many happy days with Katy at the Koco, were extremely saddened by the news."

CHAPTER THIRTY-TWO

"AT OR ABOUT the time of the February strike, the Nazis demanded that a Jewish Council be formed, which was to be called Joodse Raad in Dutch. It was very similar to the Judenrat the Nazis had set up for Jews in Nazi Germany and in occupied Poland. They were ostensibly councils that resolved problems between the ruling Nazis and Jewish citizens. They were told they would be helping the Jews. The Germans wanted the Jews to be represented by a single body, so that when they issued an order, it could be quickly communicated to the Jewish community. The Joodse Raad was also established to assist the Nazis when it came time to relocate Jewish families to Westerbork or farther east to the German camps. The Germans worked through the Joodse Raad to effectuate their rules or orders quickly and peacefully. Many times, the governing Nazis would expect the Jewish Council to refer any Jews that were intentionally disobeying Nazi orders to the authorities, although such referrals rarely occurred. The Jewish Council in the Netherlands was run by a board of Jews, headed by Professor David Cohen and Abraham Asscher. I told you, I had met David Cohen before. He and some other men were at Saul's house when I was introduced to them.

"Eight years previous, in 1933, Asscher and Cohen had organized independent Jewish organizations, such as the Committee for Jewish Refugees in the Netherlands. They were set up to assist those fleeing Germany, but now in 1941, Nazis closed those organizations."

Karyn held up a hand. "I have a question. It makes no sense to me. Why would such good men agree to serve on a Jewish council to implement the Nazi orders or relocation? That sounds like leading them to a gas chamber."

"It does, and in some ways, it was. Those who served on the Jewish Council were convinced they were helping the Jews and doing a service, and in many ways they were. The Jewish Council was created to implement orders peacefully and calmly. It's true they served as an instrument for organizing, identifying, and deporting Jews more efficiently. But their existence prevented the Nazis from running through the Jewish neighborhoods, damaging property, injuring people, grabbing whomever they could, breaking up families, taking mothers from children. Because of the existence of Joodse Raad, the Nazis agreed to act in a more civil manner. Many times it was the Jewish Council that selected people to be deported. I know it sounds awful, but Cohen and Asscher believed they were doing a good service. In the second half of 1941, the Joodse Raad was forced to provide lists of Jews to work in forced labor camps for the German war effort."

"SEYSS-INQUART WAS A man who talked out of both sides of his mouth. While he was installing a Jewish Council to resolve problems with Jews, he was a true Nazi who believed that Jews were the enemy. He gave a speech before the Nazi Party in Germany." Teddy pulled a piece of paper out of his folder and passed it forward for Karyn to read. It was a portion of Seyss-Inquart's speech. She read:

And I would like to take this opportunity to say something about the Jewish question. We do not consider the Jews to be members of the Dutch nation. To us, the Jews are not Dutch. The Jews are the enemy with whom no armistice or peace can be drawn. And would that make a difference? Do not expect me to lay this down in a regulation except in police measures. We will smite the Jews where we meet them and whoever goes along with them must take the consequences.

CHAPTER THIRTY-THREE

"IN THE SPRING of 1941, Sara asked me if I could watch Katy for the evening. Dr. van Hulst had asked her and the other teachers to join him for dinner. It seemed more like a faculty meeting than a casual social affair. Of course, I said I would be happy to stay with Katy. We went to a local sandwich shop where Katy had a chicken sandwich and a chocolate cookie. I asked her about her day at the crèche and she told me all about a picture that she was drawing, and it would be done soon. And she had been with Sylvia for part of the day. She loved her time at the crèche.

"When Sara came home, she gave me a summary of the faculty dinner. It was evident from the discussions that the situation at the Reformed Teacher Training College was tenuous. She said, 'Dr. van Hulst began the evening with a very nice dinner, and he asked everyone to please call him Johan. During dinner, talk was light, and it wasn't until we finished that Dr. van Hulst became serious. The subject matter then became worrisome, and we all realized why we were brought together.'"

"Oh no," Karyn said, "did he say that they were ordered to dismiss all the Jewish students?"

"No, he didn't. He wouldn't abide by such an order anyway, but it wouldn't be a major issue at the Reformed Teacher Training College," Teddy replied. "From the moment the Nazis invaded, Dr. van Hulst refused to abide by Nazi orders forcing teachers and students to sign the Nazi loyalty oath. Dr. van Hulst wouldn't even pass the signature pages around. He threw them away. Sara told me that the problem he wanted to discuss at the faculty dinner was one he couldn't ignore. The Department of Education was required to cut off the school's public funding.

Unless the students' families would agree to pay tuition, Johan would have to close the doors. He told us that he'd sent messages home with each of the students and he would wait for their answers. Then he lowered his eyes and said, 'I'm sure you know how that hurts me. Without additional funding, I can't pay you your salaries beyond the end of March, and I can't ask you to work without pay.'

"Sara said that she and other teachers told him that they were confident that funding would be found somewhere. It would come out of grants or tuitions or donations, but until that happened, they would continue to teach. Most of the other teachers were also happy to agree.

"I asked Sara what Dr. van Hulst's response was to the teachers' loyalty, and she told me that he cried. 'He praised us all on how dedicated to teaching and how generous we were, but we all knew he would do the same thing. He was that kind of man. Honest, principled; he would always stand up for what was right. And so would we.'

"I said, 'That's my girl,' and I hugged her for about an hour."

"THE RECENT VIOLENCE in the streets of Amsterdam had turned the city upside down. The city was on fire, figuratively speaking. A once calm, beautiful, picturesque haven had been transformed into a place of dangerous neighborhoods where shootings, beatings, even murders were commonplace. People asked why? We had surrendered. Where were the Dutch police? If the Nazis had intended the Netherlands to become a German state, why would they want to destroy it? How could it possibly serve the German interests for the citizens to harbor hate and disgust of the German rulers? It didn't make any sense. Apparently, the Nazis didn't care.

"But the citizens did. A few days later, a major strike was organized in protest of the continuing violence and the failure of the police to keep order. On February 25, 1941, the local section of the CPN, the Communist Party of the Netherlands, which had already been declared illegal by the Nazis, called a two-day strike in protest of the raid on the Jewish men a few days earlier. The action started with the shutdown of the tram transport in Amsterdam, which was how many Dutch traveled to work.

The Municipal Workers of Amsterdam, a CPN union, essentially shut down public transportation throughout the city. Over the course of two days, the strike intensified as metal and shipyard workers, white-collar workers, and manual laborers joined in the strike. It continued from Tuesday through Thursday, spreading all the way to Utrecht, to The Hague, and across the country. The CPN did something that remains to this day the only such general anti-pogrom strike to have occurred in Nazi-occupied Europe.

"The Nazis were dumbfounded by the protests. This was not something that they had ever experienced in any of their conquered countries. And the reasons for such disobedience were unknown to them. Why would the Dutch put themselves at risk in support of Jewish men? They couldn't understand that. In response, the Nazi rulers decided to turn up the heat. They sent their soldiers out into the streets, not to calm down the situation and bring about peace, but to shoot and kill the strikers. Those that weren't killed were arrested, put into German trucks, and driven to German prison camps. The cities where the strikes took place were heavily fined and the residents were forced to pay."

"ON ORDERS FROM Washington, Consul General Lee called a staff meeting and advised us that although the decision had not been made, there were forces in Washington urging us to close down the Netherlands embassy and consulate. Not that they were afraid that the Nazis would attack us; they had German embassies and German financial interests in America. Hitler was not interested in antagonizing America. The politicians who wanted us out of Europe did not fear for our embassies, they simply felt that we had no business in the Netherlands or anywhere else in Europe. These were basically the conservative America First politicians. Several in Washington, including my father and his friends, wanted us to pull out of all European entanglements altogether. They didn't want us there, so why should we go there at risk of our lives? And to be sure, they wanted nothing to do with getting mixed up in another war with Germany. My father and his friends were good men, they just thought the wrong way.

"Consul General Lee gave us the news that the State Department had tightened its rules and instituted additional restrictions on further immigration in 1941, citing national security concerns. One of the rules hit home. Any refugee with close family still in enemy territory would be ineligible for a US immigration visa. That was us!

"In the meantime, if a consulate officer was working on a specific visa and had received all the required information and was all ready to issue the visa, he would be unable to do so if the applicant had family in a Nazi-occupied country like the Netherlands. At the same time, the State Department announced that all visa applicants, regardless of where they lived, had to be approved by an interdepartmental visa review committee in Washington, DC. This decision applied to those who were granted visas in the Netherlands. Even if they could find a way to get home, they couldn't leave until the visa review committee gave its approval. It also applied to people who had received their visas and were on their way back to America. It was bound to lengthen the delays even for those refugees who had a visa and had managed to make it all the way to southern France or Lisbon, the only places in Europe from which they could embark to America. Finally, Lee went over procedures for all staffers to take in the event we were ordered to close the consulate.

"I sat there wondering whether Sara and Katy would be considered refugees or a US citizen's family members. In fact, they were a US State Department consular officer's family members. They were *my* family members."

"I have a question," said Karyn, with her index finger in the air. "What happened to Mrs. Anderson? The last thing you said was that she came into the consulate in bad shape, not being able to return to her home because the Nazis were looking for her, and she wanted to go home to Houston. So you let her sleep in the consulate, and that was against the rules."

"I caught major shit on that one. Frank Lee was out of the city at the time, and I was the acting chargé d'affaires, meaning I was responsible for the consul general's duties. Francine Anderson came to me for help. What was I supposed to do? What would you do? I remember Sumner Welles saying to me, 'Make a difference.'"

Karyn smiled. "Imagine if you let in all the people who were in trouble and didn't have a place to stay?"

"Well, that's what Frank Lee said to me. That, and a lot of other stuff. She couldn't stay in the building; Frank made that clear. So he sent Julia to locate an apartment for her in the city, and Frank sent a couple of security men with her to pick up her belongings. She didn't get to Houston, but she at least had a safe place to stay. It turned out she was a nice lady. A grandmother."

CHAPTER THIRTY-FOUR

"THE NEXT MORNING, March 13, I met Julia at the consulate. She asked me how the family was doing. I replied, 'Frazzled. It seems like the whole continent is going from bad to worse.' Then I asked her, 'Are you going to stay here in Amsterdam if the consulate closes?'

"She gave me one of those tilted shrugs. 'I don't know. I'm taking it day by day, Teddy,' she said. 'There hasn't been a final decision on closing either the embassy or the consulate. I understand that there is talk about withdrawal from all continental European countries, but mostly that's in isolationist circles, mostly Republicans. Roosevelt, Hull, and Welles are Democrats and they're firm on keeping us open. What are you going to do if they do decide to close the consulate?'

"'I'd be in a fix,' I said. 'I'm waiting to hear from my father to see if there's any way he could arrange to get all three of us home in the event the consulate closes. He said he would reach out to the people he knows. He's pretty influential in those circles, but to be frank, it would be a long shot, even for a powerful Republican like Papa Hartigan. Sara and Katy don't have passports or visas. Sara is Jewish and a citizen of the Netherlands. Katy is stateless. Sara and I are not legally married, but even if we were married in the Royal Palace and had a valid Netherlands marriage license, I'm not hopeful that would make any difference. We can apply for a visa here, even on an emergency basis, and I can pull some strings, but the bottom line is, it would have to be issued out of Washington where the State Department has placed a hold on these things. Maybe my father can work miracles. What about you?'

"'What do you think? I'm not in a bind like you are, I'm free to pick up and go home to Detroit, but I'm sort of tied down with Willem. I don't want to leave him. And like Sara, he's in Nazi Holland. Willem's family owns the hotel, and he and I have already talked, obliquely I guess, about maybe tying the knot, you know, maybe someday. Raising our kids here. Don't say anything about that to Willem, you promise? But no one knows the future, and if Seyss-Inquart permanently rules this country, I don't want any part of it. I don't want to stay here.'

"'You know, Julia, I keep looking for the bright side, but I can't find one. How does this situation change for the better? What can happen, short of a giant insurrection in Germany? An overthrow of Hitler. But I don't see that happening. Hitler is too powerful.'

"Julia nodded. 'He rules with an iron fist. The alternative for us is to leave, and it doesn't sound like either you or I are in a position to do that. Anyway, let's quit talking about the dark side. Do you want to come to dinner tonight?'

"'Are we welcome? According to Seyss-Inquart, Jews are the enemy.'

"'Don't be a jerk, Teddy, and don't ever say that again. You and Sara are my best friends. And remember, as far as any public official knows, the Hartigans are not Jews. They're American Protestants. So I want you and Sara and Katy to come to dinner tonight at the Majestic. We'll raise a glass of wine to better times and the demise of the Nazis, wherever they are!'

"'Great. Check with Willem. If it's okay with him, then we'll be there at the Majestic. But if it's a problem for him, then we'll bow out. I don't blame Willem, he has a business to run, and that crazy Seyss-Inquart would shut him down in a minute if he thought Willem was a Jewish sympathizer.'

"'If Willem has a problem with me inviting my best friends to dinner, he'll have to answer to me! But he won't. Willem is a stand-up guy, a man of principles, or I wouldn't be in love with him. I'll see you all at six thirty.'"

"THE MAJESTIC WAS abuzz. You'd never know there was a war going on. People were dressed in their finery, and the cuisine was served on silver dishes, the finest to be seen in Amsterdam. I guess if you weren't a member of the Jewish community, or out in the Jewish neighborhoods, you would think it was life as usual.

"Julia met us in the lobby and took us into the main dining room. Katy's eyes were as big as quarters. Her lips were tightly formed in a circle as if to say *Ooo*. Her head was swiveling back and forth as she took in all the sights and sounds. She'd never seen anything like this before. Julia led us to a table smack-dab in the middle of the restaurant. The table was set for five, and on one of the seats was a stuffed teddy bear. Katy looked at me and I nodded. 'It's for you from Uncle Willem.' She picked it up and hugged it. Other diners smiled and nudged each other, pointing at Katy. They looked at Sara and nodded, as if to say, *What a darling little girl you have*. No one in the restaurant knew Sara's or Katy's religious affiliations, nor did they care. She was judged for what she was: a sweet little girl.

"Willem joined us in a little bit. He was dressed smartly in a jacket and tie; I always felt like a slob in his presence. But he could carry it off, and after all, he owned the restaurant, or at least his family did. His maître d', Dietrich, also dressed in a jacket and tie, walked by the table. I smiled at him and he smiled in return. Being German, I wondered where his sympathies lay. He lived and worked in Amsterdam. Was he tolerant of the occupation? No doubt they were good for business. They threw guilders around like pennies. Then I mentally scolded myself. Shame on me. I was behaving like those I criticized. I had no more right to prejudge Dietrich than the Nazis did in prejudging Jews.

"In the midst of my mental debate, there was a shout from the other side of the room. A stocky man with broad shoulders stood confrontationally against the next table where an older man was having a quiet dinner with his wife. The shouts and insults fired at the old man were in German, so I really didn't know what he was saying, except I had a pretty good idea. So did everyone else in the room. He took the old man's plate and threw it on the floor, then knocked over his glass of wine. And then he tilted his head and roared in laughter, but he wasn't finished. He ordered the older man to get up.

"I don't know what came over me, but I jumped up and ran to the table. Willem jumped up as well. 'Son of a bitch,' he said under his breath.

The German turned around, ready to fight both of us at one time, but Dietrich appeared out of nowhere, grabbed the German by the back of his collar, and dragged him out of the restaurant like a dog. I heard the man squealing from outside in the street. People in the restaurant quietly clapped.

"A few minutes later, Willem returned, apologizing. 'There's nothing to apologize for,' I said. 'You were a hero. That German was a pig, and he was about to injure that older gentleman.'

"Willem nodded. 'So were you. Sometimes these Wehrmacht guys get out of control. We can't allow that at our hotel. Patrons have to feel that they are safe here.'

"'Aren't you afraid he'll come back with some of his buddies and tear up the place?'

"'Not at all. At any given time, there are German officers dining here. Herr Seyss-Inquart himself dines here often. On occasion, they reserve one of our meeting rooms. The creep that I tossed out begged me not to report him to Seyss-Inquart. I told him that if I ever saw him in here again, I would report him. He knows that he would be sent to the Russian front. Holland is a sweet assignment for him in the war.' Willem looked around and whispered, 'At least so far. Let's hope that changes sooner rather than later.'

"We drank to that.

"From across the room, I noticed Walter Süskind, the head of the Schouwburg, with his wife and children. I waved at him, which was a mistake. He wandered over to our table. 'How nice it is to see you, Mr. Hartigan,' he said, extending his hand. 'I haven't seen you in a while, not since you proposed that we put on *Our Gal Sunday*.'

"I shook my head. 'It was *Anything Goes*. I knew a woman in Washington who might have been interested in underwriting that production, but not anymore.'

"'Well, if she changes her mind, please let me know and I will discuss it with the board. By the way, it's been three years since my family applied at the consulate for a visa. Can you tell me where I stand on the waiting list? I'd appreciate it very much.'

"I took a breath. 'I really don't know offhand, and can't tell you here, but if you come to the consulate, we can look it up. Maybe it's coming soon.' Out of the corner of my eye I saw Julia wince.

"Walter stuck out his hand again, said, 'Thank you very much,' a couple more times, and went back to his table where his wife was waiting."

"TOWARD THE END of our dinner, before dessert had been served, Sara and Julia took Katy for a walk. Willem rose from the table and watched them leave. 'She's a lovely little girl,' he said. 'You are a lucky man.'

"'Thank you. I think so too.'

"Willem leaned forward and quietly said, 'What are you going to do to protect them?'

"'Good question,' I replied. 'Right now, we're sheltered by the United States government. Seyss-Inquart wouldn't dare storm the consulate, or arrest any of the American officers. Hitler doesn't want to do anything to antagonize the United States. Remember, he has a consulate in Washington, DC. Hans Thomsen is the chargé d'affaires operating it.'

"Using one of Julia's expressions, Willem gave me a tilted shrug. 'At the moment that may be true. But I wouldn't count on it in the future. What if America becomes involved in a worldwide dispute? Then the embassy and the consulate are no longer safe zones. What will you do to protect Sara Rosenbaum, a Jewish girl, and yourself, an officer in the State Department? Do you see where I'm going?'

"'Yeah, but you're wrong. That would be Sara Hartigan, the wife of State Department officer Theodore Hartigan. And the answer is, I hope I never have to face that dilemma.'

"'Listen to me, Teddy. Sara has been coming here along with Julia for quite some time, and I love that girl. I don't care whether she is a Rosenbaum or a Hartigan, she is always welcome here, and I will do whatever I can to protect her. Remember that.'

"'I appreciate that very much. I'm just hoping that things don't get any worse than they already are, and that I can hang around in Amsterdam for the balance of my term.'

"The girls returned, and our private discussion was over."

CHAPTER THIRTY-FIVE

"APRIL IS A beautiful month in Holland. The tulips are in bloom, the weather is agreeable, and so are all those things that make Holland a most welcoming place. Except in 1941. Instead of taking a ride down a canal, or riding a bike on a Sunday afternoon, the Dutch lived in fear of what could happen next. This was doubly so for the Jews, and all those who chose to belong to any prohibited association. The consulate continued to operate in all matters affecting United States interests in the Netherlands, and in most matters affecting the rights of US citizens, with the exception of the temporary hold on immigration and nonimmigration visas. In many ways the hold was unnecessary, because it was next to impossible for anyone to travel from Holland to America. Otherwise, we continued to perform consular operations and maintain constant contact with Washington.

"In early April, Sara and I were invited to have dinner with the Rosenbaums at their home in Utrecht. I thought Deborah would burst with joy when we walked in with Katy. She hugged her as only a grandmother could, and twirled her around while Katy squealed. They presented a doll to Katy; a little girl that looked like Katy, with long hair that could be combed with a little plastic brush.

"The chicken dinner, the soup, the vegetable soufflé were all delicious and so was the wine. Just as perfect as I had come to expect and appreciate from the Rosenbaums. After dinner, while the girls were cleaning the kitchen and preparing a dessert, Saul pulled me aside and asked that I join him for a brandy in the study. Uh-oh, I thought. Here it goes again.

"'I know you are very busy,' Saul said. 'Goodness knows these are difficult times to be a representative of a foreign government in Holland, let alone the United States. I don't suppose that you have time to keep track of the Netherlands' internal laws, do you?'

"I shrugged my shoulders. 'No.'

"'Especially those that have recently been passed affecting Dutch citizens, correct?'

"'Well, that's mostly true, although we try to keep informed. I'm sure I'm not aware of all of the laws. Those laws generally affect the Dutch, and we are temporary visitors.'

"Saul held his index finger up and moved it from side to side, as if to say, *Wait a minute.* 'There is one such law that does apply to you, Teddy. One that we should talk about. For many years, people in Holland were free to choose whether they wished to have identity cards or passports, or visas, or any other such papers issued in their name. And they were free to decide whether or not they wanted to carry such identity cards on their person. As of this April, all that has changed.'

"Saul continued, 'At the instruction of the Dutch rulers, and specifically Seyss-Inquart, a man named Jacobus Lentz, who works in the Dutch Ministry of the Interior, has devised and created an official identity card that must be carried at all times by all Dutch persons over the age of fifteen. Now that has become a law. The Dutch name for the card is *persoonbewijs*. The card is so technically advanced and displays such a wealth of information about the holder that it is impossible to fake or alter.'

"Saul pulled a small card out of his pocket. 'As you can see, a small passport photo and a fingerprint are on the face of the card, along with my address and my signature. If there is ever a question if the *persoonbewijs* is genuine or a fake, Lentz has set up a central registry to examine the fabric and determine if the card is real. What's even worse, the card issued for Jews has a large black capital *J* on both sides. I guess you know why. From this date onward, police, German soldiers, or Nazi intelligence agents are authorized to stop any person for any reason whatsoever to check the identity card. If something appears amiss, they are instructed to bring such person directly to the registry.'

"I was shocked. 'That's awful. That's like wearing a badge for everyone to see that says *Don't associate with me* or *Arrest me because I'm a Jew.*'

"Saul nodded. 'Precisely. Failure to carry the card, or produce it when asked, is a crime punishable by imprisonment or deportation to one of Germany's camps.'

"I shook my head. 'What will they think of next? What are you going to do about this law?' I asked.

"Saul lifted his eyebrows. 'You might also ask; "What am *I* going to do about this law?"'

"'Me? I'm not Dutch. The law says any *Dutch* person.'

"'But Sara is. And Katy is.'

"I shook my head. 'Nope. They're Americans named Hartigan. They are members of my family.'

"Saul lifted his eyebrows. 'Hmm. Can you prove it? Do you have something that shows either Sara or Katy is American? Or a member of your family? I understand they're not issuing immigration visas anymore, and I don't believe you have the ability at the consulate to issue an American passport. What if someone who knows Sara blurts out her name, or identifies her as a Dutch woman? You had dinner at the Majestic last night. Willem has known Sara for some time. What if he mistakenly introduces her as Sara Rosenbaum? And what if a German officer overhears him. Do you have a document to prove him wrong?'

"'Willem is a stand-up guy,' I said, 'and he's Julia's fiancé. He'd never do that.'

"Saul shrugged his shoulders. 'Not on purpose, maybe. Personally, between you and me, I don't trust him or his German manager. The Majestic makes a lot of money off those Nazis.'

"'I trust him, Saul. I think we're okay. I have a passport and Sara is my wife. But what are you and Deborah and Sylvia going to do?'

"'Take a look at the card in your hand, the one that says Saul Rosenbaum. I've had that ID card for a long time.' He took out a different card and passed it to me. It read, 'Vincent Rose.' It had his picture and fingerprints and his address, but no big, black *J* stamped on the card. He smiled. 'I thought that Vincent van Rose would be a little too much for anyone who knows Dutch history. But Vincent Rose sounded good.'

"I was impressed. I held both cards and compared them. There was no way to tell the difference between the fake and the original. 'The card looks fabulous,' I said. 'Very authentic.'

"'It is. And it's impossible to detect the forgery. Even the fabric of the paper is identical. I have one and Deborah has one. Sylvia's is in the works. We need Alice to make one for you, Sara, and Katy.'

"I shrugged my shoulders. 'Who is Alice? How does she make perfectly forged cards?'

"'She is Alice Cohn, a dear friend of mine, and a wonderful graphic artist. She was born in Breslau, and she studied cabinetmaking with her father. She moved to Berlin for a year of school in graphic arts, but when the situation for German Jews deteriorated, she fled to the Netherlands, to Utrecht, in fact. I met her when she took a class at the university. We became good friends. She has had dinner here with Deborah and me on several occasions. One night, I introduced her to a member of our resistance group, and she was overjoyed to join. "What can I do?" she will always ask.

"'This spring, when Lentz's law came into effect and everyone was required to go to the nearest office and have a card issued for them, she figured out how to duplicate them. She obtained a few of the cards from members of the group, obtained the same paper, the same ink, and the same print size and graphics. She was able to produce an undetectable forgery.' Saul stuck out his chest, he was so proud of his group. 'Now, let me take your pictures, and we will have Alice make you each a card.'

"I smiled and said, 'Really, Saul, thank you very much, but I'm an American. Theodore Hartigan. The family is all Hartigans. We don't really need Alice's cards. They're for the Dutch.'

"'My, my, Teddy, sometimes you are so shortsighted. Let me see the cards for Sara and Katy. The ones you will show to an officer if you are stopped.'

"'I will contend they are Americans, I will pull out my State Department ID and tell them they are my family.'

"Saul closed his eyes and took a breath. 'Teddy, what if Sara is walking on her way to go to work at the college, and she is alone, and she is stopped? Or, as I expect will occur in the near future, a person will have to show his identification card to enter most commercial buildings or grocery stores? How are you going to prove Sara is a Hartigan? And what if Sara and Katy are with you, and you all are stopped. What if they insist that they follow you back to your apartment to verify their identity? Hmm?'

"'I don't know. I'll say I can't . . . I'd say I'm not able right now to . . . Oh shit, I don't know.'

"Saul puckered his lips and said, 'Precisely. Let me give you another scenario. In the event the consulate shuts down operations here, and you don't have visas for Sara and Katy to go with you to America, or if you decide you want to stay here and not leave them, what identification cards will you use if *you* are stopped?'

"'I don't know.'

"'All right, just for the purpose of argument, what if the consulate is closed down? Or what if Germany declares war on the United States, or vice versa, will you walk around Holland with an American consulate identification card for you and your wife? You're an American enemy.'

"'Okay, Saul, I give in. You beat me. I can't argue any more. All I can say is when can we meet Alice and get her ID cards?'

"Saul smiled. 'I set up a meeting with Alice Cohn next Saturday here at the house.'"

"I TOOK SARA and Katy with me, although Katy was too young to need a card. Alice was very friendly. A twenty-seven-year-old woman, she had a beautiful smile and her face was surrounded with dark, curly hair. When she spoke Dutch or German, she did so with a Silesian accent. She took our pictures, copied our handwriting, and took our measurements. She asked by what names would we like to be called. Use of our real names could disclose our identity and compromise the use of fabricated cards. She said she would have cards for us in a week or two.

"The following week, we each had cards identifying us. I was William Hart, my favorite cowboy. Sara was Joy Hart, because she had a heart of joy. Katy had an ID card, even though she didn't need one, identifying her as Katy Hart; who would know the difference? Our addresses were listed at our apartment in Amsterdam. Obviously, there were no printed *J*s on any of the cards."

CHAPTER THIRTY-SIX

KARYN ARRIVED AT Teddy's retirement home a little after nine. She was met in the hall by a nurse named Eleanor. "I'm afraid you tired him out yesterday," she said. "I told him not to have any more meetings for a while.'"

"And what did Theodore say to that?" Karyn asked.

"Well, first he laughed, and then he said, 'Can't you see she's making me better? I'm bringing up old memories, people and events that have been gone from my mind for ages. Eleanor, it's the newspaper lady that brings all these memories to the surface. Don't say anything to her that will create false hopes, but I think I might be getting closer to finding out about her sister. When we talked about Alice Cohn, alarms went off in my head. I'm not sure what caused them, but when we talked about Alice, I had flashbacks. More discussions about her might bring up more clues.'"

Karyn's eyes opened wide. "He said that? About Alice Cohn? Did he say don't tell me?"

Eleanor nodded. "He didn't want me to tell you, because it might give you false hopes."

Karyn put her finger to her lips. "I won't say a thing. Silence is golden." Then she leaned forward. "Make sure you tell me if he says anything else that you're not supposed to tell me."

Eleanor winked. "Yes, ma'am."

"I STAYED UP late last night," Teddy said after Karyn arrived in his room, "maybe till two in the morning, racking my brain about the things that that happened in the spring of 1941, trying to put them all into the correct order. So much was happening, not only on the world stage, but within the walls of our consulate. This was a time when the you-know-what hit the fan. It was a time when Mr. Velvet Gloves started drafting more and more edicts containing wicked restrictions directed against the Dutch Jews, including my new family. Cards stamped with *J*s were just the beginning.

"I remember that in May 1941, Seyss-Inquart ordered the municipality of Amsterdam to provide the location of every Jewish residence. The census records already revealed the names of each Jew, and property records disclosed their homeownership, and the recent identification cards, the ones stamped with a *J*, would show the names and current addresses of the holders. But even that wasn't enough. Now the municipality was to provide a detailed 'Jew map.' As offensive and distasteful as that was, the municipality had no choice.

"The map was to be an accurate depiction of where the Jews lived in Amsterdam. In other words, where were the Jewish neighborhoods? Dots were used to indicate how many Jews lived on each Amsterdam street. One dot equaled ten Jews. At that time, eighty thousand of the one hundred and sixty thousand Dutch Jews lived in Amsterdam, and their residence was known to the municipality. And even that was not enough. The municipality was also ordered to prepare maps locating information about Jewish businesses. If you ever had a question about whether or not the Dutch authorities would cooperate with Seyss-Inquart, this was a clear answer. They did.

"My father-in-law was the great prognosticator. Saul Rosenbaum would predict what might happen next, and more often than not, his forecasts were accurate. He prophesied that Jewish municipal workers would lose their jobs, and that came true. He forecast that Jewish teachers and students would be dismissed from public schools, and that came true. It was announced that after the summer holidays of 1941, Jewish pupils were not allowed to return to their old schools. Catholic or Protestant children were also made to leave their Christian schools if the Nazis declared that some of the students were of Jewish descent.

"Starting on September 1, Jewish children were no longer allowed to attend school with non-Jewish children. There were tens of thousands of Jewish pupils in Amsterdam. Some of the grade schools had a Jewish majority and those schools became 'Jewish schools' in which all teachers and students were required to be Jewish. Non-Jewish teachers and pupils were reassigned to non-Jewish schools. The old concept of "the neighborhood school" didn't exist anymore. Surprising to the Nazis, there weren't enough teachers to fill all the non-Jewish schools. Some of those schools had to go on half-day shifts.

"New edicts soon came down that prohibited Jews in Amsterdam from shopping in non-Jewish markets. Jewish markets opened in the playgrounds at Waterlooplein, Joubertstraat, Gaaspstraat. Later, another market opened at Minervaplein. You can imagine how angry that made the owners of the markets. They lost a large portion of the customer base. Little did the Nazis care. And Jewish children could not play in non-Jewish playgrounds. Several sandwich shops, not to mention ice-cream shops, saw a huge drop in sales.

"These separation edicts hit home in several different ways. While we were spending the weekend visiting the Rosenbaums, Sylvia burst in the door crying. Ms. Pimentel had announced that the municipality of Amsterdam was requiring the crèche to dismiss all non-Jewish day care children. The overwhelming majority of the children at the crèche were Jewish, but not all of them. 'It's absurd,' cried Sylvia. 'What does a little baby know about her religion? How can she possibly corrupt another child? Many of these little toddlers are already best friends. How is a non-Jewish parent supposed to explain to her child that he or she can no longer attend the crèche or play with her non-Jewish friend? Is she supposed to say to her three-year-old child, 'We have to find another day care center because I'm not Jewish?' Does any of this make a shred of sense?'

"The crèche was the most well-respected day care center in Amsterdam, caring for over a hundred children every day. There was a waiting list for enrollment. Many pregnant mothers enrolled their unborn child so that he or she would be high on the waiting list by the time he was born.

"Saul swiveled his head in my direction and looked at me with one of his classic expressions. 'You see,' he said, shaking a finger. 'I warned you about Arthur Seyss-Inquart, who is as evil as he is ugly. His bony

face with circular eyeglasses sitting on his pointy nose, he tries to mimic
Hitler in everything he does, except Arthur doesn't have a mustache. But
it's a contest: who hates Jews the most? Seyss-Inquart has succeeded in
totally separating Dutch Jews from the balance of Dutch society. What
more can he do? It's just the opposite from our neighbor Denmark, where
everybody gets along.

"'If Germany wants Holland, doesn't it want it with a strong society?
How stupid is Seyss-Inquart if he takes away a quarter of the economy?'

"'No sense. But if he has taken away almost all we have, what is the
point of further edicts? Maybe he's done.'

"'Don't bet on it,' said Saul."

CHAPTER THIRTY-SEVEN

KARYN AND TEDDY had lunch in the dining hall for the first time since Teddy came to the retirement home. It was a banner day. Eleanor brought in a wheelchair, but Teddy insisted that Karyn push him, not Eleanor, although Eleanor followed close behind. During their lunch, Teddy raised his chin and said, "You know, the food ain't bad here. The turkey sandwich is pretty good." Karyn thought it was nice to see a smile on Teddy's face.

Toward the end of lunch, Teddy said, "I want to tell you that I've been thinking hard about Alice Cohn and her resistance group, the one she called the Utrecht Children's Committee. One member of that group is still kickin': Maggie Hovland. I reached out to Maggie and she tells me that she remembers a set of girls that were taken out by the Utrecht Children's Committee, and she thinks it was by Gwen Rothschild, although she might be wrong. Maggie is going to help us look. I know it's very little progress, but . . ."

"No, no," said Karyn, "not at all. I really appreciate all you're doing."

"Okay, I'm not finished yet," Teddy said. "Are you ready for more?"

"Fire away."

"This morning, I told you about the anti-Jewish measures that were being taken by Seyss-Inquart. It was remarkable that Saul predicted all of them. Do you remember that a few months earlier, he predicted that the consulate and the embassy might shut their doors and go home someday? The Republican congressmen and the America First Committee were lobbying hard to close all of our European embassies. They warned that if we didn't close off all contact, we would be drawn into their war, and they wanted no part of it."

"I remember."

"On July 30, 1941, Consul General Lee called for an 'important' staff meeting to take place at five P.M. He asked that the conference room doors be shut. With a solemn expression on his face, Lee began the meeting by stating that all matters to be discussed at the meeting were 'strictly confidential and must remain within the room.'

"Everyone anticipated what Lee was going to say before he opened his mouth; at least I did. Julia was sitting next to me. She reached out to hold my hand, and when Lee confirmed that the meeting was about continuing operations of the consulate in Amsterdam, she squeezed my hand very hard. Both of us had relationships in Amsterdam, and would be in a fix if the consulate were to close and all American staffers were given the right to return home.

"Lee continued. 'The German Empire has made it next to impossible for us to carry on our operations in the Netherlands. Consequently, the United States Department of State has ordered us to prepare cessation of operations, and to close our two remaining facilities until further notice. The precise termination date has not been set, but I'm sure it will be within the next few weeks.'

"Then came the crusher. 'Arrangements are being made for all consulate employees to return to Washington,' Lee said. 'Until that occurs, we are to take all reasonable steps to secure all of our documents and package them for shipping. All embassy and consulate materials are to be considered 'strictly confidential.' To that end, we have increased the number of security guards. Nonprivileged documents are to be shredded. Any of you that are engaged in local affairs outside the consulate are advised to wrap them up as soon as possible without divulging that we are closing the consulate. Public announcements will be made at the appropriate time.'

"Although Lee's address was not a total surprise, it was still a punch in the gut. You can imagine what was going through my mind. All I could think of was how to get Sara and Katy out of Holland with the rest of the consulate staff and safely back to America. I wasn't thinking about getting them visas, or passports, or any forged identification cards. I was only thinking of how the United States government was going to safely get a consular officer and his wife and child out of Europe.

"I waited until Lee had concluded the meeting, and I asked to speak with him privately. We sat in his office. He sat behind his desk and folded his hands. He looked at me like a teacher would in answering a student's question. 'As you know, sir,' I said nervously, 'I am recently married to a Dutch woman, and we have adopted a child. Because of regulations, and the current hold, I haven't been able to process visas for either of them. I want to make sure that when the time comes, and air transportation to Washington is arranged for our staff, that I will be able to take my wife and my daughter back with me.'

"Lee sadly shook his head. 'We're pretty solidly booked on the return flight, but give me your marriage certificate and the child's birth certificate and I'll see what I can do.'

"That was discouraging. 'We don't have a marriage certificate as such,' I said. 'It was a religious wedding. We didn't want to make an appointment at the Amsterdam Royal Palace for fear of the public form of registration. You know, being Mrs. Hartigan offers some protection, but disclosing her as Jewish Amsterdam woman could subject her to any number of restrictions. And the child is an orphan. She was abandoned. We adopted her but not formally. But you can rest assured that both of them are genuine Hartigan wife and daughter.'

"Frank Lee shut his lips tightly, rubbed his beard, took a breath, then said, 'We'll talk about it later, Theodore.'"

"WHEN I LEFT Lee's office, Julia was waiting for me. We walked out together. Julia knew exactly what was on my mind because it was on her mind as well. What were we going to do when the consulate closed? In many ways, she faced the same decisions; the same, but different. She wasn't Jewish and neither was her boyfriend. She didn't have a child. The orders against Jews were increasingly severe, but they didn't affect Julia personally. Sara had a forged ID, the one Alice Cohn prepared for her, but it could fail. Sara was a popular girl. Someone who knew Sara could point her out. Her birth certificate said Sara Rosenbaum, not Joy Hart.

"Julia wasn't Jewish, but maybe her identity put her at risk. She was an American, just like me, and an officer of the State Department, just like me. Right now, America wasn't a declared enemy. Hitler had his hands full on the other side of Europe with Russia. But if the US were to attack Germany or one of its allies, or should Hitler become even more ambitious than he was now, and if he were to move on the western hemisphere, Americans, near and far, would become his enemy.

"Both Julia and I had the right to return home, along with Frank Lee, Mitch, Michelle, and the rest of the consulate staff, but I wasn't about to leave Sara and Katy in Holland, and Julia didn't want to leave Willem. It was still possible that Frank could have visas issued for Sara and Katy; I was sure he could accomplish it if he wanted to, but I'd asked him about it, and all he could say was 'We'll talk about it later.' That didn't give me much hope.

"'Where are you going to go after they close up the consulate?' Julia asked me. 'If you stay in Amsterdam, I doubt that Washington will continue to pay your salary. How will you live? You don't have a large savings account here, do you?' I responded that Sara still had her teacher's salary, at least for now, but it wasn't very much, not nearly enough to support the three of us. I supposed we could stay with Sara's father, but that would be a lot to ask.

"'I don't want to be nosey,' Julia said, 'but do you have sufficient funds to stay here? I don't, and Amsterdam is expensive. I need my salary. I'm putting a lot of eggs in Willem's basket. I love him and I know he'll take care of me, but what if things don't work out and I'm stuck here?'

"'I understand,' I said. 'My father has money, but I don't know how he would get it to me. The banks are controlled by the Germans. Saul lives on a university professor's salary, which wouldn't go very far if Sara, Katy, and Sylvia all move in with him. I don't want to become a burden on the Rosenbaums, and who knows how long this occupation will continue? Maybe forever. So what are you going to do?'

"'Well, I can't afford my apartment without the State Department's stipend, so I'm sure I'll move into the Majestic with Willem; I spend most of my time there anyway. I should be pretty safe, even though the German high command wines and dines there all the time. It's their favorite place. I was there last night, and so was Seyss-Inquart.'

"'How could you do that?' I asked. 'I couldn't eat in the same room with that pig.'

"'The Majestic reserves a private dining room for Seyss-Inquart. He usually eats there. By the way, I saw Walter Süskind there last night. Did you hear what happened at the Hollandsche Schouwburg?'

"'Nothing, except the play *Our Town* is still running. I'm sure the attendance is down, but it's a pretty good play.'

"'It's not running anymore, Teddy. Walter was operating it, and he is a Jew, and because many in the cast of his production were Jewish, the Nazis barred any non-Jews from working there. They changed the name from Hollandsche Schouwburg to Joodse Schouwburg, the Jewish Theater, and ruled that only Jews can go there. Half the production was non-Jewish, so it had to close.'

"'Each day another edict comes out against the Jewish people. Seyss-Inquart must stay up all night pondering what evil edict he can devise next, although I believe that most of them come directly from Berlin. Seyss-Inquart is nothing more than a puppet.'

"Julia gave me a kiss on the cheek and said, 'I hope Consul General Lee comes through for you and Sara, and she gets her visa home. You guys need to get out of here. Give Sara a kiss for me when you see her.'"

CHAPTER THIRTY-EIGHT

"I WAS RELUCTANT to tell Sara what happened in the meeting. I wanted to hold back until I heard whether or not Frank Lee would issue immigrant visas for Sara and Katy. I felt he owed me. I had worked hard under difficult conditions for almost three years. Surely Lee had to understand that if the three of us remained in Holland, we would no longer have any protection against the murderous edicts of Hitler or Seyss-Inquart. I was an American citizen and former officer in the US State Department and Sara and Katy were Jews. They had to let us come home.

"In the few days following the meeting, the offices were as quiet as could be. Other than the occasional visitor seeking advice, or applying for a duplicate passport, or replacing a lost visa, we were all carrying out Consul General Lee's instructions not to process any new applications. Even if the US government were to relax all immigration restrictions, and it became possible to process visas for anyone who wanted one, there was no way for an applicant to get out of the Netherlands. The Nazi-run Dutch government had prohibited anyone from emigrating, effectively closing its borders.

"It was on July 29 that Lee called me into his office and shut the door. Obviously, this was the time when we would 'talk about it later.' His demeanor was dispassionate and businesslike. That did not bode well. He cleared his throat. 'Theodore, I said I would get back to you as soon as I could concerning your request to take your wife and child with you when the staff leaves for home.'

"'I appreciate that, sir. I definitely want to take them home to Washington.'

"Lee nodded. 'I know that. I also understand that your wife Sara is a Dutch woman who does not have a valid visa or passport, is that not so?'

"'Yes, sir, but she applied for an immigration visa quite some time ago, and it is pending. She's on the waiting list. I'm certain that she'll qualify when it's her turn.'

"Lee rubbed his chin. 'I know. I'm aware of all that, as well. I also understand that she is Jewish, and by remaining here, her life would be endangered. She would qualify for a hardship visa.'

"'That's true, sir, very much so,' I answered, 'and I am very grateful for your understanding. She's also married to a citizen and an officer in the State Department, so I believe that is further reason for granting an exception in her situation. All that is why I came to you and asked for your leniency.'

"Lee clicked his teeth. 'Of course, and if I could, I would do it in a minute. And it is for that reason that I personally contacted Undersecretary of State Sumner Welles in Washington.'

"'Oh, thank you sir, I so appreciate it.'

"Lee nodded his head, took a breath through his nose, and then said, 'But after looking into it, Undersecretary Welles regretfully denied your request.'

"I was dumbfounded. You could have picked me up off the floor. 'What? Why?' I said. 'Why would he reject a request made by a consul general and a consular officer? Isn't this the United States? It's not like we asked for a major departure from the rules.'

"Lee spread his hands and shrugged his shoulders. 'I said that myself, but he informed me that there are several individuals, hundreds in fact, who have special needs and special requests, and who also qualify for an exception. Issuing the visas is not the only problem. There is no way to bring them all back from Holland right now. The plane carrying consular passengers will be allowed to travel from Holland one time under diplomatic immunity. All of the seats in that aircraft are accounted for. As you know, there is no airplane or steamship passage allowed to leave the Netherlands anymore.'

"I was shaking. 'They can sit on my lap. I'll stand up all the way home.'

"Lee solemnly shook his head. 'I'm sorry.'

"I was angry, what could I do? I stood up to leave, and Lee said, 'Before you go, Theodore, I have another matter to discuss with you.'

"I wanted to say, *Stick it up your ass, I got a matter for you too, and it starts with my middle finger and ends with telling you to go to hell*, but I didn't. I stopped and turned around.

"Lee said, 'I assume that you are going to stay here in Amsterdam with your wife when the rest of us leave.'

"I was mad. 'What choice do I have? I'm not going back without my wife and child. But I'm sure going to be in a big fix. I don't know what I'm going to be doing, and I don't know how I'll support myself, but I'll figure something out.'

"Lee nodded. 'I understand. You think you've been treated unfairly, and given your commendable service, you feel you deserve more.' When I heard that I wanted to punch him in the snout, but then he said, 'But hold on. I can offer you a position. You can still work for the State Department in Amsterdam at an increased salary, but it won't be in the consulate. It will be in counterintelligence. You'd be doing your country a great service. Are you interested?'

"'You want me to be a spy?'

"'Mm, yes.'

"'What would I have to do?'

"'How well do you know your father-in-law, Saul Rosenbaum, and how much do you know about his activities?'

"'I can't spy on my father-in-law. I won't betray him so that I can get a salary.'

"'No, no, just the opposite. How well do you know Saul Rosenbaum and his activities?'

"'I know my father-in-law very well, but I don't know that much about his activities, other than he is a highly regarded professor at Utrecht University. I also understand that he's involved in an underground resistance group, but that's really all I know.'

"'What do you know about his resistance group?'

"'I know that he has assembled a group, mostly college students, that engage in activities to counter the Nazi mistreatment.'

"'And how much do you know about a woman named Alice Cohn?'

"'Some. I'm surprised you know about her, sir. Her existence is a secret, and she is in hiding.'

"'Quite right. Alice Cohn prepares forged identification cards, principally for Jews. They don't display the designated *J* in bold letters on the front or the back.'

"'I know that, sir, Sara and I each have one of Alice Cohn's identification cards.'

"Lee smiled. 'That's good. Well, let me tell you what State has in mind for you, Theodore. We think that you would be a perfect choice for a special assignment. Between you and me, President Roosevelt is concerned about American intelligence deficiencies, especially after his meeting with the senior British intelligence officer. The president requested William Donovan to draft up a plan for an intelligence service based on the British Secret Intelligence Service, MI6, and the British Special Operations Execution, SOE. Donovan has come up with a single agency responsible for foreign intelligence and special operations. It involves all sorts of things: commandos, disinformation agents, guerrilla activities, and, here's where you come in: intelligence gathering. As of July 11, Donovan is heading up a new federal agency known as OSS, the Office of Strategic Services. The OSS needs intelligence agents. Are you interested so far?'

"'Very much so!'

"'In speaking with the president, I told him that intelligence-gathering services are very weak in Western Europe. He agrees. From now on, the OSS is responsible for gathering and collecting intelligence information regarding foreign governments, including the German Reich, Western Europe, and of course, the Netherlands. If you are agreeable, you can become an OSS agent and oversee the Netherlands office of the OSS. You will coordinate with British MI6. You will also coordinate with Ambassador Biddle, who is in London ever since leaving Amsterdam last March. You will regularly report to MI6 and OSS Washington about the activities here in Amsterdam and in the rest of the country. These are things that may not be known outside the country. If Seyss-Inquart imposes an edict, we want to know about it. In the event of a military incursion, your eyes and ears will become invaluable. What do you think? Is it a deal?'

"I was flabbergasted. They were putting that kind of responsibility in my hands? 'Yes, yes,' I said, 'it's a deal. Would you like me to bring my father-in-law to the consulate to meet you? He's full of valuable information.'

"'Bring him over here? Absolutely not. That would blow his cover. If he comes into the consulate, someone will see him and make the connection. Do you understand that this building is being watched? Any information from Mr. Rosenbaum should come through you. As long as the consulate building is secured, and ostensibly open and operating, that is where you will direct the Netherlands OSS. You may use my office. It's yours from now on, or at least until we come back, which I hope is soon. You can continue to manage the building as the Department of State's consular office, and your title will be chargé d'affaires. We will provide you with adequate security guards. As long as Germany and the US are not combatants, and as long as Germany maintains an embassy in Washington, mutual diplomatic immunity should prevail for both sides and keep you safe. There should be no reason for Seyss-Inquart or any Nazi to disturb your presence here in the consulate building. Everything understood?'

"I nodded. This was a powerful assignment. Imagine going from research assistant in the basement of State, to chargé d'affaires of the Amsterdam consulate, and head of Amsterdam OSS. Quite a jump, but Frank wasn't through.

"Our discussion today is strictly confidential. It is not for anyone outside our little circle. When the assignment is over, I will do my best to bring your family back to the States with appropriate credentials. Does the position appeal to you?'

"'Yes, sir. I will do my best.'

"He reached out to shake my hand. 'We will keep the building open as long as we can, but we will be closing down consular operations. Our British counterparts will have your contact information. You will be given the names of contacts who will distribute and receive confidential information. An intelligence agent whose code name is "Gold" will deliver reports to you from time to time. You will have the use of the office teletype machine and the cable line to Washington OSS. The frequency modulation radio in the office is set to a specific channel to send and receive messages. The code ledger is in my desk drawer. Understood?'

"'Yes, sir, I understand.'

"'Good. Undoubtedly you will need to change living quarters. We keep a safe house on Berenstraat, not too far from here, but far enough away to avoid any connection.'

"I thanked him, but said we already had a very nice apartment with furnishings for all three of us.

"You could tell from his expression that he didn't care for that answer. 'I know you have an apartment, but it's in a large building. That is not sufficiently private. We will provide a single-family home, not an apartment, with adequate furnishings. Since we can no longer pay you a salary, we will arrange to provide funds through a covert account at the First Hollandsche Bank. Any questions?'

"'My father-in-law receives current information through the members of his resistance committee. May I disclose my new assignment to him and share copies of documents that might be of interest to him?'

"Lee smiled. 'He already knows. When I decided to enlist your services as chargé d'affaires, I spoke with Saul at length. Saul and I have been working together for over two years. He heartily recommended you. No doubt he will provide valuable assistance as needed, but if one of his members has delivered information to you, rest assured that Saul has already seen it.'

"'I should have known,' I said. 'I hope I am as good in keeping secrets as he is. Anyone else involved?'

"Frank tipped his head to the side. 'I am recruiting another person,' he said, 'and I think you know her very well. I have already spoken to Julia Powers. She has been with me for a number of years, and is quite dependable. She informed me that she has chosen to stay in Amsterdam with her boyfriend Willem, and will not be returning with the rest of us. She will work with you at the consulate building during the day, and stay at the Majestic at night. Other than security guards and a couple of clerks, the two of you will be the only officers left in the building. You and Julia will be working together practically every day.'

"'That will not be a problem,' I said. 'Have you already spoken with Julia about my assignment, or would you like me to do so?'

"Frank smiled. 'That's my job. She may have questions or concerns that are for my ears only. I told her I would reach out to you, and she was very happy. She said the two of you have a very close relationship.'

"'That's true. She was my first contact when I arrived in Holland. I have never known exactly what she does here at the consulate, but she is a very trustworthy person. Julia is Sara's best friend. She introduced me to Sara. Believe me, you can trust Julia.'

"'That's not an issue. For the last four years, she has been my assistant. But there is someone I want you to keep an eye on. I'm not sure about Willem, her boyfriend. You can never tell where his loyalties lie.'"

"THE MORNING AFTER I talked with Frank Lee, Julia came into my office and shut the door. 'I spoke with Frank when I came to work this morning,' she said. 'I guess you know what that was all about.'

"'It was a big surprise to me,' I said. 'Initially I was mad at him for not getting emergency visas for Sara and Katy. He told me that he tried, and maybe he did. I thanked him for that. Then he told me that you and I would be in charge of all operations when the consulate closes. That's a big responsibility. How do you feel about being the only two Americans left in the consulate?'

"'Same as you, although sometimes I think I'm nuts. I could have had a safe, sweet ride back to the States, but I chose to stay here with Willem. I wasn't planning on going back home at all. I was going to live here permanently. That is, until the Nazis came to town. Willem and I have been discussing it. Unless Amsterdam is totally destroyed, like Rotterdam was, Willem thinks I will be safe here. There is no armed conflict taking place in Europe, and Willem told me he would keep me safe. He's pretty well connected. Anyway, it looks like you and I will be hanging around together for a long time. At least we'll have each other to talk to.'"

CHAPTER THIRTY-NINE

"AUGUST 31, 1941, was the date for removing all US consulate documents and confidential materials, and what hadn't been shredded would be loaded onto the plane at the Amsterdam airfield. It was not publicly known, but I believe that word of the consulate closure must have slipped out to more than the staff. Even so, I'm sure that Berlin was happy to have all United States operations off the continent, because no efforts were made to interfere with the departure. Michelle was sure she saw Nazi agents going through our garbage, but there was nothing of importance in there. She couldn't wait to get back to Kansas. She said she would miss Amsterdam, but she was glad to get out of a war zone. Only Julia and I were left behind."

"THROUGHOUT THE END of the summer, Seyss-Inquart continued to devise scheme after scheme to injure the Jews. The Jews weren't a threat to him; they were by far the most peaceful group of people on earth. Shop owners didn't petition the government to prevent Jews from spending money in their stores. Teachers didn't ask that all Jewish children be removed from their classrooms. Henriëtte Pimentel loved all her day care and kindergarten children just the same. And the children loved her in return. There were waiting lists for her school. Ask any man on the street and he wouldn't have been able to name any reason. Only hate. Hate is the reason. Seyss-Inquart was a hateful man.

"On August 8, 1941, a financial institution called the Liro Bank opened on the corner of Sarphatistraat in Amsterdam. It opened with a big fanfare: banners, flags, and gifts for the kids. The Liro appeared to be another branch of the Jewish Lippmann Rosenthal and Co. bank, a very successful banking chain, but it wasn't. Most of the Jews banked at Lippmann Rosenthal, and many opened accounts at the Liro. But the depositors were deceived. The bank was owned and set up by the Nazis to steal money and valuables from Jews.

"It was yet another measure Nazis took to rob Jews of their money and their possessions. In fact, in late August, Seyss-Inquart's government passed a law requiring all the Jews to deposit all their cash and assets over one thousand guilders into the Liro Bank, and to register the deposit. They were no longer allowed to have accounts at other banks. In September, Jews had to fill out a form listing any real property they owned, including any buildings, any farm or mining land, and deliver the form to the government. The government didn't require them to convey anything at this time, just to register it. I don't know how many Jewish families actually followed that law, but if they were caught failing to register their real or personal assets, those assets would be forfeited."

"IN AUGUST, AND going forward, I couldn't have asked for a more pleasant person to work with than Julia. We alternated bringing lunch into the consulate, now that the kitchen was closed. And we alternated giving each other lunch breaks. Julia might go shopping or visit with Willem. I would usually go over to the crèche and visit Katy and Sylvia. Sometimes I'd visit Sara if she was on her break. We tried as best we could to live a normal life, waiting for the insanity to go away.

"During the day, we stayed alert to messages. There were evenings where we expected a delivery or a coded message, and on those nights, both of us would stay overnight. We did make use of the coffee machine, and Julia kept things neat and clean in the building."

"Didn't Sara get jealous?" asked Karyn. "Didn't this affect your relationship in some way? I mean, honestly, I think if my husband and my best friend, who happens to be a gorgeous woman, were spending every minute of every day alone together and even some of the nights, I would be jealous. Did Sara ever say anything about it?"

"Julia and I became very close friends, as close as you can get, but Sara was my wife, and she was Julia's best friend. We kept it like that. The four of us would get together when we could, in out-of-the-way places. But there were several times when we would eat at the Majestic.

"Actually, on one occasion, Seyss-Inquart hosted a huge party for the Nazis and their guests at the Majestic. We saw them walk by. You can't imagine how disgusting that was. Seyss-Inquart would always require one of the Majestic kitchen staff to stand at his table and taste his food, each and every dish, before he'd put any of it in his mouth. Even when he catered in his food and beer from Germany, it still had to be sampled in the same manner, but this time by the caterer.

"There were times when the Nazis held a raucous party at the Majestic, more than Julia could bear. On those occasions she slept in our house with Sara and me. We would all sit around talking until late in the evening, past the point when I could keep my eyes open, and I would fall asleep. Julia and Sara would keep it up until almost morning when Sara would crawl into bed with me as quietly as she could. Julia slept in the extra bedroom. There was never any indication of jealousy.

"I remember walking with Sara and Katy one evening in September. The weather was perfect. The seasons were about to change. It brought back so many memories. I had always thought of September as the start of the new year. When I was in grade school, passing from one grade to the next, it was always a big change. A time to make new friends, meet the new teachers, learn new subjects. I was a year older, a year smarter, a year cockier. With new clothes, new books, and of course, new privileges, September was a joy.

"But this September, when we turned the corner, we saw a building with a blazing red Nazi banner draped from the third floor. The sign of the devil. Then I remembered September being the month I would go to a new Sunday school class. The teacher would talk about the devil and the forces of evil. Our Sunday school teacher said that they would rise up from deep inside the earth, straight out of hell, and run all over the earth, causing damage. But if you denied the word of the devil, and rejected his evil, then you could follow the lessons of good, and the devil would be defeated. Those days, Sunday school scared the hell out of me. Get it?

"But remembering that Sunday school lesson hit home this year. The devil and his legions had risen from deep inside the earth and were conquering the world, starting in Europe. Wherever you looked there was no one who could stand up to the forces of evil. Seyss-Inquart was a soldier of the devil, a captain of his forces in the Netherlands, but he was only doing the bidding of the devil himself, ordered from his headquarters in Wolf's Lair.

"The devil had vanquished Austria, Czechoslovakia, Poland, Norway, Denmark, France, and Belgium, leaving death and destruction in his wake. Now he was doing the same in the Netherlands. All of Europe belonged to Satan. One evil edict followed another no matter where you were, except to a lesser extent in Denmark.

"Then came the announcement from Seyss-Inquart that really hit us hard. He declared that no Jews would be allowed at the Majestic Hotel. They would not be allowed to stay there, eat there, or enjoy any of its amenities. The news was delivered to Willem by Seyss-Inquart himself. 'I know that you have hosted functions for Jewish patrons in the past,' Seyss-Inquart said, 'but that is over. This property is hereafter non-Jewish in every respect.'

"Willem protested that the hotel, which was not owned by Jews, had made a lot of money from Jewish customers. Willem argued that it was a good thing that the Majestic was servicing Jews, because it was taking money from them. Seyss-Inquart didn't buy it. 'No Jews,' he said. Willem protested that he was planning on holding a big party for Julia's thirtieth birthday. Everything was set. The party would be in the large party room, the hotel orchestra would provide the entertainment, and the chef was baking his ultimate birthday cake. 'Go ahead,' Seyss-Inquart said, 'but no Jews.' Willem was distraught. He would have to talk to Julia.

"That talk did not go well. When Julia came into work, I could tell something was wrong. She recalled her conversation with Willem, and made me promise that I would not repeat a single word to Sara. Willem explained all about Seyss-Inquart's order, and said that Sara would not be able to come to Julia's birthday party. 'Do you want me to tell her, or do you want to tell her yourself?' he said. 'Neither,' Julia said. 'If Sara's not going, then I'm not going. She's my best friend.' Willem, who had spent a lot of money and made arrangements, was furious.

"'Doesn't she have one of those phony IDs?' he said. 'She can use that.' But Julia would not ask Sara to do that."

Karyn said, "I can understand Julia's position. If the real Sara was barred from attending the party, then Julia wasn't going to ask her to pretend to be someone else and attend a party where all Jews were barred. And no doubt it offended Julia for Willem to hold a party under such conditions. Right?"

"Right," said Teddy, "but Willem was out a lot of money, and it was a party for his girlfriend. In his mind, the party was going to be a smash, a gift for her thirtieth birthday, and he couldn't understand why Sara couldn't use a phony ID. She might never even have to use it. It caused a major rift between Julia and Willem. The argument kept going and then Julia said she didn't feel comfortable spending the night there. She didn't say she didn't want to go out with him, she just didn't want to go to the Majestic anymore."

"I'm sure that didn't do the relationship any good, did it?"

"No, not really."

"THAT FALL, SEYSS-INQUART ran wild. One nasty edict followed another. The forces of evil ran unopposed; that is, until the day the Japanese awakened the forces of good, and the battle was on. They were Berlin's ally, but they woke up the sleeping giant and set into motion the end of the German Reich.

"Julia and I heard the news together. We were working in the consulate, sitting by the radio in the afternoon of December 7, 1941. The news was broadcast on shortwave and on British radio. Japan had attacked Pearl Harbor and formally declared war on both the United States and the British Empire. It was no secret to Germany. Several days before, Joachim Von Ribbentrop was informed by the Japanese ambassador that the relationship between Japan and the United States was at a breaking point. Hitler had told the Japanese ambassador that if Japan became involved in a war with the United States, Germany would enter the war on the side of Japan. The attack was immediately known to all players.

"On December 11, 1941, four days after the Japanese attack on Pearl Harbor and three days after the United States declared war against the Japanese Empire, Nazi Germany declared war against the United States, blaming the US, a country that was supposed to be neutral, for a series of provocations. Germany's decision to declare war against the United States was written by Adolf Hitler himself, apparently by hand, without consultation. Publicly, the formal declaration was handed to American chargé d'affaires Leland B. Morris by German foreign minister Joachim von Ribbentrop in Ribbentrop's office in Berlin. Later that day, the US declared war on Germany. The isolationists, including my father and his friend Senator Nye, were isolationists no longer.

"When we saw that Germany and the Unites States had exchanged declarations of war, I turned to Julia and said, 'I hope you understand that as officers of a declared enemy, we are no longer "diplomatically immune." This consulate building is no longer safe. We need to get out of here before the stormtroopers come and attack our building. I'm going to take the FM radio and the teletype with me to the safe house.'

"'I'll take the coffeepot,' Julia said, 'what more do we need?'

"'Nothing more except to alert the security guards. If the Nazis come over to storm the consulate building, we need to tell the security guards that their services are no longer needed. We don't want them fighting. They may be interrogated, but they don't know anything. They were hired from an agency. I'm leaving, and remember, no one is supposed to know the address of the safe house.'"

CHAPTER FORTY

KARYN ARRIVED AT the retirement home for her afternoon session. She and Teddy originally thought they would hold the interviews outside in nice weather, but there were too many people stopping by. Though it was chilly, some still wanted to sit with them outside and listen to Teddy's fascinating stories. Many had been born during the war and wanted to know more about it. So Teddy and Karyn returned to his room.

Once inside, Teddy began. "Two months after the declaration of war, in late February 1942, Sara and I intended to spend the whole weekend with her folks. I invited Julia to join us, but she declined. Deborah was on pins and needles waiting for us. I planned to pick up Sara at the college, then the two of us would stop and get Katy and Sylvia at the crèche before heading out to Utrecht. At the teachers' college, Johan van Hulst came out to greet me. 'How are things going?' I said. He nodded and responded, 'Personally, I'm fine. The enrollment is not doing as well, but we're doing okay. Several Jewish students have withdrawn from the college, but not because I asked them to. We haven't cut back on the curriculum, and most importantly, I haven't lost a single teacher. I don't care whose God they pray to, as long as they are good teachers.'

"I moved a little closer to him and quietly said, 'Did you hear about Titus Brandsma?'

"Johan shook his head. 'I know the priest, and I know of his stance against Nazi ideology, but I haven't heard anything lately.'

"'Notice came over the wires. Three weeks ago, Father Brandsma, a Carmelite friar, undertook to deliver by hand a letter from the Conference of Dutch Bishops to the editors of all the Catholic newspapers. The letter recited that the bishops ordered the newspapers not to print official Nazi documents, in violation of the new law set down by the German occupiers. He had visited fourteen Catholic editors before being arrested on January 19 at the Boxmeer monastery.'

"'Father Brandsma was delivering an order that violated Seyss-Inquart's specific edict,' Johan said.

"'Right. So I guess it isn't just the Jews. The Nazis hate Catholics too.'

"At that moment Sara came out. 'Actually, Sara is very proud of you,' I said. 'There are several Jewish students still enrolled and attending her classes every day, despite the fact that the Reformed Teacher Training College received the orders to dismiss Jewish students and tell them to attend Jewish schools only.'

"Johan shrugged his shoulders and said, 'This is a college, and the students can stay in class as long as they want. Then they'll become the kind of teacher I would want in my school.'

"Sara and I walked across the lawn to the crèche to pick up Katy and Sylvia. There were other parents picking up their children as well. It seemed much busier than usual. While we were waiting, Henriëtte came out. We exchanged greetings. 'I have to tell you that your sister Sylvia is a treasure,' she said. 'We're so lucky to have her. We're searching for more help if you know of anybody. Our enrollment has increased dramatically, ever since they ordered the Christian nurseries to dismiss their Jewish children. I didn't have the heart to turn the extra children away. We had to convert one of the storage rooms into a classroom for toddlers.'

"Across from the crèche was the train station where we would catch the train to Utrecht. On the other side of the tracks was the Hollandsche Schouwburg, whose name had been changed by the Nazi rulers to the Joodse Schouwburg. 'Jews only.' The announcement board read: *Concert This Evening. The New Dutch Orchestra Performing Gershwin Melodies.* If that was for real, I had to get tickets. We entered the Schouwburg to look for Walter. He was backstage, but on the stage were about twenty musicians doing a practice session. In the audience were about thirty children from the crèche across the street who were brought over just to listen to the practice.

"'Is this real?' I said to Walter. 'You have an orchestra performing tonight?'

"'We sure do; some of the finest musicians in Holland. You see them right out front. They're doing a six-day run. We're almost out of tickets, if you want to come.'

"I looked at Sara, who grimaced a little and said, 'I'd love to come, but I told my mom we were going to stay until Sunday.'

"'How about six tickets, Walter? Do you have six for Sunday?' I glanced at Sara. 'We'll bring your parents, and Katy, of course.'

"Walter smiled and said, 'Six tickets for the Sunday matinee, coming up!' He handed me the tickets and said, 'Now we're just about sold out.'

"'I'm so impressed, Walter, I had no idea.'

"'They're not going to hold us down, Teddy. Seyss-Inquart ordered that this was to be a strictly Jewish theater, strictly Jewish artists performing before strictly Jewish audiences. I guess Seyss-Inquart figured that we'd never get any customers. He thought he could hold us down, but the moment we announced the program, we started selling tickets. And our community bounced back and became alive! In two weeks, Celia Bernheim will give an opera recital. She used to be with the French opera company. Get your tickets now. They'll go fast.'

"'This is fabulous. This is just what our community needs.'

"Walter's smile stretched from ear to ear. 'We are bustling. There is a string quartet and a Latin guitarist each working out a date to schedule with us. I've already booked the hall for three weddings.'

"We were delighted. I wanted to stay and talk to Walter further, but I saw our train pulling into the station, and we had to leave."

CHAPTER FORTY-ONE

"THE UTRECHT SPECIAL was only a half-hour train ride. We were giddily talking all about the programs the Jewish Theater was planning on presenting, and before we knew it, the train had arrived in Utrecht. Saul had forwarded a message to us that said, 'When you get off the train, you should keep your identification cards in your pockets where you can show them, if necessary. Keep your heads down and walk quickly from the station. Walk straight north, and look for my Opel. We'll bring you out to the house.' The Opel was waiting there and drove us northwest into the countryside to Saul's home. The driver's name was Seth; he was one of Saul's students."

"Why was it necessary to be so careful in Utrecht?" Karyn asked. "Was Utrecht just as dangerous as Amsterdam?"

"Downtown Utrecht was crawling with SS. Sixty-six Maliebaan, a large Romanesque building, was the headquarters of the NSB, the Dutch National Socialist Movement; in other words, the home of the Netherlands SS. There were far more SS in Utrecht than in Amsterdam.

"Saul lived northwest of Utrecht in a hilly, wooded area. Every day he would drive his 1934 Opel to the university, which was also west of the city. We got out of the car and Katy ran up the driveway, waving her hands and screaming, 'Grandma!' Deborah stood there with her arms wide open and swallowed Katy right up. The two of them loved each other so much. I was glad to return to the Rosenbaums' warm and welcoming home, especially the warm and welcoming cuisine. I could smell dinner cooking. Saul and Deborah had a large, wooded backyard where they had a swing, and Katy ran straight to it.

"I remember the first time I visited Saul's house, and we sat out in the back. I heard hammering coming out of the woods. Someone was banging on metal. I looked at Saul and he laughed. 'That's Myron. He's an ironworker. He works almost every day at the Royal Dutch Aircraft Factory. They produce Fokkers. The one in the back here is his private property, a hobby for him.'

"'I thought Fokker was a German aircraft company,' I said.

"'The owner and founder was a Dutchman, Anthony Fokker. He opened his plant in Berlin in 1912. Then in 1919 he moved it here. The operations are all right here in the Netherlands. It was the dominating aircraft in the Great War. Then in the '20s, Fokker built passenger aircraft. In 1923 Anthony moved to America, where he opened a plant called Atlantic Aircraft. In 1930, he combined with General Motors and formed North American Aviation, which at one time had thirty-five percent of the American market. A couple of years ago, the Fokker plant was taken over by the Germans, and now they build Bücker trainers. But there are still a number of Fokkers at the factory. Do you want to see what he's doing back there?'

"How could I pass that up? We walked over to a paved driveway that wound its way into the woods and stopped at nowhere. That's where I met Myron. He was working on an old Fokker airplane. It was a seven-year-old model that had seen its share of bumps and bruises. The paint was chipping off. 'They were going to junk it,' Saul said, 'but Myron talked them into letting him have it, if he'd tow it away. Myron is a friend of mine who fixes my Opel when it needs it, which it does all the time. We made a deal. Myron fixes my Opel, and he can use my property to repair his airplane.'

"Myron was a stocky, tough, white-haired man. He reached out his hand and said, 'Myron. Glad to meet you.' He pointed to his Fokker and said, 'Soon my Raven, she'll fly like a bird. Saul lets me use his woods where it's nice and private, and the Nazis won't bother me while I'm working. I promised him when it's all finished, I'll give him a ride wherever he wants to go.'

"'And it flies?' I said. I walked around the plane. It looked identical to a Nazi plane. Give it some fresh paint, put a large black cross on the tail, and there would be no telling the two apart. Freaky.

"'Does it fly? Mmmm, not yet. Almost. But as long as your uncle Saul lets me use his woods, I have the time to fix her up.'

"Saul nodded and smiled. 'How many people can the plane carry?' I said.

"'Oh, about six, if they're not big and fat like me.' With that he belly-laughed.

"Saul and I walked back into the house and joined the others for dinner. We made sure to take a plate out to Myron.

"It was right after dinner, when Deborah was about to serve dessert, that I pulled out the Schouwburg tickets. 'Look what we brought,' I said. 'We're all going to a concert! It's a Sunday matinee in Amsterdam.'

"'It's all Gershwin, Mom,' said Sara. 'A live concert by the New Dutch Orchestra. And we're all going. The whole family!'

"Deborah was overjoyed, but I think Sylvia was the happiest. She was a big Gershwin fan. She had seen *Shall We Dance* with Fred Astaire and Ginger Rogers at the movies, and she played the record album all the time. That and *Girl Crazy*. Sylvia spent the rest of the night dancing around and humming 'I Got Rhythm' and 'Let's Call the Whole Thing Off.'

"After dinner, Saul invited me to join him in his study, as he usually did. The girls didn't miss us at all. They were all talking about the concert and how much Katy would enjoy it. I was anxious to hear what information Saul had for me; after all, I was the consulate chargé d'affaires of the Amsterdam OSS. Would it be necessary to pass Saul's information on to any of my contacts? I mentioned to Saul that Frank Lee held him in high regard. 'The feeling's mutual,' he said. 'Frank is a fine man. I am still in touch with him on the shortwave. He asked me what happened to the consulate building since war was declared.'

"'As you know, the Germans stormed it the minute Germany declared war against the US. We had moved out everything important. The Germans are now situated there; it's a much nicer building than the one they had before. They transformed it into a Nazi government building, with two large red banners hanging in the front. Julia and I, the only two left from the consulate, have moved the entire operation into the safe house on Berenstraat, the one that no one is to know about.'

"'That's right,' Saul said. 'It must remain confidential. No one should visit you there. You have a shortwave, don't you?'

"'Oh, yes. When there is information to transmit, we send it on the shortwave. If we are to receive a package, we'll get a notice, and the package will show up at our drop spot. So, tell me, Saul, what new information should I know about? I learned that Professor David Cohen and his partner Abraham Asscher formed a resistance group called the Jewish Council? Isn't that right?'

"'Not exactly. Asscher and Cohen are fine men, but they are being manipulated. They were approached by the Nazis in February last year, during the riots, and asked to form a Judenrat, similar to the one formed in Poland. Here it's called the Joodse Raad. It's not really a resistance group. It's not undercover, it's open and obvious and available to the Jewish community at all times. It has an office for all to see. The Jewish Council is supposed to act as a mediator. When the Nazis want to issue orders or rulings to the Jewish community, they go through the Jewish Council. That way, it is supposed to be done peacefully. Suppose the Nazis want all the Jews to pay a tax. They'll go through the Jewish Council first. Maybe. So, when Seyss-Inquart wants to clear all the Jews out of a section of Amsterdam, like he's doing right now, he'll tell the Jewish Council and they will pass it along to the community and make it happen. Peacefully. If it weren't for the Jewish Council, it would happen anyway, but not peacefully.'

"I nodded. 'I heard about moving Jewish families,' I said. 'Starting in January this year, the Nazis ordered several families in outlying districts to be brought into Amsterdam.'

"'You know why, don't you?' Saul said in an angry tone. 'It is to assemble the Jews all together in a central location. Then when they decide what they want to do or where to take them, they're all in one convenient place.'

"'I've heard that. I received a message the other day that Jews from Callantsoog and the adjoining northwest coastal towns were being brought into Amsterdam a few at a time, and housed in certain apartments in an area that is already crowded. That relocation was accomplished because of the efforts of the Jewish Council.'

"'Right,' Saul said. 'The families involved were chosen by the Jewish Council and told to move.'

"'Why would the Jewish Council choose those families? They weren't rioters, were they? Weren't they living comfortable lives in small country towns, bothering no one, including the Nazis? Why choose those families?'

"'The council was ordered to fill a number,' Saul said. 'The Nazis told the council they wanted forty Jewish families brought to Amsterdam. The council was told to choose them and tell them to move. It is rumored that some or all of the men were then sent to labor camps at Westerbork, Amersfoort, Vught, or Ellecom. When they get there, they work for the Nazis.'

"Listening to this, I kept getting angrier and angrier. 'That's unbelievable. A Jewish Council is told to pick out forty Jewish families where the men are to be sent away as slaves, and the Jewish Council is supposed to readily comply? And what is to become of the rest of the family after the men are taken away? Is the Jewish Council supposed to care for the women and children who are left?'

"'Obviously not. They will be grouped together, and the council is supposed to find multiple-occupancy housing for the remaining family members in a designated section of Amsterdam.'

"My face was turning red. One, that the Nazis would make people slaves, and not just any people, only the Jewish people, and two, that a Jewish Council—a *Jewish* Council run by eminent Jewish leaders—was being used to implement the orders. 'So, tell me, Saul, what are we going to do about it? We can't just sit back and do nothing. We have to do something. We can't just watch the Jewish Council round up Jews like they're cattle, all at the behest of the Nazis. Wouldn't it be better to die fighting? Then at least we'd take a few of the Nazis with us.'

"Saul sadly shook his head. 'You know that's not the answer. You can't fight the Germans. The answer is to save as many lives as we can. I have been using my resistance group in smaller situations, like spreading fake ID cards and finding empty apartments, all in an attempt to hide the Jews. So, when the Jewish Council goes looking for Jews to turn over to the Nazis and fill their quota, some of them won't be found. Maybe they'll be hiding somewhere. Get it? The answer is to keep as many Jews away from Nazis as we can until Germany is militarily defeated, and God willing, that will be soon. Sadly, it's one thing to hide a family, or ten families, or even a hundred families, but there are one hundred and forty thousand Jews now in Holland, and we can't hide them all.' Saul lowered his head. 'It's overwhelming, Teddy. It's hard to believe that it's anything but hopeless.'

"I stood up and put my hands on his shoulders. 'You are making a huge difference, Saul, more than anyone I know and I love you for it. We just need more people like you. I stayed here, didn't I? I didn't go home. And I didn't stay here to die.'

"'I appreciate that, and so does Sara. But we have to face reality. We're badly outnumbered. Forty-five million people voted for the Nazis in the last election. The German army is over eight million strong. The Nazi Party has two main goals: expansionism and anti-Semitism. Compared to other countries, the Netherlands has a relatively large Jewish population, but it's only one hundred and forty thousand, not forty-five million, or even eight million. Do you see where I'm going?'

"'Because we're outnumbered doesn't mean we quit. You and your group have saved lives, and every life matters. We need to keep resisting, keep finding ways to disable the Nazi terror machine until they are defeated. And you know as well as anyone that we can't do it alone. You're doing it here in Utrecht. You've formed a resistance group, the Utrechts Kindercomité, but we need more groups. As many as we can form. All over the Netherlands. Saul, you know students, gobs of students, from all over the country. And the students know students, and they know other people. We need more groups, more leaders, and we need a central command post to coordinate our efforts. My safe house is a private location that no one knows about, and I have direct connections to MI6 and OSS. I'll be happy to take it on. It's only a matter of time, Saul. The Nazis made the biggest mistake possible. They took on the United States of America, and we're not going to be beaten by the likes of Hitler, Himmler, or that skinny little weasel, Seyss-Inquart. Take his armed guards away from him and Seyss-Inquart can be flushed down the sewer by the Roto-Rooter man.'

"Saul had a smile and twinkle in his eye. 'You're a very courageous young man, and you're right. We need more groups. We're going to defeat them. But my house is a better location for the command post. People can come and go here without suspicion. I have students coming here all the time.'

"We stood up, hugged each other, and went to join the women."

CHAPTER FORTY-TWO

"WE HAD AN early breakfast, then all six of us took the morning train back to Amsterdam to see the concert. In many ways I felt better. Saul and I had devised a plan. It wouldn't win the war, but it would lessen the damage and save some lives. We would recruit teams, like the Utrechts Kindercomité, the UKC, and Saul would continue to run a central command post to distribute information. Where would the Nazis strike next? What corner of the community would be their victim? Where would they send the Jewish Council to round up innocent Jewish families next? We would try to intercept their incursion and hide as many people as possible.

"As we boarded the train, we saw groups of SS standing around watching the passengers. Were they looking for Jews? They didn't ask anyone to show their ID cards. If they were barring Jews, that would have been an easy way to check. Our cards were fake and they didn't have a J. But they weren't checking. It was just the same when we reached the train station at the Schouwburg. They didn't ask to see ID cards, because everyone entering the Joodse Schouwburg was supposed to be Jewish. I didn't notice anyone writing down names or taking pictures. So really, anyone could attend.

"The Schouwburg was gaily decorated with Gershwin playbills. As we took our seats, I noticed Henriëtte Pimentel sitting with two girls. Sylvia explained to us that the two girls had been dropped off earlier in the week. The Nazis had brought four families in from an outlying town, sent the fathers to one of the work camps, and left the rest of the family members to fend for themselves. Henriëtte offered to take the two girls into the crèche until they could find a place to stay. They had been through a lot and Henriëtte brought them to the theater to cheer them up. She'd been taking kids all week.

"The Holland Jewish Orchestra was composed of twenty-two men and women, some as young as sixteen. Sara recognized Mr. Horwitz, her high school music teacher. The lights dimmed and the crowd grew quiet. Walter came out on stage for the introductions. He thanked everyone for keeping culture alive during these dark times. He said there would be more concerts, and everyone clapped. He also said that events like this were the best medicine available. The curtain was drawn, the stage lights came on, and the orchestra lit into Gershwin's 'Strike Up the Band.' One song followed another: 'I Got Rhythm,' 'The Man I Love,' 'Summertime,' 'S'Wonderful.' After a while, the conductor asked people to sing along. Sylvia knew all the songs and jumped right in. Many people joined in or hummed along. I couldn't believe how well Katy could feel the music. She could catch on to the song, and by the second verse, she could hum it beautifully. It was in her bones. Like the song said, she got rhythm.

"Two and a half hours sped by, and as though the song was written for the event, and the audience of Dutch Jews, the orchestra ended the program with, 'They Can't Take That Away from Me.'

"The applause was strong, and just what our community needed, and right at the time when we needed it. What could be a more hopeful number? That is, until they played their encore, 'Of Thee I Sing.' This was a Dutch audience, but they knew many of the words, especially the chorus, and they were counting on the United States. Everyone stood and sang it loudly. Twice. I wondered if the Nazis standing outside heard us sing, or had a clue what the song was all about, but no one bothered any of the patrons as they left the theater."

KARYN CLAPPED AND started laughing. "What's so funny?" Teddy said.

"Oh, I don't know," Karyn answered. "Nothing, really."

"Nothing? Come on, what's so funny?"

Karyn hesitated until Teddy asked her again, "Why are you laughing?"

"Do you know what the Gershwin play *Of Thee I Sing* is all about? It's about a man, John Wintergreen, running for president. His advisors recommend that he run on a platform of Love. There will be a beauty contest, in Atlantic City of course, and the judges will pick the most beautiful girl, and Wintergreen will marry her. While the judges are deciding, Wintergreen spends time talking with Mary Turner, the sensible woman who is running the contest, and she shares a corn muffin with him. The judges pick the gorgeous Diane Devereaux, but Wintergreen marries sensible Mary instead."

Teddy pursed his lips. "And you are drawing a similarity?"

Karyn shrugged her shoulders. "It's a little obvious."

"Very funny, very funny, let's move on."

"AFTER THE CONCERT, Julia greeted us when we returned to the house, or I should say, the Amsterdam OSS office. She had managed the OSS office in my absence in case anything should develop over the weekend. And it did. The Jewish Council passed along the newest edict from the Nazis. 'I heard about it in church this morning,' Julia said. 'Starting on May 1, all Jews are required to wear bright yellow six-pointed Star of David badges on the outside of their clothing with the word "JEW" in the middle. The Catholic Church in the Netherlands publicly condemned the government's action in a letter that was read at all Sunday parish services. That's how I found out about it.' She held her hand up and pointed her finger. 'You wouldn't believe the reaction in church. Some of the men suggested that everyone in the parish should also wear badges in support, but the priest advised against it. We can support them in other ways, he said.'

"I asked her if she forwarded news of the new edict to any of our contacts and she said she'd left that for me. London's MI6 answered the wire with a note that said, 'This is a very bad omen. Jews already have ID cards. The Germans already have the registered addresses of all Jewish families. What the badges accomplish is to make Jews visible from the streets for easier apprehension.'

"The British were right. The next morning the following announcement was plastered throughout the Jewish community. Teddy handed it to Karyn.

NOTICE FROM THE JEWISH COUNCIL

THE GERMAN AUTHORITIES MAKE THE FOLLOWING ORDER:

1. All Jews must register for expanded labor force or be taken to Mauthausen concentration camp.
2. Jews who do not wear a Yellow Star will be taken to Mauthausen.
3. Jews who change residence without notifying authorities will be taken to Mauthausen.

"Now it became a crime to hide. When we stepped on or off the train, the German guards eyed us carefully. They didn't ask to see our IDs. They knew that starting the next day Jews would have to wear yellow stars.

"The most disturbing message we received at our OSS office was a bulletin from Washington. There was an urgent note to be present at a shortwave conference on May 20. We had no idea what that would be about, but Washington rarely used the word 'urgent.' The conference was to be sent to London and forwarded to continental OSS offices. I was extremely nervous. What did the Americans know that we didn't? Had they intercepted a Nazi message? What terrible pogrom would be next?

"Julia tried to calm me down. 'Don't get upset before you even hear the message. It could be good news. Maybe Hitler died.'

"I smiled. Julia always looked on the bright side. But I couldn't believe that the urgent shortwave conference in the middle of the night was about good news. The Nazis had been taking men into custody and sending them to work camps. They never returned home. Sometimes, the entire family was taken and sent to Westerbork. Westerbork was originally a Dutch camp set aside by Queen Wilhelmina in the late 1930s to provide temporary housing for refugees fleeing Germany. They would be safe, and no one would be hurt. It was a welcoming camp. Now it was a Nazi prison, a concentration camp.

"Julia and I sat on the living room floor by the radio Wednesday morning at three A.M. Julia had a pad and pencil, and stood ready to take notes. There was a three-bell alert, and then the message came on:

"A raspy voice said, 'This is OSS Bulletin XND330. You are to consider the following "Top Secret" and strictly confidential. The following information is not to be disclosed to anyone, especially members of the public. Release of the bulletin is likely to cause a great disturbance. We report that a highly private conference was held in the Berlin suburb of Wannsee on January 20, 1942. This information has only recently become known. The purpose of the meeting, as described by Obergruppenfuhrer Reinhard Heydrich, was to present a "Final Solution to the Jewish Question." Washington OSS has deciphered the content of that meeting.' The broadcast went on to cover a number of details, but the objective was to present the German hierarchy's plan on how to handle the Jews in Europe. In a ninety-minute conference they decided the fate of all European Jews. In summary, it was decided that all Jews would be deported to camps in occupied Eastern Europe and killed. The broadcast concluded by the announcer stating, 'Please consider that we can and must do whatever we can to protect the Jewish people.'

"When the broadcast had started, Julia picked up her pencil and clenched her teeth. Tears rolled down her cheeks, and she continually blinked her eyes to clear them of tears so she could see the page to write. When they broadcast the report on the Wannsee decision to murder almost ten million Jewish people, she grabbed my arm, and her nails went into my skin. When the announcer ended his broadcast, and her note-taking responsibility was over, she tipped over backward into my arms, and passed out cold.

"I patted her forehead with a cold cloth. Julia awakened, but continued with convulsive crying. She held on to me as tightly as she could, and I cuddled her, rocking back and forth like a child. 'How sick, and evil, and twisted does Heydrich have to be to plan the slaughter of all those innocent human beings?' she said.

"'He wasn't alone,' I said. 'No one walked out of the meeting. No one expressed their disapproval. This was coming from the top. This was Hitler.'"

* * *

"NOT THAT HE could do anything about it, but Julia and I decided to take this information out to Saul. He should know about it. The Wannsee Declaration was the answer to all our questions about what the Nazis were doing. We had believed that they were taking groups of Jews to clear out areas for other people to live, or to provide labor for the German army. Never did we fathom that this was the beginning of a program of mass murder of an entire race of people. Julia and I made plans for our precipitous visit to Saul. We told Sara to get ready as well, but Sara said that Katy wasn't feeling well. She had been up half the night. Sara felt that it would be better if she and Katy stayed at home. She said she wouldn't go outside until we returned. I didn't like that idea. It was too dangerous. I didn't want to leave Sara alone, but our house was safe; it wasn't on anyone's register. And if someone should come calling, Sara had the fake ID. I was against it, but what was I going to do? Katy was sick. Julia and I left that afternoon."

"ON OUR WAY to the station, we saw a canvas-covered truck with people on the inside. From the sound of it, they were mostly women and children. It sent chills up my spine that they were being taken to some camp, or maybe the men had already been taken to the camp and the rest of the family was going to be dropped off in a section of town, or according to the broadcast, they were being deported to Eastern Europe to be killed. The vision caused Julia to grab my arm again. 'When will it stop?' she said. 'How will it stop? When can we make it stop?'

"We caught the afternoon train and Saul picked us up at the station in his gray Opel. I explained that Katy was sick, and that Sara had stayed at home to be with her. We all agreed that it would not be a good idea for us to hold our meeting at our house. We did not want to draw attention to our house under any circumstance. Saul wanted to know what was so urgent that I would have come all the way out here and leave them behind, and I said it would be best if we left it until we reached his house.

"We sat in his study and Saul said, 'All right, let me have it. What is the urgency? How bad is it that you would leave Sara and Katy, and come out here without them?'

"'As bad as it gets,' I said. 'Do you know anything about the Wannsee Conference?' He shook his head. 'I know that Wannsee is a fancy suburb of Berlin and an odd place to hold a conference, but that's all I know.'

"I told Saul that we were alerted that the US had uncovered a conference of the highest-ranking people there last January. It explained a lot about what had been going on. Julia, who had taken the notes and written down as much as she could, took out her notepad, and said, 'The meeting was convened by Heinrich Himmler's chief deputy and chief of the Reich Security (SS) Reinhard Heydrich. In attendance were Heinrich Müller, chief of the Gestapo, and Adolf Eichmann, chief of Jewish affairs. Also present were three more SS leaders, and chiefs of the nine top agencies of Nazi Germany. According to Heydrich, it was as high a meeting as had ever been held.'

"'The term "Final Solution" was the code name for the systematic and intentional killing of all the Jewish people in Europe. Heydrich stated that about eleven million Jews in Europe would fall under the provisions of the Final Solution.' At that point, Julia choked up and couldn't speak. I ran over to hold her while she tried to compose herself.

"I added a few more remarks I thought Saul should know. 'Heydrich said that Jews would be taken, and separated by gender, and the healthier ones would be put to work building roads in the east and other physical tasks. That is why we see Seyss-Inquart moving Jews from the outlying cities into Amsterdam. From there we see groups of Jews being by taken by truck to camps.'

"All during our recitation of the Wannsee meeting, Saul sat with his arms folded and nodded his head. When we finished, I looked to him with a question on my face and spread my hands. 'So, what do we do now, Saul?'

"Saul took a breath and then another. 'We already made a plan for the Netherlands,' he said. 'Heydrich can't kill a Jew that he can't find. Hiding is the key. Seyss-Inquart wants to bring everybody into Amsterdam; we need to take everybody out, or at least make it so he cannot find them. This is a big country with lots of places to hide. There are mountains, there are forests, there are fields, there are apartments, there are attics, there are swamps, there are gullies, there are sewers, there are cars, there are . . .' And then Saul lost it.

"We sat there while he tried to compose himself, and then he apologized. 'Let's get our student groups together,' he said. 'Let's find a way to let the people know they have to hide. I'll get the students and we'll have a meeting here.'"

CHAPTER FORTY-THREE

"THE NEXT MORNING, before we left Saul's to go home, he and I had a long discussion about the Jewish Council. I said I could not reconcile the existence of a Jewish Council that implemented Nazi orders against the Jews. While Saul and I were recruiting students to join our groups in order to save Jewish lives, we faced a most unlikely opponent, the Jewish Council.

"'The council's leaders must be corrupt, evil compatriots of the Nazis, that's all I can figure,' I said. 'Maybe they were promised money or property or something else. Or maybe Seyss-Inquart promised he wouldn't hurt them if they cooperated in everything that he wanted to do.' Bringing back an old memory, I said, 'They should be called the "Spineless Council."'

"Saul shook his head. 'I just can't believe that. I personally know the men who run the council. They are two of the finest, most well-respected Jewish men in the Netherlands.'

"'Then why are they helping to send Jews to their death?' I said. 'Seyss-Inquart was smart. Jews had good reason to respect Professor David Cohen and Abraham Asscher, and that's why Seyss-Inquart appointed them to head the Jewish Council. That Nazi bastard knew that the Jewish community was prone to believe that Cohen and Asscher would be giving them good advice, and wouldn't ask them to be doing something harmful to themselves. But of course, that's totally false. The Jewish Council is blindly following instructions from Seyss-Inquart. Cohen and Asscher are telling the community what to do. As a result, the Nazis are collecting more and more Jewish families and sending them to

Nazi labor camps with the assistance of Cohen and Asscher. If they're such good men, why are they doing it? I wouldn't care what they promised me, Saul, I would never do those things. And neither would you.'

"Saul took a deep breath. 'I know them well, Teddy. David and Abraham thought that the families were being transferred to a Jewish camp at Westerbork, and that's what they told the families. They were to reside in a Jewish town where there would be no Jewish prejudice. People had a right to respect and believe that. And so did I. Our beloved Queen Wilhelmina established that camp for Jewish refugees. She knew and loved both David and Abraham as well. She appointed them to committees. She had no reason to believe that they would betray their own people, so why should the Jewish community?'

"'The council has all the Jewish addresses. They are told to show up at a Jewish home and tell them that they are to report at a designated location to be taken to the Westerbork camp,' I said. 'The families are given no choice. The father is warned that if he does not take his family out now, they will all be subject to arrest and sent to a concentration camp.'

"'And that's true,' Saul said. 'Families believe that the Jewish Council would be truthful, and so they willingly comply. But you're right, Teddy, what choice did they have? All the Jewish families will soon be gone anyway. It's not just the Jewish Council anymore. A truck with German soldiers will show up, read off names, and put them into the truck to take them to the train station. From there they are to be transferred to Westerbork, a formerly peaceful place. At any given time, you can see families patiently waiting on the platform with a bag of their belongings.'

"Saul continued, 'The Jewish Council explained that Westerbork is a small transit camp. It isn't large enough to hold all of the Jewish families that are leaving the Netherlands. Therefore, the council said, they would be taken to Westerbork only briefly, and from there be transferred to a larger camp, or one of the other Dutch camps. The council warned that resistance will result in death. Since the Netherlands will soon be "Jew-free," it made sense to peacefully go where the Jewish community goes and join the other Jewish families. To a new Jewish settlement. Cohen and Asscher had no way of knowing about the Wannsee Conference. No one did until the US found out.'

"I shook my head. 'Why did the "well-respected" Jewish Council post that hateful bulletin a couple of weeks ago? You know, the bulletin that warned Jewish families that if they didn't obey, and register, and wear the yellow Jewish badge, they would all be sent to Mauthausen concentration camp and killed. Justify that, Saul. If Cohen and Asscher are not bad men, why did they do that? Do they follow Nazi instructions because they believe in doing things peacefully, or because they're protecting their own asses? The only thing I can think of is that they were given a position of power and security and they want to keep it.'

"Saul didn't have an answer for that, and it was time for Julia and me to go. Deborah made us breakfast, made us promise to give Sara and Katy a big kiss for her, and we climbed into Saul's Opel for the ride to the train. As we got into the car, I heard Myron hammering in the woods."

"AFTER ARRIVING IN Amsterdam, Julia and I caught a taxi to a spot three blocks west of our house, so the driver wouldn't see us going into our secret house. Who knows whether the Nazis check taxi records? It was a quiet neighborhood, and as I passed by some of the houses, I wondered how many of them were two flats or three flats and how many were empty or for rent? How many people could we hide on this block? The students could find out.

"We arrived at the house. It served as our apartment on the first floor and as our OSS office on the second floor. When I unlocked the door, I expected to hear Katy singing or talking, but it was silent. I called out, 'Sara, Katy, we're here!' But no one answered. I looked downstairs and Julia searched the upstairs, but no one was home. The last thing Sara had said to me was that she wouldn't go outside. Now what?

"I started to panic, but Julia calmed me down. 'There could be lots of reasons,' she said. 'Sara could be getting groceries. Or they could just be taking a walk. It's a nice day. Katy was sick, so maybe Sara went to get medicine.' 'Or she could have been taken,' I said. So, we sat and waited. And waited. And each passing minute, my stress level grew. After a while, we both started to panic.

"Finally, we decided that Sara might have taken Katy to a doctor. The

alternative was too horrible to consider. Julia went to scour the directo-
ries looking for the names of doctors and clinics in our neighborhood.
I decided to walk around the neighborhood. Maybe someone saw them
or knew something.

"There was a young boy two doors down, throwing a ball against
the side of his house. I asked him if he saw anyone come or go from our
house at any time. 'Did anyone get out of a car and go into my house?'

"'Do you mean like the Germans?' he said. He shook his head. 'Nah.
I haven't seen anything like that. But the lady who lives there took her
daughter and walked down the street. She was walking pretty fast and
carrying the little girl.'

"'Do you know where she was going? Did she get into a car or a taxi?'

"'No, sir, there was no car or taxi. They were going to the doctor. He's
a nice man and he's not too far away. I go to him too.'

"'I sure do appreciate your help. Thank you very much. How do you
know that's where she went?'

"''Cause my mother told her to go there. The girl, Katy, is not feeling
very good.'

"'Can I talk to your mother, please?'

"'I don't think so. She doesn't talk to strangers. I'm not supposed to
either, so you should probably go.'

"'I'm not a German or a bad man. Would you please ask your mother
if she would talk to me for just a quick minute about my daughter?'

"'The little girl is your daughter?' The boy thought about that for a
second, said, 'Okay,' and ran into his house. I hoped he would return
with his mother, and that she didn't scold him for talking to strangers. A
moment later, a woman pulled back the curtains and peeked out of the
window. Then she opened the door a bit. 'Sara took her daughter to Dr.
Dop,' she said. 'Her daughter is sick and she asked me if I knew a doctor
nearby. I recommended our pediatrician. He's not very far.' She wrote
down the address for me and pointed in that direction. 'I'm sorry if I was
overly cautious, but you can never tell these days,' she said.

"Julia and I walked straight to the doctor's office. The door read *Dr.
P. H. Fiedeldij Dop*. In the waiting room were several children and their
parents. It was very crowded. After giving me the third degree, his nurse

246 RONALD H. BALSON

walked us back to one of the examining rooms. Inside, Katy was lying on a bed sound asleep. Sara sat beside her. She looked almost as bad as Katy.

"'How is she?' I said. 'She doesn't look very well.'

"'I don't know what's wrong with her. Dr. Dop examined her and ran a few tests. Katy was a very good patient. She didn't cry a bit. She has a high fever. We were waiting for the test results. Now we're waiting for medicine. We've been here for a few hours.'

"Waiting at the doctor's for a long time to get test results or medicine didn't sound right to me. Usually they take the tests and call you when the results come in. I asked Sara, 'Did you give them a phone number?'

"'No.'

"'Did you give them our address?'

"'No.'

"'What happened when you came here, Sara? You walked in and then what?'

"'The nurse asked me all those personal questions and I wouldn't give her any answers except to say that my baby was very sick. Then the doctor came in. He asked me those questions too, and when I hesitated, he said, "Are you Jewish?" I said I was and so was Katy.' Sara started to cry. 'What could I do, my baby was sick. I would have told him I was anything.'

"'What did Dr. Dop say when you said you were Jewish?'

"Sara answered, 'He said "Don't worry about it. You're welcome here." He asked me for my ID and I showed him the Joy Hart ID. He squinted. Obviously, there was no *J* on the card for someone who says she is Jewish. Then he smiled and said, 'Of course. Alice Cohn.' He asked my real name, and I told him Sara Rosenbaum. He opened his eyes wide, and asked me if I was related to Saul Rosenbaum, and of course I said he is my father. "And this is Saul's granddaughter?" he asked, and I nodded. He said he'd give us some cold medicine and told me to take Katy out to my father's. "Deborah will take good care of her," Dr. Dop said. "She'll make her well. Little Katy has a cold." So, we're here waiting for the cold medicine.'"

CHAPTER FORTY-FOUR

WHEN KARYN ARRIVED at the retirement home for her next session with Teddy, she was told that he was in with the doctor; it would be a few minutes. "You must be writing quite a book," Eleanor said. "You and Theodore have spent a whole lot of days together."

"That would be putting it mildly. How is his health? Is the doctor in there seeing him for any emergency reason?"

"You know I can't discuss that," Eleanor said with her hands on her hips. "Patients' medical records are strictly private. You want me to lose my job?"

Karyn shrugged her shoulders. "Only if I could get you a better one."

Eleanor laughed and said, "He's okay for a ninety-two-year-old buzzard. It's just a checkup. I know one thing; he makes a lot of phone calls trying to find out information for you. Why don't you go down to the cafeteria, and I'll come for you when he's ready."

TEDDY WAS SITTING up with a smile on his face and a lollipop in his hand when Karyn entered the room. "You must have been a very good boy for the doctor to give you a lollipop."

"I demanded it. As far as I'm concerned, a cherry pop is an essential part of an examination."

"Eleanor tells me that you have been making phone calls."

Teddy's expression went from chipper to sad. A frustrated look covered his face, and he hung his head. "I'm a failure," he told Karyn. "I've hit nothing but brick walls. I thought when we started that I had a good shot at finding someone who could find out about Karyn Sachnoff and her sister. But I can't. You know, when I came to the part of the story when I saw the orchestra at the Schouwburg, it sparked a bunch of memories and I called a few people, but . . . I'm sorry. I wouldn't blame you if you stopped writing the memoir. I don't have a right to keep you here any longer."

Karyn smiled. "I was there, Teddy. I was at that Gershwin rehearsal. Me, with Miss Pimentel, Annie, and a girl named Lois. Do you hear me? It wasn't on the Sunday that you were there, but Miss Pimentel took a few students across the lawn to the Schouwburg each day that week to listen to rehearsal. I heard the orchestra play Gershwin, and it went deep inside. I've been singing 'Who Could Ask for Anything More' all my life. That tune has been in my head, and I never knew why. That's where it came from. I never made the connection until yesterday. I can see us all sitting there, including my sister. And in your narrative, for that brief moment, I was back there sitting with my sister Annie, listening to Gershwin. Do you see what you did for me? You brought my sister back to me. So, you keep right on going, Mr. Hartigan. Bring back more memories. Please. Good ones. So, let's go!"

TEDDY CONTINUED. "FOLLOWING doctor's orders, we traveled straight out to Utrecht to the Rosenbaums'. By then Katy had improved a bit, and showed some energy, especially when she saw her grandmother. It was early July, and the weather was warm. Unfortunately, we knew from our intelligence dispatches that mid-July meant that the Nazi mass deportation plan was about to be launched. Something had to be done. We couldn't fight the Nazis; we were outnumbered a million to one. We couldn't escape from the Netherlands; the borders were all sealed shut. But we couldn't just sit back and do nothing while people were being deported to Nazi death camps. Up to now, it was truckloads of Jews that were being deported. Now it would be trainloads. We had to do something, and I knew that Saul and his group were making plans to safeguard the Jews in some way. In advance of our visit, Saul had arranged for his group of student rescuers, the UKC, to schedule a meeting.

"Seven students attended the evening meeting. They discussed the progress that had been made in finding hiding places for Jewish families. The young people were very social, and their contacts were all over Holland. They were also fearless. They knew what was right and they wanted to do whatever they could to counter the Nazi tyranny. Whenever they were able to move four or five families into concealed locations, it was time for a celebration. There were some vacant second-floor rooms, some empty wooden garages, and some attics that were still available in Utrecht. Now they needed to branch out. The students felt good about what they were doing and they wanted to expand their operation.

"The students reported that efforts were underway to locate students in other towns. With Saul's help, they had been able to form a group in Amsterdam. Those students were very active, and had connections with young men and women all over the country. As a result, Amsterdam families were being interviewed and moved, and the word was getting around. Some cities were so crowded with Nazis, German soldiers, and SS, that it was harder to run the operation. It was better to take a family from a crowded city and move them ten miles away, where the Nazis weren't searching.

"One of the students, a tall blond fellow about twenty years old, stepped forward and said that he and two others had traveled all the way up north to Friesland. It was in the northwest peninsula of the Netherlands. He knew some students connected with a nearby college. They went around to homes that the college students knew, inquiring if they had extra space they could make available to Jewish fugitives, or if they knew of friends who did. The students were shocked to discover that people around Friesland had never heard that Jews were being deported. They couldn't believe that the Nazis had plans to remove all Jews from the Netherlands. The students had to convince them it was true. That unless a Jewish family could avoid being captured, they would be killed. Even little children. And the only way to do that was to find a place to hide. But these were good people up in north Netherlands They said they would spread the word and coordinate with the students.

"Saul warned them all that as of June 1, the Amsterdam chief of police, Sybren Tulp, had founded an office he called the Jewish Affairs Office. Tulp said that the Amsterdam police were better equipped for tracking Jews than the Germans, because the local police knew the city better. 'You may have noticed that many more street arrests have taken place. A police car will drive by, spot a person wearing a Jewish star, and pull him into the car. They go straight to the police office located in downtown Amsterdam. If any of you know Rudolf Dahmen von Buchholz, an NSB member and blatant anti-Semite, he's running the office.' Some of the students already knew this, and one of them said, 'I heard that his car keeps getting flat tires.'

"After a while, there was a knock on the door. It startled me. What if it were SS? Saul looked through a peephole, smiled, and opened the door to reveal a young woman. Saul smiled at her, and they exchanged warm hugs. She was unrecognizable because her head was covered almost entirely with a scarf, but when she removed it, the students instantly knew her and greeted her warmly. 'Welcome, Alice,' they said. It was Alice Cohn. She had brought a box full of phony IDs. She had been working on them and now needed the students to deliver them. For those families that wouldn't or couldn't leave, Alice supplied them with these IDs, which were the next best thing.

"Finally, with a grim face, Saul turned the floor over to me. 'We have received word on the teletype that as of July 20, the Germans will be commencing mass deportations of all the Jews in the Netherlands. Up to now the Nazis were removing about a dozen families at a time. They pick them up and hold them in some warehouse or school until space is available on a train going deep into Germany. Sometimes that takes a week, sometimes a few weeks. From Amsterdam they are taken who knows where. Most likely they are taken to a concentration camp like Mauthausen, Auschwitz, or Sobibor. Now, as of July 20, the Nazis will be implementing mass arrests and deportations in order to remove one hundred percent of the Jewish population as soon as possible.'

"The students gasped. They couldn't believe it. 'July 20 is next week,' one of them said. 'Are they going to be dragging the Jews out of here starting next week?'

"'That's not a very nice way of putting it,' Saul said, 'but yes. We don't have a moment to lose. Remember, every life is precious. Let's expand our student rescue squads the best you can and as soon as you can.'"

CHAPTER FORTY-FIVE

"WE TOOK THE morning train back to Amsterdam. Despite the Nazis' plan to round up one hundred and forty thousand Jews and deport them all to a concentration camp, and despite the fact that the Netherlands was infested with thousands of Nazis, the city of Amsterdam was still commercially viable. Dutch citizens were going to work every day. Restaurants were open, drugstores were open, and the taverns were open, even in the morning. But not the theater. There was a sign outside the Joodse Schouwburg reading: 'Schouwburg closed. All performances canceled.'

"I saw Walter standing by the door and I went over to talk with him. 'What happened?' I asked. 'You were sold out of most performances.'

"He nodded. 'Yes, we were. Ever since they decreed it was exclusively a Jewish theater, we sold out the house for nearly every date. And we had talent, oh, what great talent, lined up through September.'

"'I could make a pretty good guess,' I said, 'but what happened?'

"'David Cohen came over here. He was a friend; I've known him for years. We belonged to the same synagogue, until they shut it down. But he came here on business. He was representing the Jewish Council. He said that there would be a number of Jewish families moving out of Amsterdam. It's not their choice, the Germans are deporting them to a camp somewhere, they say it's the Westerbork. They'll be bringing them here to the theater, and putting them on a train. Their intent is to keep them here until the entire group is assembled and ready to go. That could be a while.

"'Let me see if I have this straight,' I said. 'They're going to arrest families—men, women, and children—and hold them in the theater until they're all collected and the train comes.'

"'That's right,' Walter answered. 'And so I asked David how many people were in this group that was going to be transferred on the train, and he said he wasn't sure how large the groups would be. I said to David, "You just said groups, with a plural. How many groups?" David shrugged and said, "As many as it takes. The entire Jewish population of Holland is going to be deported."'

"Walter put his hand on his forehead. 'As crazy as that sounds, David was serious. They were going to arrest and take the entire Jewish population to some camp somewhere, probably a concentration camp. I said to him, "If you and your buddies, the Nazis, are going to kill all these innocent people, you sure as hell aren't going to use my theater." David shook his head and said, "I'm sorry, Walter, but that has already been decided. The Jewish Council isn't going to kill anybody, we're trying to make it all as peaceful and humane as possible. We're going to use the Schouwburg and I want you to stay and manage the theater until they have all been transferred. I know you don't want to do that, but if you don't, then the Nazis will staff the theater themselves and treat the families as cruelly as possible. You know that's true. We need you, Walter, to take care of our people, with food and water and the basic amenities."

"'David looked at me with a kind face and said that I was the perfect choice. I knew the building, I was Jewish, I could relate to the Jewish captives, I was kind, I was this, I was that, blah, blah, blah. This is what the Jewish Council is all about: trying to make the best out of a terrible situation.'

"'So, you took the assignment?' I asked.

"Walter nodded. 'What would you do? David said I would be a fool to turn it down. It was that or be sent to a concentration camp myself. So, I'm going to live on the premises and manage it for the benefit of the captives.'

"'Did they say when they thought the deportations would start?'

"'David wasn't sure, but he thought it would be soon.'

"'We heard that mass deportations would start on July 20,' I said, and Walter nodded. 'Sounds about right.'"

* * *

"RETURNING TO THE house, Sara, Katy, and I were met by little Tommy, the boy next door. I guess we weren't strangers anymore. He asked how Katy felt, and she said, 'I feel fine.' Then Tommy said that two men had come to our house and knocked on the door. 'They stayed for a couple minutes,' he told us, 'walked around the house, and looked in the windows, but they couldn't see much because the curtains were closed. Then they asked me who lived there, and I said I don't know. They asked how many people lived in there, and I said again, I don't know. Then they said, "What is your name?" And I didn't answer. One said to the other one, "Ach, he's a dumb kid, he don't know nothing." And they walked away.'

"'Good job, Tommy. Very smart, but you should never talk to strangers.'

"Now I was worried. Julia was supposed to be in the house. If the Nazis gained entrance, they'd search the house and find all our OSS materials, and arrest Julia. You have to wonder; why were they interested in our safe house anyway?'

"'Do you think they know who we are?' Sara said. 'Do you think they were looking for us? Should we move?'

"I shook my head. 'They were asking who lives here. And they were asking how many live here. That sounds like they don't know who is living in this house or if it's vacant. They could be canvassing houses that aren't registered. I'd just be guessing. Remember, we're just Joy and William Hart. But I am worried about Julia. Maybe we shouldn't have left her alone.'

"We entered the house, and no one was home. Nothing seemed disturbed. All of the OSS equipment and materials were in place. Julia's clothes were in her closet. The kitchen was clean, the stove was cold. It was like Julia hadn't been there in a day or more. I was worried as hell, but there wasn't anything I could do about it.

"I went up to our second-floor office to see if there was anything new on the wires, and there was quite a bit, though most of it was war news. The British had secured a beachhead at El Alamein in Egypt, the Americans and the British were landing on the beaches in Algeria and Morocco. But there was nothing new going on in our neck of the woods. Europe was held securely by the Nazis.

"Sara said that she and Katy were going to take a walk to the crèche. Sara thought she should check in with Johan van Hulst at the college to see if he needed her help this week, and she would take Katy by the crèche for a while. Katy loved it there. She missed her teachers and the other children that she knew. But I wasn't going to leave Katy alone; I told her I would go with her. I knew that Sara wasn't wearing the yellow Star of David, and that her ID said Joy Hart, and it wasn't stamped with a black *J*, so there shouldn't be any reason for the SS to arrest her on the street. But still, I didn't want her out alone. Actually, Johan suggested that given the times and the needs of her family, Sara should consider taking a leave of absence. She'd be welcome to come back to work whenever she chose. He was that kind of man. Sara did take advantage of the offer, and said that for the time being she would come in as a substitute teacher, if he needed her."

"HENRIËTTE PIMENTEL WAS outside in the yard playing with a class of children and her dog Brownie. I asked her if she had heard about the planned deportation, and she had not. I told her that I had heard that large numbers of Jewish families were going to be taken from Holland and sent to a camp somewhere. The deportations were supposed to begin at the end of next week, on July 20. 'The Nazis intend to clear the Netherlands of all Jewish people,' I said. 'One hundred percent. I know for a fact that is the order. Walter learned it from David Cohen of the Jewish Council. I know it doesn't make any sense, I just know it's going to happen, and you have to prepare.'

"Henriëtte said she had heard wild rumors, but there were always wild rumors floating around. If what I was saying was true, if the arrests were going to start next week, then she had a job to do. She had to inform her day care families when they came to pick up their children. 'They need to know,' she said. 'Do you suppose that you and Sara can help me?' I said, 'Of course.'

"Henriëtte gave me a hug and said, 'As you may know, ever since

Seyss-Inquart issued his order on schools, everyone in the crèche is Jewish. That means all the children and all the teachers are Jewish. I don't want the Nazis coming by and sweeping them all into their trucks. My crèche is a place of learning, and joy, and friendship, not a pen to collect children for the Nazis. We need to get them all out of here and close the crèche for good.'

"Sad, but we agreed. We asked her how we could help. What would she like us to do?

"'First, we need to inform all my teachers. Then we'll meet with the parents as they come to pick up their children. They need to know what we have learned.'

"I told her it would be best if she was the one who informed the teachers. No one would believe such a wild story if came from Sara or me. Henriëtte agreed, and said, 'The teachers will stay to inform each of the parents when they come, but there are one hundred students in attendance today. In order to inform all of the parents, and to answer their questions, I'd appreciate it if you and Sara and Julia would stay until the last parent has come and gone.

"We went home to ask Julia to help us, but she wasn't there, so we returned to the crèche. We stayed there while the parents were told that the crèche was closing immediately, and this would be the last day. We told them to take all their child's school belongings with them. When they expressed their astonishment, or their anger, we had to be truthful.

"We gathered them in groups and told them the news: 'We have learned that the Germans intend to capture and deport every Jewish person—man, woman, and child—and we don't know to what destination. They have said it will be to Westerbork, but Westerbork is a small camp, not large enough to hold anywhere near the size of the Jewish population of Holland. You need to protect your children as best you can.'

"The parents were predictably shocked. They would gasp, they would swear, they would say it was preposterous. Their eyes opened wide, their mouths hung open, their jaws dropped. and practically all of them shed tears. They said, 'How?' 'Why?' 'Who could be so cruel?' All those questions for which there were no answers, other than 'It's the Nazis.'

"In a saner moment, the parents would pull us aside and ask, 'What

are we supposed to do?' 'What do you recommend?' 'What are you going to do?' I said I was going to try to stay away from the Nazis and avoid
them the best I could. That was the key. Become invisible. I was going
to try to find a place to hide my family. 'Hide?' some would respond.
'That's impossible. How am I to take my husband and our four children
and hide somewhere until the Nazis are gone? That is, if they are ever
gone?' I felt so bad for them, but then, we were in the same boat. I just
responded, 'Find a big hiding place.'

"Some of the parents said that they were willing to do that, but they
didn't know where to go, or how to find a place to hide. I agreed that such
places are hard to find, and that sometimes you had to search far outside the city, where there were groups being formed to help find places. I
thought about Saul's rescue squad, the UKC; his group of students who
were already searching for hiding places. Maybe they would be willing
to help the crèche's parents. 'Look,' I said, 'I know of a secret organization that is looking to find places to hide Jewish families all throughout
the Netherlands. It won't be the Taj Mahal. We're talking about barns,
attics, garden sheds, toolsheds, garages, basements, whatever. If you
would like me to pass your name along to the group, I'll be happy to do
that. Write down your name and address. No promises, but maybe it's
an opportunity. It's a long shot.'

"Many of the parents lined up to give me their names and where they
could be reached. Some of the parents were too cautious, and really, who
could blame them? Maybe going to a camp was better than staying in
an attic. Some didn't want to give me their name and address. What if
it fell into the wrong hands? At the end of the day, I had the names and
addresses of fifty-two families.

"It was a rough afternoon. Poor Henriëtte. She had to close the door
on her crèche, her baby, the institution she had built and worked on for
so many years. Having to say goodbye to all those children was a knife in
her heart. When she bent down and kissed Katy goodbye, the raw emotions were more than even I could take, and I was supposedly a strong
man. I thought I could handle it without emotion, but I was wrong."

CHAPTER FORTY-SIX

"IT WAS A dark, moonless night, and it was drizzling by the time Sara, Katy, and I reached home. We had stopped at one of the few delis that were still in operation and picked up sandwiches for dinner. Poor Katy was starving. When we walked into the house, there was Julia sitting on the couch, and she was in a bad way. A big red suitcase lay at her feet. Sara walked over, sat down, and put her arm around her. She didn't say a word to Julia, she just sat there in silence like a good friend would. Julia would speak when she wanted to.

"After a while, Julia lifted her chin and said to Sara, 'It's over, I left for good.'

"Sara nodded. She didn't need to ask. It was obviously about Willem. 'He doesn't care,' Julia said. 'I went to talk to him tonight. You know, we had a lot of good times together. I really loved him, and he said he loved me. He was kind and generous to me, but at the same time, the Majestic was catering to the Nazis. While the Nazis were making plans to arrest and deport one hundred and forty thousand innocent people, his Majestic Hotel was hosting a party for Seyss-Inquart and eighty Nazis. Music, food, dancing, and girls. Oh, lots of girls. It was disgusting. They were hanging all over the Germans. I asked Willem how could he allow his hotel to engage in such debauchery? To fete a group of slugs who were seeking to injure or kill innocent people for *no reason*! It's like he willingly invited Satan and his minions from hell to hold a party. 'Did you give them your good bottles of wine?' I asked him. 'No,' he said, 'I *sold* my good bottles of wine to the Germans at a nice profit. That is what I am in business to do, Julia. I'm a businessman, and this hotel is my family's business.'

"'I got more upset with every word. He looked at me, shrugged his shoulders, and with a sarcastic look on his face, he said, 'It didn't seem to bother you when you were eating and drinking wine here, did it, Julia? Or when you were sleeping here for free? That was pretty sweet, wasn't it? But now, you want me to kick my biggest client out and go broke. You just don't understand business.'

"Julia bowed her head and cried. 'And I guess he was right,' she said, 'but the comment infuriated me. I slapped him across his face and said, 'I can't stay here anymore, and I can't stay with you.' And do you know what his response was? He just tipped his head to the side and said, 'That's up to you, Julia.'

"Sara wrapped her arms around her and cried with her. 'He wasn't worth it,' Sara said. 'I don't care how much money he has. He doesn't have a soul.'"

"IT WAS THE middle of the night, and I heard Julia sobbing. She had been crying on and off all night long. Sara was sound asleep, so I quietly left the room and went down the hall to Julia's room to ask if I could get her anything. She looked at me with her bloodshot eyes and said, 'I stayed in Holland because of him. I could have gone home to Washington with Frank and the rest of the staff. But no, I stayed to be with Willem. That's what love will do to you. It makes you blind and stupid. Seyss-Inquart would be having dinners at the Majestic in his special, private dining room, but I would go right past it and take the elevator up to my room. Or Willem's room.'

"I listened to her confessions, but what could I say in response? I told her I'd made the same decision. 'You are welcome to stay with us in the safe house for as long as you want.'

"With tears flowing, she put her head on my chest. 'You and Sara are all that I have in the world,' she said. She kept sobbing and then said again, 'I should have gone home. Now I'm going to die in this stupid country. I'm a target. I hate the Netherlands!'

"'You're not going to die. We're going to survive. You just have to have faith.'

"Julia could hardly speak, and when she did, she made little sense. 'They're going to arrest me on the street, Teddy. They're going to grab me and arrest me and send me away to some concentration camp.'

"'They're not going to snatch you off the street, Julia. They're not even looking for you. You don't have a yellow star, you're not Jewish, and you're not even registered,' I said.

"'Are you nuts? It's worse. I'm an American spy. Just like you. What do you think they will do to me when they catch me? They'll torture me to death, that's what. I want you to do something for me, Teddy. I want you to ask your father-in-law to get me a cyanide capsule. I won't be tortured by the Nazis. You should ask for one, too.'

"'I won't, and you won't. We're going to survive, I promise you. We came over here to Holland as officers in the US consulate. A dream posting. A job that made everyone envious. But then the war came, and everyone with any sense went home. But not you and not me. Why? Ask yourself why. There must be a reason. We stayed here for a reason, Julia, and it's because we can make a difference! We can save lives. You and I can't beat Hitler. It will take armies of soldiers, millions and millions of soldiers, but you and I, two small people, can make a big difference. We can save a life. Or two lives, or maybe twenty. Lives that will live beyond this horrid war and discover a cure to a disease, or invent an artificial limb, or pull a tooth or drive a bus or sing a song. Lives that will create other lives to do other wonderful miracles. Julia, don't criticize yourself, praise yourself. We were meant to stay here. We were meant to make a difference.'

"With that, Julia nodded, gave me a kiss on the cheek, and flopped down face-first on her bed."

CHAPTER FORTY-SEVEN

"I WAS REALLY worried about Julia. She was in such a state when she passed out on her bed. I tried hard to sleep, but I only managed two or three hours. I showered, dressed, and walked by Julia's room. The door was wide open but Julia wasn't in there. All kinds of thoughts raced through my mind. Where could she have gone? I went into the kitchen. Sara was feeding Katy her breakfast. I said to Sara, 'Julia's gone again. I have no idea where she went.'

"Sara smiled. 'She's upstairs in your office. She seems okay this morning. She's the one who made the pot of coffee.'

"I went upstairs, and Julia was sitting at the teletype, reviewing messages. 'What's happening?' I asked.

"'Where do you want to start?' she asked. 'North Africa? The North Atlantic? Russia? The Pacific Ocean? All are very active.'

"'How about Western Europe?'

"'Nothing. Dead as a doornail.'

"'I have fifty-four names and addresses of Jewish families who would like a rescue squad to find them a hiding place for the duration of the war. I'm going out to Saul's this morning. Maybe the UKC can find places for those families. Maybe those students up in Friesland know of a place or two.'

"'I'll go with you.'"

"WE CAREFULLY WALKED to the train station, all four of us. Sara pushed Katy in a stroller. I told Sara and Julia to bring an overnight bag;

we couldn't get back on the same day. It was more dangerous than ever to be on the streets. Every now and then, a car would pull up to a street curb, two or three men would get out, grab a person, throw him in the car, and drive away. With Heydrich's Wannsee Declaration commanding an arrest of every Jew and a transfer to a concentration camp to be murdered, every Nazi soldier, SS agent, or German officer became a potential executioner. So, we kept our eyes peeled and stayed off the main streets as much as we could. We were going to the train station, but we had some stops to make along the way. First, we had to talk to Johan at the teachers' college. Sara wanted to make sure his classes were covered while she was on leave. He appreciated her concern, and he confirmed that it was okay for her to be on leave, and stay away. He didn't need her. The next stop was the second point of the triangle: the crèche.

"Poor Henriëtte. The crèche, that well-known primary school and day care center, was her whole life, and it had been since the mid-'20s. Henriëtte was one of thirteen children born to a wealthy Jewish-Portuguese family. Seven of her siblings were still alive. Raising and caring for children was all she cared about. I told her that we were on our way to visit Saul in Utrecht and give him the list of names and addresses. She asked me to wait a minute, she had a couple more, and she turned to walk into her building. Katy cried out, 'Miss Pimentel,' and reached out for her. Henriëtte came back and asked if it would be okay for Katy to walk with her, she'd be right back. Watching the two of them walk into the crèche together, hand in hand, was enough to touch my heart. I still see them in my mind, and it still does.

"When Henriëtte came back outside, she brought a few additions to the list. Katy brought a lollipop. Henriëtte asked how we were getting up to Utrecht. I answered, 'On the train. It's too far to walk,' and I motioned across the lawn to the train station. Henriëtte's response was in the negative. 'It's crawling with Germans. For all we know there could be soldiers all around the Schouwburg and in the station itself.' I agreed, and I said I'd take a careful look.

"I told the group to wait, and I'd go check it out. The station was quiet, no one was waiting on the platforms. I glimpsed Walter standing near the door of the Schouwburg. I thought I'd have a word with him, but he waved me off and tipped his head toward the theater. Obviously, there was somebody, or somebodies, inside. Walter crossed the tracks and walked over to me. 'You can't come over here anymore,' he said. 'There are German guards inside and out.'

"I told Walter that we were planning on taking the train to Utrecht. He shook his head. 'You can't do that. You can't come anywhere near this area. Any minute, the Germans are bringing trucks full of Jewish families to unload at the Schouwburg. They'll wait there until others come, and when they collect enough, they'll bring the train for Westerbork.' As we were talking, we watched a car full of SS agents pull into a spot in the Schouwburg parking lot. 'See there,' Walter said. 'Taking a train is out of the question for any of you.'

"So, I thanked him for the warning, turned around, and went back to the group, convinced that we would need to find other ways to travel to Saul's. We walked back to the house and gave Saul a call. I explained our dilemma. We couldn't take the morning train. He groaned, cursed the Nazis, and said he would drive down and pick us up in an hour. I said that would be great, and I asked him if he would please call a meeting of the UKC during our visit to Utrecht."

"IT WAS EARLY afternoon when the gray Opel pulled up in front of our house, and we all squeezed in. 'My name is Kendall,' said the driver, a boy of about twenty. 'Saul said to tell you that he's getting the group together for a meeting this evening. He said something about there being a list of families that needed places to stay.'

"'That's right,' I said. 'Nice, quiet, out-of-the-way places where they won't be found.'

"'Yes, sir,' he replied, 'that's the UKC, that's what we do. That's what we're all about. We travel everywhere and find places for families to stay. We'll find some for your list, too.'"

"UPON ARRIVAL IN Utrecht, we handed the list to Saul. He looked it over and clicked his tongue. 'Fifty-four more families, some with two or three children,' he said with consternation. 'That's rough. A garden shed wouldn't work for a large family. Neither would an attic. But maybe a garage, a basement, or a vacant second-floor unit. Who knows? We'll discuss it all at the meeting.'

"Deborah was glad to see us, and especially Julia, whom she hadn't seen in quite a long time. She'd met her three years earlier, when Sara brought her out for a weekend. Sara introduced her as her best American friend. She had met her at the college where Julia and a couple of consulate workers were taking introductory Dutch classes. They had stayed close since then.

"The meeting of the UKC started after dinner. The dark of night shielded the squad members on their way to Saul's. Saul stood up and showed them the list. 'The reason we called you all here on short notice was this list of families. Nearly all the families live in the concentrated Jewish sector of Amsterdam,' he said. 'Many of them were forced to move there during the past year. Starting last February, dozens of Jewish families who lived far out of town were brought into the sector by order of Seyss-Inquart. Now it won't be long till they are transferred to some camp. Finding hiding places for all those families is not going to be easy, especially for the larger ones.'

"'He's right,' said a student named Einor. 'I located an attic in South Utrecht for a family, but it was just large enough for a man and woman, a husband and wife. I know if they had children, the owner wouldn't have accepted them.'

"'Same thing for a basement,' said Vernon, another student. 'Even if it's a good-size basement, if they try to take in a big family with children, especially babies who cry, the property owner may not permit it. People who go into hiding have to be silent. If the Jews are caught, they go down, and so does the property owner. It's a crime to hide a Jew.'

"'I have a thought,' said one of the students. 'Suppose there is a Jewish family that wants to hide out through the duration of the war, but they have a two-year-old boy and a crying baby. You can't put that family in a quiet hiding place in someone's attic. Agreed? Well, what if the family were to split up? The husband and the two-year-old could go into one place, and the woman and the baby to another?'

"'Well, that may be workable,' Saul said, 'but it makes our search doubly difficult. And, maybe the families don't want to be split up. A man is not going to want to leave his wife and baby. And, splitting up doesn't solve the problem of a noisy child or a crying baby.'

"'Just a minute,' Julia said, standing up. 'I know this sounds a little cold, but what if we're only trying to find a place for the baby, not the whole family? Just the baby. I mean, what if the UKC locates a Christian family that would love to take in a baby and keep him for the duration of the war? Or a Christian family that would take in a two-year-old boy? I'll bet there are plenty of good-hearted people who would agree to take in a child. Or what if there's a family that already has a little child and would love to have a two-year-old playmate? Then you've placed the children in nice homes and saved their lives. Then it would be easier to find an attic for the husband or the wife. Do you think that's doable?'

"'That's a very good idea,' Saul said. 'Of course, the parents would have to agree to split up and leave their children. The parents would have to know that their child is going to live in another family's home, whatever they do, or wherever they go. And there would be no guarantee they'd ever see their child again. The people that take in a baby have to understand that they may be adopting it for life.'

"A woman with dark, curly hair walked into the room and said, 'I like Julia's idea. She's a sharp woman. I hope you all agree. But I see an inherent problem.'

"Saul interrupted and said, 'For those of you who don't know her, this is Alice Cohn, the brilliant drafter of the ID cards that many of you carry. Alice also heads a rescue group of her own that she calls the Utrecht Children's Committee. She has saved several children already.'

"Alice smiled. 'Like I said, Julia's idea is an excellent one, and most likely the only way to save the members of a family from ending up in a concentration camp and certain death. But there is a problem. It's a human problem. An emotional problem. If you were to split up a family, which might be the only way to save their lives, you would take that baby from its Jewish family and give it to a non-Jewish family, probably a Christian family, where it would grow up without fear of being arrested. You would give that sweet little baby to a family, and ask that family to raise, and care for, and love that child as their own until the end of the war. Bear in mind, we might be talking about two, three, or four years, or more. The last war went from 1914 to 1918. What happens at the end of the war? Does the Jewish family come back out of hiding and want their baby, now a five-year-old? Wouldn't that be traumatic for everybody? Imagine the bond that would be formed between the baby and the surrogate family over that period of time. Imagine the love. So, what happens at the end of the war?'

"'I see your point,' Julia said. 'If the mother and father survive in the attic, and return for the baby at the end of the war, the child wouldn't even know them. The child would only know the surrogate parents.'

"Correct. I would think that in such a situation, when the baby's natural parents place their child, they should understand that the child is placed without any guarantee that the natural parents would ever see him again. But maybe that's the way the surrogate family and the baby would want it.'

"'You're right,' Julia said. 'As tough as that is, the family would have to give up parental rights to the child completely. It must be equivalent to an adoption. The parents cannot ever come back. Face it, there's no guarantee the natural parents of the baby would even live to come back, but if they did, they would have to seek permission to even visit with the child.'

"Alice nodded. 'You have a very smart squad member, Saul. Everyone must agree to those terms. In fact, I would suggest that the Jewish family not be given the name or address of the surrogate family. In the case of a baby or a small child, I would suggest that the child's name be changed to the surrogate family's name. Otherwise, it would be too confusing for the child.'

"I grimaced. 'Alice, I don't know how a parent could be strong enough to do that,' I said. 'That child is their flesh and blood.'

"'But if you want the baby to live, that might be the only way. The Nazis are murdering babies. Upon arrival at the camp they are slain without a second thought. If the baby stays with her Jewish parents, and they cannot find a place for all of them to hide, it is likely that all of them will die.'

"Einor put his hand on his forehead. 'So now the UKC is not only looking for places to hide families, we're looking for surrogate parents for babies. It's one thing to locate a property. I can find hiding places. But finding a family to take in a child, that's another story, and I don't think I'm qualified. That's way too big an assignment.'

"'Totally correct,' Alice said. 'The UKC can only do so much. But the Utrecht Children's Committee has a number of students who are being educated in early childhood education and nursing school. Those girls are perfect for trying to locate families who are willing and able to take in a child. And you are all right, the conditions must be clear. The placement must be under the circumstances we discussed. I do concede, however, finding parents may be very difficult to do.'

"'I don't think so,' said Julia. 'I would take in a baby in a minute.'

"'Where would you even look for such parents?' said Kendall.

"Saul held up his hand. 'We have made very good progress today. We have identified our goals, now let's go out and do our searches. Do your interviews!'"

KARYN CLAPPED LOUD and long. "That's me," she said. "They're talking about me! I was the Jewish child placed with a surrogate family. Somebody, maybe the Utrecht Children's Committee, found a home for me! And maybe Annie!"

Teddy nodded. 'Maybe. And maybe that's enough for today. I don't know about you, but I'm tired. These sessions are draining me, Karyn. Truly, I don't have much left. Maybe we've covered enough material for my memoir. I doubt my grandchildren will read it all anyway. What do you say we call the project finished?"

"Finished? After bringing me this far? Oh no, you don't," said Karyn. "Don't you quit on me now, Theodore Hartigan. Do you understand you have taken me back to my long-forgotten childhood? My earliest childhood. I just asked you to try and find out something about my sister Annie. But you have found *me*. You have found Karyn. I can see myself in the crèche. I can see them coming for me and for Annie. Every day my memories are just a little clearer. I can see the rooms in the crèche.

I can see Miss Pimentel. In your narrative, when Katy hollered, 'Miss Pimentel,' I could hear her. It was like I was there. Please don't stop yet."

Teddy nodded. "Okay, we'll pick it up tomorrow morning."

"Thank you so much. Get a good night's sleep."

CHAPTER FORTY-EIGHT

TEDDY AND KARYN resumed the next morning. Teddy began, "I woke up early the next morning at Saul's. Too early, but I was immersed in the aromas of coffee and pancakes. 'I must be dreaming,' I said. 'Am I in DC?' I flipped over and realized I was alone in bed. Sara must have gone down to the kitchen. But how did a Dutch girl know how to make pancakes that smelled like Walker Brothers? I also heard the pounding and banging coming from the woods. What the hell was that all about? It was all too much for me. I got up and went downstairs.

"I should have figured. It was Julia, a Detroit girl, frying up flapjacks. Sara was making a bowl of fruit and Katy was eating her cereal. 'Mom and Dad are not up yet,' Sara said. 'Dad left a note telling us to take a cab back to our house, it costs three guilders, so let him sleep.'

"We left him a plate of pancakes and a thank-you note. It was raining and the streets were quiet. Later that afternoon, I decided to take a walk over to the crèche, and share some of the thoughts we'd exchanged at Saul's the night before. Henriëtte was alone in her empty crèche. What a turnabout. The liveliest place in town was now dead silent. You could hear a diaper pin drop.

"Henriëtte thought that Julia and Alice were correct. Splitting up the families might be the only way to save the children. But she also knew the parents who dropped their children off at the crèche each day. They were tough. They might believe they could survive the persecution. And she knew how deeply they loved their children, and how difficult it would be to walk away from them.

"I asked her if she thought any of them would be amenable to letting their children hide with a non-Jewish family if it also meant they would never see them again? How would they feel about that?

"She didn't want to guess. She said that if any of her parents inquired, she would bring up the options available. 'The problem is that people believe they might not be arrested. Maybe they won't have to die at all. Maybe the war will end before that occurs. Maybe the German plans will change. What if Heydrich's monstrous Wannsee Declaration becomes public knowledge all over the world, and the whole world condemns Germany and takes up arms. Maybe the outrage would be so great that his own people would rebel. Maybe then the Germans would withdraw the declaration and there would be no more murders of Jews. Maybe it's not a sure thing that everyone will be snatched up and sent to concentration camps. I know all that is far-fetched, but Jewish parents are searching for excuses to keep their family together.'

"I nodded. It was a horrible thought to send your child into hiding. But as months went by, and thousands of people were arrested, all the excuses started flying away.

"In November, the deliveries of human families to the Schouwburg became so frequent that the theater and the outside lot became overcrowded. People were shoulder to shoulder. Walter told me that sometimes it took two or three weeks before the Westerbork train would come to take Jewish prisoners from the Schouwburg. Then within a week or two, a train would come to take two thousand or more prisoners to the camp. But what they didn't tell anyone was that another train would come and take them from Westerbork to a concentration camp in Germany or Poland. Westerbork was really nothing more than a transit camp.

"The Jewish Council, with the Nazis' permission, had appointed Walter Süskind, the director of the Schouwburg, to continue managing the theater building and the captives being held there. It was always a large crowd, and Walter did the best he could. Though it was staffed with several Nazi guards, they couldn't have cared less about the captives' welfare. That was left to Walter. It was also his job to keep a register of each prisoner in the Schouwburg, every Jewish man, woman, and child. Even the babies. When the Westerbork train would load, they would read the names off the register, one by one, and check them off as they boarded the train.

"Walter was Jewish, and he felt the prisoners' pain. He did his best to make their stay as comfortable as possible until their names were read off to board the train. Cohen and Asscher, directors of the Jewish Council, knew Walter and that's why they appointed him. Walter talked the Nazis into letting him have eight Jewish helpers, four men and four women, who would work there all night and all day without fear of being sent to Westerbork. They were given the promise of leniency, but truth be told, they would have worked there anyway. They passed out food and drinks. They cleaned the washrooms. They washed the diapers. They kept order.

"Try as they might, the nonstop noise of crying babies and wailing toddlers, the smell of dirty diapers amidst the crowded, sweaty surroundings, was more than people could stand. More significantly, it was more than the Nazi guards could stand. It was nerve-racking. The captives couldn't sleep, and sleep was the only escape from the torture of confinement. And it was cruelty for the children. So, Walter approached the Germans and suggested that he be allowed to ask Henriëtte Pimentel to reopen the crèche and house the babies and toddlers until it was time for them all to board the train. The Nazis, who were equally annoyed by the racket, readily agreed. But Walter had another idea that he wasn't about to disclose to the Nazis.

"Walter called me and asked if Sara, Julia, and I would meet with him at the crèche. That afternoon, he walked across the tracks, pushed through the hedge, and across the lawn to the crèche. The building was empty except for Henriëtte and a couple of her assistants. It was a lovely building, artfully designed to care for one hundred twenty babies. Now it was empty.

"Johan van Hulst was sitting with Henriëtte, when Sara, Julia, and I came in. Walter walked in a few minutes later. He told us that the situation in the theater was so oppressive that the Nazis readily agreed to his suggestion to ask Henriëtte to reopen the crèche. He turned to Henriëtte. 'I asked the Germans if the crèche could be reopened,' Walter said. 'The conditions over at the Schouwburg are miserable. There's nowhere for the kids to play or run or even nap. There are about seventy children in attendance today—babies, infants, toddlers, and young children. The Germans don't know what to do, and they get mad. Those kids need a nursery and a day care program, like the one you used to run, Henriëtte. It's the humane thing to do. Not that the Nazis are the least bit humane, they just want the children out of their sight. That way the Nazis wouldn't have to be bothered by the noise and the crying and the smell. They could run their transit program smoothly. They would also supply the crèche with sufficient food and milk and diapers. Whatever you need.'

"Henriëtte, who loved children more than life itself, said, 'I can't run the crèche by myself. I need at least six staff members.' She was amazed that Walter assured her he would be able to finesse such an arrangement for the welfare of the children. 'Thank you,' she said. 'You're a blessing.'

"'I'm sure they'll allow the workers, though you'll have to hire them yourself. And when I say hire, I don't mean for money. I mean that they will probably have the same benefit as the Schouwburg workers. They will not be arrested, nor will they be sent away. At least for the time being,' Walter said. 'Maybe forever, I don't know.'

"'Why were Sara, Teddy, and I requested to meet with you here this afternoon?' Julia asked.

"'Good question,' Walter said. 'I don't know how long it will take Henriëtte to find suitable assistants. In the meantime, I was hoping that you and Sara could help out. The Nazis expected me to take the children out immediately. You know them, they want everything done at once. I can delay a few days, but they expect me to take all the children out of the theater by the end of the week. And here's another thing. If the Nazis are employing the crèche to keep the babies away, they aren't going to come here. So they won't bother anyone in here. It will be safe in here.'

"Henriëtte was shaking her head and saying, 'How can that be done? Sara and Julia agree to help on the day shift, but that's not nearly enough to staff the crèche day and night.' Johan van Hulst, who had been sitting there listening, said, 'Some of the student teachers at the college might be willing to help. We'd give them full credit, and they would be trained to do it. One way or another, we'll get it done.'

"Walter tapped me on the shoulder and asked me if I could speak with him in private. So, he and I went into the other room. 'When I first made the suggestion to the Germans about the crèche, they discussed it among themselves,' he said. 'They were loud, brash, and they didn't care who heard them. They complained about the babies. They didn't want anything to do with babies or the little children. They didn't like being babysitters. They were Nazi soldiers, not nursemaids. That's when I told them I could take the youngsters and babies across the lawn to the crèche. They were delighted.

"'But, some of the parents in the theater overheard them. A few of them loudly objected. They said, "I don't want you to take my son away from me and put him in some nursery. If we are being transferred somewhere else, then we're all going together as a family." The Germans replied, "You'll go together, believe me, but for the time being, your son will go with the other children to the children's building." One German said, with a smile, "You know, Jewish families used to pay good money to send their children to the crèche. Your kid gets to go for nothing. I'm sure he'll like it better than this crowded theater."

"'But the parent didn't care. "I want my child to stay with me, under my protection," he said. "I don't know what will happen to him when he's out of my sight. And no one knows what will happen after we get on the train. It's just a lot of talk." The German shrugged and walked away.

"'A couple of the fathers, who seemed better informed, pulled me aside,' Walter said. 'One of them said, "We're not being fooled. Everyone in here is going to a concentration camp. The sentence is death. When our sons come back from the crèche, they will have to go with us, won't they? But when our sons are in the crèche, in the midst of all those children, wouldn't it be a simple thing to make them disappear? What if my son doesn't come back to the Schouwburg? The Nazis wouldn't know who came back and who didn't; they'd just load people onto the train. Maybe the workers at the crèche could place my son with a nice family, and he'd survive. How do we make that happen?"'

"'A parent said that to you?' Julia said. 'Because I was thinking the same thing. Those fathers wanted someone to take their child to a safe home. They had the courage to come forward.'

"Walter nodded. 'His name is Jacob. He wants his son to live. Standing there talking to them, I was stunned. I shook my head. 'It's not as easy as that,' I said to the two fathers. 'What are we supposed to do when the Nazis call out his name to board the train, and he doesn't come forward? He can't come forward because he has been placed with a non-Jewish family. Each of the children is registered by name. Even the babies. I write their names in the registration ledger. For example, when the train is boarding, they will call out the so-and-so family, and they will know it is a husband, wife, and two sons. The Nazis will check off each member of the family as they board the train. What are we supposed to do about that? And even if we could sneak your son out, and erase him from the registration, and trick the Nazis, where is he supposed to go? Do you know a Christian family who is ready to take him? Where are we going to find a parent to take your son and raise him?' And you know what the two fathers said to me? They said, 'You're a righteous man, you'll figure it out.'

"I looked into Walter's eyes as he relayed this colloquy. 'Are we supposed to figure this out, Walter?'

"Walter nodded. 'You do your part and I'll do mine. I'm in charge of the registration ledger. The child's name will disappear. You find him a home.'"

"A WEEK LATER, Walter called me. He said that a hundred children were ready to be brought to the crèche from the Schouwburg. 'We'll be walking them straight from the theater. I'll have a few assistants with me, and of course, a couple of Nazi guards. I hope the crèche is all set up to accept one hundred children. Thirty of them are infants, fifty are toddlers, and the rest are between five and eight years old. Please have Henriëtte and her staff ready.'

"Later that afternoon, a parade of children walked down the sidewalk to the front door of the crèche. The toddlers were walking hand in hand. The babies were all in strollers, buggies, or carts with wheels, with their names on their clothes. Each of their names was written on the register. When they got to the crèche, Walter checked off the name of each one as he or she entered. At such time as the group returned to the Schouwburg, they would be reunited with their family, checked off the register, and put on the train."

CHAPTER FORTY-NINE

"THAT EVENING, I messengered Saul. *Please arrange a joint meeting of the UKC and the Utrecht Children's Committee as soon as you possibly can.* Four hours later, I received a return message: *Tomorrow at 2 P.M.*

"The four of us arrived before lunch. That was deliberate. There was no telling what Deborah was preparing, but it was bound to be delicious. Katy had put in a request. It was round and had sprinkles. As soon as we arrived, Katy went straight to the kitchen, where her grandmother had a plate waiting for her. Then Deborah turned to Sara and Julia and said, 'I need help. My husband has invited thirty to forty young people to a meeting today at two, and you know how they love to eat.' So, while Julia and Sara were putting on their aprons, Saul and I retreated into his study.

"'Walter has successfully arranged for all of the children to be housed in the crèche,' I said. 'It's healthy and for their own good. The plan is for them to stay in the crèche until it is time for them to return to the Schouwburg to board the train for Westerbork, or wherever it will take them. A few able helpers have been assigned to Henriëtte from among the Schouwburg prisoners. They are capable women who were caring for the captives. Even though they are Jewish, they have been released from confinement at the theater and given a promise of a lesser sentence, though no one knows if that promise will be kept. I suppose it was predictable that many of the married women declined the service and did not want to leave their husbands' sides, but some did, and along with some single women, they volunteered to watch the kids at the crèche.'

"'I don't blame them. It's the honorable thing to do, irrespective of the Nazis' illusory promise,' Saul said. 'The children will be kept under humane conditions and the female volunteers from the theater will also be under clean, humane conditions. They'll be given promises of a temporary reprieve. So tell me, Teddy, why did you call this meeting today?'

"I took a deep breath. 'Because a hundred children are being housed in the crèche for a limited period of time. When the train comes, they will leave the crèche, return to the Schouwburg, and join the rest boarding that train. They will ultimately be transferred to a concentration camp, and you know what will happen. Maybe some of the mature, healthy, strong prisoners, men and women, will be put to work in labor centers. The women will most likely sew garments, the men will do heavier labor. The older men and women will be murdered and so will the children. To the Germans, children are a costly nuisance.'

"'We all understand that,' Saul said. 'So, you called a meeting. Why? What do you want us all to do?'

"I repeated the conversations between the two parents and Walter. 'Those parents want their children saved, and so do I. I want us to rescue as many children as we can. We can't rescue all one hundred at the crèche, but maybe we can rescue two, or five, or twenty. Who knows? Every rescued child is given the chance to start a new life. A rescued child will grow up to be a doctor, a craftsman, a pianist, or a mother. Who knows? I want those futures to be realized. Right now they are all foredoomed. I want to save them, all of them. I know that is a fantasy, but damn it, we are going to save some.'

"'Okay,' Saul said. 'I'm with you. And how do you propose we do that, Teddy? We are way outnumbered. There are fifty of them to every one of us. They have guns and tanks and planes. What do we have to fight them with?'

"'Maybe intelligence. Maybe wisdom. Maybe God. I'm a Lutheran who never goes to church, but I believe in God. And if you believe in God, you know that Hitler won't win this soulless war. Goodness will win. In my whole life, I never thought I would say something like that, but now I believe it. How are we going to save people? I don't know all the details yet. I trust that you and I and the UKC and the Utrecht Children's Committee can all put our heads together and come up with plans.'

"Saul gave me a pat on the shoulder. 'A noble idea, my son-in-law, and I believe it too. But there are some mighty mountains to climb. The population of the crèche will change every two to three weeks, because that is how long the captives remain in the Schouwburg before boarding the train. So, in each case, you only have a limited number of days to work with each group. There are one hundred and forty thousand Jews in Holland, a lot less now, and at the rate the Nazis are going, the entire Jewish population will be deported from Holland within eight or nine months. We need to hide as many as we can, or place as many children as we can, as quickly as we can.'"

"THE STUDENTS OF the UKC and the Utrecht Children's Committee began to filter in and pretty soon we had about thirty men and women. They made their first stop at Deborah's kitchen table. Then, when all were present, we gathered in the basement. The UKC reported that they had located thirty-six new hiding places, some large and some tiny. They were contacting some of the families on the list to inquire if they wanted to go into one of these hiding places. The Utrecht Children's Committee reported that fifty-three hiding places had been filled. They planned to still keep searching for more. They understood that the Friesland rescue group had located ten or fifteen.

"Saul welcomed them all and thanked them for getting together on such short notice. 'Given the subject matter of today's meeting,' Saul said, 'short notice was and is required. I also thank Alice Cohn and her Utrecht group for joining us. It is now my pleasure to turn the floor over to Teddy, otherwise known as William Hart.'

"I stood up and faced the group. Undersecretary Welles's words echoed in my mind. 'Go and make a difference. You're there for a reason.'

"'I asked Saul that you all be assembled here today, and I apologize for the short notice. Maybe some of you already know that Walter Süskind is the director of the Joodse Schouwburg, the marvelous Jewish theater. I hope that someday we'll all enjoy wonderful performances there again. But right now, the theater is being used as a holding cell for captured Jewish families. Walter was assigned to manage the theater on behalf of the captives until they all leave for Westerbork and beyond. Because the theater has become overcrowded and noisy and smelly, Walter was able to convince the Germans to allow the small children to reside in the nearby crèche until they are to be reunited with their parents and put on the train. For those moms and dads, it's too late. There's nothing that can be done for them. They're going to board the train and be taken to their destiny. I know that's cruel, but that's the truth.

"'At the moment, the crèche is holding about one hundred children until the train comes to take them all to Westerbork. If you saw what I saw, a parade of little children walking down the sidewalk and into the crèche, children who are the sweetest things God ever made, children who never did a single thing to harm a single soul, then you would do what I am trying to do. I am trying to rescue as many of those children as I can before they are sent away to certain death. I want you to help me.

"'What can we do?' a woman asked.

"'Alice Cohn and Saul Rosenbaum have been carefully devising plans. I want you all to listen to them and then dedicate yourselves to making them work.'

"Alice stood up and cleared her throat. 'Excuse me, it's hard for me to speak; I have a lump in my throat. I agree with Teddy one hundred percent. Condemning those children is the most evil, dastardly act imaginable. That condemnation has been ordered by the Germans, and is being carried out by Seyss-Inquart. Every step possible must be undertaken to save as many as we can. Obviously, what we are already doing is finding a place for them to hide and never be captured, and that is the best solution. To that end we have all been working very hard. Fifty to eighty families are now in hiding and are difficult for the Germans to find. We must increase our efforts and make it hundreds, maybe thousands.'

"She continued, 'Today we are talking about devising plans to rescue as many children as we can before they return to the theater to board the train. One hundred of the youngest children are being housed at the crèche. We can't save them all, but we can save some. We can save a portion of that hundred. So, the question is, how do we know which ones we can save? Which ones do we choose? How do we take those few away from the rest of the group? The identity of each child was checked when they entered the crèche. They are noted on the register. When the train is ready to leave and the children are sent for, how do we account for the missing child? If we sneak them out, where do we take them? If we are going to give them to a family, how do we find the family that is willing to take them? These are all questions that need answers.'

"'Alice is right,' I said. 'Those questions need answers before we can save a single child. For some of these questions, I have obtained answers. Before the children were taken to the crèche yesterday, two fathers of little Jewish children took Walter aside and told him that they didn't want their children coming back to the Schouwburg. They wanted them to be left at the crèche. They knew that if their boys came back, they would join their fathers and be put on the train with everyone else. And they would be victims. "Find a home for them," their fathers pleaded. "Sneak them out of the crèche and place them with a family somewhere." Those two fathers have put their two boys up for adoption. Alice posed the rhetorical question, "Which ones do you choose?" but we know that we have been given permission to choose those two boys. Walter said that he is sure there are many parents who would give permission to place their children with a family rather than return them to the theater.

"'Alice raised questions that I don't have answers for,' I said. 'I'm not sure how we will account for a missing child when the group returns to the theater. They are all checked in and checked out. They are identified on the register.'

"Saul raised his hand. 'I think I have an answer. Walter said he has a sharp eraser. I'm sure he could finagle the register. One day a child is listed, and the next day he is not. His name has been erased. The Nazis wouldn't know the difference. But I have to say, I agree with Alice that there are questions that need answers. For example, we need to find a sufficient number of Christian families willing to take in little Jewish children. How are we going to do that? This was also the dilemma mentioned by Einor the other day. How do we go about finding surrogate families? You can't go door to door, knock on a door, and ask them if they would take in a baby. You can't make a public announcement or the Germans would find out.'

"'May I make a suggestion,' said Sara, who had just walked in from the kitchen. 'A little while ago, my Katy was ill, and we had to find a pediatrician. We went to the offices of a pediatrician we had previously used, but he was no longer there. His practice was closed. Jewish doctors have been barred from practicing by order of Seyss-Inquart. We were told that the practice of three doctors were merged into the pediatric practice of Dr. Fiedeldij Dop. The records of all the patients were now going to Dr. Dop. His practice deals exclusively with children. Parents took their children to him and found him to be a warm, kindhearted man, in addition to being a very good doctor. That was my experience, as well. So now he has a huge practice. He meets with mothers every day, all day long. Wouldn't Dr. Dop be the perfect source for finding young parents who would be amenable to taking in a child? If you want me to, I'll be happy to talk to Dr. Dop.'

"'Very good suggestion,' Alice said.

"'Wonderful!' said Saul.

"That was my wife and she made me very proud. I wanted to go over and give her a big hug and kiss, but I didn't. Instead, I said, 'Now we have one more problem to solve, and I have to believe that the UKC and the Utrecht Children's Committee can make this happen.' Now I had the attention of all the students. 'The problem is how to get the child from the crèche to the adoptive family. We can't have these parents come to the crèche and pick up one of the babies. There are Nazi guards. They're watching the door.'

"Einor popped right up. 'We all have bikes,' he said. 'When we get the word, we'll come over to the crèche and put the child in a carrier and ride to the address.'

"Some of the students laughed out loud. 'What if the adoptive family is in Groningen or Friesland? That's two hundred kilometers away. You going to ride your bike with a two-year-old on the handlebars, or a baby in a basket?'

"'Hey now, don't do that,' I said. 'He said a carrier. Einor has a good suggestion. You can't drive a car up to the crèche and load a child. The Germans would see it. But if we could sneak a child out the back door and carry it away on foot in a basket, or take it in a bicycle carrier a short distance to a waiting car, or a meeting place, these are methods that could work. As to how to get the child out of the crèche, I'll have to talk to Miss Pimentel about that. We'll come up with a solution.'

"Rising to his feet, Saul said, 'We have made excellent progress here today. I doubt there is much we can do about the current group of children at the crèche, we just can't put it all together that fast, but if we all work as hard as we can, we can rescue children from the next group. Not all, but some. We need to find parents who give permission for others to adopt their children, families that are willing to adopt, and find a way to get the child to them. Good work today. Let's all get started.'"

"SARA, JULIA, KATY, and I got out of a cab a few blocks from our house. As we walked along, Sara said, 'That was a positive conference. We got a lot accomplished, and we should feel good about ourselves. But the two fathers who talked to Walter and told him that they didn't want their boys coming back to the Schouwburg, they wanted him to find another home for them so their lives would be spared, that makes me feel sad. Doesn't that make you feel sad?'

"'It does,' said Julia, 'but these two men were the ones who prompted Walter to talk to Teddy and Henriëtte, and that turned everything around. In many ways those two men lit the fire. They were instrumental. But like Saul said, we probably don't have time to put our plan together before the children are returned to the Schouwburg. If that happens, the two boys won't be saved.'

"I agreed with Sara and Julia, it was sad, but the meeting was encouraging. As we neared our house, Tommy, the little boy next door, ran over to us. I held up my index finger, waved it back and forth, and said, 'I don't think you're supposed to talk to strangers, Tommy. Mom's rules.'

"'You're not a stranger,' he said. 'And my mom said she would like to talk to you, Mrs. Hart.'

"We stood and waited while he ran into his house. A moment later the woman appeared in the window and motioned for us to come to the door. 'How is the little girl?' she said, and Sara put her arm around Katy and said she was fine. She thanked the woman for her recommendation and said that Dr. Dop appeared to be a very kind and caring person.

"The woman nodded. Then she added, 'I wanted to tell you that a man has been snooping around your house. Late last night, after midnight, he drove up and parked his car in front of your house. It was a black sedan, like the ones the Nazis drive. He told the driver to wait while he went to the front door and found it to be locked. He rang the doorbell several times, looked in the window, walked all the way around your house, came back to the car, shrugged his shoulders at the driver, and then they drove away. He didn't seem to me like someone you were expecting.'

"'Definitely not,' Sara said. 'Thank you for telling us. We'll keep an eye open.'

"'I agree,' I said. 'If you see a few students taking things out of the house, though, it's because we asked them to. Don't be alarmed.'

"'I'm not alarmed. I'm cautious. My name is Vera.'

"Sara introduced us to Vera and then she said, 'We very much appreciate that you alerted us, and I appreciate you sending us to Dr. Dop. We won't trouble you anymore.'

"'It's no trouble,' said Vera. 'When you said that students would come by and remove things for you, would they be the same students that are trying to find places for Jewish people to stay?'

"I nodded my head. 'Could be. How do you know about that?'

"'I've got eyes and ears. I can see who you are. You're good people. I'm a Lutheran. There's talk in church. The Dutch must bond together in hard times. We know that people are looking for places to stay so they don't get caught by the Nazis. Do you all need a place to stay? I couldn't take all of you, but a couple. I certainly could take this adorable young girl.'

"'You have a kind heart, Vera, but right now, we're okay. We have the place right next door and our identification is sound.'

"Vera nodded and shrugged. 'I'm just saying I wouldn't mind letting another person, or a child, move in with us until this terror is over.'

"Julia's eyes opened wide. 'Did you say you would take in a child? Would it matter if the child is a Jewish baby, maybe a year and a half old?'

"Vera pointed at Julia. 'You're part of them, aren't you? The ones who are trying to place Jewish babies before they are sent away. Isn't that so?'

"'We're some of them, Vera. There are a lot of us trying to save children's lives.'

"'Well, I would take in one. There is a lot of love in this house. Enough to share with another child.'

"'It's not temporary, Vera. You'd have to adopt him. His parents are going to be shipped away.'

"'I understand. I would adopt a Jewish baby.'

"Sara looked at Julia. 'That's one less to place.'

"'Vera,' Julia said. 'There may be a child waiting for you right now. Are you ready?'

"'I have a high chair and crib sitting up in my attic,' she said with a smile. 'Bring him over.'"

"LATER THAT AFTERNOON, Henriëtte went into the backyard, to the row of hedges that separated the crèche from the teachers' college. She lifted Jacob's baby over the hedge to a college student on the other side. The student put the child in a carrier, took the baby into the college, out the front door, and walked down the block. Walter would be told to erase the child's name from the register. We were there when the child arrived at Vera's. He was a beautiful boy. Everyone shed tears of joy. We had saved a life."

CHAPTER FIFTY

"THREE DAYS AFTER Jacob's son was rescued, the entire group of children was marched out of the crèche and down the sidewalk. Minus two."

Karyn interrupted. "I know where this is going," she said. "I know all the characters too well."

"Oh, you think so?" Teddy said. "Where is it going?"

"The children minus two. I know Jacob's son went to Vera. And the other? I bet a dollar it was picked up by Sara."

"But Sara already had taken in Katy, one of the crèche children. She was a Jewish woman on the run. There were already Nazis snooping around our house. There was no way to properly raise and care for another young child. It would be way too dangerous for a child if Sara were to take him in."

Karyn nodded her agreement. "Mm-hmm. Did you tell Sara all that?"

"I certainly did."

Karyn's smile went ear to ear. "What did she name him?"

"Danny Hart."

"A TRAIN WAS sitting on the tracks waiting for them when the group of children returned. Fifteen hundred people boarded the train that afternoon: men, women, and children. The Nazi guards were glad to see them go. They were tired. They needed a rest. So they said.

"But the guards' rest was not for long. Trucks drove into the Jewish sector of Amsterdam. Family names were announced through a bullhorn. The same names were posted on flyers nailed on trees. They were ordered to report to the Schouwburg by December 19. Anyone who failed to report would be considered a hostile enemy. All who refused would be hunted, captured, dealt with severely.

"Before long, the Schouwburg was once again filled, with even more Jews than before. An announcement was made that all children under the age of eight were to be separated, lined up, and taken to the crèche. To soothe the parents' distress, they were told that the separated children would be housed under humane conditions. The separation would only be temporary, only until the Westerbork train came. Then they would be reunited with their parents and taken to the Westerbork camp, where other Jewish families stayed. They didn't tell them it was a transit camp.

"Thanks to Walter and a few of the Jewish helpers at the Schouwburg, a message was secretly circulated among the parents. The message said that it might be possible to have some of the children placed permanently with non-Jewish families, families who would agree to adopt them. Those who were willing to allow their children to be adopted, and who would relinquish their parental rights, were advised to notify Walter Süskind.

"At the same time, notifications were circulated among the Christian churches. Notices were passed to Dr. Dop and social agencies. I know that Vera made the information known to the bishop at her Lutheran church. The bishop conveyed the information to Holland's other prominent religions, and soon adoptive parents were found in Catholic and Protestant churches. Dr. Dop, who had direct connection with hundreds of parents, more than any other individual, made sure that his patients' parents were informed.

"As positive responses were received, Saul and Alice recorded their names and addresses. This information was passed along to Walter. Walter kept record of all those captive parents who wanted their children to live, even if it couldn't be with them, and agreed to an adoption. When those children were each identified at the crèche, Henriëtte and her helpers would separate them from the others. At a convenient time, these children would be taken into the backyard, and lifted over backyard hedges to students at the teachers' college. Johan van Hulst had set aside a certain number of classrooms that would serve as bedrooms. The children would be kept there until it was time to be smuggled out and taken to adoptive parents.

"One week later a large green delivery truck with 'Friesland Laundry Company' stenciled on the side pulled up to the teachers' college. The driver opened the back door, took a load of laundry out, and carried it inside. A few minutes later, sixteen little children and two twenty-year-old student teachers were loaded into the truck. Bedding and pillows lined the truck. When all were comfortably settled, the truck departed for Friesland, 329 miles to the north. The truck made several more journeys, once with forty-five children. These remarkable rescue operations went on all throughout the months. Each month, the number of adoptions increased."

TEDDY LOOKED STRAIGHT at Karyn and said, "There is a famous quote from Johan van Hulst that is now on display in the Garden of the Righteous at Yad Vashem in Israel."

"I think I know about it," Karyn said, "but I don't remember the quote."

"He said, 'Now try to imagine eighty, ninety, perhaps seventy or one hundred children standing there, and you have to decide which children to take with you. That was the most difficult day of my life. You realize that you cannot possibly take all the children with you. You know for a fact that the children you leave behind are going to die. I took twelve with me. Later on I asked myself: 'Why not thirteen?'

"It took men like Johan van Hulst, and Walter Süskind, and great women like Henriëtte Pimentel, along with all the students and volunteers of the Utrecht Children's Committee and the OKC, to save the lives of so many families and so many children."

"UNFORTUNATELY, AS THE months went on, Saul and I heard that the SS were searching outside the Jewish sector for Jews who were hiding. In April, we learned that the SS was searching for two American spies that used to work in the consulate. One of them was a woman that used to live in the Majestic Hotel. Julia, Sara, Katy, Danny, and I made plans to move out of the safe house. One of Saul's students had a truck. We took the consulate equipment, our clothes, and beds for Danny and Katy, and took them to Saul's. From there, we moved into a small house near Saul.

"In May, my picture was circulated among the SS offices and the police departments. Where they got that photograph, I didn't know. Maybe it was taken at the time we had our engagement dinner. The night I asked Sara to be my wife. Maybe it was the time that I had the run-in with the fat German soldier. We almost came to blows, and lucky for me the security man at the Majestic broke it up. It might have been at that time that my picture was taken. It wasn't hard to believe that someone at the Majestic had cooperated with Seyss-Inquart.

"One night in late May, while the women were cooking another spectacular dinner, Saul asked me to take a walk with him. We took a couple of flashlights and walked through his backyard. Outside the yard, there was a path. We followed the path deep into the woods. After a while, we came upon a large machine covered by black tarpaulin. Saul pulled up the corner of the tarp.

"'Oh my God,' I said, 'it's a German Fokker.'

"'It's not German,' Saul said, 'though it's been painted to look like one. Myron says it's ready to go.'

"I was astonished. So all that pounding and banging had actually paid off. 'You mean he fixed it up and he's turning it over to the Luftwaffe? How much are they paying him?'

"Saul smiled and shook his head. 'Do you think that Myron would repair an airplane for the Germans? Nope. He intends to give it to the British.'

"'What? How is he going to do that? And for what purpose?'

"'He's going to fly it to England, silly. The British will make whatever use of the plane they desire. Maybe they'll study it, maybe they'll use it to spy? I don't know.'

"'That's insane, Saul. It will be shot down by the Germans before it can reach the sea, and if it makes it past them, it will be shot down by the British as an enemy aircraft.'

"Saul tapped me on the shoulder. 'You think we haven't thought about that? No, my boy, the Germans will be told, through an underground contact we know, that the plane is flying to the English coast on a very dangerous surveillance mission. They will let it complete the mission. As for the British, we will use the consulate equipment to contact British intelligence as we have before, and we will tell them that the plane is ours, and it carries Allied personnel.'

"'Who is going with the plane? What Allied personnel?'

"'You, Teddy. You and Sara and Katy and Danny and Julia. And maybe Sylvia, if I can convince her to go. We're going to get you out of here. They're looking for you. It's only a matter of time. We know they've been asking around in Utrecht. We have the opportunity to fly you to safety. You have to leave.'

"'But the job isn't finished. For once in my life, I feel like I am making a difference. I need to stay and save as many as I can.'

"'You think you haven't already made a difference? You and the others have saved seven hundred babies to date. Seven hundred little lives who would have been sent to concentration camps to be killed on arrival. Seven hundred, and it's not finished. There aren't many Jews left in Holland. In a month or two they will all be gone. But not the seven hundred, or the ones that will be saved out of the final group. We made a difference.'

"Saul continued. 'Seven hundred saved, and that's not counting the families that have gone into hiding. We have been told that hiding places were found for almost thirty thousand Jewish people. Thirty thousand are living somewhere, not in a camp. So don't think you haven't made a difference. Thirty thousand, seven hundred people would contradict you. They are proof we made a difference.'

"'How do you know it's thirty thousand, seven hundred?'

"'We know. We do the math. There were one hundred and forty thousand Jews left in Holland when the Nazis started their pogrom. There are about five thousand left. According to Walter, the Nazis have deported about one hundred and nine thousand. We know from the records of the hiding places we obtained and from the children we rescued, that at least thirty thousand seven hundred people survived, and that proves that you and the others did make a difference. Your job is over. It's time for you to leave.'

"'What about you and Deborah? You deserve to leave more than I do. You go, and I'll stay behind. I'll make it.'

"'Nah. We're two grizzled old Dutchmen. I'm an aged professor and Deborah is a kindly old woman. Don't let her hear that I said that. They're not searching for me. I've covered my tracks pretty well. You're young and your lives are just beginning. And you have a story to tell.'

"It was hard for me to talk. I didn't know what to say. 'Does this old plane fly? Has it ever flown?'

"'Myron says it will fly; he's betting his life on it. Has it ever flown? Well, maybe once, a long time ago. Not recently. I suppose you just have to close your eyes, cross your fingers, and have faith in Myron.'"

"THE DAY CAME. We were all called together at Saul's. The weather was clear, Myron had brought over several gallons of fuel, and I helped him gas up the Fokker. Myron, Saul, and I sat in his study, planning the trip. We planned to land in Bradwell Bay, an RAF airfield, on the southeast coast of England. I contacted British OSS on the teletype. They were advised of the mission, and not to shoot us down.

"When it was time to go, we gathered our papers: Julia and I had passports, we had a visa that Julia and I had issued for Sara, and we had visas that I issued for Katy and Danny, who were now fast friends. We packed a small bag of essentials, and we were ready to go. We couldn't convince Sylvia. She was too connected to Holland. She wanted to stay.

"I stood by Saul's side as Myron climbed into the cockpit. He had a leather cap and goggles. He gave us a thumbs-up and I pulled down on the propeller. Once, twice, once again, and the thing came to life. Noisy, but smooth. It worked! 'You doubted me?' Myron said.

"We pulled the Fokker out onto the street in front of Saul's, a long straight street. Sara, Katy, Danny, and Julia climbed up the stairs into the plane. Saul and Deborah stood by the side of the street and waved us goodbye. Everyone had tears in their eyes, except Myron, thank goodness. The Fokker, a silver plane with all the German insignias, propellers whirring, rolled down the street. Faster and faster, it bumped and bounced along, took one big bounce, and lifted off into the air. We were England bound!

"The distance to England was two hundred and forty miles. The distance to Amsterdam was only fifty miles, and we looked out the window at the crèche, the Schouwburg, the consulate, and all our memories below. We said goodbye to those memories, good and bad. It gave us a series of heartbreaks. We also saw German soldiers on the ground, but they were not about to shoot at a German plane. We turned and headed out to sea. Before we knew it, we were circling to land at Bradwell Bay, near Maldon, Essex, England. From there, we took a bus to London Heathrow, and Frank Lee provided a military flight home to Washington."

TEDDY SAT BACK and folded his hands. "That's it," he said to Karyn. "We made it home. That was the end of my time in Holland. So may I say the Dutch phrase for The End: *Het Einde!*"

Karyn rose to her feet. She clapped. "That was a wonderful story. You've had a courageous and extraordinary life. I will write it up and you can share it with your grandchildren. I am honored to be the one to scribe it."

"Thank you," Teddy said with a tear in his eye. "You have no idea how deeply I appreciate it. By now you know me very well, and you know that it wasn't always easy for me to tell things. It was the same with my family. Now they will know what I couldn't tell them. Not only about me, but about their grandma Sara. You have done that for me, and I'm very sorry that I couldn't keep my word and do my part for you. I failed. I failed to find a way to connect you with your sister Annie." He shook his head. "I tried but I failed."

"Oh, you're so wrong," Karyn said. "I'm going to write your story, and I'm going to send it to each and every one of your grandchildren, like I promised, so that they will know and appreciate their wonderful grandfather and their grandmother. Then I'm going to have your story published. And when this story is published and widely circulated, like I know it will be, Annie is going to hear about it. I know she's still alive, I can feel her. She'll read your story, and she will know that it was all about children like the two of us. She'll know it was written by her sister because my biography of Theodore Hartigan will be dedicated to her, and children like her. And when she reads it, each page will bring back memories, just like it did for me. She'll see the crèche, and she'll remember being taken to her new home and her new parents. She will have grown up wondering about her sister, just like I did, but when she reads Theodore Hartigan's memoir by Karyn Sachnoff, she'll know it was written by her sister. And she'll feel what I feel. She'll say, 'That's my sister! She wrote this story about us.'"

Teddy smiled. "I had hoped to put you together in person, and I'm sorry I couldn't do that for you."

"But you're wrong. You did put us together. In my mind, we're together like never before, and who knows, maybe it will come true. We sat down to write a story about Theodore Hartigan, and we did. And you were the star. Your grandchildren will know about their grandfather and what a star he was."

Teddy bowed his head. "Thank you. But the real stars of the story are the children who were taken into custody, smuggled out through the crèche, adopted by wonderful people, and grew up to work magic. You were one of them, Karyn."

They hugged and they jointly said, *"Het Einde!"*

AUTHOR'S NOTE

A Place to Hide is a work of historical fiction. It is a story of wartime Holland, as told through the eyes of fictional characters that I have created. I have woven those characters through the actual times, people, places, and events as they occurred. In every way I have endeavored to stay true to the historical facts. My fictional main characters are: Theodore "Teddy" Hartigan, Broderick Hartigan, Betsy McCutcheon, Sara Rosenbaum, Julia Powers, and Saul and Deborah Rosenbaum.

Karyn Sachnoff is fictional, but based upon a true story relayed to me by a woman whose grandmother is a celebrity, and a survivor of the Nazi occupation of Holland. She lectures at Jewish events and is a docent in Los Angeles. She was just a small child when the Nazis came to Holland. She was separated from her parents and raised by a foster family. Because she was so young, she had only a sketchy memory. Standing in line at the Bank Leumi in Israel, a man heard her speaking Hebrew with her accent and said she sounded Dutch. Amazingly, they made the connection. He knew the foster family that raised her. She went back to Amsterdam and reconnected. That formed the starting point for my novel.

Nazi Germany's attempts to arrest and murder all of the Jewish residents of the Netherlands was absolutely true and reported as accurately as I could. So were the heroic efforts of citizens who formed rescue groups, hiding places, and adoptive homes for the children. Almost one thousand children were rescued from the crèche and taken to new homes.

Henriëtte Pimentel was real. She was the director and operator of the crèche in Amsterdam. Her heroic wartime activities were correctly described. During their last sweep of the crèche, the Nazis took Henriëtte along with the children to the Westerbork transit camp. From there she was transferred to Auschwitz, where she died in September 1943.

Walter Süskind was the director of the Hollandsche Schouwburg, and operated the building as a holding cell when the Nazis dropped off Jewish prisoners to wait for the Westerbork train. He helped to rescue Jewish babies and children by obtaining their parents' consent, erasing their names from the registry, and assisting in saving them for their adoptive homes. When the Nazis had finished their arrests and deportations, and contrary to their promise, Walter was arrested, along with his wife and child, and taken to Westerbork. His wife and child were murdered and Walter died shortly thereafter.

Johan van Hulst was in fact the director of the Reformed Teacher Training College. He and his teachers accepted the babies and small children who were lifted over the hedges and took them to classrooms, where they stayed until an adoptive home was located. His quote in the book is accurate, and for some time I considered calling the book *Why Not Thirteen*. Johan served as a member of the Netherlands Senate from 1956 to 1981. He died in Amsterdam in 2018.

Alice Cohn lived in Utrecht and formed a group to forge identification cards. She also formed a group of resistors called the Utrecht Children's Committee, which rescued thousands of children. In 1947, she returned to her home in Lichtenstein. She engaged in a career as a graphic arts designer and a designer of children's books. She died in 2000.

Arthur Seyss-Inquart was appointed by Hitler to be the Reichskommisar of the Netherlands in 1940. During his reign he carried out numerous anti-Semitic edicts designed to fulfill the Wannsee Declaration to murder every Jew. He attempted to arrest and deport every single Jewish person in the Netherlands to concentration camps to be killed. He managed to deport 104,000. At the end of the war, he was arrested and sentenced to death by hanging at the Nuremburg war trials. His sentence was stated with particular reference to his reign of terror and atrocities committed against the Jews. He was hanged on October 16, 1946.

Amsterdam was liberated on May 5, 1945, the date that Germany agreed to surrender German troops to the Allies. The Liberation Day is celebrated every year as Bevrijdingsdag.

ACKNOWLEDGMENTS

Once again, I express my heartfelt gratitude to all those who helped bring this project into being. To my supportive group at St. Martin's Press: my editor, George Witte; his colleague Brigitte Dale; the marvelous copyediting done by Christina MacDonald, and the St. Martin's Press art department for the beautiful cover. Thanks to my literary agent, Mark Gottlieb of Trident Media Group, for his efforts and his guidance. Finally, to my tireless wife, Monica, a woman of boundless energy, brilliance, and love, who carefully read the manuscript pages as they came out of the printer, who caught my mistakes, smoothed out the rough passages, and provided invaluable suggestions. Thanks to you all.

ABOUT THE AUTHOR

Monica J. Balson

RONALD H. BALSON is an attorney, professor, and writer. His novel *The Girl from Berlin* won the National Jewish Book Award and was the Illinois Reading Council's adult fiction selection for the Illinois Reads program. He is also the author of *Eli's Promise* (Target Book Club selection), *An Affair of Spies, Defending Britta Stein, Karolina's Twins, The Trust, Saving Sophie,* and the international bestseller *Once We Were Brothers.* He lives in Chicago.